The halls were confusion to allow Ma room. He spotted him l _____ by a short woman. Matt knelt down as if to tie his shoe. They passed him and Tommy went into the boy's bathroom. The tiny woman stood sentry. While she was looking the other way. Matt stood and pulled the fire alarm down as quickly as he could. There were startled looks from students and teachers alike. One of the teachers said, "What a horrible time for a drill!"

Teachers called to students to get in their lines. The elfin woman opened the boy's room door to clear it out as Tommy appeared wide-eyed. She sent him next door to his class. "Go with them. I will tell your parents to meet you outside." She pushed him along and hurried back to the office.

Tommy was the last one in line and followed his class outside. When they reached the double doors and stepped outside, Matthew reached for the boy's hand. Tommy looked up and pulled away, eyes full of recognition and fear. Matt leaned down and spoke directly into his ear.

"Come with me Tommy, you will be okay."

"Leave me alone!" With a sharp tug, the boy pulled his hand free and ran to the front of the line. "Mrs. Johnson! Mrs. Johnson! Help!"

Trevor

by

S. Hilbre Thomson

Trevor

Cover Art by *Kristian Norris*

The Wild Rose Press, Inc.
PO Box 708
Adams Basin, NY 14410-0708
Visit us at www.thewildrosepress.com

Publishing History
First Edition, 2022
Trade Paperback ISBN 978-1-5092-3974-0
Digital ISBN 978-1-5092-3975-7

Published in the United States of America

Dedication

To my husband Dave, who encouraged me to follow my passion for writing and for never letting me give up on this book. Also, to my daughters Riley, Brynn and Colby who cheered me on every step of the way.

Acknowledgments

I would like to thank the people who helped me with this book. First and foremost, my family who kept encouraging me to get back to it and complete the manuscript. My editor, Ally Robertson, was patient and wise in her guidance. This version is a much better one than the original! There were a few others who stepped up when needed with readthroughs and technical advice. Thank you CN and MG. Your input was invaluable.

Chapter 1

Trevor's cries brought Jesse out of the greenhouse and into the backyard. Tears filled his wide brown eyes and fell down his cheeks. She looked for any obvious signs of injury. No stains, scratches, bumps, or bruises. He threw himself into her legs and cried.

"What's wrong?" Jesse asked, checking him more closely.

With a trembling hand, he pointed to the back fence. "The Badman. He was here."

Over the past few weeks, Trevor had been saying that a man was watching him. At school out at recess, the park, during soccer practice. He even said that the man was following the bus one day. Smoothing his dark blond curls away from his face, Jesse tried to reassure the child. "Trevor, there is no bad man. We've talked about this. It must have been a deer, or something, maybe the wind."

"Mommy, he was here. Right there in the woods. He called me Tommy." New tears fell as Trevor twirled her hair between his fingers. His whole body shook as he turned back to look at the fence.

Wanting to prove to him that there was no one there, she asked, "Can you show me, honey? Where he was?" Trevor buried his head in her legs again. "Come on, kiddo. You can do it. Spiderman would." Lately Spiderman was the be all, end all. The mere mention of his name would convince the child to brush his teeth, take a bath, or help set the table. She waited.

Slowly, he let go and looked up at her. Then at the fence, and back at her. With a determined nod, he edged toward the back of the fenced-in yard. After the first few steps, he slowed and reached for his mother's hand. Holding it tightly, he led her to the edge and pointed to an opening between two pine trees where a small patch of grass grew along their fence. Years of pine needles littered the forest floor. Their scent lingered and usually brought back memories of playing in these very same woods as a child. Jesse was caught between believing Trevor and thinking it was part of an elaborate fantasy in his mind. She crept forward and peered over the fence. Was her imagination playing tricks on her? No, clearly outlined in the grass were two footprints, large indentations pressing down on the spring grass. Letting a small gasp escape her mouth, Jesse pulled Trevor away from the woods. "Let's go inside and get some juice."

"Did you see him too, Mommy? Isn't he scary? Are you gonna tell Daddy?" He alternated between looking at Jesse and the fence line.

"Everything's okay, hon. Let's just go inside and get a snack. We'll put on a show and take a rest." She tried to make her voice light but could hardly keep herself from running into the house and locking all of the doors. Something else was pulling at her mind. Something was wrong in the forest, but she couldn't see anything out of the ordinary. One last look past the swing set into the darkening woods, she picked up the pace and they entered the house.

Closing the door, she hesitated and then locked it. Never could she recall feeling the need to lock the house. In fact, they never had a key that she could remember until her father passed away and her mother asked Steven to change the locks. She said it was the only way she could feel comfortable in the big old house by herself. It was one of her subtle ways of asking not to be alone in the house. As the bolt clicked into place, Trevor turned at the unexpected sound. With a small furrow in his brow, he suggested they call Daddy for dinner. Shooing him into the den to find a movie, she phoned her husband, Steven, at work.

****

Jack, Steven's partner, picked up the phone. "Hunter-Reed, can I help you?" The two men had tossed a coin to see whose name would appear first in the company name. Jack won and claimed it was the first time Steven hadn't cheated to come out on top. After five years of working at competing architectural firms in the city, the longtime friends decided to go it on their own.

"Jack, it's Jesse. Is he in?"

"Sure is, whatcha cooking for supper?"

Jack's wife, Jen, was in San Diego leading a seminar for startups. They had promised to look after the quasi-bachelor for the week. "Uh, chicken, rice pilaf, and salad. Can I talk to him?"

"Sounds great. You all right?"

"I'm not sure. Trev saw the 'Badman' again. This time I think there might be something to it."

"Hang on. He's right here."

"What's wrong, Jesse? Let me guess, the Badman?" Steven's voice was mixed with concern and frustration. He had been getting upset with Trevor because he thought maybe the boy was making this all up to get more attention from his parents. He was feeling bad enough for not being home much. Getting upset only added to the guilt.

"It happened again, this time right in the backyard. When I went to check it out, I saw footprints by the fence. Everything else looked fine, but that's weird. I can't shake this chill. Something's up." Jesse slumped into the bench in the breakfast nook.

"What do you mean footprints? Like a whole bunch? Could they be mine? Or yours?"

"Not unless you have been outside of the fence, in the woods. Steven, the woods felt weird. I can't explain it, but I wish you could come home and check things out. It would make me feel better. Bring Jack. He can get a fresh meal, and we can get his take on the whole thing." Her voice was pleading. She hated to sound vulnerable, but hoped it was enough to convince her husband to come home early for the first time in months.

"Are you really that concerned? We're in the middle of something here." She could hear him mumble something to Jack. "We'll take..." The phone went dead.

"Steven? Hello?" Jesse pushed the button and there was no dial tone. She tried it again beginning to panic then rushed into the den to check on Trevor. He was pointing the remote and clicking it continuously. The screen was black. "Mommy, did you forget to pay the bill again?"

A small giggle slipped out. "No, hon, I think the power went out." Her anxiety continued climbing as she realized that without electricity, it would be dark soon. "Let's go and get my cell phone out of the car." The six-year-old followed but mumbled that he was missing his favorite part of the movie. They went through the kitchen door that opened to the garage, and Trevor climbed into the Ford Explorer to retrieve the phone. It had been their last splurge before starting the business. As she pushed the button for Steven's cell, she forced herself to try to relax. Trevor was watching her every move, and she didn't want to scare him any more than he already was.

"Jesse? What happened? Are you guys okay?"

Jesse let her breath out in a burst. "The phone went dead, and the power is out. Should I call the police?" Visions of a tacky horror movie flashed through her head as they stood in the garage.

"We are on our way, just sit tight. Call over to the Johnsons." The Johnsons lived next door, which in this neighborhood, meant down the street and around the corner. There was an old path that cut through the woods between the houses. No one really used it anymore, but it did save time when they were younger.

"Okay, good idea. See you soon." Jesse hung up the phone and said to Trevor, "Daddy and Jack are coming home."

"Daddy and Jack, Jen too?" Trevor adored Jen because she always played games with him and let him win.

"Jen is in California working, but your dad said he and Jack will be home soon. Let's go inside." As she shooed him into the kitchen, the side door to the garage caught her eye. It was ajar. Had she left it open? With her heart in her throat, she cautiously approached the door flashing back to her childhood days. She and Kristen Johnson were best friends. They used to play Nancy Drew and pretend that they were detectives. Inventing and solving countless mysteries, they usually ended up in trouble for sneaking through the house or peoples' yards. If only this was one of those mysteries. Jesse reached over, flung the door shut, and dashed back into the kitchen. After locking the doors and checking all of the windows, she found Trevor playing with his Legos. She called the Johnsons whose power was out as well. Mrs. Johnson suggested that an animal had gotten into the transformer. That happened at least twice a year.

The next half hour passed slowly, as Jesse and Trevor made a small Lego town. It was quarter past five. "I'm going to start supper." Trevor barely glanced at her as he was immersed in his own pretend world.

As she absentmindedly rinsed the vegetables, she stared into the woods from the kitchen sink. What had been tugging at her mind about the woods? Something was different, but she couldn't put her finger on it. As she watched the trees, some bushes moved off to the left. Gripping the knife she was using to cut up the lettuce, she leaned forward to get a better look. A deer burst out of the bushes, ran along the edge of the fence, and disappeared again between the two pine trees that Trevor had pointed to earlier. That's what had been bothering her. At any time of day or night, there were noises from within the forest. Whether it was squirrels arguing, birds calling each other, or the random drop of an acorn or pinecone, there was always something. When she was looking at the footprints in her backyard, the woods were silent. It was as if someone had pressed pause. There was no noise and no movement. The deer was the first sign of life she could remember in the last hour. Something had scared the animals into silence. Walking in to check on Trevor, she found him putting away the toys. When did he start cleaning up after himself?

"Where's Daddy? He should be home by now." Trevor looked expectantly at Jesse.

"He'll be here soon, hon. Can I ask you a couple of questions about the man you saw earlier?" Jesse sat on the floor next to him and helped him clean up the small plastic pieces.

His eyes filled with fear again. She felt bad bringing up the topic, but she needed some answers. "When you saw him today, what made you look for him? Did he say anything?"

He shook his head, and his dirty blond curls shifted back and forth across his wide eyes. "He called me Tommy, so I looked up. He was standing there, staring at me." Trevor shivered and crawled into Jesse's lap.

"What did he do when you saw him?"

"When I yelled for you, I guess he went away."

"Where did he go?"

"I don't know. The woods I guess." He looked down. "I was scared, I just wanted you."

"It's okay, honey. You did the right thing by getting me." They both jumped as a crash came from the garage. Laughing they recognized the sound of the garage door being pulled up. That meant Steven and Jack were home. "Daddy's here!" Trevor jumped up and ran into the kitchen. When the door opened, the boy was standing on a chair with his arms open wide.

Trevor sailed into his father's arms almost knocking him down.

"Well hello to you too." With Trevor still clinging to him he hugged his wife. "There was a big accident. Apparently, someone drove off the road into a telephone pole tearing down the lines. According to the police officer at the scene, they should have the power back up in the next hour or so. So that's one mystery solved, anything new here?" Steven set Trevor down, and he immediately jumped onto Jack's back for the mandatory piggyback ride. Until now Jack had been standing quietly by the door.

"Hey, buddy, let's go for a ride." Jack winked at Jesse and Steven and took off through the house with Trevor yelling commands.

"Thanks for coming home. I know it sounds crazy, but I do think I saw footprints." Jesse let go and sat down.

"What did Trevor say happened?"

"Well, all he said was that the guy stood there and called him Tommy. Then he disappeared into the woods when Trevor called for me." She pointed to the yard and then to the patch of grass by the trees.

"Why don't Jack and I go check it out? You can stay here with Trevor and get supper ready." He went off in search of Jack. Judging from the racket, they were in the spare room right above them upstairs.

She went back to the salad as the boys came down the stairs. Jesse went to preheat the oven to only remember that the power was still out. "While you're outside, why don't you start the grill? Power's still out." Jesse flipped the light switch on and off as if demonstrating the lack of electricity.

"Will do. Be back in a few."

Trevor reluctantly pulled out the placemats and began to set the table. "Are they looking for the Badman?"

"Um... I think they are checking out the fence and looking where you saw him. When they come back, they'll probably want to talk to you, okay?"

"I guess so...do we need spoons?" Jesse barely heard him as she watched the men walk along the edge of the fence pointing, shrugging, and nodding. Steven turned and saw Jesse watching them. He signaled that they were going into the woods. Holding up two hands with the fingers splayed he then pointed to his watch. Ten minutes...and they jumped the fence. Jesse was pretty confident that whoever was there earlier was long gone, but her stomach churned with anxiety. Finishing the salad, she helped Trevor with the table.

"Can we have Corn Flake chicken?" Trevor loved the recipe handed down from her mother. He liked smashing up the Corn Flakes and dipping the chicken in the eggs and crumbs. It wouldn't work tonight because she had no idea if it would cook right on the grill.

"No oven tonight, we will do it another time."

"I miss Grandma. I wish she was still alive." Trevor sat at the table with his chin in his hands.

"I do too, but it's nice to tell stories about her. What's your favorite story?"

"Um, I think the one when she went swimming in her clothes! Tell me again!"

Jesse remembered the day well. It was a brutally hot day in June. They were invited to the neighbor's house to swim. While getting her sisters, brother, and cousin ready, she forgot to pack her own suit. The kids spilled out of the car when they got there and sprinted to the pool. Without even saying hello, they jumped in. Her mother walked around to the back yard and was embarrassed to see her kids swimming before greeting their host. Torn between understanding and being embarrassed she tried to scold the children for their lack of manners. However, Mrs. Cook came out the back door mid-scolding. She walked up behind her mother and slyly nudged her hip. With hands full of towels, snacks, and pool toys, her mother fell into the pool. The children were silent as they waited for her to surface. With a completely straight face, their mother walked up the pool stairs and dropped the soggy items on the pool deck. Then she strode to the diving board and cannon balled the group. That was Trevor's favorite part.

"She did a cannon ball?" He asked the same question each time the story was told.

"She sure did and because she forgot her suit, she just swam in her clothes."

"You should do that, Mom." Trevor walked over to the picture hanging in the hall of the grandmother he never got the chance to meet.

"Maybe, let's go put the chicken on the grill." Carrying the platter of marinated chicken, she led Trevor into the backyard. Neither could help themselves from looking at the place the strange man had stood and where Jack and Steven had hopped the fence. The spitting of the chicken going onto the hot grill hid the noise of the two men returning from their walk. Both Jesse and Trevor jumped when they heard the chain link fence clanging.

"Sorry to scare you." Steven brushed hair from Jesse's cheek. "Hey, Trev, go show Jack how high you can swing."

Jack took Trevor's hand and led him away so his parents could discuss what they saw. "Well?" Jesse asked.

"We found something interesting, but we aren't sure if we are overreacting." Steven turned the chicken on the grill. "There are what look like footprints that go all the way around the fence. There are also small piles of cigarette butts in five or six places around our yard."

"Steven, someone's been watching us for a long time!" Her hand flew to her mouth where she nervously worked a nail.

Taking her hand in his, Steven said, "It does look weird. Weird enough to at least call the police, we think. I just don't want to freak out Trevor any more than he already is." He paced back and forth in front of the grill. "Also, no one has seen him besides Trevor. Will they even listen to us?"

"Joe will." Jesse saw the expected grimace on her husband's face. "We should call him and at least get his take on it." She understood why Joe wasn't Steven's favorite person. She dated him through most of high school up until she left for college. They had remained friends, and he had helped the family when her father was sick and she was living in the city. Jesse considered him a dear friend more than an ex-boyfriend.

"I don't know," Steven protested.

"It makes sense, Steven." Jack had returned with Trevor in tow. "Who else can you call unofficially to get some questions answered? You want a beer?" Trevor giggled when Jack pointed to him. "Come help me, little man." The two went into the house in search of drinks.

"Two to one, I'm going to call him and see if he can come by." Jesse already had her phone to her ear and was dialing his number.

It was the right thing to do, Steven couldn't let his ego get in the way of his family's safety. But did his wife really need to have her ex's phone programmed into her phone? Turning the chicken, he cut into it to see if it was cooked. "Just a few more minutes," he said to his friend as Jack slapped a beer into his outstretched hand.

Jack had nodded to Jesse in a silent question of, "She's calling him?"

With an arch of the eyebrow and a slight nod Steven acknowledged the fact that they did indeed need to contact Joe. Jesse walked away to talk. As she paced the length of the garage explaining the situation, Steven remembered the years that his father-in-law was sick. Like it or not, Joe had made it easier. Whether it was checking on Jesse's parents, driving them into Boston for doctor's appointments, or keeping up the yard... Joe had acted more like a son-in-law than Steven himself. Was it actually guilt that stoked the jealousy he felt toward the man? Steven's first job was in the city. He and Jesse had found an apartment in the Back Bay and neither had a car. The monthly parking rental was almost more than their apartment. With his student loans and Jesse finishing nursing school at Mass General Hospital, there was little money for luxuries, like cars, square meals, or cable. Jesse's family was forever grateful for Joe's generosity. Though if you asked Joe himself, he was 'just doing for family.'

Joe's parents were shadows compared to the Martins. He would have been looking at the law from the other side of the bars, had he not had Jesse and her family to help him through high school and beyond. Swallowing the last of his beer and some of his pride, Steven approached Jesse to hear the last of the conversation.

"Thanks, Joe. Supper is almost ready, why don't you join us, and we can talk more?" Jesse gave Steven the thumbs up. "Okay, see you soon."

"What's up?"

"He was just heading home, so he will come by here on his way. We have enough for him too, right?"

"Jack won't get a doggie bag, but that's okay."

"I'm going to get the rest of the food on the table. Will you watch the chicken and Trevor?" Jesse glanced at her son, swinging high. Jack was pretending to get kicked in the head with each pass. Smiling and shaking her head, she headed inside to finish supper preparations.

Chapter 2

"Daddy!" The small boy reached for his father, his hands grasping the torn collar of his father's bathrobe. "Daddy, why did you hurt me?" Big brown eyes filled with tears, and a bubble of blood escaped his lips. Too quickly, the frail body slumped in his father's lap.

"What have I done?" Rocking back and forth in the hallway, the big man held the now still body of his son. "Oh my God, oh my God, oh my God... Somebody help!"

"Hey, buddy, are you okay?" The rough hand touched his shoulder bringing Matthew Stone back to the present. He was lying on a bench in the state park. Clutching a tear-stained blue scrap of fabric to his chest, he looked up to see a man in jogging shorts standing over him.

Wiping his eyes on the piece of his son's blanket, he stood up. "Yeh, I'm okay. I uh, must have dozed off." Another blackout—that had happened a few times in the past.

"You sure you're okay? You look pretty upset." The stranger bent down to look closer at Matt, no doubt noticing that he hadn't shaved or possibly even bathed in several days.

"I took a few days off to collect myself. My parents died, and I'm up here cleaning out their house. The funeral was Monday." Matt had no idea where that explanation came from. Then the truth hit him. After running across the road and causing a car to crash, he must have sat down to rest. He stood up quickly to go. The police would be looking for him.

"I'm so sorry for your loss." The man crossed himself silently. "You sure you're okay?"

Matt nodded and walked away. "Hey," he called over his shoulder to the man, "Thank you. I'll be okay." Then to himself, he thought, "Well there are some pleasant New Englanders." He had always heard that Yankees could be cold and untrusting. In the few months he had been here, he had not bothered to make an effort to meet people. He kept seeing his Tommy, sure that it was him. Deep down, he realized it wasn't possible, because Tommy had died in his arms years ago, but this little boy looked and acted just like him. As much as he knew it was going to get him in trouble, he couldn't help himself from trying to catch a glimpse of him each day.

After the hearing in North Carolina, Matthew packed a few belongings, drained his bank account, and hit the road. Even with the acquittal, there was no way he could stay in Charlotte. There were too many memories, too many whispers. He felt there were some who believed he had done it on purpose. Some even went as far as saying that he was responsible for his wife's death too. With Carol gone, there was nothing left for him there. Matt decided to explore the country and try to start over. At the very least, he might be able to escape the nightmare that had become his life.

Matt had just been able to sleep through the night when he first saw Tommy get on a bus at the school. He followed the bus and saw where the boy lived. Now each waking moment was filled with the uncontrollable desire to hold his son again. He needed to be more careful. The boy had seen him and started yelling. The woman in the car might be able to describe him. He could probably be charged with stalking. The police were taking that very seriously now. With a kid? Much worse. He needed to get his head on straight, leave this place and move on. That way he could keep himself out of trouble and try to forget the past. As he drove back to his motel, he decided to leave the next morning.

Feeling better having made the decision to leave the small town, he stopped for supper at a small Italian restaurant. He looked in the rearview mirror and was not shocked to see deep hollows around his eyes. Using fingers and some spit, he combed through his hair, tucked in his shirt, and got out of his rusty Taurus. The hostess gave him a quick once over and with a 'humph' led him to a small table in the back. That suited him just fine. He had plans to make and wanted some time to think without distractions.

The waitress was more pleasant. Her name was Terri and reminded him of a long-lost cousin from back home. She had a husband who had been a truck driver and wanted to know if he was one too. Not knowing why lies came so easy to him now, he said that he had just finished a long weekend of fishing and was looking forward to a real meal. She laughed and bustled off with his order. The chicken parmesan was delicious. Matt surprised himself by finishing the heaping plate of pasta and cutlets. When the waitress offered dessert, he said yes and asked her to pick the best one. The tiramisu was the best he had ever had, he had told her without lying this time. Matt left Terri a generous tip and allowed himself a smile as he left. The old red vinyl booth creaked and the man in the painted mural on the wall forever rowing his boat but never getting anywhere. He related to the guy, stuck in time with nowhere to go, and no way to go back.

****

Dinner was more than a little uncomfortable. The adults tried to make small talk while the young boy peppered the policeman with questions. Trevor had met Joe before, but it wasn't often he saw him in uniform, and most certainly never at his own kitchen table! Joe skillfully asked him questions. What did he do at school? Were there any new teachers, or janitors? Did any new friends move into town this year? How often did he go out for recess, or play at the park, or in his back yard? Then he asked Trevor the big question. Where had he seen the man before? Trevor had been eating quickly, talking fast, being very animated. Until the mention of the man. He sat back in his seat, grabbed his mother's hand, and looked out the kitchen window.

"I don't want to talk anymore." His voice was soft, and he looked smaller than he was, almost curling into himself. Trevor was putting the pieces together. Joe was here and he is a policeman. So, either he was in trouble, or they finally believed him. Both ideas were scary.

"It's okay, Trev, Joe wants to help us," Jack intervened. "If you tell him about the man, Joe can talk to him and find out why he was here."

"I've seen him a buncha times. He watches me. At school during recess. He's been at the grocery store, the library, and here. Mommy and Daddy don't believe me, but he's everywhere."

Steven reached out to take Trevor on his lap. "I'm sorry, champ. I didn't know what to think."

"You believe me now?" Trevor looked from Jesse to Steven and then Joe and Jack.

"Yes, we do. Can you tell me what he looks like?" Joe leaned forward slightly, his weight tipping the table slightly.

"He's big, like you, Dad, but not as big as you." Trevor pointed at Joe.

Ouch. Joe was built like a linebacker, while he himself was more of a quarterback. *Bet I could beat him in a race...*

"What else can you tell me? What color eyes and hair does he have?" Joe was discretely writing notes on a small pad he had pulled from his pocket.

"He has crazy hair. It's all sticking up. Sometimes he has a beard, sometimes he's just messy looking." Trevor was animated again, pulling his hair straight out and doing his monster face.

"Good job, Trevor. What color is his hair?"

"Brown-y, black." He pointed to Steven for the brown and Jack for the black.

"Is it long? Short? Curly like yours or straight?"

Trevor waited for a minute. "Too long for a guy." He put his hand below his ears. "A hooligan, like Nana calls the kids who skateboard in the park."

Joe straightened up. "Is he a teenager?"

"No, he's old, like you."

Joe laughed while Jesse tried to apologize for Trevor. Score one for the Daddy, Steven silently tallied.

Joe pressed on, "Have you seen his eyes?"

"They look dark, shiny, but he has big eyebrows, so they are hard to see."

"Good, good. Now, do you remember what he was wearing?"

"Pants, like Jack's." Everyone looked at Jack. He was wearing jeans. "But his were messy, like torn up. He wears a sweatshirt too. It has some kinda picture on it, but I don't know what it is."

"Do you remember what color it is?"

"Blue, I think. But he wears that one and a red one. Nothing else." Trevor crawled from Steven's lap to Jesse's. "He scares me. What does he want?"

"Honey, we don't know. But Daddy, me, Jack, and Joe will figure it out. Okay?" Jesse's fingers twirled Trevor's curls around and around. "Right, boys?" She looked purposefully at the men gathered around the table.

"Of course. I have to check into a couple of things tonight. Let me talk to a few people, and I will call you tomorrow." Joe addressed the group. To Trevor he added, "Hey, little guy, would you like to go look at the cruiser? I will be out in a minute to show you some of the cool stuff." He motioned to Jack to take the boy outside for a few minutes and waited until they left to talk again.

****

Trevor ran ahead screaming, "This is so cool!" He jumped up and down trying to see in. Jack lifted him up so he could peer in the driver's window. Jack looked through a window in the house, watching his friends talking with the policeman. He had been observing Joe interacting with his friends during dinner. Jack could honestly say there didn't appear to be a reason for Steven to worry over the ex. Jesse was polite, friendly even, but she constantly had her hand on either Trevor's shoulder, or holding Steven's hand, wiping a tiny crumb from his lip, playing with the hair at the base of his neck. All things she did on a regular basis that were reminders that these boys were her world.

Joe was like having an old friend around. Easy going, quick witted, and concerned for the safety of his friends and his town. He was at ease in the house, grabbing the milk when Trevor asked for a refill, and knowing where to find the paper towels when he washed his hands before dinner. If Jack had seen a glance that lasted too long or anything indicating that Joe was holding onto memories, he would bring it to his best friend's attention. Calling the cop was a good idea. Jack would die if anything happened to Trevor. He tapped the boy on the shoulder and said, "Tag, you're it!" They took off running across the front yard.

****

"I think we need to take this seriously. Trevor has too much detail to be making this up. He also repeated the same descriptions again and again tonight. If it wasn't real, there would be subtle differences. I want to see these footprints you saw. So why don't we go for a quick walk out back? I will look closer when the light is better tomorrow." Joe stood up, raised his eyebrows as if asking if it was okay.

Steven stood up. "Come on, I will show you what Jack and I discovered. You coming?" He looked at Jesse.

"No, I'll clean up and stay with Trevor. Do you want Jack to go?" Jesse jumped as the power came back on. The TV blared from the other room, the ice cubes dumped from ice maker into the freezer and Jesse dropped the salad bowl. "Shit! That scared the life out of me!" They all leaned down to clean up the scattered vegetables. "I've got it. You two go."

Steven put his hands on her shoulders. "Are you sure you are okay? You almost jumped out of your skin there."

"I'm fine, go before it gets too dark."

She tried to sweep up the lettuce, but it ended up making more of a mess. Getting down on her hands and knees to pick up the pieces, Jesse remembered playing on the floor as her mother ironed or cooked. Sometimes she would color or play with her plastic animals. Sometimes she would just listen to her mother humming. Her mother could never remember the words to any songs but loved music. Her parents had eclectic tastes. In any evening they would listen to the Boston Pops 1812 Overture, Pete Seeger and Arlo Guthrie folksongs, and Harry Belafonte. The sound of the needle dropping onto the vinyl record was like a cattle-call for her sisters and brother. The kids would come running into the living room to dance and sing. Jesse shook her head, bewildered how she could get so sidetracked. Finishing with the salad mess, she turned to the sink. Steven and Joe were walking slowly outside the fence. They would stop every once in a while and squat down. Joe took notes and snapped a few pictures on his phone. When they disappeared into the woods, she finished up the dishes.

Outside, Trevor was back at the police car sitting in the front seat pretending to drive. He was whooping like a siren and make screeching sounds as he accelerated and braked in his imagination. Jack walked over and gave Jesse a hug. "Are you okay?"

"I don't know. This is crazy. Why would someone be watching Trevor? Is he a pedophile? What does he want?" Jesse pulled away and shivered, despite the warm evening air.

"I don't know, Jesse. But I think Joe is taking it seriously. It's good to have friends in high places, huh?"

"Yeah, it must be killing Steven to have to take his help. I don't think he likes him very much."

"Joe isn't his favorite person. However, I know he wants to keep you guys safe, not play Superman and think he can do it himself."

"Mommy, look at me! I'm a cop!" Trevor looked tiny behind the wheel. His head barely reaching the top of the steering wheel.

"Awesome!" Jesse put Joe's hat on his head. "Now you look more official."

"Now I can't see, I'm going to crash! Screech! Bam!" Trevor yelled at the top of his lungs and threw himself around the front seat of the cruiser. Giggling, he peered out from under the rim of the hat. "Where's Joe?"

"Right here. Did you crash my car?" Joe leaned into the window and straightened his hat on Trevor's head.

"No, I was just pretending. Sorry, Joe." Trevor put the hat in the passenger seat and moved to climb out.

"Hang on. Push over." Joe slid into the driver's seat and flipped on the siren.

Trevor's eyes were as round as saucers as he put his fingers in his ears. "That's cool! What's this? And this?" His little hands touched everything in the car.

Joe named a few of the buttons, then promised to show him more tomorrow. "I bet it's time for you to start getting ready for bed. I am going do some work tonight and talk to your parents in the morning." He ruffled Trevor's hair as they climbed out of the car. The boy looked back as he walked up the steps with Steven and Jack and waved.

"So, what do you think? Did you see anything?" Jesse leaned against the car and looked him directly in the eye. Joe would tell her the truth. They might not be together, but she could read him like a book. That was nothing new.

"There's a fairly visible path from the backyard into the woods. I want to look at it more closely tomorrow. We both know kids use the woods to party, but these new trails are too close to your property, and the path looks recently worn. Also, there are piles of cigarette butts. If I am right, they correspond to spots where he could watch Trevor either in the front yard, the back yard, his room, or the family room. Whoever he is, he is trying very hard to keep tabs on you guys. I am going to guess that he is watching Trevor, because Trevor is the only one to have seen him. Tomorrow I think we should have him talk to the sketch artist. Maybe they can come up with a picture?"

"So, you think there is reason to worry?"

"Well, he appears to be stalking Trevor, and we really don't know for how long. We are being very careful with this lately. Especially with a kid. I will have a car come by several times through the night and call you in the morning. I am not sure about school for him. Let me talk to a friend of mine at the State Police. They probably have dealt with things like this. You

S. Hilbre Thomson

okay with that?" Joe reached out and laid his hand on Jesse's shoulder.

Jesse reached up and gave him a quick hug. "I hate that this is happening but am glad we called you. You have always helped us out." Jesse stepped back and leaned against the car again.

"Well, your parents basically saved me. Without them, I probably would have dropped out of school and...who knows what." Joe kicked the dirt on the driveway. "I'd do anything for them. For you." He looked past her, into the woods that separated their property from the Johnsons'. Years ago, he would meet Jesse there and hide under the branches of the willow tree. They would share their dreams, their worries, and more than a few kisses. It never failed though, that before they could get too serious, one of her sisters would come giggling by and remind them that they weren't in their own world. Evie was the closest one in age to Jesse, and as they got older, the relationship had changed from tormenting her little sister to protecting her. One time, Jesse and Joe had fallen asleep under the tree. Evie woke up in the middle of the night. Before panicking, she slipped out of the house and checked the willow tree. After scaring the hell out of them, she helped Jesse sneak back in. Joe's parents weren't even aware he was gone, so he just walked home.

"Hello. Earth to Joe..." Jesse waved her hand in front of Joe's face.

"Sorry, spaced out there. I should go. Lock the doors and call me if anything comes up." Joe reached for the handle, grazing Jesse's hip.

"Thanks, Joe." Jesse slipped past him, looking where he had just been staring. Nodding to herself she realized he was probably looking at the willow tree. Those were some of the best times in her life. She had a great family, parents who would give her the moon if she asked, and was dating the captain of the football team. It was all so easy, back then. No responsibilities. She just had to get good grades and do her chores. Now, as a grown up, everything worried her, Trevor, Steven, the house, the bills, the future, the past. It all changed when her dad got sick her freshman year of college.

The sound of the engine turning over jarred her back to the present. The look on Joe's face told her he could tell that she, too, was reminiscing. They shared a bittersweet smile before he made a quick three-point turn and drove down the long driveway.

****

Jesse watched him until the taillights blinked out as he rounded the corner. Not wanting to be alone outside, she hurried up the steps and into the house. She could hear Jack, Steven, and Trevor laughing upstairs. Touching the picture of her parents as she walked by, she said a silent prayer. "Mom, Dad? Please watch over Trevor. Help us keep him safe." Putting on a smile, she walked into Trevor's bedroom, where she could see that the shades had been drawn. Were they blocking out the world, or blocking them from the world?

"Hey there, guys...ready for bed?" Jesse laughed at her own joke, as the bed was in shambles. The sheets were hanging from the top bunk to make a fort. Every stuffed animal ever sold appeared to be in the fort or spilling out onto the floor. Her son's sweaty face peered out from the pile.

"Mom, Jack made a zoo!" Jack looked sheepishly at Jesse while arranging more animals on the top bunk.

"I can see, how 'bout we put these creatures back in their homes?"

"No! I want to sleep with them. All of them." Trevor clasped his hands together in mock prayer.

"Pick a habitat." Steven tried to negotiate. Animals were Trevor's favorite. He could tell you where almost any creature lived. His vocabulary was unbelievable for a boy his age.

Trevor scanned the animals, no doubt looking to see which animal habitat was represented the most in his homemade domain. "Um, the rainforest?" Pleased with his choice, they organized the animals. As they sorted, he mumbled the habitats as he threw them into the storage bins. "Dessert, forest, tundra…"

The adults stepped in the hall as Trevor sorted and said goodnight to his animals. "So, what did you and Joe talk about?" Jesse asked Steven.

"Well, we walked the fence line, and I showed him the cigarettes and the path. He seems to believe Trevor and thinks we need to be very careful. I gotta admit I feel awful not believing Trev. I figured he was just pissed at me for working so much." Steven dragged his hand across his face.

"Hey, we all thought he was imagining it. Let's come up with a plan with Joe tomorrow and try to get the guy." Jack peeked into Trevor's room. He was still sorting.

"Joe said he was going to call a friend of his from the State Police. He's going to tell them everything we told him and see what she says." Jesse bent over to pick up some pine needles that had stuck to the bottom of their shoes and dropped on the carpet. "I will feel much better once they find him."

"Mommy! I'm ready!" Trevor's voice floated into the hall.

"I'll tuck him in. You going to hang around?" Jesse asked Jack.

"I'll probably hit the road. Jen will be calling soon."

"Take one last look around the yard with me?" Steven asked his friend.

"Sure, 'night, Jesse." Jack kissed her cheek and followed Steven downstairs.

"Drive carefully, and thanks for your help tonight." Jesse blew him a kiss and slipped through the door.

Jesse read Trevor his favorite books, giving in for the fourth book, though three was the usual limit. Jesse lay in bed with him, loving the way his hair smelled, the soft rhythm of his breathing, and the way he rubbed the tail of a panther between his two fingers. She would do anything to protect him. She slid out of the bed and tiptoed to the door. Clicking on the night light, she could see his head poking out from the animals on his bed. Jesse went downstairs to find Steven sitting on the couch drinking a beer.

"Hey there." Jesse took the bottle from his hand and helped herself to a generous sip. "Thanks, what are we going to do?"

Taking the bottle back, he drained it and peeled off the label. She hated it when he did that because then they couldn't get the nickel back when they recycled. Tonight, she let it slip. "I am going to stay home tomorrow and work from here. Jack will cover the meeting with Connelly-Burbank. Are you scheduled to work tomorrow?"

"I'll call out. Meredith will kill me, but I can't leave now. Should I tell her what's going on?"

"I don't know. Let's wait and see what tomorrow brings. I feel like I should patrol the yard or something. Sitting in here makes me crazy. But Joe said to act as normal as possible. He thinks that's the only way we might catch the guy. If we up and change things, he'll know we know, you know what I mean?"

"No," Jesse answered more playfully than she felt. Steven kicked his feet up and laid his head in her lap. As they flipped through channels, Jesse stroked his hair. "Pretty soon you'll have to start coloring this."

"What?"

"Your hair. The salt is winning the salt and pepper war." To emphasize her point, she plucked a gray hair and showed it to him.

"Ouch, that's cruel. If I dared mention an imperfection of yours, you'd cry and shut me off for weeks!" He pretended to sniffle.

"True, but it's the cross you bear, being the greater sex and all." Jesse flicked his ear.

"I'll show you greater sex." Steven used his dirty man voice, a trick he used to make her laugh. He could turn any phrase into a sexual inuendo with a drop in his tone. Though "I'll clean your dishes" said with a leer and a grope, didn't get her juices flowing, it did make her laugh.

Steven had pulled her down for a kiss. Having him home at night was a novelty. Even with the unusual circumstances, she found herself giving into the kiss and lying next to him on the couch. Soon they were entangled and fell to the floor. The audience on the television was applauding at all the right times, both on the screen and off. Afterward, they lay in each other's arms.

"Was I as good as I think I was?" Steven joked.

"Not bad, for an old man. Especially one who's out of practice."

"Zing, way to kick somebody when they're down. Pun intended." He waved his hand at his crotch.

"You can make up for it…" Jesse rolled over onto her stomach, hoping he would take the hint and rub her back.

"You want it doggie style?" Steven arched an eyebrow.

"You wish—did you hear something?" Pulling the blanket over her she sat up and put her finger to her lips.

"No, wait…" There was a distinct thumping sound coming from the front hall. "I think Trevor's coming down!" As they both struggled to get into their clothes, Steven tripped and fell over the coffee table. Jesse was unable to control her laughter as he landed with his ass in the air and pants around the ankles.

"Careful, you are showing off your assets." Jesse tossed her tee shirt over her head, smacked his bottom, and went to intercept Trevor.

"Pig," he called as he wriggled into his pants.

"That's why you love me," she called back.

Jesse's sense of humor was not for everyone, but he loved it. Shaking his head, he pulled on his shirt and tried to act casual.

"Did you fall, Mommy? I heard you crying." Trevor looked from one parent to the other.

"I wasn't crying, I was laughing." Jesse mouthed OMG over Trevor's head.

"We were just fooling around, and Mommy thought I was being funny." Steven looked proud of himself for coming up with a clever reply that neither lied nor told the truth.

"Why are you up?" Jesse asked Trevor.

"I can't sleep. I'm scared. The Badman, Joe coming over, you know." Trevor nestled himself between his parents.

"How do you feel about today?" Steven asked.

The young boy shrugged. "I don't know. I'm scared. Why does that man keep coming here?"

"We don't know why, honey. But your mom, Uncle Jack, me, and Joe will keep you safe. The doors are locked, and we're right here with you. Do you want to watch some TV?" Jesse reached for the remote, which she couldn't find. Ironic, because ten minutes before, she knew exactly where it was, jamming into her butt. She had tossed it off to the side. Reaching under the coffee table she pulled out two pairs of socks, an Iron Man figure, and the remote.

"Yeah, I wanna watch Spiderman." Taking full advantage of his parents' goodwill, he settled in.

Luckily it was a movie they all liked. Jesse and Steven exchanged looks over their son's head. Would they need to worry for his safety much longer?

Chapter 3

Matt had gone back to his motel room after picking up a few maps at a gas station. The young gas attendant asked if he had an iPhone. "You don't need those dinosaurs if you have the map app," he said as he pointed to the dusty rack of maps and local attraction brochures.

Ignoring the barb, Matt picked out maps for New Hampshire, Maine, and Vermont. After paying for some sodas and chips, he walked back to his car. He would look over the maps and see if anything jumped out at him. Maybe he would go fishing.

Back in his room, he spread them out looking at the lakes in particular. He circled Lake Sebago in Maine and Lake Winnipesaukee in New Hampshire. They both looked big enough that he could blend in without causing a stir. Smaller lakes do mean more seclusion, but also smaller communities and less chance to fade into the background.

Popping the top of a can of Sprite Zero, he pulled up Safari on his iPhone; he did have one but didn't care to share that with the kid at the gas station. He surfed the web for a couple of hours looking at motels around both lakes. He would make up his mind in the morning. The comfort of knowing he had a plan to move on relaxed Matt into a sleep that was restful and more importantly, dream free.

****

Hundreds of miles away, reporter Karen Copeland looked at the story ideas her editor Mr. St. Germain had asked her to follow up on. She had worked for *The Weekly*, a small weekly newspaper for two years. It wasn't her first choice of jobs, but it did pay the bills. The paper had a Where Are They Now? column. Her job was to review the previous years' articles for that week and update any interesting stories. It looked like she had three prospects. Joanna Fields, the woman arrested for abusing foster children; Peter James, a lottery winner; and Marlene Downs the married, mayor mother of four, who was caught with the pool boy. How cliche. Boring, even more boring, and possibly coma inducing. Joanna would most likely be in prison awaiting a trial. Peter will have spent his fortune and was back working at the gas station. Marlene would be onto her next conquest, with her fool of a husband turning a blind eye so he could enjoy the life his wife's inherited wealth he had grown accustomed to. There had to be something better. Something with a punch. She kept scrolling through back copies. A picture caught her eye. A tortured looking man, cradling a framed picture of a young boy. The headline screamed "Murderer or Mourner?" She quickly read through the first few paragraphs of a story she couldn't believe she hadn't heard of. It read like a movie script. A man who lost his wife to a home invasion was being accused of killing their only son five years later. He had been acquitted of the manslaughter charges. She typed the name Matthew Stone into Google. More than one hundred hits. This story might have what her boss called 'meat.' She would have to convince him that this was something worth looking into. Understanding that this man's misery was causing her to almost giggle in anticipation, Karen put her guilt in a mental pocket and continued to research Matthew Stone well into the early morning hours.

Chapter 4

Joe sat at his computer plugging in the day's notes while sipping a Corona. The beer tasted flat, but he had run out of limes. Eating lime flavored corn chips was the closest he would get. He looked over today's calls. There was false alarm at the bank, a dispute over a fence placement, and a warrant he helped deliver for someone who jumped bail and went to his mother's house to hide. Idiot. The two interesting calls were the accident with the running man and Jesse's call. He found that typing his notes helped him organize his thoughts and kept him from forgetting details. He did this every night, even though the guys down at the station called it his 'Diary.' Dismissing their insults and the never-ending stream of flowery books with tiny locks and keys that mysteriously appeared on his desk, Joe found the practice therapeutic. Occasionally, he found a discrepancy and saved himself or a fellow officer an embarrassing mistake. He typed in the time the accident was called in. 4:25 p.m. Renee Poulee was the driver. 56 years old, renting the Gibbons' place in East Woods. Her home address was in Branford, Ct. He had no idea where that was, but he did know where the Gibbons house was. She had been checked and released from the hospital, but most likely would need a rental car. He would look in on her tomorrow. As he read over the description she had given at the scene, something clicked in his mind. Tall, broad shouldered, unruly dark hair, dirty clothes, and a wild look in his eyes but no eye color was noted. She said he was wearing a gray sweatshirt and 'workpants.'

Joe flipped though his notebook and found Trevor's description of the man he saw. 'Big, messy dark hair, dirty jeans, and a blue sweatshirt.' Blue and gray were often confused by people. There were so many shades of both colors, and they tend to blend. Seeing the two descriptions side by side, Joe recalled something else. Jesse said she called Steven at 4:15. He pulled up a map to confirm that the hill behind the Reeds' house had trails that led to many neighborhoods, including the one that the woman had almost hit the fleeing man. Joe slammed down his beer. How could he have missed that? It was the same man. The one Trevor has been seeing. Joe saw that his beer was foaming over and quickly sucked it down. He would have to bring a sketch of the man to Trevor. If he recognized him, it would answer at least one question. Why had the man run carelessly into the road? If he was familiar with the trails, it meant he might be fairly local, but not from this town. Joe knew almost everyone in town.

He called into the station to remind the dispatcher to send a car by Jesse's. He flipped through the channels not finding anything that interested him or that could take his mind off of the mysterious man. He settled on a 'true stories' show. This episode featured a daredevil rock climber who saved the lives of two fallen hikers. Opening another beer, he sat in his recliner letting his hand drop to pat his dog's head. Mutt was his name and that's what he was. No one could even guess the dog's lineage. He had the short legs of a Cocker Spaniel, a fluffy brown coat like a retriever, the muzzle of a bulldog, and German Shepherd ears. Too ugly to be cute, too cute not to love. Mutt nuzzled Joe's hand licking the salt from the chips on his fingers. Joe kept one ear trained on his radio as he drifted off to sleep.

****

Halfway through the movie, Trevor fell asleep again. Steven carried him up the stairs and gently put him back to bed. The boy mumbled something and curled up in the middle of his bed.

"He looks so vulnerable," Jesse whispered over her husband's shoulder.

"He'll be okay. We'll make sure of it." Steven closed the door halfway and led his wife down the hall to their bedroom. They brushed their teeth and got ready for bed quietly, each lost in their own worries. Jesse fell asleep wrapped in Steven's arms.

After an hour of trying to fall asleep, Steven slid out from under the covers. First, he went to Trevor's room and found him sprawled on the bed like a puppy. The animals, long forgotten, had fallen to the floor. He moved through the house silently, checking the doors and windows. Sitting in the family room he stared out the picture window into the forest. The bright moon cast a silver covering over the tips of the trees. It was hard to imagine anything bad lurking in there. There was the occasional rabbit caught by a coyote. Once a baby owl had fallen from its nest. Trevor wanted to nurse it back to health. Instead, they brought it to the wildlife rehabilitation officer. She kept the owl until it was healthy. Then it went to the sanctuary to become part of the birds of prey program.

Now the hairs on Steven's arms stood on end. He walked to the window with the feeling he was being watched. Straining his eyes to see into the forest, his mind played tricks on him. Shadows moved, the leaves rustled in the wind, and Steven willed the man to show himself. He almost yelped when something came into his sightline underneath the window. It was a skunk. A huge one. As his pulse settled into a normal rhythm, he laughed at his reaction. Man up, he chided himself.

Steven decided he would sleep on the recliner. At least then he felt like he could protect his family better if someone tried to get in. Just as he was about to nod off, he heard the telltale sound of tires on the driveway. He checked the clock on the cable box. It was blinking. They never reset it after the power came back on. Getting back up he went to the front window to check. It was probably the patrol car he told himself pulling back the curtain and peering outside. As the cruiser pulled into the driveway the headlights blinded him momentarily. Steven watched as a flashlight scanned the bushes. His emotions were conflicted, glad the cop was taking this seriously, but wounded because once again the mighty Joe was coming to the family's rescue. When the beam came to the front of the house Steven moved out of its way to remain invisible to the outside world. The officer drove away, apparently satisfied that the Reeds were safe. Steven climbed back into the recliner and tried to get some sleep.

Chapter 5

"Daddy!" Trevor jumped onto his father.

"Umpf. Morning." Steven nudged his son's knees out of his crotch. "Careful there, you might want a brother or sister one day."

"Uh?"

"Nothing, give me a hug." Steven bearhugged Trevor and tickled him with his unshaven cheek. Trevor's squeals of delight brought Jesse into the room.

"Hey, you sleep down here?" She brushed his cheek with her lips and ruffled Trevor's hair.

"Sure, if you can call it that." Steven rolled Trevor onto the floor and stood up.

"Long night?"

"Mm, Joe, or an officer, drove by."

"Good, I wonder when he'll call," Jesse looked at the cable box, then her watch. "7:00, think it's too early to call him?" She played with the buttons on the box until it read the right time.

"Let's wait until 7:30 and see if he calls us. Meanwhile, let's eat breakfast...pancakes, buddy?"

"Animal pancakes?" Trevor was now standing on the recliner and rocking back and forth.

"Sure, give me a few minutes." Steven stretched, bending down to touch his toes. Jesse could see that his boxers were inside out and remembered their rush to get dressed the night before.

"I see London, I see France, I see Daddy's underpants!" Trevor shouted with glee as he jumped off of the chair and tried to give his father a wedgie. He was at a distinct disadvantage because he only came up to his father's waist. Leverage was a problem.

Jesse helped out by giving the waistband a yank, and whispered, "They're inside out, Swifty."

He blushed at the memory and went into the kitchen to start breakfast. "We need to cancel Shannon. We won't need her today."

Jesse picked up her phone to text the babysitter giving her the day off. The sun was peeking through the trees from the east side of the hill. Usually, a favorite part of the day, Jesse didn't want to sit on the porch with her coffee like usual to 'greet the day' as her father called his morning routine. She preferred the comfort of the walls of the house between her and whomever was watching Trevor.

She felt a small hand reach around her leg. She put her hand on his shoulder and said, "So how'd you sleep?"

"Okay, I woke up real early, it was still mostly dark. I saw Joe in his car. I waved, but he didn't see me."

"Oh, he was probably just checking up on us. He'll be by again." It was nice to know that the cruisers were patrolling last night. She wasn't sure whether or not to send Trevor to school. She didn't want to scare him by keeping him home, but she also didn't want to let him out of her sight. She would have to talk to Steven and Joe. "Let's go help Daddy with breakfast."

****

Joe had been awake for hours. He went to the station to see if he could get a copy of the sketch of the man from the accident. He also wanted to talk to the other officers to see if there were more witnesses. Staring at the drawing, he got the feeling that the man he was looking at was possibly homeless. There weren't too many issues with that in this town. Sometimes there were a few that walked or hitched into town. Middlefield was right between Route One and Route 95. A lot of truckers pulled off the highway to get a meal or sleep for a few hours. Occasionally they picked up hitchhikers along the way. Once or twice a year they were called to clear someone out of the park.

The man had a haunted look. Joe's officers would show the picture around and see if anyone recognized the stranger. He wanted to get to Jesse's house to check out his idea that it was the same person Trevor had seen. He needed to walk the paths behind the house and see if there were any signs that he had run over the hill and into the road. It was probably less than a mile away 'as the crow flies.' None of the officers that reported to the accident yesterday were in that morning. Looking at his watch he assumed that they would most likely be sleeping. He decided to head over to the Reeds'. He would call Jesse along the way but wouldn't share his suspicions yet. At least not until he had a chance to look around some more.

****

"I want to wear my Red Sox shirt today," Trevor announced, putting his dish in the sink.

"Sounds good, I'll wear mine too." Steven reached to wipe the syrup from Trevor's chin. Seeing the napkin coming, the boy quickly wiped his mouth with his pajama sleeve and ducked under his father's arm. "Be right back!"

"The shirt is in the dryer; it probably needs to be ironed. You sure you can handle that?" Jesse raised her eyebrows. She never missed a chance to remind Steven that he was a mama's boy. Before they met, he had never ironed, or even laundered a shirt before. As he left the room, they shared a look. It was understood that they would do whatever it took to keep their son safe.

****

Arriving at the Reeds' house Joe saw no signs of life. He was just about to turn the car around and drive to the other side of the hill when he saw Jesse wave at him from the upstairs window. He put the car in park and walked to the front door. Steven opened the door before he could even knock.

"Morning." Steven stepped into the hall to give Joe room to enter.

"Morning, quiet night?" Joe took Steven's outstretched hand.

"No problems, saw the patrol come by. Thanks." Steven led Joe back to the kitchen. "Pancakes, coffee?" He waved at the remaining pancakes.

"No thanks, just finished my second cup." Joe leaned against the counter, while Steven sat at the table and signaled the other man to sit with him. Really too antsy to sit still, Joe sat anyway.

"So, do you know anything new?"

Joe decided to tell him his theory that the man who caused the accident might have been the man Trevor saw in their back yard. Hearing it aloud made it seem all the more plausible, but maybe too easy. Steven had been nodding and seemed to agree with the idea. "Let's go walk the paths, see what we see."

Jesse and Trevor walked into the kitchen as they were getting up. The men excused themselves, saying they were going to get another look around, leaving through the back door. Trevor was much shier that morning, hiding behind Jesse's legs and peering out to watch them leave.

"Mom, are they going to get him?"

"They are just looking around. Let's do the dishes and clean up this mess." Trevor rolled his eyes but grabbed the step stool and dragged it over to the sink. Usually, he loved playing in the bubbles, but today he was just swishing the suds around listlessly. Jesse allowed him to rinse and pass the dishes to her. She dried them and put them into the cabinet lost in her own thoughts.

Jesse was grateful to have Steven home for the day. She had understood there would be sacrifices when Steven and Jack decided to open up their own firm but didn't count on feeling like a single parent. Many days she only saw her husband as she was walking in the door from the overnight shift, and he was rushing out to start his own twelve-hour day. They would schedule date nights, only to cancel them both feeling too guilty to leave Trevor with the sitter again. Jesse took weekend shifts whenever possible to make up some of the money they still owed for her student loans, and the mortgage on the office building.

With the dishes done, and nothing to distract them, she asked Trevor if he wanted to hear a story.

"I want to see Joe's car again. Please?" His curly hair bounced up and down as he ran to the front of the house.

Jesse ran to keep up with him. "Why don't we wait for him to come back?"

"Mom, please? Can I look at it?"

Jesse saw no harm in him looking at the cruiser. They walked out the front door and over to the car. Trevor jumped up and down trying to get a good look in the windows. Jesse picked him up and held him on her hip so he could see better. Trevor reached out a small hand up to touch the roof lights. "These are cool." He slid from her arms and ran around to the front of the car. He was examining the grill lights and asking questions Jesse really wasn't listening to. It wasn't until Trevor was grabbing her shirt that she realized she was spacing out.

"Mom, can I please just sit in the front seat? I won't touch anything…"

Jesse looked around the corner to see if the guys were back. There was no sign. She figured Joe wouldn't mind, so she opened the door and let him clamber in. He reached for Joe's hat. "Officer Reed, you are quite handsome." Jesse took out her cell phone and snapped a picture. Trevor sat on his knees and pretended to drive the car. As his imagination took him on a chase, the small boy bounced back and forth. He lost his balance and fell into the passenger seat, pushing a stack of papers onto the floor.

"Oh, shit. I mean shoot. Okay Trevor, that's enough. Time to get out." Jesse opened the door to let him out and went to the other side to straighten out the papers.

Trevor sheepishly put the hat down and walked around to look over Jesse's shoulder as she cleaned up. "Sorry, Mom, it was a axed-i-dent."

She smiled at his approximation of the word and stood up with the stack in her hands.

"Mom! That's him! The Badman!" Trevor backed away from the car pointing at the sketch on the top of the pile.

"Huh?" Jesse looked at the man in the picture. "You sure? This is the man you saw yesterday?"

Trevor could only nod and continued to back away. Jesse looked at the picture more and saw yesterday's date on it. Confused, she set the pages down on the seat and took Trevor into her arms. "Let's call Daddy."

****

Joe and Steven walked in silence, both scanning the floor of the forest for any telltale signs that someone had gone through recently. Joe pointed at a broken twig or a bent blade of grass along the path. Steven nodded but really didn't see what the other man did. When Joe saw what appeared to be a skid mark in the dirt, he pointed at it and said, "Whoever ran through here almost wiped out. See, he caught himself with this branch." A tree limb was hanging at an unnatural angle and the new wood splintered through the bark.

"Yeah, that makes sense. If he was trying to get away, he would have been rushing, maybe looking behind him to see if anyone was following him," Steven offered.

Joe nodded. "Let's keep going, the trail leads this way." The men picked up their pace.

They continued on to see more signs that someone had come through there recently and in a rush. When they came to the top of the hill, Steven's phone rang. "It's Jesse. Hang on."

Joe stopped and sat on a rock. He listened to Steven's side of the conversation.

"What's wrong?" Silence. "He did? Where?" Silence. Steven looked at Joe. "Wait, Jesse, let me put you on speaker." He pushed the button, and Joe could hear Jesse's voice, near panic.

"The picture, the picture in your car, Joe. It's the man. The man Trevor's been seeing." Steven looked at Joe, who didn't look as confused as he should have in this situation.

"What picture, Jesse?" Steven asked.

"It's the sketch of the man who ran into the road yesterday, causing the accident that took out the power lines," Joe interrupted. "I was going to show it to Trevor this morning." There was silence on the other end.

"Jesse? You there?" Steven asked.

"Yeah, can you come back? Trevor is really upset. This is really freaking me out."

"We will be there as soon as we can." Joe finished talking as both men turned to walk back the way they had come.

"Let's get back." Steven started to run. Joe easily caught up with him and could have taken off at a sprint, but sensed Steven would be pissed if he was faster, so he eased back. The men jogged back without another word.

Chapter 6

Karen had woken before her alarm went off. She wanted to get into the office early to see if she could get more information on Matthew Stone. If she could dig up even a scrap of news on the man acquitted of killing his own son, maybe Mr. St. Germain would let her proceed. After a quick shower and a healthy breakfast of a Diet Coke and a Pop Tart, she was in her car on the way to the building that held the inner workings of *The Weekly*. She would need something really interesting in order to persuade her boss that this was a good story.

George, the maintenance man/security man, let her in with a comment on her early arrival. "Hot story, Karen?"

"Maybe, George. I need to do some digging first. I'll be in the 'Hole'." She waved to the old man as she headed toward the closet that served as her office. It had no windows and you had to take five steep steps down and go around a narrow corner before squeezing between her desk and filing cabinets. Thus, it was dubbed, the 'Hole' by her colleagues. But it was hers.

She plugged Matthew's name into Google search and opened up her second diet soda of the day. The first link was a blurb that appeared to come from a local Charlotte bulletin.

Young mother dead as husband and son recover from house fire.

Thursday, April 16, the body of Carol Stone, 25, was found in the ashes of her home. Her husband, Matthew, 26, and newborn son, Thomas, were dragged from the burning house by neighbors. Reports from people at the scene said that Mr. Stone was barely conscious with many injuries, while the baby seemed to be okay other than minor smoke inhalation. Authorities have not commented on the cause of the fire.

The next was an article that went into more detail. Karen skimmed it to find a gruesome story.

Young mother dead from brutal home invasion.

Police and fire arrived at 22 Birch Tree Lane yesterday at 5:30 to find the house ablaze and neighbors tending to a father and newborn son. They are now asking for the public's help in finding the men responsible for the death of Carol Stone and the attempted murder of Matthew Stone and their son Thomas. Authorities are not giving out much information but have said that Matthew came home from work where his wife and two-week old son were being held by what is believed to be two men. Stone himself was then bound and beaten and left for dead when the intruders set the house on fire and fled. Neighbors reported seeing a dark blue Chevy pickup with a dented rear fender in the driveway earlier in the afternoon.

"I was going to drop off some cookies, but saw that Carol had company, so decided to wait." Hailey Brown, neighbor and longtime friend said before

breaking into tears. That was around 2:30. Her husband saw the flames as he came home around 5:15.

"I yelled to Hailey to call 911 and ran right over." John Brown reported, "I broke the window and saw Matt tied to a chair. I was able to get him and Tommy out. I didn't know Carol was on the couch. It was completely on fire. I couldn't get her," Brown said from his hospital bed where he is being treated for injuries sustained during the rescue.

Matthew Stone remains under sedation but is expected to recover. Thomas, 'Tommy,' suffered only from smoke inhalation, but is being kept at the hospital for observation. At this point there is no description of the intruders, but another neighbor believes he saw two men in the truck as it sped away a few minutes after five.

If you have any information that you believe could help police locate these men, please call the Charlotte police department at 704- 555- 2121.

After reading a few more articles, Karen was able to piece together more information, but a follow up story done around a year ago gave the most details of what actually happened inside the house that day. The more she read, the more upset she became. It never ceased to amaze her that human beings could be so evil.

****

Matt initially felt good when he woke up in the morning. He had a job to do and packed his clothes. Maybe fishing in New Hampshire or Maine would clear his head and give him a chance to think of plans for the future. Wanting to hear what the weather would be like, he flipped on the local cable station. The top story was the accident that took out the power for the northern section of town for hours. Matt froze and listened to the story of a disheveled man running into the road, causing a woman to swerve and drive into the junction box. According to the reporter, the driver had described the man to the police, and they were working on a possible connection to another local case.

Remembering the media coverage, first from his wife's death and then from Tommy's, his legs trembled. He had to sit down. Matt couldn't believe that it might happen again. Stuffing the rest of his few belongings into his duffle he glanced around the room for anything he might have missed. As he was just about to close the door, he spotted the tattered blue scrap from his son's blanket tangled in the sheets. Bringing it to his face, he was taken back to their house in Charlotte.

"What do you want?"

"We've already gotten what we want, you just interrupted our dinner." A deep voice spoke down to him.

"Let's bring him inside," the other voice growled.

"What the f...?" With fear and anger, Matthew tried to get up and rush to Carol. His vision blurred as another explosion rocked through his head. The last thing he saw was the bat he had bought when he found out they were having a boy. 'Little Slugger' danced before him as he came to in his living room. The bat had been thrown on the living room floor. Across the room he saw his wife tied up and naked on the couch. In a rush, he pushed up and forward to find that he was tied to a chair.

"Carol!" Matthew screamed only to be hit again from behind.

"Look who's back." Matt tried to turn to see who was talking.

"Don't look at me! You look at your wife, see what we've done, what we are going to do. If you fight us, we are going to kill this." The taller man pulled back the blanket that was covering the bassinet. It was then Matt saw the man was wearing a ski mask. The stranger picked up the baby. "See your Daddy? Helpless and weak? He can't help you. Or your Momma." The baby was put back in the bassinet. "Now be a good boy and let us have some fun." Throwing the blanket back over Tommy, he got in Matt's face. "You be good, or we start in on him." The stranger's eyes were a startling green, shot with burst blood vessels.

"Who are you? Why are you here?" Nausea crawled up his throat. "Is she alive?" Straining against the ropes he begged them to leave. As the first man ran his hand up Carol's leg, the other wrapped duct tape over Matt's mouth and around his head. He still had not seen the second attacker other than from the corner of his swollen eye.

"I hope so, I'm not finished yet." The first man threw a glass of whiskey on Carol's face. She moaned and rolled her head in Matt's direction. The green eyes glared at Matt as the man licked the whiskey off of Carol's cheek. Barely conscious, she looked at him with terror. Matthew cried and strained against the ropes. That earned him another hit with the bat, and pain rocketed through his body.

"Shut up and sit still. Don't forget about the brat." The man nodded at Tommy who was now crying loudly.

Utterly helpless, he listened to the men rape and beat his wife again. He could not watch so he squeezed his eyes shut and begged God to end this nightmare.

A shrill ringing brought everything to a halt. The men froze and Matthew looked at the phone helplessly. "Hi guys, it's Tammy. I was hoping to catch you before supper, but I'm running late. I'm dropping by with a lasagna, hope you haven't eaten yet!" The line went dead as their friend hung up.

"Well, guess that's our cue." The taller of the two stood up, pulled his jeans up, and walked over to Matthew. "Thank you for your hospitality." He took off his mask, and long hair spilled over his shoulders. A small scar above his lip was more pronounced when he grinned wickedly. The rancid breath from the liquor and garlic of whatever they had eaten, stung his eyes.

Instantly, Matt understood why the man had taken off the mask. He was going to die. Using the last of his strength he pushed forward, and head butted the man in the stomach sending him sprawling on his ass.

"Now you really shouldn't have done that." Matthew watched again as the second man walked into the garage and came back with a large red plastic jug. The smell of gas filled his nostrils as the heel of a boot came down on his temple. His last memory was the howl of his house going up in flames.

Matt sat on the edge of the bed sweating and gasping for breath. He went to the bathroom sink, splashed his face with some cold water, and grabbed his bag again. Stuffing the tattered cloth into his pocket, he closed the door and headed to the motel office to settle his bill. He was never going to truly escape this nightmare. Once he was on the road, he hoped he would feel better, safer.

****

Karen read through several more stories before her breath caught in her throat.

Mourner or Murderer?

Tragedy has struck the Stone family once again. But is it just a tragedy, or is it treachery as well?

Early this morning state police were summoned to the home of Matthew Stone in Dilworth. The body of five-year-old Thomas Stone was discovered when the police answered a 911 call. Officers found Matthew Stone holding the body of his son, who had died from a gunshot wound. It is reported that Mr. Stone woke up to what he believed was someone breaking into the apartment. In an attempt to scare away the intruders, his gun went off, fatally injuring the boy. Stone was taken into custody pending an investigation.

Karen sat back in her chair. She downed the rest of her Diet Coke and continued searching.

****

As Matthew began to drive toward Route 95, he couldn't get Tommy's face out of his mind. He felt as if he was leaving him on the coroner's table all over again. Dizziness swept over him, so he pulled to the side of the road. There was no way he could leave Tommy. This might be his only chance to see his son again. Feeling trapped by the confines of the car, Matt got out and walked around to the other side. Leaning against the door, he struggled to get his breath. His heart ached to see his son, hold him, read a story to him. The ache became unbearable. Reaching inside the car to pull out a bottle of prescription anxiety meds, he saw the scrap of Tommy's old blanket on the seat. He brought it to his face and inhaled. The scent was there, barely. A mixture of baby shampoo, oatmeal, and well, just innocence. A whole new wave of grief almost took Matt to his knees. Tucking the piece into his pocket he opened the glove compartment. He had never liked taking medication, not even an Advil. Since the attack, he took anxiety pills every day with a second pill he used for extreme situations. Like when he hyperventilated or felt like he was being crushed by memories and emptiness. Dry swallowing two pills he tilted his head back to look at the sky. The bitter taste was welcome, knowing soon he would get some relief. Matt sat on the ground and tried to focus on the tops of the trees on the side of the road. He practiced some of the deep breathing the therapist had taught him. Sometimes it worked, sometimes it didn't. Either way, this time it was helping. Slowly his breathing returned to normal, and he was able to see straight.

Matthew returned to the car with a new plan. He would drive by the school just to see the boy one more time and then be on his way. This would be it, he promised himself. Then he would put this mess, and the whole town, behind him.

Chapter 7

Jesse and Trevor were waiting for the guys in the kitchen. Out of breath, Steven handed Joe a bottle of water before getting one himself.

"Dad, Dad, I saw him. Joe had a picture in his car!" Trevor jumped up and down and then apologized for messing up Joe's stuff.

"It's my fault, I let him sit in the front seat." Jesse was biting her nails again.

"No problem. I was going to show it to Trevor anyway. Do you have it?" Joe finished the water and crushed the bottle.

"I put it back in the seat."

"Be right back."

"Did you guys find anything back there?" Jesse asked sitting down next to her husband.

"Yeah, Joe was able to find where he ran through the woods. We stopped when you called."

"Here it is." Joe reentered and sat back down. "Trevor, can you look at this again?"

Trevor nodded and slowly walked over to the table. Steven pulled him on his lap and then he peered at the sketch. "It's him, the Badman. How did you get his picture?"

"Well, this is from an accident yesterday. A woman almost hit him as he ran in front of her car."

"Did you catch him?" Trevor looked at Joe.

"No, not yet. But now that we know what he looks like, we can find him more easily." Joe looked from the boy to his parents. "Since Trevor says he's seen him at the school, I think we should bring it there to see if anyone else has."

"Okay, should we go now?" Steven asked.

"Yes," Jesse answered. She wanted to get out of the house. It was starting to get very creepy knowing this man had been watching them for months. What did he want?

"Okay, we can all go." Joe nodded and stood. "I want to get a few people here to check the path again and collect those cigarette butts." He left to make some calls.

Jesse reached over and took Trevor's hand. "I'm sorry, honey. We should have listened to you."

"S'okay," he smiled. "Why does he watch me?"

Jesse shook her head. "I don't know. Let's get ready to go to school."

****

Opening a new can of soda, Karen shuddered as she pulled up the next account of the Matthew Stone saga.

...Over the next few years, Matthew slowly built a life for himself and his son. He had voluntarily taken part in therapy sessions to try to relieve some of his guilt for not having been able to save his wife from the horrible beatings and repeated rapes. He felt responsible for the attacks because he had not returned home earlier. Had he been there, maybe it never would have happened. Then having to watch as those men tortured Carol and threaten Tommy as he sat helpless in the chair was beyond what he could handle himself.

Friends tried to help by stopping in, watching Tommy, and keeping Matt busy. However, there was no consoling him. When Matt mentioned getting a gun to help him feel secure, no one thought it was the best idea. But who could blame him? The killers were still running around free. After taking a safety course, his friend Jon went with him to pick out a gun and file for the owner's permit...

****

Walking into the school, Trevor was between his parents, holding their hands. He had never been to the principal's office before and wondered what it would look like. Did it look like the doctor's office, all neat and clean? Or like his dad's, messy with piles of papers he wasn't allowed to touch? Most kids were in trouble when they had to go there. Was there a jail cell where she kept the naughty kids? He squeezed his parents' hands, hoping she wouldn't put him there if there was one.

Jesse looked down at him. "You okay?"

He nodded but looked uncertain. "Am I in trouble?"

Steven stopped and knelt down. Parents dropping off their kids tried to move around them, so they moved to the bench just off the sidewalk. "Of course you're not in trouble. We are just going to talk to Mrs. Hemingway and your teachers. We want to see if they have seen anything that will help us."

****

From his car in the school parking lot, Matt scanned the front of the building and saw Tommy sitting on a man's lap. The way that the man was holding Tommy suggested he cared deeply for him.

56

Matt's mind slipped in and out of reality. Tommy, no, the boy, looked up at the man holding him. Wait who was holding Tommy? He used to hold his son that way. In fact, it was how he held him the last time he saw him. Matt leaned his head against the back of his seat.

Before going to bed each night, as well as any time he entered the small apartment, Matt checked each window and the door to make sure they were locked tight. That evening, before going to sleep, he had checked the door three times. The night before had been filled with dreams of his wife's murderers coming back to kill him and Tommy, the only witnesses to their crime. Failing his family haunted him every night. After reading four stories to Tommy, the small boy had finally fallen asleep.

Matt always watched television as he lay in bed waiting for sleep to come. Many nights, he wished for a drink, to calm his nerves. However, the memory of the steamy, alcohol laced breath of the intruders was a reminder of that dreadful night. He couldn't even choke down a beer without an anxiety attack. Sheer exhaustion finally took over, and he dozed off. An hour or so later he awoke with a start and sat up in bed. His heart banging in his chest so hard he could barely hear. Forcing himself to calm down, he was able to make out a faint, but undeniable sound. Someone was in the apartment. Matt reached for the gun he kept between his mattress and box spring. Quickly deciding what to do, he dialed 911 and put the phone under the pillow so he wouldn't give himself away to the person down the hall. The police had to respond to all 911 calls, and he had to get to Tommy.

Matt crept to the door in the near dark, it was always kept open so he could hear if Tommy needed anything in the middle of the night. As he worked his way into the hall, he heard whispers, but couldn't make out what was being said. That meant there were at least two people. Should he make noise and scare them away? Things started feeling eerily familiar as the shadows got closer and closer to the hallway that led to his and Tommy's bedrooms. A cloud formed around his brain as he heard voices from years ago... "We've gotten what we came for." His chest felt like it was in a vise, and he struggled to get a breath. Fury took over.

As the intruders entered the hallway Matt caught a glimpse of one of the men's boots, boots similar to the ones worn by one of the men who killed Carol. Summoning all of his anger, sadness and energy, Matt hurled himself toward the intruders. Hearing his own voice bellowing from years of pain, he pushed the handgun in front of him. Startled, the men turned the corner to see what was coming. Matt saw the barrel of a shotgun swing up in an arc to level at his head. Looking at the man's shotgun, Matt squeezed the trigger. The kickback made him stumble while a shot thundered down the short hall. At that exact instant he saw a tiny blur of blue jump out of the door behind the man in boots. Both of the men had fallen to the ground, one on top of the other. Matt's ears were ringing from the blast. He froze as the strangers clambered to get out of the apartment. In the rush, a small table in the hall was knocked over. Matt's eyes never left the blue blur. It had stopped moving. There was his only child, all he had left in this world, curled in a ball just over the threshold of his bedroom. "They're gone, they're gone," Matt tried to reassure his son. It took him a second to see that there was something very wrong. Picking him up, bright red blood spilled between the small hands clutched to the front of the pjs. Matt looked into Tommy's eyes as the question formed on the child's lips. "Daddy, why did you hurt me?"

Matt screamed for help as his son closed his eyes and left him forever. The next thing he could remember was fighting the police who were trying to help Tommy. Paramedics took over and worked to revive his son, as Matt was led into the living room. There was a crunching sound. Absentmindedly he looked down. The only picture he still had of Carol and Tommy lay torn under broken glass. Matt collapsed into unconsciousness clutching the blue blanket.

Matt's heart broke in two as he saw the man cradle Tommy. Without warning, the couple stood up and disappeared into the building with his son. No, the boy. His mind spun. *That was his son.* No one was going to take him away again. Matt's breaths were becoming ragged. It was all he could do to stop himself from jumping out of the car right then.

How could he get Tommy back? There was no way he could just walk in and take him. Or could he? A plan spun into motion. Matt calmed his breathing and exited the car. He went quickly to the side door where children were still streaming in. Walking next to a couple of children he held his phone to his ear pretending to have a conversation as he passed the teacher at the door. "I am just dropping them off now. Yes, they have their lunches." He looked quickly at the teacher and flashed a smile nodding to the two youngsters next to him. She let him pass without concern. Once inside the building he followed the group halfway down the hall where he saw a bathroom labeled "adults only." Matt slipped inside and locked the door. Letting his breath out slowly he finished mapping out the rest of his plan to get Tommy back.

****

Trevor and his parents entered the main office area and waited for Mrs. Hemingway. Trevor sat quietly on his mom's lap playing with her locket his dad had given her. The tiny picture was of Jesse and him smiling at the beach. About five minutes passed until the principal opened the door and said to come in. Trevor stepped cautiously into her office. He looked from wall to wall seeing a map, pictures of the school, a few hand-painted pictures from students, and a giant yellow smiley face. Trevor grinned. It was a silly thing to have in a principal's office.

"Good morning, Mr. and Mrs. Reed, and Trevor," Mrs. Hemingway shook hands with them, and bent down to greet Trevor eye to eye. "I have spoken to Officer Marchand, and he gave me a brief rundown of what has been going on." She nodded to Trevor. "Would you like to play with some toys?" A basket of toys was on the floor next to Steven. With a look at his parents, Trevor slipped his hand from his dad's and pulled out a coloring book. He sat on the floor and began to color.

"Joe, Officer Marchand, will be here soon. He was right behind us." Jesse explained. While they waited for Joe to arrive, they discussed the pros and cons of keeping Trevor at the school. Routine was good for kids, and he would never be alone. A teacher or assistant would be assigned to him during transitions, lunch, and recess. Only the Reeds or a police officer could pick him up. He would not ride the bus to school or home. There were too many stops along the way.

"Do you feel comfortable with that? I believe we can keep him," she nodded again toward Trevor who was now lost in his coloring, "safe during the day, and we can ask for an officer to be here at both arrival and dismissal to keep an eye out."

Steven and Jesse exchanged a look. Jesse was gripping Steven's hand while his other hand went to Trevor's shoulder. "Well, it sounds okay, but I want to run it by Joe."

"Mom? I have to go to the bathroom." Trevor stood and rocked from foot to foot. "Real bad."

"I can have Mrs. Gooding take him," Mrs. Hemingway suggested.

Mrs. Gooding, the secretary, looked like a pixie fairy. She almost floated through the halls giving Mary Poppins a run for her money. All of the kids and half of the parents seemed to believe she had some special magic that made you feel good just by being near her. Trevor jumped at the chance and was led into the outer office.

Once Trevor was gone, Mrs. Hemingway looked directly at the couple. "Now, Mr. and Mrs. Reed, is there anything else you want to tell me? If you don't mind me asking, was Trevor adopted? A stepchild from a previous marriage?" She was known for her cut to the chase manner but when Jesse and Steven sucked in a breath, she followed with, "I don't mean to pry. We have had issues surrounding custody with families in the past. We have to ask these questions."

"No, no...he is ours," they said in unison.

"I can't think of anyone who would want to harm him, or us for that matter," Jesse added, her grip on Steven's hand turned her knuckles white.

"Well, I have to ask. Many times, parents aren't forthcoming with private matters. So, there is no chance this is someone Trevor knows?"

"No, I mean not that we know. Only Trevor has seen him. And some lady possibly that have might have seen him running away from our house."

"Hmmm." The principal swung her chair side to side. "I still believe Trevor will be fine here with us. But you have the final say of course." She stood up and looked out the window. "Let's wait for Officer Marchand and get his input. He says he has a sketch for the staff to look at. We really can't pull them together until after school to discuss the issue properly."

"Let me call him and see where he is." As Jesse reached for her phone, the fire alarm sounded.

Chapter 8

The children were still coming in and putting coats and backpacks away. The halls were noisy, and there was enough confusion to allow Matt to slip out to look for Tommy's room. He spotted him being escorted by a short woman. Matt knelt down as if to tie his shoe. They passed him and Tommy went into the boy's bathroom. The tiny woman stood sentry. While she was looking the other way, Matt stood and pulled the fire alarm. Collectively, students and teachers jumped and then swooped into motion. One of the teachers said, "What a horrible time for a drill!"

Students were ushered into lines. The elfin woman opened the bathroom door to clear it out as Trevor appeared wide-eyed. She sent him next door to his class. "Go with them, I will tell your parents to meet you outside." She pushed him along and hurried back to the office.

Trevor was the last one in line and followed his class outside. When they reached the double doors and stepped outside, Matthew reached for the boy's hand. Trevor looked up and pulled away, eyes full of recognition and fear.

Matt leaned down and spoke into his ear. "Come with me, Tommy, you will be okay."

"Leave me alone!" With a sharp tug, Trevor pulled his hand free and ran to the front of the line. "Mrs. Jones! Mrs. Jones! Help!"

Mrs. Jones turned and looked like she was going to scold Trevor for not behaving during a fire drill. Matthew could see his son pointing at him and crying. The teacher's eyes followed Trevor's outstretched hand pointed at him. The teacher and he stood there looking at each other for a split second, then Matt backed away from the building. Survival instincts kicked in and he started to run.

As Matt raced around the corner to the parking lot he almost ran right into Jesse, Steven, and a few other staff members. "That's him," Jesse yelled.

Matt made a bee line to his car. What the hell was going on? The fire alarm blared, and children poured into the yard. Tommy had looked terrified, and that was the last thing he wanted. Why was he so frightened? He should know that his daddy only wanted them to be together. Jumping into his car, he yanked it into reverse and hit the gas. A crunching sound had him looking back at the Caution, Children Crossing sign he'd hit. A raw scraping sound came from his undercarriage as the car lurched into forward. Horrified parents and teachers pulled their children closer as the sign was dragged, showering the ground with sparks. As Matt hit a speed bump going at least twice the legal speed limit the sign broke clattering to the side. He looked for Tommy in the rearview mirror, but it was hopeless, he would never see his boy again. A horn blared startling Matt and he swung the car to the right. He overcompensated and his side view mirror clipped a tree. Matt's heart thudded against his chest seeing that he had almost hit a cruiser. Leaving Tommy behind, Matt concentrated on getting away from the school, away from the people staring and pointing at him. He swung onto the main road as the fire engines and more police cars barreled toward the school. Somehow, the tattered remains of Tommy's blanket found its way into Matt's hand. Rubbing it on his face, it caught the tears falling down his cheek. He had let his son down again.

Chapter 9

Joe let Mrs. Hemingway take him to the Reeds. As they got closer, he could hear Trevor talking.

"He called me Tommy and said I would be okay if I went with him. I screamed and ran to my teacher. I didn't see you anywhere." Trevor buried his head in Jesse's leg.

"Joe, it was him, he came here! He almost got Trevor!" Jesse's voice faltered and her color drained from her face.

"Let's get them to my cruiser." Joe led the way to his car which was parked halfway on the curb with the door still open. He settled Jesse and Trevor in the back seat and leaned against the open door to talk with them. Steven told Joe what Trevor said again. As more information came in, Joe realized that he had probably just passed the guy. In fact, he had almost hit him. "What color was the car?" He posed the questions to the principal and Mrs. Jones, who had joined their little group.

"Uh, it was old, brown? Tan maybe? The plates weren't from here. The same color, just a different style," the teacher offered.

"There will be damage on the rear bumper, that's for sure." Mrs. Hemingway added. "He crushed that sign over there." She pointed near the exit where a mangled Caution sign lay.

"Well, I'll bet anything that the alarm was a cover for this. The school should be cleared in a minute or two. Do you have cameras rolling yet?" Joe looked to the principal.

"No, not yet. They are due to be installed this summer." Security upgrades were passed at the last budget hearing. Schools everywhere were adding more security. "I have to see to my staff and students. I will be back."

Joe excused himself to check in with the fire chief. He left Jesse and her family huddled near his car.

Chapter 10

Pushing away from the desk, Karen shook her head. Wherever Matt Stone was, he wasn't drawing the attention of the police or media anymore. Several searches in surrounding communities produced no more information. This wasn't going to be easy, that was for sure. With every sentence she read, she was convinced there was a story that needed to be told. However, she wasn't going to get the go ahead from Mr. St. Germain without something new. She decided to go back to the original story to see if there were friends or family mentioned that she could talk to. But first, she needed to refuel. She grabbed her purse and went off in search of breakfast, something chocolate maybe.

****

Once inside the police station, Trevor's curiosity overcame some of his fears and he walked in a close circle around the big desk. Joe had set them up in his office while he spoke with the chief. Trevor had a juice box and crackers from a vending machine, and Jesse and Steven swirled what was supposed to be coffee. One sniff and Jesse put hers down. "How do they drink this stuff?" Steven gulped half of it down, then coughed at the bitter taste.

"Is that why they call it cough-ee?" Trevor asked innocently.

It was a laugh they all needed, and it earned them a few looks from officers outside of the room. Steven excused himself to update Jack, who had called several times already. Jesse wandered the room looking at pictures of the town, its leaders, and commendations sprinkled across the pale-yellow walls. She stopped at the bulletin board with several pictures and announcements on it. The left side held photos of the known sex offenders in the county. There were eight. She carefully studied each face not surprised to see some scruffy looking men, some with missing teeth, or messy hair, or both. Only one looked somewhat clean cut, in a button-down shirt. But the eyes, they were all the same dark, bottomless evil. Wrapping her arms around herself she turned to see Trevor watching her. Another officer, this one a woman she vaguely recognized, brought out a small box of toys. A Jacob's Ladder, a container of Silly Putty, some Matchbox cars, action figures, paper and crayons. Toys from a much easier time. A more innocent time.

Jesse's parents never worried about them getting abducted. They would joke once in a while. Mom saying, "Come home when the streetlights come on. You wouldn't want a stranger trying to take you."

To which her dad would answer, "Good luck to that person, they'll pay us to take you back!" It was never a real concern.

Back then all the neighbors played together, ruling the street, pulling pranks and pointing fingers when they got caught. Even their mischief was innocent. Ding-dong ditch-it. Pulling the stakes out of sleepover tents. Taking money from mothers' change jars when they heard the Ice-Cream Truck bell ring. Now parents supervised the playdates. "A date to play?" Steven nearly choked the first time she mentioned it. "Is his prom date and college planned too?" Jesse hadn't thought how ridiculous it sounded until he said it. She thanked the policewoman and sat on the floor with Trevor. They played for a while, and Steven came in to join them.

Joe walked up and was watching the family play and talk to each other in subdued tones.

"You could have it too, you know," a voice behind him said. It was Sarah Dixon, the only female officer in town. After hooking up a couple of times they came to a mutual agreement that it was a bad idea. They remained close, in fact she was the person he turned to when he needed to talk over a case. He warned her off of a couple of the guys who were jerks and saved her some heartache. There was mutual respect and they looked out for each other.

"Yeah, some day. A first date would help." He walked over to break up the little union. "Sarah? Can you come hang out with Trevor, while I talk to his parents?"

Sarah plunked down and introduced herself to the child. She gave Joe a wink, and he led the parents into a conference room. "How are you holding up?" he asked the pair. They answered with shrugs. "There are a few things we need to do to get rolling. First, we need to get your fingerprints for elimination purposes, so we can check the house to see if he has been in it."

Jesse's hand flew to her mouth. "He's been in the house? I hadn't even considered that!" Steven reached over and took her hand. "This is a nightmare!"

"We don't know if he's been inside but need to check it out. I'm also contacting the State Police. They usually handle things like this." Joe continued trying to separate personal feelings from his job. This was his first attempted abduction case and to be honest, he was scared. In fact, no one in town had any experience dealing with a situation involving abduction, attempted or otherwise.

****

Karen entered the Quick Mart on autopilot. Completely lost in her thoughts, she was unaware that someone was calling her name until the woman waved her hands in front of Karen's face.

"Earth to Karen..." A high-pitched sound that could cut through lead assaulted her almost physically.

"Oh, hi...Wendy." Karen stepped back to make space. This voice from the past was so distinctive that she hardly needed to look at the face to know who it was. The girl who had it all. All the looks, all the grades, all the boyfriends...even those who weren't hers to begin with. That was years ago, Karen silently reminded herself. People change. She must have been going to the gym based on the clothing. "How are you?" Looking at Wendy's toned body and tanned face she reached for a granola bar instead of a brownie.

"I haven't seen you in such a long time!" Squeal, air kiss, and a tiny hop. Really? "What have you been up to?" her ex-classmate exclaimed.

"Not much. How 'bout you?"

"Well, just got married, you know," Wendy stuck her left hand in Karen's face. She had no idea about diamonds, but anything that big must be heavy. "Five carats, double inlay of sapphire, like my eyes... it's so pretty..." she breathed. Looking back up at Karen, "Anthony is just a doll. He didn't want me working, but I teach Yoga twice a week." Prance, prance, pose. Now that caught the eye of the teenager behind the counter. Karen could almost hear his blood pressure skyrocket. "We opened up a studio in Meadowview. I'm the boss! I could never work for anyone else. I have to be in charge. Top Dog, you know." Smile, wink.

Top dog all right. Karen hoped her ex-classmate was not a mind reader. Top of the class, top of the pyramid, on top during sex... Karen only knew that last part because her best friend, Sam, had roomed with Wendy their first year of college. That was until she came home to find her boyfriend underneath that Top Dog. Karen continued the monologue in her head. I'm going to pull a muscle if I keep smiling like this. "Well, it was nice seeing you, I have to get to work."

"Wait, here I am jabbering away. How is work? Anything interesting happening around here?" She actually stopped for a moment and gave Karen her full attention.

Without thinking, she told Wendy about the story she was looking into. Was she trying to make her life seem more interesting, important? "So that's what I am doing. I have to do more research though. The guy seems to have dropped off the face of the earth."

Wendy tapped her cell phone and switched screens, looking intent. "Sorry, hang on. I think I might have someone you can talk to." Tap, tap, tap. "That was such a horrible story. Charlie, my ex, is from Charlotte. He wasn't friends with that guy, but his cousin was Matt Stone's wife's old neighbor, or something like that. I can call him and see if he could help you find out more information? I still have his number, see?" She flashed the phone toward Karen.

"That would be great." Karen wanted to kick herself for holding onto old grudges. Maybe a leopard can change its spots.

"Can I have your number? I will call Charlie today and get back to you ASAP!" Wendy seemed almost as excited as Karen was. They exchanged numbers, and Karen thanked her genuinely. As the woman turned to leave, her giant purse caught the edge of a snack rack, toppling the pastries Karen usually called breakfast, and truthfully, sometimes, lunch or dinner. When Wendy bent to pick them up, Karen saw the cashier's face light up. She had to gulp down a burst of laughter when she saw a leopard print thong creeping out of the top of Wendy's yoga pants. Leopard. Spots. The thought made her giggle out loud.

Chapter 11

After a little more discussion, Joe told Steven to take the family home with a two-man crew to watch over them. They holed up in the family room waiting for Joe to call with more information. Steven tried to work from home but gave up and called Jack to answer a couple of questions and cancel some appointments. Jesse and Trevor played games and watched a movie. After some time, Trevor fell asleep. She slid quietly from the couch and found Steven in the dining room looking out the window. Her arms encircled him from behind, and they just stood there for a minute. "You okay?"

Steven turned around to face her. Smudges of purple beneath his eyes spoke to a sleepless night. "I don't know. This is so surreal. I just want to get in the car and drive as far away from here as possible and hide."

"Me too. He, whoever he is, can't get Trevor if he can't find him," Jesse murmured. One of the officers got out of his car and stretched. "We should see if they are hungry. Are you hungry?"

"Not really, but it's something to do. Doing nothing is driving me crazy."

"Well, you go ask…find out their names while you are there. I feel like we haven't even said hello or thank you." Jesse went to check on Trevor while her husband jogged down the front steps to talk to the policemen who were watching over them.

Trevor was still sleeping, clutching something furry. A dog, bear, something…he looked angelic. Jesse thought back to when he was just learning to walk. He had been doing this bum scooting thing, where he used his legs to drag himself across the floor, like a dog scratching its bottom in the grass. Although it got him from here to there, he always wanted things that were just out of his reach. So out of frustration, he pushed himself up, forgetting to hold on and fell every time. He would grunt and shake off any help. She and Steven would laugh as he pushed himself into a standing position, totter like a drunk, stabilize, and repeat the process until he got where he wanted to go. It was painstakingly slow, but his determination was remarkable. Within a couple of days, he was walking, climbing, and pulling things down. Sometimes she missed the days where he would stay in one place and let her hold him for hours.

In the kitchen she pulled out bread, deli meat, mayonnaise, and mustard. The lettuce had not been returned to the refrigerator last night and looked like discarded seaweed. She tossed it into the wastebasket and turned back around to make Steven's lunch. His preference was to eat a little bit of everything. She searched for pickles and was startled when he came through the door from the garage. Hitting her head on the edge of the fridge, she dropped the jar. It rolled under the table. "Jesus, Steven! You scared me half to death."

"Sorry, are you okay?" He bent down to retrieve the pickles, "Hey, look what I just found!" Dust and

Cheerios scurried across the floor as Trevor's old blanket was pulled out. It had been missing for weeks and thought to be left at a restaurant.

"Blankie!" Trevor and Jesse said at the same time. He had just woken up, ran to his father, and grabbed his old friend. "Where was it?" he asked rubbing it on his cheek.

"Behind the bench. Along with a bunch of cereal and…" he plucked some dried peas from the dirty fleece, "your veggies."

"Eww. They look like warts." Trevor tried to smooth the blanket out on the floor. "Mom, can you wash it? It smells yucky."

"Of course, go throw it in the washer, I will do a load after lunch." Jesse was getting teary-eyed and wasn't sure why. She turned to finish lunches.

"I'll throw a load through," Steven offered and disappeared into the adjoining bathroom/laundry room.

Jesse took lunch to the officers. As she was walking back in, Joe pulled up the drive. Eager to hear what he had to say, she waited on the porch for him to finish checking in with the officers. They walked in together, this time surprising the boys at the kitchen table. Steven had two Cheetos sticking out of his mouth like teeth. He abruptly flipped them in his mouth. Trevor stopped laughing and greeted Joe with a salute, then crawled onto his dad's lap to pick at his sandwich.

"So, what is happening?" Jesse sat next to Steven and indicated for Joe to sit.

"Well, first off, there will be a crew here shortly to check things out more thoroughly. That means cameras, collecting fingerprints, the cigarettes, and checking out the yard. You might want to take Trev somewhere while we do this. It might get hectic and confusing." Joe looked from Jesse to Steven. "But first, there will be an officer from the State Police coming by to talk to you as well. We still need to coordinate a few things, but they are taking it quite seriously. Until we know who this guy is, we have to assume the worst."

Jesse swallowed hard and bit her lip. "Where would we go?"

"You could go to a friend's or Steven, are your folks nearby?"

Steven shook his head. "We could go to Jack's." Trevor had been there before and would be comfortable. He looked to Jesse who nodded in assent. "How long do you think we should plan to be there?"

"I would plan on at least one night. I really want to wait and see what comes from the fingerprints, if we find any. The cigarette butts should give us that, and other DNA if we need it."

"Um, I guess I will go and pack a bag or two. Trevor, you go grab a few videos and toys. Put them in your backpack. Steven, can you call Jack?" Trevor slid to his feet and ran into the other room. Jesse shook her head and stood up. "Joe, what do you think is going on? Do you think he really wants to take Trevor?"

"It's hard to say. But from the looks of it, he's certainly obsessed or something. He called him Tommy. Does that mean anything to you?"

"I have a cousin named Tom, but we haven't seen him in years. And he's like forty-five or something." Steven looked hard at Joe. "Have you checked the sex offender's list?"

"One of the first things I did. Looking at pictures only, there were no matches. But without a name, I'm not sure." Joe patted Jesse on the arm and stood up. "I'm going to make some calls. Find out when they want to talk to you." When he was gone, Jesse and Steven stood in the kitchen holding one another.

Chapter 12

Matt drove north on Route 95 for about an hour and needed a break. Seeing an exit that looked desolate, he pulled off. Fields of salt marsh hay gave way to industrial parks. Three giant wind turbines sliced slowly through the air in the distance. He chose a parking lot with several tractor trailers lining the back edge, slipped between two, and turned the car off. Resting his head on the steering wheel, Matt tried to regroup.

Where should he go? He needed to dump this car, which meant getting a new one. Luckily, he had a large amount of cash on him and access to a bunch more. The insurance settlement from Carol's death was meant to provide Tommy with whatever he would need. Matt had not touched it beyond basic living expenses after he lost his job due to PTSD. His disability kicked in which provided most of what they needed to survive. After Tommy died, he had no intention of using the insurance money. But when the stares and whispers kept coming long after the acquittal, he felt trapped by the past and needed to escape. He looked in the backseat of his beat-up Ford Taurus. There were the few belongings he bothered to take with him. Matt could name each item by heart, the picture of Carol and Tommy, smeared, but he could still make out the images. He had considered laminating it because he felt if the image faded completely, he would lose them all over again. There were a few of Tommy's drawings that had been taped to the refrigerator door at the apartment. Most people wouldn't be able to tell what they were of, but Matt could. The first one was a family portrait, complete with an angel with wings. She was above them, because Matt told his son that Mommy was watching over them. They were holding hands and looked like snowmen touching their stick arms together. The other was a fireman, what Tommy said he wanted to be when he grew up. He said if he were a fireman, he could have saved Mommy. That's the story Matt told. There had been an awful fire and his mommy couldn't get out in time. Matt wiped a tear at the memories. The rest of the belongings were more of necessity, clothing, toiletries, camping gear, and some food he kept restocking just so he would have it. And of course, the money, tucked in the hidden compartment. Hell of a way to sum up 37 years of life.

Rubbing his eyes, he tried to focus on the here and now. "Where the hell am I going to get a car?" Matt said to the dashboard. Looking at the turbine, its movements made him think of a swimmer in an endless crawl. Just like his life. Pulling his eyes away from the hypnotic sight, he googled used car stores in the area. He pulled up each location to get a picture of it. The one that had no website or picture was the one he wanted figuring it for a low traffic, need to sell outfit. He plugged the address into GPS and was happy to see it was fifteen minutes away on Old Route One. The tiny map on the screen suggested that the road he was on connected 95 and Route 1. So, he started up the car and took a right passing more industrial parks, an elementary school, and a police station. Jesus, that was ironic. The whole state might be looking for him and he drives right by a barracks. He pulled his hood tighter and consciously obeyed the speed limit. He came to a set of lights and saw a quaint little restaurant. The Kitchen Counter promised comfort food and fast service. He needed both but couldn't risk being seen. He opted for the McDonalds across the street. With a number two meal, he was on his way again. The hot greasy food did nothing to settle his stomach, but it was fuel for his weary body and the caffeine helped his mind. Heading north on Route One, he looked for Jim's Auto Sales on the right. Matt hoped this dealer wanted money more than a perfectly legal sale. He needed to get in and out quickly.

A rundown sign propped against a tree announced he had arrived at Jim's Auto ales. The S lay in the dirt at the base of the sign. Matt eased to the right and bumped along the rutted dirt driveway. His eyes scanned the lot, using the term 'lot' loosely. Five cars sat scattered in a circular drive, with a mobile home serving as an office. The tiny building had cracked siding, blue tarp on parts of the roof, and a step that served as a porch. A trash barrel sat to the side of the steps, and a quick peek in told Matt that the owner was a smoker and a frequent flier at Dunkin Donuts. He tapped on the front door and stepped off of the creaking landing.

While waiting for someone to answer, he mentally whittled down his choices. Of course, the one without tires was out, as was the Ford Taurus with the cracked windshield. That left a green Hyundai, an electric yellow Chevy Cruze and a dark grey Saturn. The yellow was too recognizable, so that was out. It was between the Hyundai and Saturn. Matt could hear someone approaching. A high-pitched voice said, "Hold yer' horses, I'ma comin'."

Matt was startled by the large man who opened the door. He peered past the man's shoulder to see if anyone else was there. "Can I help you?" The giant man spoke in a voice several octaves above what Matt expected. Stubby greasy fingers were rubbed on an already stained tee shirt. The jeans were held together by a button closure that looked tentative at best. Filthy grey socks encased feet that were wedged into old moccasins, the suede worn almost translucent. Not a shrewd businessman, but maybe just the type of businessman wanted at the moment.

Matt cleared his throat and explained that he needed a car today. The man looked back into the trailer. It multitasked as an office, dining room, and apparently bedroom. Trash was strewn around, a blanket lay pooled at the foot of a Lazy Boy recliner, and it all faced a large screen TV that was set atop a set of dresser drawers like a monument to life outside of this squat, smelly trailer. The man he assumed was Jim, sole employee of Jim's Auto Sales, looked torn between leaving the relative comfort of his home and making a sale. The internal struggle lasted long enough for Matt to ask, "You selling those cars out there?"

"Yeah, yeah, lemme show you." He grabbed a handful of keys from a hook near the doorway. Taking the steps like a toddler, he reached the ground and already sounded winded. "Whatcha lookin' for?" His voice reminded him of a friend from high school who, when punched in the face, broke his nose. For the week after, he walked around with cotton balls stuck up his nostrils talking like a cartoon character. It was hard for Matt not to laugh at the memory.

"I am heading north and need something more reliable. Someone sideswiped me. Took off my mirror and I hit a guard rail. Mostly it's aesthetic, but it needs new tires and there's a squeak under the hood. Probably a belt, but I don't have time to fix it. Mine's a '13, almost 160,000 miles on it. Use it as a trade towards one of these two?" Matt pointed at the two he thought would best suit his purposes.

"Well, I don't know what I would do with that." The man wrinkled his nose in disgust. As if his standards were higher than Matt's. "Let's see if you like one of these, then we'll talk trade in value."

Matt walked around the grey Saturn, popped the hood, and turned over the engine. He checked the fluid levels, tire pressure, and looked underneath to see the carriage. Many cars were shipped north after Hurricane Katrina. People bought cars that had sat in water for weeks, dried out, and passed off as sound. This one looked good. A couple of spots of rust on the body, but Matt didn't care what it looked like, as long as it ran and blended in. He also liked the color. People couldn't always tell the difference between green, blue, and grey, especially in the dark. If the police caught onto his switch, that might confuse them some. This was the one, he didn't need to check out the other. "How much you want for it?"

"Five grand?"

"How 'bout three? I can pay cash," Matt countered, "Plus you have my trade in." He nodded to his car, still clicking, a telltale sign that the cooling system was on its way out.

"Four, and you got a deal. I can get the paperwork in order by this afternoon."

"Thirty-five and I take care of the paperwork, leave with it now." Matt was getting nervous. Nothing suggested this man cared about paperwork, titles, insurance, even checking out the car he was getting. Matt tried to keep his expression even.

"Why you need it so quick?"

"Listen, I just want to get away, start over. My wife and kid left me, and I have to make a change." Matt coughed to clear the lump that formed in his throat, and his voice cracked.

"Oh," the man's tongue clicked like an old lady. "That sucks. I know about women leaving, they just don't appreciate what we give 'em."

Matt nodded and mumbled a vague reply, just wanting to get the hell out of there. The big man stood there, as if he wasn't sure what to do.

"Well, I'm trying to pick up and carry on." Matt waved one hand over the car hood while the other wiped a tear. "We have a deal?"

"Yes, brother to brother. We have to stick together." Turning on his heel, the man lumbered toward his trailer/office/home. "Lemme git the title."

Matt went to clear out his car. He double checked the glove compartment, under the seats, and the trunk. He glanced over his shoulder to see if Jim was watching. Once he was sure it was all clear, he pulled hard on the back of the rear seat. With some force, it popped open. Matt reached in and grabbed two piles of cash wrapped in brown bags. He stored the money there, thinking it was safer than in his duffle in a hotel room. All told it was probably around fifty thousand dollars. He slipped it into his backpack after peeling off several one-hundred-dollar bills. Then he removed his license plate to put on the new car. When Jim came back out, Matt was standing next to a pile of his belongings checking the local news website on his phone for anything that might mention the incident at the school earlier that morning. He looked up as he heard Jim jingling the keys to the new car.

"Here's the title. There's only this key. Guess the other guy lost the spare. You can get another made if you want." Matt felt the man was ready to drool when he saw the stack of bills in his hand. For a moment, he wanted to hold it above his head to see if he would actually jump for it.

"Thanks, Jim. Here's your money, and my keys." Matt was relieved to get rid of his car and get going again. "Let me just put this stuff in and I will get outta your hair."

"Sure, nice doin' business with you." Jim turned on his heel and was back in the trailer in a blink. Matt chuckled to himself, thinking of the man practically skipping back to his recliner.

Once the plates were attached and he was in the new car, Matt adjusted the seats, mirrors, and headrest. The drive was going to be long, and he wanted to be as comfortable as possible. Before he left, he slid his hand inside his front pocket. Just as quickly, he pulled it back out to check the other. Panic set in. Where was Tommy's blanket? He checked his bags, the floor of the car, and got out to look for it in the lot. Matt's breathing got heavy as he ran to his old car. Where is it? He needed this last reminder of his son. He knelt on the ground and felt around under the driver's seat. His fingers grazed the edge of the scrap. It had fallen between the seat and the middle console. Once he tugged it free, he leaned against the car holding the fabric to his eyes. After a minute, he got into the Saturn and drove away.

Chapter 13

Karen drove back to work nibbling on her granola bar. It promised chewy satisfaction of chocolate, peanut butter, nuts, berries, and tree bark, or something like that. The first bite wasn't too bad. The second and third left a nasty, earthy aftertaste and perhaps a splinter. This just can't be good for you, she thought, stuffing the bar into a grocery bag she used for trash. She took a giant swig of Diet Coke, swished it around her mouth like Scope, and swallowed. "That's better," she said aloud looking for a Krispy Kreme drive through. A girl cannot live on mulch alone.

Armed with a glazed raspberry filled donut, Karen entered her office, hoping to dodge Mr. St. Germain. As she was shutting the door, he stuck his head in the doorway. A brief cartoon-like vision of her popping his head like a balloon flitted through her mind. "Karen? Do you have a minute?"

"Uh, sure…" She sat down at her desk, and he looked for a chair. No one ever visited her, so there was no need for a second seat. When she offered him her chair, he waved her off.

"Karen, I am going to cut to the chase. The newspaper is being bought by Media Nation." He was referencing the multimillion-dollar company that was buying up and consolidating smaller newspapers and radio stations. Many syndicated columns and wire stories were switching to web pages instead of hardcopy issues. The radio stations moved to pre-recorded countdowns and tracked deejaying. All advertising was handled by the pared down New York staff and the local news stations sent over a brief news cast via the internet. This was not good news. Pun intended.

The young writer sat stone faced, while her boss perched a butt cheek on the corner of her desk. It molded like Silly Putty, and she wondered if it would stay like that when he stood up. Her mind had a tendency to wander. "We are going to have to make some cuts." He was looking past her just over her head, probably seeing a picture of her and her brother, Teddy, at their college graduation party. They were twins, both went to school in North Carolina. She went to at Chapel Hill, he to High Point. Teddy chastised her unhealthy habits, and she called him a dumb jock. They were best friends, often phoning each other just when the other needed to hear a friendly voice. Neither believed in telepathy, but it was uncanny at times. He would probably call her tonight, if Karen could read what was coming.

Mr. St. Germain was saying something about a good reference. She was young. It was a good time for an adventure. Maybe she should look outside of North Carolina. All good ideas from a man who was likely looking at the end of his own career. "They have offered everyone decent severance packages," he said. "They will give you four weeks' pay, on top of your two weeks paid vacation. They're shutting things down by the end of this week. Apparently, this has been in the works for some time." Karen could not hide the shock on her face.

"They are giving me three days' notice. Is that even legal?" Karen stood up and would have paced but that would put her in her boss's lap.

"Well, they don't have to offer you the full four weeks. This is them being nice. It's happening to all of us. We're closing down. I can stay with the company but would have to move to some place...I don't know, Podunk, Nebraska." He sighed. "Don't know what I am going to do. Is it cold in Nebraska?" He was not really expecting an answer.

"So, are we even putting out an issue this week?" Karen's mind quickly moved back to the story she was chasing. Either way, she was holding that for herself. If it turned out to be something, she could sell it as a freelancer.

"Just a mini-issue, highlighting some of our bigger stories, and announcing the changeover. It will mostly be archive stuff, and I will write a letter from the editor thanking the community for their support. Corporate actually wrote most of it. I will just add a few personal touches. We don't even need to come in the rest of the week, officially." He got up and stuck a hand over the table. Karen shook it, and he held on for a moment. "Let me know if you need anything." He maneuvered between the furniture and walls and left with a sigh.

Still dazed, Karen watched as he left. "What the hell?" she said to the dingy walls. Even though she complained, she would miss the cramped quarters, stacks of papers, and the old wooden desk she rescued from the cellar. It was slated for the dump, but she liked the worn spots where the previous owners must have rested his or her elbows. There were scratches on the sides from being moved from room to room, and the two drawers squeaked when she pulled them open. In the right light and angle, she could even see indentations from where someone had written some notes. The date 1978, the name George Schw...and 'total', were etched in the grain. On slow days she wondered if it was an unsolved mystery, an obituary, or just random words. Someone flushed a toilet. She wouldn't miss the sounds from the adjacent restroom. Would she miss knowing the gastrointestinal habits of her coworkers? Probably not.

Karen didn't know what to do next. Should she work on her resume? Start cleaning out her desk? Go for an early lunch and get loaded? Her day was most certainly not going in the direction she was planning on. Crap, she hated being a grown up!

Chapter 14

Officer Thomas Paine finished up inside the elementary school carefully cataloging the fingerprints he found on the fire alarm. The outside cover was smudged with fingerprints, dust and God knows what other sticky substances. Inside, there was only what looked to be one set. The janitor's prints had been taken for exclusionary purposes, and Thomas felt he had one full and a couple partials that just might belong to the man they were looking for. He had also taken a bunch from the men's bathroom. There were only a few males who would use it on a regular basis, but on the weekends the gym was used for community sports. He was less hopeful to find anything useful there.

Outside, the parking lot had been cordoned off with cones. The principal had asked that police tape not be used, and teachers who had classes facing the front of the school were asked to close their blinds. This was all done to try to lessen anxiety with the students and parents. Thomas slowly walked the lot looking for anything helpful in identifying the suspect's car. The caution sign remained on the ground bent in half near the speed bump. He took pictures of it from a few different angles and saw some paint chips on the ground. He bagged them and saw that the color was that weird brownish green color on army fatigues. What an ugly color for a car he thought to himself. Paine's back was killing him from last night's workout. As he stretched out his muscles, he caught a glimpse of metal shining in the grass down the drive. He wandered down scanning in a grid-like search for anything on the road and surrounding area. Nothing of real interest, but plenty to raise the eyebrow. He saw beer bottles, fast food wrappers, and a condom wrapper. Those were not the lollipop sticks, candy wrappers, and old baseballs that you might expect at an elementary school. When he reached the spot where he had seen the metal he slowed and crouched down farther. There he found broken glass, more like a mirror. He photographed it, in situ, from different angles and with a ruler to give a size reference. He then bagged and labeled the pieces not knowing if they had anything to do with the case. If it turned out it did and he ignored it, his boss would string him up. If it didn't, at least he was thorough. There were new tracks in the dirt, like someone had swerved off of the road quickly and then recovered. It would explain the glass, a side view mirror hitting the tree branches. He looked at the tree, a crabapple, and found the branch. It was broken at the height just above his hip. It seemed right, so he took pictures of that too, and walked down the rest of the entrance and back to the lot. Nothing else caught his interest, so he called Joe to tell him what he found.

"Good catch on the mirror." Joe sounded tired. "As I came around the corner to the school, he was leaving. We almost sideswiped each other."

Thomas smiled to himself, knowing that Joe was a stickler on details. He had only been working at the station for three months, and this was by far the most serious case they had. "I will run the prints through our system and send the other stuff to the lab. It should take a week for the glass and paint."

"Yeah, hold off on that. I am meeting with the State Police in about a half an hour. I will tell them what you found. Maybe their labs are faster?" Joe hung up with a quick thanks.

Thomas' ultimate goal was to join the State Police. This might be a foot in the door. He drove back to the station with a new sense of purpose.

****

Joe briefed the detective from the State Police who arrived a short while later. Avery Price was tall, moved with grace, and spoke little. His friend has said she was the real deal. While he talked, she wrote notes, going back and forth to add details. Nodding understanding or stopping him only for clarification, she was all business. He liked her demeanor, no unnecessary questions, no ego. When he was done, she took a minute to look over her notes. Staring past him, he could see her mind working. It also gave him a moment to check her out. Shoulder length hair, chestnut with a wave, outlined an oval face. She was definitely pretty. When she moved, it was with purpose. He looked away before he was caught, he hoped.

"What's your take on the parents?" She clicked her pen against her teeth. "Any chance there could be something there? Trouble in paradise?" Her eyebrows arched, and she looked directly at Joe.

"I have known the family for a long time. Jesse, the mom, almost all of my life."

This information made the stare more intense. "How well do you know her?"

"We grew up together, grade school through high school. And yes, Jesse and I were together, for three and a half years."

"That going to be a problem?" Detective Price cut to the chase. "With you, her, or the husband?"

"No, it was in high school. We are on friendly terms. I think Steven has gotten over any jealousy."

"He has. Have you? Lingering feelings, a chance to win her back?" Tap, tap, tap, went the pen against her teeth.

"Jesse and I parted on great terms. She was in college. I stayed home, went to the academy, and helped out the family when they needed." He paused. "They helped me out too." Joe stood and paced the length of the room. "It could be complicated, but it's not. I would do anything to keep her family safe, but I would do that for anyone." Joe stopped, put his hands on his waist, and returned the stare.

"Okay, fine. I had to ask. You have their trust?" He nodded. "Then you come with me for the interview. Can you think of anything else?" She was gathering her things, tucking them into a slim shoulder bag.

"No, I've told you everything. I think talking to the teacher who saw the suspect at the school, and the driver of the car who almost hit him yesterday near the park would be a good idea too. Maybe they have remembered something more." He led her out of the conference room and into the main office. Several officers had arrived for the shift change, and others lingered to hear more news on the man hunt. An air of excitement buzzed. This was big news in a small town. Joe escorted Avery out the back and caught Sarah's eye. He beckoned her over with a nod of his head. She quick-stepped across the room and met them outside.

After brief introductions, Joe asked her to come along to the Reeds'. Trevor had already met her and appeared comfortable with her. She could hang with the child when they spoke to the parents. "Ride with me?" Avery suggested. Sarah slipped into the state issued sedan. Price would likely ask her about his relationship with Jesse. Sarah had his back. He led the way letting his mind wander back to the night he and his co-worker had first hooked up.

****

Sarah had been on the job for six months. Some of the guys tried to mess with her. She proved to have a sharp tongue and fast reflexes. The first to grab-ass had his face slammed into the wall. "Sorry, you startled me. You trying to re-define 'cop a feel'?" she said loud enough for the whole squad to hear. While they were laughing, she leaned in and stated in no uncertain terms what would happen if he ever tried that again. The ten-year veteran left rubbing the lump on his head and mentally massaging his bruised ego. Others were smoother, asked her out or bought her a drink when they went out as a group. She shut them down with tact but left no question. She did not mess around with co-workers.

After a funeral for a fallen firefighter, they found themselves sitting on the back steps of the widow's house drinking beer. The man had died trying to help Sarah during a domestic abuse call. The wife was trying to set her husband on fire. Sarah thought she had it under control but then it all went to shit. The fireman arrived just as the women lashed out at Sarah. When she ducked, the flaming bucket landed on the off-duty fireman instead. Without his turnout gear, he was engulfed. He died after two weeks in a coma. Sarah felt like it was her fault.

Tipping back the bottle, she downed it in seconds. "Thirsty?" Joe asked sarcastically. She burst into tears. Joe gave her his shoulder and let her get it out. After, she apologized and leaned in to hug him. They kissed, both shocked. Within minutes they were on their way to her apartment. The rest, they say, is history. There were a couple more nights, full of fuzzy memories and impulsive emotions. However, nothing lasted beyond the next morning. In the end they decided it wasn't in either of their best interests to continue. When Joe made Sergeant a few months later it solidified their decision.

****

He pulled into the Reeds' driveway with a smile. It had been fun while it lasted. Back in work mode, he climbed out of his car to hear the women talking quietly. With a wink, Sarah let him know everything was okay.

After meeting with the Reeds, Detective Price went to her car to make a few calls. The family was packed and ready to go to Jack's apartment in Boston. They were just waiting for the final decision from Price as to whether they would go or stay in a nearby hotel for easier access if there were questions.

Joe found himself looking at the pictures in the hallway, and his mind wandered back to when Jesse's dad brought him to get his license. His own dad was nowhere to be found, and his mom was nowhere near sober enough to take him. The appointment had been made, and Mr. Martin came home from work early to take him. Joe felt more comfortable with him than his dad anyway. When he passed the test, the man who was more a parent than either of his patted him on the back and said, "Good job, son." That feeling stayed with him for a long time, and he was as loyal to the Martins as he would have been to his own family.

He was pulled out of his thoughts when his phone rang, startling everyone in the room.

"Marchand."

"It's Paine. I have a possible make and model of the perp's car. Sending you a picture now."

Joe waited. A positive ID on the car might help them locate this mystery man. When his phone dinged, he opened the file. It was a Ford. "I only caught a glimpse, but that looks about right. Any numbers?" he asked referring to the license plate.

"No, everyone was too freaked out."

Joe looked up to see Jesse and Steven staring at him. "Thanks for the information, I'll check back later."

Before he could explain, Detective Price knocked on the door. "Okay, change of plans. We need the techs to go over this place, but my boss wants you guys to stay closer. Is there a hotel in town you could stay in for the night? We will be quick here, but I think Trevor, and you"—she nodded at the Reeds—"would feel less put upon if you weren't here."

"Can we go to the one with the water park?" No one had noticed Trevor at the door.

Sarah jogged in behind him with an apologetic look. "He has to go to the bathroom."

"Can we? It has a tunnel slide!" Trevor was jumping up and down, with excitement or maybe the need to pee. Jesse hustled him off to the bathroom with a whatever you want look to her husband.

"Do you think that it's safe? A water park is an easy place for someone to get in." Steven looked at the police officers.

"It should be fine, for one night. Just stay next to Trevor at all times. From the description of this guy, he would stick out like a sore thumb in a place like that," Joe said.

"Yeah, and our people will be there watching over you too," Price added. "It isn't quite tourist season, so you should be able to get a room."

Trevor ran back into the kitchen wiping his hands on his pants. "We can go. I'll get my suit!" He ran upstairs.

"Okay, guess I should make a call," Steven said. "At least it will keep Trevor occupied." He wandered into the other room to make the reservation.

"Once you are gone, my team will come in and gather whatever evidence we can find. We will be as neat as we can, but it's not going to be perfect. I will ask them to clean up when they are done, but there will be residue. We will check the house, yard, and the woods behind, all the way down the trail to the park. It will probably take the rest of the day."

"Well, tell them to help themselves to any food or drinks. We don't have much, but they are welcome to it," Jesse offered. It was weird thinking there would be so many strangers in her house without her being here.

"Thanks, Mrs. Reed. I will tell them." Price smiled. It was against policy to eat or drink at a crime scene, but the offer was kind. "Two officers will be here soon to go with you."

Chapter 15

Karen cleaned out her desk quickly. She copied the columns she had written on a flash drive and put the framed pictures of her family into a WB Mason box. There was a plastic figurine from a young boy named Peter. He had given it to her after she finished a story on his dad. The brave man had saved the lives of a bunch of school children when their bus careened off of the road and went into a ditch. The man was able to free all of the passengers, except the driver, who was pinned between the seat and the steering wheel. When the bus exploded into flames, his dad was still helping the driver. She had done a follow up on how the family was doing during their 'Hometown Heroes' week. The boy wanted to thank her for keeping his daddy's memory alive. He gave her the Batman toy, because it would remind her to try to be a hero too. Wiping a tear from her eye she laid him atop the pile in the box. She decided to go see how her co-workers were doing.

Karen saw a white ball sail through the air. Jose was sitting with his feet on his neighbor, Deb's desk. They were shooting baskets with wadded up paper. Neither was doing very well in the contest. "So, what are we going to do?" she asked grabbing her own piece to crumple.

"We have decided to become pole dancers, since this basketball thing isn't going to work." Jose had a strange sense of humor, and his smile slowly rolled across his face as he sunk a paper ball by bouncing it off of Karen's chest.

"Nice, can I watch?" She grabbed a Twizzler from the never-ending supply Deborah kept on her desk. Skinny bitch, ate like shit, never exercised, but was an easy size two. She was smart, quick witted, and could drink anyone under the table. Deb would make an excellent pole dancer, Karen decided.

They chatted for a while as a few other employees joined them. Deb announced that they should go to the bar down the street and drink their sorrows away. While others talked about stories or books they would write, Karen decided to keep her Matt Stone story to herself. Her co-workers were good people, but now they all needed a job, and a good story was something that made journalists forget where their loyalties lie.

****

Matt had driven back to the highway and headed north. He figured he would decide later if he would cut across Vermont into New York, or just hide away near the Canadian border. His mind kept wandering back to the time when he and his parents had gone fishing. Even though it was the hottest week of the year, and their car had no air conditioning, Matt loved the two day drive up the coast to the big lake. They drove an ancient station wagon, and Matt sat in the backseat with his face out of the window. He loved the sights, the giant bridges, and the fast food. Once they reached the lake in New Hampshire, they stayed in a Veteran's Lodge. It was hot and sticky, and he slept on the floor in a sleeping bag, but it was the best week of his life. There were arcades, fried dough, and a huge boat that would toot its horn when Matt danced and jumped up and down on the pier as it left the dock. That was the last time the family was together for a vacation. The next year, his father was injured at work and out of a job.

When the highway split off, Matt saw a sign for Lake Winnipesaukee. He veered off to the left and took Route 16 heading to the Lake Regions.

Chapter 16

Jesse and Trevor loaded into Steven's car and drove off to the hotel, following an unmarked car with a two-person team in it. The crime scene techs filed onto their property to find any evidence that would tell them where the stranger had been and who he is. The yard was being processed, with a focus on the spots Joe pointed out on the outside of the fence. A few men walked the path to check that out too. It was a good thing the State Police were involved; this would take the town's small department days to process. Joe watched from the patio answering any questions he could.

Detective Price was on the phone talking animatedly while she paced around the garage. Joe liked the way she moved. Long legs covered the ground quickly. She absently stopped and leaned down to pick a leaf off of a weed. She pinched it in half and brought it to her nose. The scent brought a smile to her otherwise stern face. Joe remembered that was where the mint grew that they used to pick and put into their lemonade. Jesse told him that when she was little, her friend tried to make gum by mixing it with marshmallows. It was an "epic fail", but they did sell it to the boys down the street who claimed to like it.

Price was shaking her head walking over to him. "My boss wants an APB put out on the car state-wide.

We will need a better description of it. The school have any cameras?" Joe shook his head. "He also wants to get the sketch on the evening news. He thinks with the exposure we can flush him out."

"Or put him into hiding." Joe scowled. "If he sees it, he will disappear, and Trevor won't be safe."

"True, but with cell phones in the hands of almost every person in the state his picture will spread like pollen in the spring." Price stopped and looked Joe right in the eye. She raised one eyebrow, cocked her head toward the house, and walked in. Joe was left to follow, which he did, casually noticing her rear profile. Smooth and firm, he was an admirer of fine things.

Inside, the team was focusing on Trevor's room, the windowsills, and the doors. Joe frowned at the dusty film on the surfaces. A place so full of good memories should not be covered in fingerprint powder. He had made a note to get their friend Jack's and the nanny's prints too and texted Jesse to ask for their contact info. Hopefully the family would enjoy the indoor water park.

****

Thomas Paine sat ramrod straight in his chair as the computer scanned the fingerprints from the school. His belt was new and cut into his side if he slouched at all. A spit shine on his shoes and a newly pressed uniform signified his eagerness to impress his bosses. He studied criminal law at the local university, the captain working his shifts around that schedule. Paine loved his job but didn't seem to fit in with the other officers. They had grown up here or in a near-by town and seemed to understand the community and what made it tick. He had moved from Connecticut to follow his girlfriend to graduate school. They broke up a few months later, but he was in the police academy and decided to stay put.

He watched the computer skip over hundreds of prints per minute. His gaze wandered across the room into Joe's office. Neat as a pin, everything lined up, papers in a vertical file, and every pencil sharpened to a fine point. He couldn't decide if Joe was anal or just needed to get laid. Most were aware of Joe's history with Jesse Reed and from what he understood, there had not been a serious girlfriend since. Joe had dates, and the occasional 'get together' with Sarah. They didn't know he knew, but one night while on patrol he drove through Sarah's neighborhood and saw them going in, arms around each other.

Sarah was sexy, but he had heard of her near lethal offense. After his girlfriend dumped him, the last thing he needed was another ego spanking. The computer had slowed down and pinged. There was a match! Thomas stood up so quickly that his chair rolled backward into the radiator. The loud crash got everyone's attention. "Where's Joe?" he asked.

Chapter 17

Karen was enjoying her beer. The fancy drinks her friends were drinking were too expensive and gave her an instant hangover. They were playing pool and darts, being somewhat raucous and drawing scowls. Most of the other patrons were families and older couples out for a quiet meal. They had no way of knowing the group had collectively just become unemployed.

When Jose started doing body shots off of Deborah, Karen decided to call it a day. The group was dwindling, and people were getting less sober and more somber. She said her goodbyes and promised to keep in touch. On her way to the car her phone vibrated. She had missed a call from her brother. No surprise there.

She hit the callback button and waited for his voice. "Hey there, what's up?"

"You tell me, the hair on the back of my neck was crawling. It was my Spidey senses telling me to call you."

"Got laid off." She let the statement hang.

"You got laid? Now that's something to talk about!"

"No, I got laid off! Jerk."

"What? What did you do?"

"Nothing, jackass, the company was sold to a huge outfit, and they are downsizing. I am out on my butt."

She sat behind the wheel caught between tears and anger.

"That sucks. How much notice?"

"Two minutes, plus or minus a minute. But a pretty decent package." She chewed the inside of her mouth. "Think I will freelance. I have a story that has potential." She filled him in on the Matt Stone saga. He seemed to think there could be something to it.

"So, Bendy Wendy might be your best lead?" Teddy remembered her well. Most of the guys in their class did. "Use her, kiss up if you have to. It can't hurt."

Karen smiled at the nickname, remembering Wendy's pretend disgust with it. She had earned it and didn't seem to mind it at that time. Karen drove to her apartment and brought her belongings in. Plopping on the couch she powered up her laptop and continued her search on Stone.

Chapter 18

Trevor slid down the plastic tube and landed in the shallow pool with a splash. He was having the time of his life. While Steven played along, his mind was reeling. How had this happened to them? Had he become so preoccupied with work that he ignored the warnings? Guilt built on layers of guilt like a giant onion. He and Jesse hardly ever talked anymore. Really talked, getting into conversations covering anything from the inane to the profound. They were a playful couple, silly, passionate, and connected. Now, they were robots, just going through the motions. Last night was like a flashback to the good old times. Even in the midst of all the confusion, they found each other and well, connected. Now they were in the middle of a crazy situation with no answers.

"Can we, Dad? Please?" Trevor was jumping up and down and splashing him.

"Um, what?" Steven looked down.

"The big slide, that one." He pointed to top of a red tube near the ceiling that actually extended outside of the building in a loop and jetted down into a separate pool. Steven wasn't sure Trev was ready for it but said yes. He gestured to Jesse who was talking to the female officer, Sarah, by the tables. Taking Trevor's hand, they walked to the other side of the indoor water park to get an innertube for the slide.

****

"So how long have you worked at the station?" Jesse asked Sarah.

"Five years." Sarah was aware of the history between Joe and Jesse. She didn't think it would help anything if she let on that she knew.

"Do you like it?" As the two women tried to make small talk, people were checking them out, Sarah being in uniform, and another officer was at the main entrance. Jesse asked if it would be possible for them to change into street clothes. She recognized a few people by sight from the school and one woman from their pediatrician's office there with her kids. Tongues were wagging for sure. She turned back to Sarah waiting for an answer.

"Let me text Joe and ask. Good idea." The message was sent along.

Jesse nodded her head and excused herself to get a drink. "You want anything?"

Sarah shook her head and looked at Trevor and Steven landing in the pool. She doubted the guy would come here but needed to be vigilant. She checked in with Sean, her partner on this detail. He hadn't seen anything but needed a restroom break. Watching the small water park from the door she noted, "Try to be quick." She was uneasy because she couldn't see the area where Trevor and his dad were.

****

Joe listened to Paine explain that he had an ID on at least one of the prints from the school. It was Matthew Stone from North Carolina who was accused of shooting his son while trying to scare off intruders. He had been acquitted and released. That was several

108

years ago. Paine was online looking up contact info for the man. The picture on file didn't really look like the man that had been described to them by any of the people who had seen him here. The rookie cop was sending him a copy of it as they spoke.

Avery saw Joe's back stiffen while he was on the phone and walked over to see what was up. He was jotting notes down in a tiny notebook he had pulled from his breast pocket. She sat down at the kitchen table to wait for him to finish. "That's great, Tom, I will pass it on and get back to you. Keep looking and let me know."

"We have a match to the prints from the school." Joe was glad they got the first lead. "The picture is coming in a minute. Matthew Stone. He's from North Carolina." He raised his shoulders in question. "Don't know what he's doing up here."

Avery was tapping away at her laptop like a frenzied bird. She flipped it around just as Joe pushed his phone screen at her. The picture on the screen showed a clean cut, grief-stricken man in his early thirties. The picture from the local artist was of a much older, grizzly loner with long stringy hair. But the same eyes portrayed an emptiness that could be felt through the screens. The detectives looked back and forth between the photo and the sketch. Joe covered the hair on both pictures, and the face beneath looked like a father and son. It was as if the man aged twenty years in under five. "What's his story?" Avery mused, tapping some more. She brought up the arresting officer's report. With Joe reading over her shoulder, they got their first impression of Matthew Stone. Continuing to read, they learned about the home invasion years earlier.

"Jesus, if it weren't for back luck, this guy has no luck at all." Joe leaned back and let out a long sigh. His phone dinged, and he looked down at the message from Sarah. He showed it to Price, who nodded. He sent back the okay for them to change into street clothes.

"With all that, he appears to have finally gone over to the dark side." Price tapped her teeth with a pen. "Do you suppose he is looking to get back his son?" She pecked away some more and brought up a photo of Matthew's son. It was an autopsy photo, so the young boy looked like he was asleep, with damp hair combed straight back. Joe grabbed a photo from the fridge of Trevor. Side by side, there was a resemblance, but Trevor's curls and tanned face made a comparison difficult. Avery pulled up a picture of Tommy Stone from Matthew's case.

"They look the same age." Joe read some of the details. "Same size, same color eyes. Are there any pictures of the boy…" He looked back at the article. "Tommy, alive?" Joe snapped his fingers and stood up. "The perp, Stone, called Trevor 'Tommy' at the school!"

"Okay." Avery joined him, standing, bouncing on the balls of her feet. The woman could not sit still. "It's starting to make some sense."

"Now let's see if any of the prints from around the property match the ones from the school." She snapped her fingers in the direction of a younger tech who practically skipped over.

"Woah, that actually works for you?" Joe whispered.

"They fear me," she whispered back with a smirk and moved forward to meet him halfway. She spoke with authority and directed them outside to help with the collection by the fence and in the woods. Speaking to Joe again, "We should focus on where we know he has been."

"I'll get the APB out with his name and pictures." Joe called back into the station to start that rolling. He felt good having the lead, but worried for Trevor. With what the man had gone through, who knows how far off the rails he had gone?

Chapter 19

Karen's phone buzzed from somewhere on the floor. She must have nodded off. Tripping over the blanket she had wrapped around her legs, she nearly hit her head on the corner of the coffee table. She grabbed her phone just as it was going to voicemail. She hit the call back button and untangled her legs.

"Karen?" Wendy's voice was loud in her ear.

"Hey there, Wendy, sorry I couldn't find the phone for a minute." She sat on the edge of the couch waiting for any information.

"Okay, my ex called me back. His cousin didn't really know him well but did remember a few things." She sounded like she was reading notes. "Three, maybe four months ago, he got tired of everyone looking at him like he was either a killer or a pathetic loser, my cousin's words, not mine. So, he packed up his stuff, emptied his account, and drove north. A couple of friends said that they got a few postcards from him. Basic 'hello, I'm okay,' kind of stuff, no details. He hasn't heard anything else for at least a month." She was out of breath.

Karen wrote it down and thought for a few seconds. "Do you think Stone has a phone with him? Anyone have that number?"

"I don't know, I can call back and ask if you want. It's getting late, he has a baby now. Acts all Father of the Year." The disappointment in her voice was clear. Karen wondered if that was a sticky subject for the former couple.

"If you don't mind, or if you think he would talk to me, I could just call him." Karen figured it would be easier to talk directly to him in case other questions came up.

"No, no, I don't mind. Most exciting thing to happen to me in years." Wendy's voice slowed. "That's sick of me. This poor guy, so much crap, and I am excited to be prying into his life."

"Welcome to my world," Karen muttered. It was hard for her sometimes to dig up people's emotions. They weren't always open, or ready to talk to a stranger. "Hey, I appreciate your help. Teddy says hi." Teddy was one of the guys Wendy toyed with. Once she was bored, she left him in a corner and moved on. Teddy said it hurt at first, but then he was glad to have only been a momentary diversion for her.

"Oh, Teddy! How is he?" The squeal was back. Karen wondered if she had a trophy wall or something to track her conquests. She filled her in on Teddy's situation, living with a girlfriend, just getting a new job. They hung up with a promise to connect in the morning after giving Wendy some time to get in touch with Charlie again.

Just before she settled down, she sent Wendy a text. "If you can find out where the postcards were from, that would be huge. Thanks for all of your help."

****

The APB was issued right away, and the news stations promised to air Matthew Stone's pictures, both the new and old ones, in case he had cleaned himself up some, at the late newscast. It announced that he was a person of interest in two incidents, one involving an attempted kidnapping of a child.

****

Matt hit traffic almost as soon as he turned off onto the Spaulding Turnpike. There was major construction, and the road was down to one lane in either direction. He drove in stop and go traffic for two more hours when another headache took over. He knew it wouldn't get any better without sleep, so he pulled off looking for a place to bunk for the night. The first exit that said Lake Winnipesaukee, he took. Matt saw several mom-and-pop type places but was unsure if a smaller or bigger place would be better. Bigger places would want ID, while at a smaller place he would stick out more. Dry swallowing some medicine for his headache he pushed farther down the road.

The Lazy Man's Inn was next to the lake and set into the woods with a dirty half-full pool in a small clearing. The season had not really begun, so most places wouldn't be open. He decided to take a chance and see if there was a vacancy. His head was pounding, and there were black spots in his peripheral vision. This was going to be a bad one. Matt backed the car into a spot that had a hand painted "Welcome, visitor!" sign. He tucked his shirt in and straightened his hat. The screen door complained as he pulled it over the warped step.

"G' afternoon. Looking for a place to stay?" The man behind the counter turned to him from his stool and smiled widely. His eyes were clouded over. Cataracts?

"Yes, please, just for the night."

"Passing through?"

"Yup, just tired of driving, need to rest up." Matt tried to sound casual and ease up on the southern drawl, because he was worried the man would somehow know about him.

"Just you? By yerself?" The man squinted and peered over the counter.

"Yup, going fishing."

"Hmm, man needs to get out by himself sometimes, just him and the fish." His hands slid over the cracked laminate and turned the register toward Matt. "You can sign in here. Sixty bucks a night. There's HBO, and there's your continental breakfast." He nodded to a box of Hostess crumb cakes and coffee pot and laughed with a phlegmy cough.

Matt scribbled an illegible name and placed the money in the old man's hand and took the proffered key. "Number three, right across from the pool. Don't recommend swimming yet, just got opened yesterday. Probably looks like a swamp. Smells like one. If you're hungry, there's a great clam shack just down the road. On a good day, I can smell it from here. My name's Red, if you need anything."

"Thanks, I might just check it out." The idea of food made Matt's stomach turn. He needed a bed and sleep. Pulling his bag out of the car, he headed into the small cabin. That door creaked too; the whole place could use some WD40. The undeniable musty smell was not altogether awful, but it did tickle his nose. Dropping the bag on the couch earned him a cloud of dust. He looked for a glass in the curtain covered cabinet and turned the water on. It ran cloudy for a few minutes and once it was clear and cool, Matt filled it up. He downed the liquid and flopped on to the bed. In a couple of minutes, he was fast asleep.

Chapter 20

Karen woke with a start with a stiff neck and a burning need to pee. Stretching while she walked slowly to the bathroom, she wondered what time would be too early to expect a call from Wendy. She ran her tongue over her teeth. They felt like the inside of an old sock. She had fallen asleep without brushing or even changing her clothes. She should be upset over getting laid off, but the mere promise of a good story excited her.

The water spray cleared her head as she brushed her teeth in the shower. The heat eased the muscles in her neck. Karen wondered how she should go about getting information on Matthew Stone. She was stalking him and should feel bad about it. It looks like he is trying to get a new start. Would he welcome her intrusion? Probably not. She would have to be tactful. Would she back off if he didn't want to talk?

Toweling off, reality hit, she had to figure out the work stuff first. She needed to know when the severance package would be available. How much money did she have in savings? She wandered over to her kitchenette. The drawer on the left served as her home office, imperfect as it was. She fished out her checkbook and played with the numbers. Rent, car payment, and credit card all were due in two weeks. It would be okay even without the severance pay. If the newspaper money came in soon, she would be fine for a while. But she really should look for a job. She wouldn't be alone in the search either, they weren't the only paper closing down. Maybe she would join Jose and Deborah pole dancing. The phone dinged, indicating there was a text waiting. With her hair in a towel, she plopped back down on the sofa. It was from Wendy. *--No news yet. Will call him if he doesn't call me by noon--*

--Thx, I appreciate it. Pls tell him I said thx too-- It was nine. Three hours seemed like forever. With the TV on in the background, she powered up her laptop, with the intent of looking for a new job. As she refreshed her screen, the Google search scrolled down. There were several hits with 'Wanted, Matthew Stone in connection to attempted child abduction.' "What the hell?" She clicked on the first one, a news story from a Massachusetts station, her heart pounding in her chest.

A blonde woman looked directly into the camera and delivered this report. "The police are looking for this man, Matthew Stone, in connection with a hit and run accident in Middletown. These are two pictures of him, the one on the left is a more recent artist's rendering from a witness." The right side of the screen brought up an archived picture of Matt leaving a North Carolina courthouse with lawyers by his side. "Matthew Stone is no stranger to the law." Karen sat, dumbfounded as she saw her story unfold in front of her eyes.

A small map shown on the news clip showed the town is just north of Boston. So, he was heading north. She had to call Wendy.

"Oh. My. God! Did you see the news?" Wendy's voice hit a note only dogs could hear.

"I know, what the hell? Could you talk to Charlie for me? I am hoping to get the scoop on this." Karen paced, finishing her soda and stifling a burp. "I think I am going to New England." The words came out before Karen had processed them herself. Surprised at her rush decision, she grabbed a duffle from under her bed.

"Really? Are you sure that's safe?" Wendy voiced her concern. Karen was surprised by that.

"Um, yeah, the newspaper laid everyone off yesterday. I have nothing else to do." The words kept coming out. She packed as Wendy promised to call her ex right away and push him to follow up with his cousin. Not knowing exactly where and for how long she was going, she threw in jeans, shorts, tee shirts, sneakers, socks, underwear, and bras. Tossing her toiletries on top, she zipped it closed. In the small living room of her apartment, she gathered her laptop, chargers, a notebook, and some pens. Finishing, she sat quietly on the edge of the couch. Looking around the tiny space, she was caught on how little there really was in her apartment. Some pictures of her family and some friends sat on the mantel of the gas fireplace. There was a stack of magazines with the pages marked of items for 'when she got a real place.' Well, that was a long way off for sure now that she lost her job and was becoming a roving investigative reporter.

Suddenly hungry, she opened the refrigerator. Just as empty of anything of value, she popped open another can of soda, and sniffed a container of Chinese food from a few days ago. Nope, even she wasn't that desperate. She tossed that, along with the fuzzy cheese, and what might be shriveled peaches or maybe nectarines. Those were bought a few weeks ago in a momentary delusion of healthy intentions. With that, some low-fat feta and lettuce that left a green pool at the bottom of the drawer were added to the barrel. "Pop Tarts never go bad," she thought out loud. With the fridge no longer a HAZMAT issue, she tore open her foil-wrapped meal. Standing over the sink, she waited for the phone to ring.

****

Jesse had fallen asleep sometime after three a.m. She had tossed and turned, trying not to wake the sleeping child next to her. He had worn himself out, Steven did too. They stopped counting at seventeen how many times they went up the three flights of stairs and slid down the giant slide. After a quick meal of chicken nuggets and cold fries, they tromped up to the room. Sarah and Sean, now in plain clothes, were in tow. Jesse had offered to buy them dinner, but both refused. When she saw them set up two chairs in the hallway a few feet from the room eating dinner from vending machines, her anger at the situation returned.

The sun peeking through the curtains told her morning had come. She looked over at Steven in the next bed and was happy that he was getting some sleep. The past couple of days were a blur. Was it a dream? No, what would today bring? More questions from the police? Guarding Trevor from a crazy man? Would they find him? Why was he doing this? Too many unanswered questions. She slid out of the bed and went into the bathroom. The face staring back at her was older than it had been just last week. Hints of her mother stared back at her. The high brow line, the slim nose, and those baggy earlobes! Ugh! It was a family trait for sure. All of her sisters and brother had them. Trevor had Steven's neat little ears that tucked back nicely. A quick shower might help her feel better or at least look better. Jesse turned the knob to hot and waited for the steam to fill the mirror before stepping in.

Chapter 21

Matt woke with a start to the sound of a train barreling by. The walls shook and the dishes in the cabinet clattered. Steadying himself, he peered out of the window to see it was really just a caravan of trucks passing by. Going back to the road work he figured. Rolling his neck and rubbing his jaw, he tried to work out the stiffness that had set in overnight. Once the trucks were gone, he turned to see the smooth surface of the lake. The rising sun caught the front of a small house on the other side of the inlet. He watched as someone walked out onto the dock. From behind the man a dog jumped into the water. The ripples slipped across the cove in a hypnotic dance. Matt watched them until they disappeared from view. He was starving and decided to take the old man up on his continental breakfast. Pulling a new shirt over his head and combing back his hair with his fingers, Matt walked across the small parking lot to see if the office was open.

In the early morning light, Matt got a better view of the place. What looked like old green paint was really mold and dirt clinging to what was left of the white paint. Shutters hung at odd angles, and the pool did in fact smell and look like the swamp. Kind of reminded him of the frogging ponds he used to play in as a kid. That was something he wished he had been able to share with Tommy, frogging. Shaking the idea from his mind he pulled open the door and stepped back in the office. The manager was there, on the same stool. It was almost as if he hadn't moved from the night before. He looked in Matt's direction, the cloudy eyes didn't seem to focus on one thing. Stepping a foot to the left Matt saw that the man's eyes didn't follow him. Red addressed the space Matt had left, "How was yer night?"

"Great, I fell right to sleep and slept right through." The man's head jerked to track Matt. "Mind if I take you up on that breakfast? Fell asleep before I could get supper."

"Sure, take what you want. Haven't made coffee yet." As the man stood, he felt his way around the counter. Matt was right, the man was either completely blind or his sight was quite impaired.

"I can make it, no problem," he offered and stepped to the small table to start the coffee brewing. "Fishing any good round here?" Matt asked hoping to sound casual.

"Depends. If yer lookin' for a prize winner, no. Solitude and relaxation, yes. Great little coves and tucked away inlets to meander all day. Drop the line in, drink a few beers, it's paradise." He sat back down. "You have a boat?"

"No, wasn't sure where I was going to land, didn't want to tow it too far."

"You're from the south, what parts?"

"Carolina," Matt answered quickly then caught himself. "South Carolina, Greenville," he added, kicking himself for slipping.

"Mmmm, never been farther south than Boston. Went there once to see the Red Sox play. Wanted to see that Green Monster for myself." Matt looked at the man. "That was when I was younger, before the eyes went." Red tapped his head. "Damn thing, getting old, ever'thing breaks down. Be lucky to get around much longer. Arthritis, ya know," he said matter of factly, not looking for pity. He continued. "Once yer my age, they say each day is a blessing. Not sure I agree. Would like to see my Celia again." The voice softened, and his eyes misted over.

Matt felt his pain. "Celia your wife?"

"Yeah. Damn cancer took her. Been ten years. Miss her ever'day." He wiped a rough hand over his face. "Lookit me, whining on like a baby." The older man cleared his throat. "So, do you think you'll be movin' along or hanging here for a bit?"

Matt paused for a minute. The coffee had finished brewing, and he took his time pouring two cups. A blind owner, an out of the way place, and an entire lake to get lost in. Maybe he could hole up here for a few days before moving on. "I was thinking of staying a little longer, try out those clams and the fishing."

"That'll be great..." Red let it hang for a second. "Didn't get yer name."

"Greg." He used his middle name, because he was so caught off guard, he couldn't think of another.

Red extended his hand in Matt's direction. "Nice to meet you, Greg, from South Carolina. Welcome to the lake."

After shaking his hand, Matt said, "Thanks, think I will look around. Thanks for breakfast." He grabbed two of the plastic wrapped cakes and stepped outside.

Walking back to his little cottage, Matt saw the car he had bought the day before. Hopefully it would buy him some cover. He needed some time to let things settle down. Maybe then he could try to start over somewhere.

Chapter 22

Joe relieved Sarah at the hotel before the sun was fully up. He asked her how the family seemed before they went to sleep.

"Trevor was exhausted, looked like he almost forgot why he was here. Jesse and Steven? They're putting on a brave face. She checked on us close to midnight to see if we needed anything. Haven't heard much since."

"Thanks, go home and rest. I will call you if anything else comes up."

"Don't worry, Joe, everything will be okay." Sarah patted him on the shoulder. She and the other officer left, leaving Joe to his worries, waiting for the family to wake.

Joe took out his notebook and compared notes to what Avery had emailed him during the night. While he nursed a cold cup of coffee, he read the Matthew Stone file.

September 9, 2011 7:12 a.m. State Police Barracks, Charlotte, NC

Report written by Jefferson Tinely
Arrested Matthew Gregory Stone Age: 30 DOB 06/12/1981
Charges: homicide

Victim: Thomas G. Stone Age: 5.4 DOB 05/02/2006

Location: 254A Winslow Avenue, Pineville, NC

Officer's notes: Officers Tinely and Melton arrived at scene approximately 12:46 a.m. following a 911 call from the address. Neighbors had reported hearing gunshots and screaming. Apartment was on second floor of three floor walkup. Security door on main level, locked. Approached second floor and heard calls for help from unit 254A. Front door was open, identified ourselves as officers and entered unit. Found suspect on floor in hallway between first bedroom and the living area. He was holding male child with gunshot wound to the chest. Melton called for ambulance and back up to secure the scene. Tinely checked victim for pulse, found none. CPR was administered. Handgun on floor near second bedroom, broken glass on floor in hallway. Melton secured gun, and cuffed Matthew Stone after suspect stated, "I killed him, oh my God I killed him." CPR continued until EMS arrived. Child transported to Union, pronounced DOA.

After victim was removed, Matthew Stone reported that he had heard someone in the apartment. He was trying to protect his family.

Tinely observed a window in kitchen open and the screen on fire escape floor. Flecks of what appears to be white paint were on the kitchen floor near this window. Several drawers were opened and appeared to be rifled through. iPad, wallet, and watch found in driveway below window/fire escape. Wallet had Stone's ID and two credit cards in it. No cash. Evidence points to break in. Neighbors heard shot then screams. Mr. Stanley

Phillips, 256A reported motorcycle 'screeching' out of parking lot minutes after shots.

Transcript of Matthew Stone interview:

This will be recorded for both your protection and ours. Do you understand your rights as they were read to you?

Please voice your response so the recorder can hear it.

Yes.

Please state your name and address.

Matthew Stone, 254 Winslow Avenue, Pineville, North Carolina.

How old are you?

Thirty years old. How's my boy? Can I see him? I didn't mean to. There was someone in the apartment. They were going to hurt him; I was trying to protect him. Can I see him? Will he be okay? (subject agitated)

Mr. Stone, we will get to that. Who else lives with you?

No one. My wife died. That's why I have to be with Tommy. There's no one else. Please, tell me how he is!

Mr. Stone, please tell us what happened.

Not until I see Tommy. Where is he?

Mr. Stone. Tommy died. He...

NO!!!!

taped transcript ended. Officer added:

Suspect became very agitated and uncooperative. Restraints were used for his safety and the safety of the officers.

Interview ended, suspect became catatonic and was transferred to Union in restraints with escort.

Joe sat back and reflected on what he just read. The rest of the information included that the man had been tried and found not guilty. Several references indicated that due to the stress from the loss of his wife and the beating he had taken during that break in, the jury felt Stone had not meant to kill his child. A few believed he may have staged the break in, but that was later resolved when a woman turned in Carol Stone's cross and necklace. She had bought it at a pawn shop. The woman had seen an article on the shooting and the only item believed to have been taken during the break in. The owner of the pawn shop could not identify who had brought it in originally. The necklace was returned to Matthew, who later buried it at the cemetery where his wife and son were laid to rest.

Joe wanted Avery to call so he could see if she had contacted the police down south. Just as he was going to call her, the Reeds' door opened a crack.

"Joe?" Jesse's whispered but showed surprise. "You weren't here all night, were you?" She slipped out, placing the metal security latch between the door and frame to keep it ajar.

"Nope, got here a half hour ago. How is everyone?"

Jesse must have showered, for her wet hair hung limply around her tired face. She had pulled a sweatshirt on, and the shoulders were starting to get wet. Noticing it, she knotted her hair in a twist. She sat down in the chair next to Joe, pulling her bare feet underneath her. "They are still sleeping. Trevor wore himself out on the slides. Steven too."

She looked expectantly at him. Joe didn't know if he should share the new information or not. This was new for him. He hadn't read up on the rules of how to let your ex-girlfriend, daughter of the people who practically raised you, mother of an attempted kidnapping victim, knowing that the man after her son was probably in the middle of a mental breakdown. Nope, he must have missed that day at the academy. He gave her the standard line, "We are looking into some possible leads."

She was just about to say something when they heard Trevor call for her from inside. She leapt up and went to him. "Mommy's here," Joe heard her say before the door closed with a soft click.

****

Joe looked at an email from Detective Price. Avery said she would extend the APB for Stone's vehicle into bordering states. If that plate went through a toll, hopefully they would get it. If Stone had an EZ Pass, it could be figured out in minutes. But not all drivers had one. North Carolina has a Quick Pass, but it works in the EZ Pass system. If he went through a manual one, it would depend on if it was covered by cameras or not. That would take longer, because those only took screenshots of the plates if the driver didn't pay. Then the driver would get a bill and a fine in the mail. All cars were recorded, so the files would have to be checked manually. Joe waited for Avery in the hall balancing his laptop on his knees and reviewing his handwritten notes. Drinking his coffee, he wondered why cold coffee tasted like shit, but iced coffee was good. He decided it would remain a mystery, while he checked emails and listened for signs of life from inside the Reeds' room. He could hear low murmurs, which led him to believe that Steven was still asleep.

He looked up to see Price walking toward him looking refreshed and neat. His own uniform was rumpled, but he had showered and changed before the sun came up. Joe loved the uniform, but sometimes wished he could wear a suit and tie, add some personality. He stood up to greet her. As they shook hands, he noted that they were the same height, and that she could make a button-down shirt look remarkably attractive.

"Morning. How are you?" Joe gestured to the other seat, as if they were in an office and waited for her to sit. While she was his superior, he still had manners. Jesse's mom always said, "Manners matter, not money, power, or position. Pull out the lady's chair!" Holding back a smile, he waited for her to speak.

"Well, I assume you read the file." Joe nodded. "He has quite a history. I think there's a good chance he's lost his grip. We should consider him dangerous. Possibly armed. We know he's owned a gun in the past. I sent out the APB for the car. I am waiting for more information from North Carolina, but from what we know, he is traveling alone, right?"

"No one has mentioned ever seeing another person with him. He was alone at the school, we can assume, because he was driving the car. If there was another person, don't you think they would have driven?"

"Most likely." Avery bent over to pick up a pen she dropped. Joe saw the no nonsense bra peeking out of her shirt. Quickly, he averted his eyes. She popped back up and adjusted her collar.

Joe was looking down at his laptop and working hard to look engrossed on the empty screen. "So," he asked. "Can the family go back home?"

"Let's just check with the CSI's and see if they can think of anything else they might need. Then we can release the house back to them. Do you have the manpower to leave a team on them?"

"Yes, I do. For a few more days. We are spread a little thin with this case and the upcoming festival." Joe was referring to the Craftsman's Festival. It was a craft and artisan fair held every year on the town common. Vendors from all over New England vied for a table there. It wasn't a rough crowd, by any means. Just a lot of out of town traffic and details to be filled. On a sunny day, 3000 people walked through the booths and shopped for one-of-a-kind gifts, decorations, and homemade food products. The strawberry shortcake line formed at nine and curled around the building for six straight hours or until the berries ran out. One of the perks of the uniform was line cutting. He was sure to get a big serving of warm biscuits, juicy strawberries, and whipped cream. His stomach growled audibly. "Would you like something from the hotel bakery?"

"Um, do they have Boston creme doughnuts?"

"They should, this is a tourist hotel, the vacationers want a taste of local fare. They probably have Boston Beans too, if you want."

Avery made a sour face. "Gross, bad combination. I'll stay here, if you don't mind getting our breakfast."

"No problem. Coffee?

"Cream, Splenda, shot of caramel if they have it." She was back to her laptop tapping away before he even stood up.

He had been dismissed. Price was smart, pretty, definitely sexy, but didn't seem to be aware of it. Which added to the sexy. Girls caught up on themselves were a real turn off. He turned the corner and rode the elevator down to the main level. Another cop was in place, in plain clothes. Joe himself was in uniform because he was not on the detail. With a nod, he acknowledged his presence and went into a small cafe. The girl behind the counter eyed him. After he gave his order, she whispered, "Is there a VIP here or something? We were told the police were around. Usually that means like someone important is here, like Taylor Swift, or Jay-Z. Oh. My. God. is One Direction here?" Her voice got louder, and she looked around.

"No, no. No one is here. At least no one you would know." Joe shut the conversation down politely and waited in silence for his order. The chastened teenager quietly filled the cups and wrapped up two donuts. Feeling bad for shutting her down he tried to make nice. "You know cops and their doughnuts. We can't get through the day without them." He flashed his best smile, but she stared blankly at him. He turned and walked back to the elevator bank.

Chapter 23

Waiting was not Karen's strongest character trait. She even considered going for a run but promptly dismissed the idea and called her brother. Most likely he would be returning from his run and squats or thrusts or something exhausting. She would save him from himself and get some advice, she hoped.

"Hey there, I was thinking of calling you. How are you doing?" Teddy's voice was a comfort. In the last twenty-four hours her life had taken a definite turn for worse, or for better? That remained to be seen.

"I'm okay, I guess. Trying to decide what to do."

"Bendy call you back?" Teddy's smile could be felt through the phone.

"She did, but no new info. He was all over the news today, you see it?"

"No, you know I don't watch TV." Teddy felt television was the top of the slippery slope to mindless, self-centered, overweight societies. She filled him in on what she had seen. Teddy was silent for a while. "You still thinking of following the story?"

"I'm thinking so. He's going north, he's been in Massachusetts for sure. If I were him, I would continue north into the woods of New Hampshire or Vermont. Disappear, wait for this to go away," Karen shared. "Unless he comes back for the little boy." She paused. "Do you think he's dangerous?"

Her brother was silent for a while. Karen did have a habit of asking for then ignoring advice. "I think you should wait for more information. Let Wendy talk to her cousin's friend or whoever, then make a plan. Don't go off blind."

"But the story is out, if I don't follow it others will. I might have information they don't by using Wendy." Karen was worried she would lose her edge. And then the story.

"You're gonna go no matter what, huh?" Teddy was concerned. But he knew his twin sister, and common sense wasn't her strongest trait.

"I think so. It's an adventure, but without the mountain lions and peeing in the woods." Remembering their trip always brought a smile to her face. She could hear him laughing.

"All kidding aside, you need to be very careful, Kare. You have no idea if he is crazy, or if you will get into trouble for interfering. I would get in touch with the local police when you get there. Make it seem like you have info they need. Then you might get something back."

"When did you get so smart? I'm going to head north and get that much closer. Wendy can call me while I am on the road."

"You're already packed, aren't you?" He managed to say it in a way that made her feel small, like their parents used to.

"Uh, yeah," she answered. "But I have a plan. Or at least directions to New England."

"What did you do, MapQuest 'north'? Karen, you have to be careful. I'd go with you, but my new boss would be pissed. Anyone from the paper a good choice?"

"Hmm, Jose and Deborah. They would be flashing people on the highway, drinking beer for breakfast. Deb makes me look like a health nut. I don't think she's ever eaten anything with an expiration date."

"Ha! That's the pot calling the kettle black," he interjected.

Karen ignored him. "Plus, they are really pissed about losing their job. I would rather go it alone."

"You have to promise to call me morning and night. What are you going to tell Mom and Dad?" Their parents worried, especially about Karen. They viewed her profession poorly, unless she was writing for the New York Times, People magazine, or perhaps as a speech writer for the president. Then they would brag. Teddy had to give her credit for following her dream regardless of their not so subtle criticism. Plus, she would have sucked as a teacher, which was what their mom was and wanted her daughter to be. Karen had little patience, and flashbacks from her babysitting days with the triplets down the street steered her away from anything having to do with kids.

"Mom and Dad don't need to know. I will tell them about my job later. If you talk to them, be vague. Very vague. I will call them at the end of the week like usual. Play it cool, like nothing's changed."

Teddy inhaled deeply, a calming technique. The best route was to support her and slip in pieces of advice. "Promise you will call me. Every. Damn. Day. Let me know where you are staying, where you are going. Be sure to let the police know you are there. Keep your phone charged."

"Yes, Dad. I packed clean underwear, I won't talk to strangers…well actually I will, but not in dark alleys. You won't have to ID me from dental records, or DNA from a woodchipper. I will be careful."

"Not funny, Kare. Be careful. Promise."

"Promise."

"Love you."

"Love you too." Karen hung up; she didn't like putting more stress on Teddy. He always looked after her. Kept her out of trouble, covered for her a few times. Before she left for her impromptu trip, she made sure the windows were closed, turned off the lights, and locked the door. As she walked down the stairs to her car, she was excited. Nervous too, but excited. This was the biggest thing she had ever done. She took a deep cleansing breath like her brother had taught her and dropped her bag in the backseat. Once she was in the driver's seat, she looked at herself in the rearview mirror. "This will be good. Here we go," she said turning the key in the ignition.

Chapter 24

Jesse and Steven spoke to Avery and Joe about going back to their house. As of now, Trevor would not return to school. The family would go home with officers around the clock. With Stone's picture on the television and internet, they were hoping he would stay away and that someone would see him and call in.

"We are waiting for reports from traffic cameras to see if we can track his car. If he has gone through a toll, it might get picked up. More likely, we will have to weed through hundreds of false leads. The public has a bad habit of wanting to help when they really have no info. Imaginations work overtime, and memories get twisted into what feels important." Avery delivered this news frankly. Counting on a reliable lead from regular citizens was foolish in her mind. Once in a while something turned up, but it was the proverbial needle in a haystack.

"Okay. So, we lay low. Keep Trevor out of sight. How long do you think it will be?" Steven asked.

"No way of knowing. Don't want to take chances. Can you both get time off?" She looked back and forth between the parents.

"They won't be thrilled, but there's no other choice. They should understand," Jesse offered.

"I can work from home. My partner can cover most of it," Steven added, but worry lines framed his brow.

"Okay. You can check out of here, go back to your house, and wait for news from the traffic cams." Joe stood up and waited for the Reeds to get their bags. Trevor looked tired and less excited to see him than before. The novelty was wearing off. Joe was aware of how important routine was for children. He never had it, and he remembered feeling on edge most of the time. As a kid, he longed for someone to make him eat breakfast, tell him to clean his room or to do his homework. School was one of the only places he felt noticed. So he went, every day. Clean and eager to please. Coming back to the situation at hand, he put a smile on his face and asked Trevor, "So, you have fun at the water park?"

Jesse and Steven walked slowly behind, in silence. She reached for her husband's hand and squeezed it. Steven pulled her close and brushed a kiss across her forehead. It was a distracted gesture but a hint of their recent intimacy.

****

Jim ran a hand over his face as he slowly woke up on the dirty recliner in his small trailer. With his eyes closed, he reached for the bag of chips on the floor. Digging to the bottom, he found it empty. Damn, he was hungry. Flipping the remote off, he pushed himself out of the chair with no shortage of grunts and groans. He stuffed his feet into the worn moccasins. Taking a moment to tuck his shirt into the back of his sweats, he deemed himself presentable to the drive through cashier at McDonalds.

He stepped down the front steps gingerly, it usually took a few minutes for his body to adjust to being upright. Jim ambled over to his truck, a weary Toyota pickup with the gate rusted shut. It complained as he settled in and drove onto the main road. McDonalds was just down the street, but it would never have dawned on him to walk the distance. The radio had broken years ago, and since he didn't go far, he left it hanging from the dash from an ill-attempted repair.

Moments later he arrived at the drive through and ordered breakfast. The girl at the window accepted the money from his outstretched fist but quickly pulled her hand back to the safety of the window. The large Cokes were handed over in the same manner. She basically threw the bag at him and mumbled, "Have a good day."

Jim would have been insulted if he hadn't been diving into the bag with pleasure. The smell alone brought a smile to his face. Before arriving back at his home/car lot, the sandwiches were gone, and he was working on the hash browns. He threw the empty wrappers and bag into the barrel by the door. Dishes done, he thought to himself. Time for his shows. As he was entering the house, Matt's car caught the corner of his eye. He got a good price for the Saturn, and he would probably just sell the Taurus for parts. A couple times a month, the guy from the junk yard drove by looking for scrap metal and parts. He would make out on both ends. The ex-bitch would never know and therefore never ask for a piece of it.

Jim waddled back to his chair and eased himself into it. Pointing the remote to the TV he gulped down the rest of the first Coke. Before he could change the station, the newscaster caught his attention. "Police have released this picture of Matthew Stone, wanted in connection to an attempted abduction at the elementary school in Middletown yesterday." At this point another feed came up on the screen showing parents outside of the school telling their version of the story.

"When the fire alarm went off, we all panicked," said a woman with two children pulled tightly to her chest. "I tried to go back in to get my daughter, but then this guy pushes right past me! He looked crazy, I tell you. The teachers were chasing him, and he knocked down that sign over there when he drove off. When we heard that he tried to take a little boy, I almost fainted. Once my Cara was out of there, I just wanted to take her home." Tears fell from the mother's face.

Then it cut back to the reporter. "Local police will not comment on the ongoing investigation." The pictures of Stone flashed on the screen again with the tip line number scrolling below.

Jim nearly spit out the soda and jumped out of the chair in an uncharacteristically agile movement. "What the fuck?" He watched the screen with interest as he made the connection to the man he had just sold a car to. While the photograph didn't match the person, he had seen the day before, the sketch did.

The reporter continued. "Our own researchers found that Matthew Stone is no stranger to the law. Two years ago, he was found not guilty in the accidental death of his five-year-old son in North Carolina. With this latest development there might be some question as to whether that decision was the right one." Then the reporter went on to explain what had happened to Stone's family.

Jim paced in the small trailer. The man was wanted. By the police. Shit. He listened to the reporter describe the incident in which Stone shot his own kid. His mouth dropped open as she continued to share the home invasion years before where he lost his wife too. No wonder the guy wanted to get away. Murder suspect? Attempted kidnapping? This guy was bad luck. And now, Jim was knee deep in it. He should call the police and explain that he sold a car to the guy. But then he would get in trouble, they might think he had something to do with it. What if he had to pay taxes, or give the money back? No, maybe he could just play dumb. According to his ex it was a role he was born to play. That's what he would do. Play dumb, claim he never saw the news. Sitting back down, he changed the station and tried to put it out of his mind.

Chapter 25

Walking back into their house felt cold and scary.
Strangers had been there, touching their things. Jesse
felt the need to clean everything. Dropping the bags in
the kitchen, they silently looked around at the
remaining evidence that the police had been there. Joe
said he tried to clean up, but fingerprint powder was
tough to clean. Smudges could be seen around the
doorknobs and on the windowsills. Jesse pulled a spray
bottle and a roll of paper towels from under the sink.
She got to work trying to erase any reminder that their
world had been turned upside down. Trevor ran to his
room to see if all of his stuffed animals were still there.
Joe waited quietly by the door. Steven went into the
family room to call his partner. After scrubbing the
counter and refrigerator, Jesse turned to Joe and
stopped.

"Why is this happening?" She sank down onto the
floor, leaning against the cabinets. "Why Trevor? Why
is this man so far away from his home?"

"I'm sorry, Jesse." He sat at the table. "I don't
know why. Trevor does look like his son. And he is just
about the same age when he died. I think he has
slipped, or something, and thinks he can replace him
with Trevor."

Putting her head in her hands, she finally allowed
herself to cry. She tried to be quiet, but it was ugly

crying, full on snot and red splotches covered her face. Joe looked on, clenching his fist in frustration. After a few minutes Jesse raised her head and tried deep breathing to try to stop the flow of tears. Grabbing a paper towel from the roll, she hastily swiped the mess away. "What if he gets him?" she whispered. "How do we keep that from happening?"

"He has most likely left the state. No one would stick around once their picture was plastered all over the news and papers. We will find him and keep Trevor safe." Joe sat down on the floor too. "I promise." His voice was low, and sincerity was etched on his.

Joe had always tried to protect her. There was no denying their history, he had become as much a member of her family as her sisters and brother. He was a pall bearer at both of her parents' funerals. You could see his handiwork in almost every room of the house and the yard too. He wanted to help but be respectful of boundaries at the same time.

Steven entered the kitchen looking at the pair sitting on the kitchen rug. Jesse looked up to see that her husband's face had lost all color. "What's wrong?" She jumped up.

"My dad. He had a heart attack. He's in a coma." Steven sat on the bench seat and shook his head.

"Oh my God. What do they think? Will he be okay?" Jesse knelt in front of him and held his hands.

"They don't know. It just happened this morning, my mom came in from her walk and he was on the kitchen floor. She tried CPR until the ambulance got there. They say it is a waiting game, but it doesn't look good." Steven looked up, eyes on Jesse. "I have to go see him. What are we going to do?"

Joe stood up; this was a private moment. He let himself out the door and into the garage, giving them a few minutes. This would definitely complicate things. If he remembered correctly, Steven's folks had two houses, one in Florida and one in New Hampshire. Which house were they at now? He should call Avery but needed to wait for more details. After a few minutes, he knocked gently on the door.

Jesse answered, "Come in, it's okay."

Joe opened the door to see Steven rubbing his face and Jesse wringing her hands. "Where are your parents now? Down south?" Joe asked.

"Up north, at the lake. He's in Hawkins Memorial. Joe, I have to go to him."

"I know. We will get you there. Just have to figure out a few things. Would you all go?" He didn't know what the plan would be for this. There was no precedent set. Yet another thing not covered in Cop 101.

"I don't know what's best. I don't want to leave them, but I don't know if it is safe for Trevor to be traveling. Also, he hasn't seen his grandfather this year. We skipped the trip in February because of work. If he...if he dies, this will be the last time Trev can see him." Steven leaned back and let out a long breath. "Damn it!"

"Dad?" Trevor peeked around the corner, with the blue blanket hanging around his neck. "What's wrong?" The small boy looked from face to face of the adults in the room. No one could muster up a cheery front. Steven and Jesse turned to Joe.

He kind of shrugged, raising his eyebrows as if to say, "It's up to you."

Steven cleared his throat. "Um, your grandfather. He's sick."

"Wumpy? What's wrong?" Trevor climbed onto his dad's lap. When he was younger, his 'g's and 'r's were slow to come out right. The name stuck but was at odds with the formal man. Deep down, they suspected that Andrew, Steven's dad, liked it. Old age had mellowed him some. Not much, but there was a soft spot for the grandkids.

"He's in the hospital. We are waiting to hear what the doctors think." Jesse leaned in and took Trevor's hand.

"How's Nono?" No-no was his name for Steven's mother. Whether it was because he couldn't say Nana, or because she was always saying 'no-no' to Trevor when they went to visit, no one could say.

"Nono's fine. She's with Wumpy," Jesse answered and looked back at Joe. "Can we all go? See them? I wouldn't want..." She let the statement hang in the air. Joe knew she had not been with her father when he passed, and never forgave herself for it.

"Let me talk to Detective Price. We will have a lot to figure out. I'll go call. Steven, what's the name again, of the hospital he's at?"

"Um, Hawkins, it's in Wolfeboro." Steven got up setting Trevor back down. "Let me call my sister, see what she knows. Tanner is on his way up." Steven didn't talk to his siblings as much as Jesse did.

Joe and Steven left to make some calls and Trevor was left staring at Jesse. His brown eyes bored into her; his little mouth was set in a straight line. Grabbing onto the ends of his blanket, he cleared his throat. "Mom, is Wumpy going to die?" It was a logical question. Both her parents were gone, and they had talked about the fact that as people got older, their bodies got weaker. Sometimes, people got very sick and died. How would he handle it if Andrew died?

"Trev, I don't know. I hope not. The doctors are working hard to help him get better. I really don't know."

"Will I get to see him before…?" His voice trailed off.

"I'm not sure. We have to see. It's super complicated."

Trevor jumped up. Anger flashed across his face. He balled up his fists, and his beautiful brown eyes filled with tears. "I hate the Badman. He's stupid, I hate him!" He ran out of the room, and Jesse heard him flop onto the couch. She hated the stupid man too. Rolling her head slowly to let some of the tension out of her neck, she walked into the family room. Her heart almost broke to see him staring at the pictures on the table behind the couch. Family pictures, her parents, Steven's, aunties and uncles and Jack and Jen. He reached out and touched the picture of her parents. "Help Wumpy get better, please?" Trevor whispered the words, but she heard her own voice in them. She, too, often asked her parents for help. Sending her own silent prayer, she pulled him into her arms.

That's how Steven found them and joined the family hug. Jesse could see a tear slip from the corner of his eye. Joe had walked in but backed out of the room. He decided to wait in the driveway.

****

Avery Price had been busy. Matt's plate was tagged going through the Hampton tolls on Route 95 in

New Hampshire. But it wasn't on a Taurus, it was on a later model greyish Saturn. The tape was not clear, and the cameras only caught a quick view of the rear end of that car when the driver behind him didn't pay. That was around one o'clock yesterday. Consensus was he was heading into the northern woods of New Hampshire. He could veer off to the west and go into Vermont or New York. Then again, he could go east and hit Maine. There was no shortage of remote places he could hide. The APB was adjusted to update the car model. They still needed to find the Taurus, but now the Saturn took priority.

Tapes from the Dover and Spaulding Turnpike tolls were being checked. She wanted to have the tapes from the Hookset Toll and Maine tolls checked too, in case he changed course. But her boss said to wait for the Dover results. She didn't want to waste time. This guy had her worried. It appeared that he was in the middle of some sort of breakdown. People with a tentative grasp on reality made foolish decisions. Her phone buzzed, and she checked the ID. Joe Marchand. Interesting guy. Handsome, in a rustic way. Not really her type, but where had her type gotten her? Divorced and lonely. "Price."

"Detective Price, this is Joe Marchand. Sorry to bother you again." Joe had left a couple messages this morning already. She was entangled in a few other cases and had been double checking the toll information. She hadn't even listened to her messages.

"Call me Avery, and sorry I haven't gotten back to you. Busy morning. Stone switched cars. Caught his plates at the Hampton toll. One o'clock yesterday, 1:17

to be exact. He's in a Saturn now. I updated the APB. Still checking tolls farther north."

"You sure it's him? He could have switched plates. Any picture of the driver?" Joe hated to be negative, but that would be an easy way to put them on the wrong trail.

"True, could have. But I have a feeling it's him. Going to check parking lots in strip malls and factories for his car. Lots of turn offs on both Routes One and 95. Tons of factories, big trucks to hide between. Weigh stations, rest stops, all being checked."

"This guy has you worried, huh?" Joe hesitated.

"So, what's on your mind. Three messages in two hours. What happened?" Avery was sitting behind her desk tapping her pen on a blotter. She heard him inhale deeply. Oh boy, what now?

"The family got through the night fine. No issues. Trevor had fun in the water park. However…"

"I hate howevers."

Joe laughed. "Don't we all? There's been a serious emergency in Steven's family. His father had a heart attack and is in a coma. He wants to go see him of course."

Price could hear him pacing. She took a beat and then answered, "Okay, that makes sense. We can try to arrange an escort. Where is the dad?"

"New Hampshire, Lake Winnipesaukee to be exact." He echoed her earlier words.

"No shit." Avery closed her eyes and shook her head. "Seriously? The entire country, and the grandfather is in the same state we think our suspect is in?"

"Yeah, they summer up north, winter in the south."

"Snowbirds, huh? Well, I have to think on that. It's like tempting fate. Can you stall them?" She blew out a stream of air. "I mean I get it; the guy wants to see his father. What if the wife and kid stay here?"

"Steven won't go for that. There's no way he'd leave them now. I think they'll be a package deal." Joe let out a breath. "Can we rush the toll cams? If we know he has turned off and maybe driven to Vermont or Maine…"

"Let me see what I can do." Tap, tap, tap. "Tell them I am working on it."

"I have a kid who would work overtime on this. I can send him to you and give you another set of eyes. He's good with all the technology, might be able to really help."

"Sure, if you can spare him."

"I can. Where should I have him meet you?"

"I am going to be in the Danvers office. A colleague from the Boston FBI field office is meeting me to review this case and a few others. He is working on a missing persons case involving a boy from the South Shore."

"Connection?" Joe's voice was raised. The FBI got involved with all kidnappings. If this guy had kidnapped other kids, it brought it all to a new level.

"I don't think so. But it can't hurt to be thorough. Send your guy any time. There's a whole team working the films now, he can join in."

"Will do. His name is Thomas Paine. He looks green, but he's sharp. Found some clues the initial crew missed at the school."

"Good, I'll get back to you ASAP."

Chapter 26

Matt decided he liked Red, and the blind man offered him more cover. Even though he wasn't as far away as he really should be, Matt figured he could get a haircut, shave, and try to stay mostly out of sight. With a different look and a new car, it might just work. The car bothered him some. If the guy from the lot remembered him, the cops would be one step closer. He turned on an old radio on the counter in the miniature kitchen. Fiddling with the dial, he found a station that was broadcasting from Boston. Before he could unwrap the crumb cake, Matt heard his name on the radio.

"Boston area police are asking for the public's help in locating Matthew Stone. Witnesses describe him as six feet tall, around 190 pounds, long brown hair, and beard. He was last seen wearing jeans, a grey hooded sweatshirt, and a baseball cap. He is believed to be driving a grey or green Saturn in New Hampshire. You can see a picture on our website at WXKB.com. Call the State police at 1-781-555-2121."

The cake fell to the floor as Matt stood up, the chair toppling to the floor. With his heart hammering against his chest, he rocked back and forth in the small cabin. "What am I going to do?" he said to the mildewed walls. Throwing the few belongings he had taken out back into his duffle, he felt the walls closing in on him. The need for fresh air took over, and he stepped onto the tiny landing at the door. Gulping breaths, he willed himself to calm down. Eventually his heart rate slowed, and he sat on the stoop. "Think," he said to himself. Maybe he should just turn himself in. He was broken, beyond fixing, but he certainly didn't intend on hurting Tommy. No, the boy. He needed space and time. That's why he left Charlotte. Damn, he had messed everything up. Matt looked at the Saturn, the only car in the lot. There was a Jeep across the road with Rhode Island plates on it. That gave Matt an idea. He could change the plates with another car, going in a different direction than he was. New York, Connecticut, Rhode Island. Any of those would work and hopefully get the cops off of his trail. His pulse quickened again, but not in an awful way. He could stay here, hide out, and lead the police on a wild goose chase. Matt liked the idea. He just needed to find the right car. It should look similar to the Saturn, same size, same color. There was a parking lot just down the street, near that clam place Red mentioned. He could walk down there and see if there was a good choice and eat. He hadn't eaten in almost eighteen hours. Glancing at his watch, he saw that it would have to wait at least a little while, until the place opened for lunch. He picked up the cake from the floor, blew on it, and took a bite. That would hold him over until the clam place opened for lunch.

Back in the kitchen area of his cabin, Matt searched through the few drawers. Scratched and bent silverware, rusty set of knives, a can opener were in one. The next held a pile of fliers from local restaurants that delivered, a worn deck of playing cards, two pencils, and a collection of ketchup, salt, pepper, and duck sauce packets. The third drawer had a mismatched collection of cooking utensils including an ancient pair of scissors. Hopefully they would work on his hair.

Matt picked them up and walked to the bathroom. It was sectioned off with a plastic accordion door that was cracking from age and use. The face staring back at Matt was unrecognizable. Gone were the laugh lines, the easy smile, and what Carol had called the mischief in his eyes. Instead, a hollow cheeked, mangy looking stranger stared back at him. Greasy long hair, unshaven, pale skin, and empty eyes had taken over. The scissors cut through months of neglect. Tossing the strands into the trash barrel, Matt felt a weight being lifted off of his shoulders. Next, he shaved, carefully trimming off hap-hazard whiskers that grew around the scars from the attack. The scars. Crap, maybe he should have kept the beard. Too late.

Stepping back from the mirror, Matt saw the shadow of the man he used to be. Still hiding, but there. Angry, sad, terrified, but there. He stripped and took a long, hot shower. The water was from the lake he guessed. The pressure sucked, but it was heated in a tank behind the cabin. Washing away the fear and dirt, Matt thought he would be okay. Switching the plates will work he determined. Emerging from the bathroom, Matt felt that he could pull it off. Hide out here while the cops looked in another state for him. Time to heal without all of the painful memories beating him down. There was enough money to stay out of sight for weeks. Toweling off he selected a newer, cleaner tee shirt, jeans, and threw on a different baseball cap.

Matt stepped into Red's office to see if he wanted something from the clam shack. Red had his back to him and was cleaning the breakfast counter. "Greg, that you? Kin hear those boots scuffing across the lot."

"Yup. Hey there, I am going to go check out that clam shack. You want anything?"

Red turned around to face him. "Sure. Fried clam plate. Might's well grease the arteries!" He chuckled to himself, reached into his pocket, and pulled out a thin fold of bills. "Here, take ten. Tell 'em it's for Red and they'll add extra onion rings. Don't need to worry 'bout my breath no more. Celia used to hate it when I ate them. I use garlic salt instead of ketchup. Breath to drop a dragon, she would say." The smile on Red's face made Matt long for Carol. She had often talked about growing old together. Who would feed who, would their kids visit them in the nursing home, or keep them home?

"Will do. Going to do some exploring before, so it'll be a while."

"No hurry, I'll be here."

Chapter 27

Joe had entered and leaned against the bookcase opposite of Steven. "I told Avery, Detective Price, about your dad. She needs a little time to figure out the right plan. Meanwhile, we have his license plate circulating in the surrounding states. The cameras at the tolls can see if he goes through, but we need to review each tape. More men are being pulled in to do that. Weeding through that takes time."

Steven slumped back into the cushions. He looked defeated. "Joe, thank you. I mean that. This just can't get any crazier, can it?"

Joe looked down at his phone. "I have to go back to the station." There was a reporter from down south who thought she had information related to the case. He wasn't going to tell Jesse and get her hopes up or add to her worries if it turned out this lady was off her rocker. "Call me if you need anything."

****

The ride back to the station was done on autopilot. Joe's mind was swirling. How quickly life can change. Just last week he and a friend were complaining about the dreary routine of their lives. While he loved his job, he yearned for more excitement. Careful what you ask for, as the saying goes. He wanted to find this guy and put an end to this quickly. Not just because of his connection to Jesse, but failure was not something he tolerated well. After growing up in such an unsettled manner he craved control. His heart raced. Maybe this reporter had some useful information and wasn't just looking to nose into his investigation. Pulling into the parking lot he saw Sarah climbing out of her car.

"Hey, Sarah," Joe called. "Wait up." He collected his things and jogged to catch up with her. The strap on his briefcase gave way, and he stumbled trying to keep the leather case from opening as it hit the ground. He must have looked funny, because as he straightened up, his friend was laughing.

"Quite the manly skip you got there." She mimicked his dance-like movements. "How do you keep the women away?"

In spite of his heavy thoughts on the drive over, he found himself chuckling. It felt good. A little levity in the situation pulled him away from a dark place. Sarah was always good for keeping him sane. He brought her up to speed on Steven's father and the reporter on her way in.

Sarah held the door for him. "The Reeds must be going crazy. Do you think we can help him get up there to see his dad?"

"Waiting on that too. Price is working on it. Knowing Stone is likely in New Hampshire, it seems risky to let them go. But it sounds like his dad is in really bad shape. Can't deny them what very well might be their last chance to see him." Joe poured himself some coffee and leaned on her desk. "I really don't know what I would do if it was me."

"If it was you, this would be a different story altogether. You haven't heard from your dad in thirty years or so."

"As I said, I don't know what I would do." Joe pushed himself away from the desk and walked into his office. His butt barely hit the seat of the chair before Detective Price entered. Standing up straight took effort. He was tired. Extending a hand, he welcomed her back. They both sat before speaking.

"Okay. It took some doing, but we can get Mr. Reed up to his father. I will send an escort. My hope is that he will go alone, much safer to keep the boy as far away from Stone as possible. If he pushes though, we will add two more and make it a short trip." Avery looked up from her laptop, a hint of pain behind her eyes. "Lost my mom a year ago." She coughed. "I can't keep the guy from his dad." She met Joe's gaze for a moment, then quickly looked away. Using the laptop to distract her, she let a slow breath out. Her composure back, she was all business. "I can have the escort ready in two hours. Call the family and let them know our plan. Not exactly sure how we will handle a funeral, depending on where it is." Realizing that might have sounded cold, she cleared her throat. "I think we need to be prepared for the likelihood he will pass in the next twenty-four to forty-eight hours. You have any idea as to where the services would be?"

"Family's from Massachusetts, but the parents haven't been here for years. Don't know for sure. Steven's siblings are scattered around too. I'll ask. Now, we have this reporter coming in. Should be here in an hour, maybe? She's been doing some digging into Stone for a human-interest story, a check-in to see how he's doing since the shooting. Guess she's getting a real story, bigger than she bargained for."

"I am having my colleague, Agent Buchanan, meet us both here. I figured we could save a step and just meet altogether. Hopefully there isn't a connection with his case. I really hope there isn't. I would rather be dealing with a first timer than a pro. More likely a rookie will slip up. Either way, having an agent's opinion can't hurt." Most cops hated working with the feds, but Price had ambitions. Taking every opportunity to network was a step in the right direction. She had worked with Buchanan on a few cases before and they had an easy rapport.

"Any help is good. When do you expect him?" Joe was hungry and wanted to grab something to eat before the agent got there.

She checked her watch. "Twenty minutes."

"You hungry? I am going to grab a sandwich. I can get you anything?"

"More carbs? Usually I'd say no, but I feel like I've been running a marathon. Turkey club please, and an iced coffee would be great." She reached for her wallet, and Joe waved her off.

"I got it. Be right back." Joe disappeared down the hall.

The detective watched his exit carefully. "Not bad," she whispered to herself.

"Quit drooling, Price. Makes you look like a Doberman." Agent Leonard Buchanan had come through the door on the other side of Joe's office. His arrival startled her, and she nearly toppled from her seat. Buchanan's laugh made her laugh too. His was kind of like a wheezy donkey. Completely at odds with the Cosmopolitan profile the man worked so hard at. There was not a hair out of place or a speck of dust to be found. His laugh was the result of taking an iron pipe to the throat during the take down of a suspected terrorist. Almost crushed his neck and severely scared his vocal cords. His voice was deeper, but he was okay.

"You scared the shit out of me." Price rose to shake hands with the man who was a head taller than she was in heels.

"Good, heard you were full of shit anyway." Buchanan set his briefcase on the other visitor's chair and removed his coat.

Cashmere, most likely. Avery knew nice things when she saw them, and the coat was very nice. She did her best on her budget but was getting tired of combing the sale racks to find the designer clothes at the discount price. Half of the time she couldn't afford that price either. Maybe she should marry up. Find herself a sugar daddy. All of that flew in and out of her head in the time it took for him to sit down. "Thanks, good to see you, too." Their collaboration on a few cases over the years lead to a mutual respect for the other's talents. She might have even pursued the man himself if she didn't know he was taken.

"He'll be right back," she said, nodding her head in the direction of Joe's desk. "Ran out to get some food. You want anything? I could call him."

Leonard shook his head. "I wanted a minute with you anyway. My case, Weymouth." Down to business, he pulled up a file on his laptop. "Six-year-old boy, missing three days now. Last seen at school, at the end of the day. Mother usually picks him up. Meeting him outside with the other parents. Teacher said she shook his hand, waved to the mother, and then turned away. Mom reports that he signaled to go to the playground.

She waved yes and was talking with other moms just a hundred yards away. Poof, kid is gone. Took her eye off him for a minute."

"Clues? Ransom? Father?" The questions were fired in a staccato manner. The hairs on the back of her neck stood on end. Stone tried to abduct Trevor from the school. Boys were nearly the same age, and from the picture on Buchanan's screen they looked to be the same size and colorings.

"No ransom, father is in the Navy. On a ship two hundred miles offshore. Came back last night, looks like he stepped on a grenade. Too broken up to be involved. Only clue is the boy's backpack. It was at the edge of the woods behind the swings. There is a small pathway that leads to a neighborhood behind the school. No one saw anything."

"Well, there are some definite similarities, the age, appearance, and the woods. Our suspect used the wooded area to stalk Trevor. From what we can tell he's been around for a while. Only approached him the one time, but the boy has seen him on several occasions. No one believed him, family just thought he was looking for attention."

"Looking for attention? Problem with the parents?"

"Not that I can tell, dad works a lot, mom works some overnights, kid is sometimes with a sitter. But since this went down, both parents haven't left the kid's side. We have a lead on the suspect and believe he is targeting Trevor because of the similarity to his own son, Thomas, deceased." She was prepared to continue, but the agent cut her off.

"Read the reports." Business like, Buchanan recited the facts as he remembered them. The incident at the school, the car accident, even details like Joe's connection to the family, Jack. He also had facts about Stone that she had no idea of how he knew. But then again, he was with the FBI, better access to records, files, and information than the State Police. Even in the age of streamlining on a computer base, some had more than others. "So, what's not in the reports? Your gut?" Buchanan looked expectantly at Price.

"I really think this guy, Stone, has lost touch with reality. With his history, it's not a big leap to think he is trying to replace his lost son. No evidence of the man being violent in the past, completely the opposite. He's been a victim of some horrible things. It can change a person. I'd like to think that since he is trying to replace his son, he wouldn't hurt Trevor, were he to get him. He would try to make him his own. However..."

"You hate howevers," Buchanan inserted.

With a nod, she continued. "Stone doesn't have much more to lose. Lost his wife, then kid. Uprooted himself to try to start over. That, as we know, hasn't gone so well. Thinking he could leave the past behind only caused him to try to create a new reality he can live with. Now, he is on the run. Alone. Clearly starting to deteriorate. If he got cornered, he could do some bad things. We can't give him that chance."

"Okay, let's just review our cases again to see if there is any connection we might have missed."

Chapter 28

Matt wandered down a narrow path that cut through the backyards of camps facing the water. Most were older, somewhat run down. The cabins showed years of activity. Water skis, kayaks, and life jackets were tucked under porches, while plastic covered boats rested on rickety metal trailers, waiting for their owners to take them on the lake. He read signs, hand painted and nailed to trees: Olsen's Hideaway, Auntie's Hideaway, Tyrone's Treehouse, all pointing down a dirt driveway that opened to a small cove. As he walked along, he saw evidence of new construction. A paved driveway led to a foundation surrounded by pickup trucks, Bobcats, and a flatbed layered with two by fours. The lot had been cleared, save a few taller pines. A barge was on the lake dropping huge boulders into the water. Must be building a breakfront Matt guessed. A group of men were leaning against the foundation smoking and drinking coffee. They were talking and laughing. Matt missed that too. Just a normal day at work, sharing a joke with a co-worker. He hadn't had that in years. Back home he tried to go back to the garage where he had worked but couldn't escape the crushing panic attacks. The smell of gas brought him right back to that fateful day. Tried other jobs too, but never lasted more than a month. Disability checks came twice a month, and opening them brought down a cloud of depression and regret. Soon he just had them automatically deposited into his account. He wondered briefly what happened to them when he closed that account.

"Hey there! You looking for work?" One of the men on the worksite was calling to him, waving him down.

Startled, Matt just shook his head and walked away. The trail continued through the woods until it opened up to a small parking lot very much like Red's. There were a few cabins and a small store. He went to the front. "The Loon-y Bin" sign showed two cartoon loons sipping coffee on a small boat. He had heard the lonely unanswered call of the bird the night before. It matched his mood exactly. As Matt stepped on the weathered boards of the landing, he saw several initials carved into the railing. RET, BHT, and CAT were here, CW + PZ, crossed out and a TA replaced the PZ. Love is fleeting. Matt shook his head as he opened the screen door. Inside, the shelves were lined with canned soup, tuna, ketchup, cookies, and various snacks. Opposite were shelves filled with batteries, flashlights, candles, matches, decks of playing cards, and anything else a camper might need or want. The cooler held sodas, waters, and beer next to milk, juice, and worms. Tee shirts with the store's logo could be had for fifteen dollars, sweatshirts thirty dollars. Fishing gear, fireworks, and lifejackets were stashed here and there. Matt grabbed a bottle of water and a banana from the counter. The woman behind it was perched on a stool set so she wouldn't need to get up to reach cigarettes, the lottery machine, or cash register.

"Morning, how are you today?" She glanced up from the magazine she was reading and flashed a smile.

"Just fine, you?" Matt pulled out a few dollars from his pocket, not making direct eye contact.

"Good as can be expected. Season's starting up soon. We'll be busy-busy before you know it. Makes the days go faster." She took his money and made quick change.

"I imagine it would. Thank you, have a good one." Matt turned to leave.

"You from around here?" The woman called after him.

"Nope, just passing through. Y'all have a good day." Matt stepped through the door and let it fall shut behind him. He had to be careful not to draw attention to himself by either being a jerk or overly friendly. He tried to keep most of his interactions short and sweet. He hadn't had a cigarette yet that day. It had become more of a nervous habit than something he enjoyed. When he was smoking, people tended to keep their distance. Lighting one from the pack he bought last night, he remembered the fight with Carol before Tommy was born.

"They will not smoke in front of the baby," she scolded him as they planned a party for their friends who had just gotten engaged.

"But it's their party. What do we say?" Matt countered.

"We say no smoking. They don't like it, they don't have to stay." Her mind was made up, and nothing was going to sway her. He smoked occasionally when he was out with the guys, but had to shower and change

164

before she'd let him get into bed. Matt would figure out a way to smooth it over with his friends.

He took a deep drag on the one thing he and his wife didn't agree with and kept on walking. Up ahead there was another parking lot where a few boats were being set into the water. The accuracy of the drivers maneuvering the trailers down the narrow ramp was amazing. Matt sat on a bench under a tree full of young leaves. He pulled his cap down lower and stared out at the lake. A few boats passed with dogs in the bow enjoying the windy ride.

Slower, lower boats skimmed the water as their passengers trolled fishing lines. A giant white boat pulled around the bend of the bay. The same boat from his childhood visit to the Weirs. He had rushed to the dock as the mammoth boat pulled up, yanking his father's hand. "Can we go? Please, Dad? Please?" He waved frantically at the captain, hoping he would blow the horn. When there were several children waving and jumping up and down, the captain would give a short toot earning cheers from the people standing dockside. They watched the passengers getting off and the next batch loading. His mother slipped her hand into his father's and murmured, "Next time, Matty." There would be no next time, Matt found, but he still loved the memory of watching the boat come in with his parents. Afterward, they had gone to the arcade and played Skeet-Ball.

Matt watched the boat approach and dock with hardly a bump as it came to a stop. Thick ropes were set around the cleats on the dock. A few tourists waited patiently for the crew to secure the boat and then walked aboard. Maybe he would do that one day. He checked his watch. 11:20. The morning almost gone. Halfway through another day. He'd walk back to the cabin and go get lunch for him and Red.

****

Karen was relieved to see the signs announcing the exit for Middletown, 14 miles. This drive felt endless. The motel she stopped at last night was sketchy to say the least. She would have pulled the bed over to prop the door closed had it not been secured to the floor. Just off of the highway in Connecticut, the sign boasted "Clean rooms, low rates, free movies." The clerk handed her the room key attached to a block of wood. First class all the way. She should have known it meant adult movies and that the word 'clean' was up to interpretation. The first thing she did was text her brother to let him know where she stopped in the not so off chance she was chopped up that night. Sleeping with one eye open was just an expression, she thought. All night people walked by her door, laughing, screaming, and crying. She must have checked the lock a hundred times. Before lying down, she spread several towels on top of the bedspread hoping they had been laundered more recently than the stained blanket. Karen slept in her clothes, was showered and out the door by daybreak. She felt the need to throw away the clothes she had worn but tucked them in a plastic bag to wash later.

Armed with a Diet Coke and breakfast sandwich from Dunkin Donuts, she pulled back onto the highway for the last leg of her trip. Her GPS promised a straight shot up Route 95 for three hours. Stopping once for a bathroom break and to get more gas, she was almost at her destination by noon.

She was nervous. This was turning into a much bigger thing that she had imagined. Was Stone dangerous, or just disturbed? He was now running from the police. Would he hurt the child? Karen doubted it, feeling she understood the man some. But what did she really know? Reading some articles, talking to the very distant connection to Matt's family, did that really tell her who he was? Her last conversation with Wendy gave her the number for Charlie's cousin what's-his-name. Turned out what's-his-name was Randy. Randy was very forthcoming with information. She ran over the call with him in her mind. He recounted the first house invasion, then the death of Tommy and how friends were scared for him and even worried he might be suicidal. When Stone talked about going north, they were concerned and made him promise to keep in touch. The last piece of information turned out to be the most important. "Stone had a friend buy the phone he uses so it wouldn't be in his own name. He was hoping to fool the reporters or anyone else looking to track him down."

Karen interjected there. "The phone is in his friend's name?"

"Yup, the friend thought he could call him whenever he wanted. But the guy doesn't answer. Last text from Matt was that he was fine, just needed to be alone."

"Do you think I could get the number from the friend who got it for him? That would be a huge help. I think he's really in trouble. He tried to kidnap a boy yesterday."

S. Hilbre Thomson

"What? Who?"

"I'm not sure. It's just what I heard on the news earlier. There's a bunch of accounts on the internet, but I can't tell what's true." Karen was quiet for a minute. "Was there anything you know that would make you think maybe the shooting wasn't an accident?"

"Not that I know of. He was a real stand-up kind of guy. Before all that shit happened. Maybe he's changed. Maybe he's really pissed at the world and has started acting on it. Lemme ask about the number. I don't want the friend to get in trouble for giving him the phone either. Can I call you back on this number?"

"Yes, please. And thank you, Randy." Karen had pulled off onto a rest stop during the conversation and wrote a few things down on the back of a receipt. Gripping the wheel as she pulled back onto the highway, she was no longer tired from her sleepless night. Miles passed as she mentally explored all of the possible ways this story could go.

****

Matt entered the office with his hands full of grease-stained bags. Red appeared from behind the curtain with a smile on his face. "Hmm, must be you, Greg. Clam Shack has its own distinct fragrance." He inhaled deeply through his nose and swiped a hand across the counter making sure it was clear. Set it right here, please. You get some for yerself?"

"Couldn't resist. Got the same thing as you. Grabbed you a Coke too." Greg looked around for another stool. He was tired from the walking and was also mentally exhausted. A normal conversation might be good for him.

168

"Forgot my manners, lemme grab you a stool." Red shuffled behind the curtain and came out with a matching seat. Matt imagined him and Celia, whose picture, he guessed was the one hanging on the wall, sitting behind the counter during the busy season signing in guests.

The two widowers set up and dug into the bags. Matt found himself in an easy silence with the older man. Both were lost in their own memories. Afterward, they wiped the oil from their hands and faces and Matt was tying the remnants tightly in a plastic bag.

"So how long ago did your wife pass?" Red's question startled him.

"My wife? How'd you know I was married?"

"A person's voice tells a lot. What they say, and what they don't say. Yours told me that you understood my loss like only another widower could. Mind if I ask what happened?"

Matt's eyes watered, and he was glad the old man couldn't see it. "Um, she died in an accident. My son too."

"Jesus, Greg, I'm sorry. Man shouldn't have to bury his child. Wife neither." Red wiped the counter dropping the crumbs onto the floor. "How long's it been?"

"Seems like forever and just yesterday at the same time." Matt pushed open the door. "Thanks for lunch, Red. I'm gonna go lie down."

Red watched the shadow of his new friend disappear around the corner. "Poor guy," he said to the empty room. The Red Sox were on. They were playing the Oakland A's. Red settled into his chair to listen to the game.

Chapter 29

Jesse tried to keep busy neatening up the house and playing with Trevor, who asked an endless stream of questions distracting her some. Her patience was growing thin when a phone rang. She and Steven each grabbed their cell phones. It was his. Jack was calling for an update. Jesse listened as her husband filled his partner in on the latest news. She could hear Jack's concern and offer to come and stay with Trevor and Jesse while Steven was away.

"I appreciate it. But don't know if I can leave them, even with you here. Plus, we have that second meeting with the contractors tomorrow." Steven circled the room, running his hands across his face. "That was today? Jesus, I am so turned around. How did it go?"

He listened for a while, seemingly pleased with the results. "Thanks, Jack, it's been so crazy. Can you handle the office for a while longer? I am going to ask if Jesse and Trevor can come with me. I don't think I could leave them. I just said that didn't I?" He laughed at himself.

Jesse could hear Jack reassuring her husband. They were lucky to have him as a partner. If this deal fell through, the business would take a huge hit. Getting this account would give them the reputation to go against the larger firms with bigger contracts. More clients might mean she could quit working the overnights. Most importantly, with Jack handling the office Steven could concentrate on his dad, and Trevor.

When Steven hung up, he came to her outstretched arms. "You okay?" she asked.

"Yeah, no. I don't know." Steven spoke softly, stroking her hair. "Wish I could fix this, all of this. Trevor, my dad. What will my mom do if he dies?"

"We'll figure that out if we need to." When they were first together and her parents were so sick, they had discussed moving home and living with them. It was agreed that living with her parents might be doable. His not so much. But now things have changed. She wondered what Steven would want. First, they had to figure out this Matthew Stone guy. Catch him, put him away. God, she hoped Andrew would be okay, but the nurse in her knew that that was unlikely based on the little she had been told.

"Wish Joe would call back. I am going out of my mind doing nothing." Steven checked his watch. "They said they would figure it out in a couple of hours. It's been two. I'm going to call him." He picked up Jesse's cell phone and pushed the button for Joe.

****

"Okay. So, we are all on the same page here, right?" Buchanan had taken the lead for the meeting. They had ruled out the likelihood of the missing boy from Weymouth and Matthew Stone being connected. The timing didn't fit, and there had been no sightings of Stone, his car, or evidence at all on the South Shore. With that taken care of, they could focus on the business of getting Steven Reed to his father. "It's trickier than it probably needs to be. Neither of you have any jurisdiction across state lines. You, Joe, have none outside of your town." Both Joe and Avery nodded, not insulted. "Given the attempted abduction, and the fact that we know this guy has crossed state lines, it becomes my case." He put a hand up to stop Joe from interrupting. "Don't worry, Joe, you're still on it. Vital in fact. We just need to go by the books. I will send two of my people along." He stopped there and looked at Joe. "You think there's no chance of him going alone?"

Joe shook his head. "None. He feels so guilty for ignoring Trevor's reports of seeing this guy that he won't leave him."

"Figured. Okay. So, two teams of agents will go with them. You are welcome to send someone too. We just don't want to look like a parade. New Hampshire looks small, but we have to be careful. Too many places to hide, turn off, or change direction. The family stays together, with an escort 24/7. The agents can take turns with breaks. If it goes longer than two or three days, we will send in another team. If and when funeral arrangements come up, we will regroup." Agent Price's phone sounded, and they all jumped.

She looked at the screen and she excused herself. Looking at Buchanan she added, "Okay, the plan sounds good, do you want me to talk to the family or would you?"

"Let's go together. They trust you. Just need to line up the escort.".

Joe cleared his throat. "There is the matter of the reporter from Charlotte. She's on her way here. My gut is to hear what she has to say, see if there's anything of value." Joe valued input from others and liked to vet the person himself. While he liked control, he understood

172

the value of cooperation, and keeping reporters on his good side.

"What's her ETA?"

"This afternoon. The front desk took the call. The woman's been driving for two days, appears very eager to talk to us."

Buchanan mulled it over. "Okay, it can't hurt, I think. We don't give her anything we have, just listen to what she says. Play it close to the chest." He was typing on his laptop. Price popped her head in.

"Um, I gotta go. A DB two towns over. Eighty-year-old found by the neighbor after seeing a strange car in the driveway. Waiting on the coroner, but I'd like to check the scene before more people tramp through. I'll call you from the road."

A quick run-through to recap the plan and she was gone. Leonard returned to his computer. Joe was being dismissed, but they were in his office. He stood awkwardly for a moment and then excused himself to go check in with Sarah. Joe wanted to know her opinion on one of them going with Jesse and her family. He found her at her desk, searching the internet for information on Karen Copeland.

"What's that?" Joe asked sliding some papers aside and leaning on the desk.

"Make yourself at home." She slapped his leg and rescued her coffee from the edge. "Karen Copeland, the reporter coming in. Working at *The Weekly* a small newspaper covering local news, mostly human-interest stories. Went to University of North Carolina, Chapel Hill. Graduated with a degree in journalism. One brother, her twin. No priors, a couple of parking tickets, seems normal so far."

"That's good. Wouldn't want to invite crazy on purpose." He grabbed Sarah's coffee and took a gulp. It was cold, and nutty. "What the hell? You're drinking designer coffee now?" He wiped his mouth with the back of his hand. She stuck her tongue out at him and pulled the cup back. "You got a minute?" She nodded. "The Reeds will be going together to see Steven's dad. And I was thinking one of us should go with them."

Sarah minimized the screen and focused on Joe. "Who else is going?"

"Buchanan will be sending two teams. Said we could send someone too. I think it is a good idea, but don't want to look…" he hesitated.

"Clingy? Too attached? Third wheel?"

"Exactly. So…"

"You want me to go." She looked around the room, spread her arms. "And leave all this?"

"Yes, I would like to keep a close eye on them but think it would be better if someone with less of a history went with them." Joe lowered his voice. "Price has asked me several times if our past relationship was a problem."

"She asked me too. I said it was cool, no issue. But I see your point. Sure, I can go. Any idea how long?"

Joe shook his head. "They are planning on at least a couple of days. You'd be in plain clothes, no jurisdiction. Another set of eyes and someone Trevor knows. I'll figure out the overtime." He raised his eyebrows. "You okay with that?"

"No problem. A couple of days dogging the family, hanging out at a hospital. Sounds relaxing." She stood and stretched. "When will we leave?"

"Not sure, couple of hours. Buchanan is putting together his people, and we need to tell the family." He stood too. "You want to go home and pack a bag? Feed the cats?"

"Asshole, I don't have any cats. Single, but not lonely." She looked at the front desk. Standing there was a young woman, bearing a striking resemblance to the picture they had just seen on the internet. "Your roving reporter?"

They moved toward the greeter's desk to hear her announce her name. "I'm Karen Copeland, looking for Officer Dixon, or Marchand?"

The greeter turned as Joe called over, "Hi, have a seat for a minute, I will be right back to get you." He went back to his office to let Agent Buchanan know she was here.

Sarah followed behind whispering, "She's the reporter? Looks so much younger than she sounded on the phone. Her picture did her no justice."

"Switching teams on me?" Joe said over his shoulder.

Sarah retaliated with a kick to the back of his knee which caused his leg to buckle, and he nearly fell into the room.

****

Thomas Paine hunched over the computer desk, scanning the photo stream from traffic cameras at the Dover Toll Plaza in New Hampshire. Traffic was moderate being in between seasons. The nearby mall attracted people at all times, and the area was forever expanding with supersized stores like Wal-Mart, Home Depot, and Kohls. Thomas' eyes were nearly rolling back into his head when he caught the last three letters of the suspect's plate...D89. Hitting rewind and then pause, he stopped to check it again. It was the car. There was no way to see who was driving, but Matt Stone's plate definitely passed through the toll at 4:16 the day before yesterday. He took a screen shot of the license plate, then zoomed out to a better picture of the car. Grey Saturn four door. No markings on the rear, a quick cross check gave Thomas the make and model. 2003 SL. Another screen shot was sent to the color printer across the room. Paine dialed Joe but got his voice mail. He stood up to tell the person in charge at the State Barracks. Avery Price was nowhere to be found, so he told another officer checking tapes who promised to pass it along.

****

Buchanan looked up as the pair noisily entered the office. One he had quickly made his own by pushing Joe's papers aside and placing his laptop and files in their place. Joe scowled at the sight. "That reporter is here."

"Okay, we'll get to her in a minute. I just got off the phone with Price. She will be tied up for a few hours. I have the escort team ready to go for 14:00. Need you to inform the family. I will go over after the interview with the reporter."

"Um, I'd like to be in on that," Joe inserted.

"Of course. Who else is familiar with the family?"

"Sarah, Officer Dixon." Joe hitched his thumb at her. "Been in on this from day one. Has a good rapport with them. I would like her to go with them to New Hampshire. I think it will make the family feel more comfortable and will keep us up to date."

Sarah straightened up. "I can go. Anything they need to know other than the time?"

The man twirled his pen for a minute. "Sounds reasonable. You go talk to the family, let them know we will be there soon. They should pack for a few nights. Let's talk to this reporter." Buchanan stood, dismissing Sarah.

"We have a conference room down the hall. Probably more comfortable in there." Joe led the way, asking Sarah to bring Copeland back to them.

****

"Thank you for meeting with me." Karen stuck out her hand with a mixture of excitement, curiosity, and caution. This was by far the biggest story she had ever been involved with. She eyed the two men standing against the counter.

The local cop, Joe Marchand, leaned in to shake her hand. He was the one in the uniform with a five o'clock shadow starting on his chin, a nice build and that boy next door face that mothers ate up. Then there was the man in the thousand-dollar suit. Clean, manicured, GQ model looks. Choices, choices. On another day she might attempt some subtle flirting. Today she was all business.

"What do you know?" Karen took out her iPad and got ready to take notes. She caught Joe looking at her curiously as he pulled out a tattered notebook from his back pocket.

"Miss Copeland, this is Agent Buchanan from the Boston FBI office. I thought it would be helpful for you to share what you have found out regarding Matthew Stone." Officer Marchand relinquished the stage to the agent, who was extending his hand.

"Pleased to meet you." His hand was as manicured as his face, but it felt warm and strong. Still, she preferred some callus, something that spoke to hard work. She returned a firm shake and cleared her throat.

"Well, you probably know most of what I know. I did talk to one of his old friends, actually a friend of a friend." Stop sounding flaky, she chastised herself. "No one's talked to him for a few months. Just a few texts. Last info was he had packed up his car and was heading to New England to get some time and distance."

Buchanan straightened. "Wait, he has a phone?"

Karen was excited, she had something the Feds didn't. "Yes, a friend bought it for him so the reporters couldn't track him down. They said it was nightmare, he couldn't go anywhere."

"Reporters can be like that." Buchanan looked directly at her. "But that would explain why we haven't been able to track him with one."

"You have that number?" Officer Marchand had his pencil at the ready.

She shook her head. "No, working on it though." Looking at her notes, she got back to her information. "North Carolina had nothing left for him. He told his friends he would get in touch when he found a place to settle. He was plagued by anxiety, depression, and felt deeply responsible for what happened to his wife and son. He stopped working and is living off of savings, disability, and insurance." Karen finished, surprised that she was out of breath. She was nervous, afraid to give out incorrect information, and didn't want to be told to stay away from the case. The story was taking on a life of its own, and she wanted to help. She sat on the edge of her chair and watched the men, waiting for a response.

They stood there with curious looks on their faces. She just had thrown stuff into her car and driven north. Her clothes were rumpled, and her deep brown hair tossed back in a messy bun. The makeup she had hastily applied this morning was smudged. She must be a sight. Clearing her throat, she took the plunge. "What can you tell me?" she repeated.

Joe looked to Leonard. "Normally we don't work directly with journalists, but given the fact that you are sharing information, and might have more leads..." He stopped there raising an eyebrow. She had nothing to add, so waited him out. "How did you track him here?"

"His friend said that he has received some postcards from him. One in D.C. and another in Mystic, Connecticut. I took a chance and figured he was following 95 up the coast. That friend mentioned he loved to fish and had always wanted to go deep sea fishing. That and the postcards led me north. Then I picked up the story on the internet, and that brought me the rest of the way." She sat down and eyed the plate of donuts on the table.

Joe saw her. "You're welcome to them, but I have no idea how long they have been there." He picked one up and tapped the table with it. A hollow *thunk* answered back.

"Oh, no thanks," she laughed. "I'm not that hungry."

"Did the postcards mention Stone's son, or the boy?" Leonard asked bringing the conversation back to the task at hand.

"Not that I was told. More like, weather's nice. I'm doing okay." Karen made a show of checking her notes, but she had memorized them. "I can call back and ask." She was excited to offer the help.

"Umm, let me think about that. It might be better if one of us contacted them." Leonard looked to Joe while tugging at the crease in his pant leg. It was sharp enough to slice a tomato.

Karen hid a smile as Joe smoothed his wrinkled uniform that probably hadn't been changed for a day or so. Still, rumpled and scruffy, Joe was sexy. She didn't want a man who was higher maintenance than herself. And that wasn't asking for much. Type A Leonard quickly took a back seat in her ever-single mind. Who said she couldn't multitask?

"Thank you for the information. Do we have a number to contact you if we have further questions?" the agent asked, as if saying, "Don't call us, we'll call you."

"Um, yes, I can give it to you again. I would like to keep following the story." She held her head high, hoping to look professional and not like an eager puppy.

"We will contact you if anything else comes up. But we don't want you in harm's way." Buchanan was now pulling rank, Karen noted, keeping her in her place.

Deflated, she wanted to protest, but held back. Standing, she left a business card with her cell number on the table. "I'll walk you out," Joe said steering her out the door.

Once out of the agent's earshot, he pulled up short. "Sorry about the bum's rush. He's just doing his job.

Are you staying in town?" Was he keeping tabs on her, or being nice?

"Not sure. Is there anywhere to stay?" She had tunnel vision as she followed Siri's directions to the station. Karen was so excited, she hadn't even asked to go to the bathroom, which was desperately needed now. She looked down the hall. "That the ladies' room?"

"Yes, pull the door hard to shut it, the latch is temperamental. I'll write down some places to stay. Nothing fancy, but they're safe."

Karen nodded; they couldn't be worse than what she stayed in last night. She didn't want this to end here. She had to play her cards right.

Chapter 30

Sarah pulled up to the Reeds', not surprised at all to see Jesse open the door and meet her on the walkway. She had been waiting for news.

"Mrs. Reed. How is everyone holding up?"

"Jesse, please. Okay, I guess. Steven's ready to climb out of his skin. Trevor is confused, scared. I'm waiting for this crazy ride to stop. I want to get off." She stopped halfway up the stairs. "Sorry to complain. Are we going to be able to get to New Hampshire?"

"That's why I'm here. We will all go in a couple hours. Your family, me, and some agents. A team from the New Hampshire office will check out the hospital and any other place we need to go while there." Sarah looked at Jesse who had stopped to lean against the door frame. "You okay?"

"This is insane. Agents, following us around, escorts? I appreciate it, I really do, it's just that..."

"It shouldn't have to be this way?" Sarah put a gentle hand on Jesse's arm. "You're right, it shouldn't. But we are going to do everything we can to keep Trevor safe."

They were interrupted by Steven and Trevor. "Any news?" Steven asked. The subtle lines in his face, which just yesterday added character, today added years to the man. He looked exhausted, scared, and angry.

"We are all going." Jesse answered. "Us, Officer Dixon, and some agents."

"When?"

"Two hours, give or take. Agent Buchanan and Detective Price are setting everything up. Can you be ready?" Sarah asked.

"Of course. Just need to throw a few things in a bag." Steven turned to go back inside but stopped. "Trevor, you head up and pick out a few stuffed animals. No more than three." He watched Trevor run up the stairs. "Is this really safe? I want to see my father, but don't want to put Trevor or Jesse at risk. Are you sure it's safe?" he repeated.

Sarah explained the protocol again, adding a few more details like no unnecessary stops, they would travel in the government car, and the family needed to keep the agents abreast of any changes or requests.

"Jesus, I can't believe this is happening." Steven drew in a deep breath and tried a brave face. "Thank you. I really mean it. I'm not at my best right now, sorry." Looking over Sarah's head, somewhere into the distance, Steven seemed to be steeling himself for the trip north, whatever it might bring. "We'll be ready." Turning quickly, he went back inside leaving Jesse and the policewoman alone. He returned in a second, "We should probably pack a suit, a dress, you know, if…"

As Jesse welled up and nodded, Sarah assured her that everything possible was being done to help the family. Jesse smiled and thanked the woman again.

Sarah checked in with the officers that were there and left to get herself packed. Not much to do. Just grab a few clothes and ask a neighbor to take in the mail. No pets, not even a plant. Her apartment was simple, clean.

No one to say goodbye to, nothing to complicate her life. A complication might be nice, she thought.

Chapter 31

Matt woke in a sweat in the small cabin. He had dreamt again of the day Carol died. This time though, he saved her, but lost Tommy. He had been through that day a million times. Wondering what he could have done differently. How could he have kept it from happening? Fear, regret, and a bottomless loneliness overcame him and, without warning, the greasy meal rushed back up his throat. Matt lurched into the bathroom and emptied his stomach. When that was over the unmistakable signs of a migraine crept into the edges of his vision. He crawled to his bag where he shook out two more pills. They were getting low and would need a refill. That was a detail he hadn't planned for when he fled. Swallowing the tablets, he pulled himself back onto the bed and prayed for a dreamless sleep.

****

Just across the parking lot, Red stirred from his own nap. He heard cries, like a wounded animal coming from nearby. Scared at first, he waited for his heart to calm down. Straining to hear where it was coming from, he rose quietly and made his way to the back door of his small room. Pushing it open just a crack allowed him to hear more clearly. Through muffled cries he distinctly heard the name Tommy repeated several times. He walked as quickly as he felt was safe across the small lot to the cabin Greg was in. The cries had stopped, and he heard the man throwing up. Red waited by the door until it stopped. A few minutes passed, and Red heard the springs of the old bed creak and he guessed his tenant was lying back down. Satisfied the man was okay, Red crept back down the stairs and returned to his place. He hoped the guy would be all right.

****

A few hours later, Matt woke with what felt like a hangover. He needed caffeine and something light for his stomach. When he walked to his car, he was surprised to see the sun setting over the lake. He must have slept most of the day away. Remembering his dream, Matt was torn between wishing he could forget everything in the past and wanting to keep Carol and Tommy alive, if even it was only in his memories. If only he could control which memories. His mind wandered again, this time seeing Tommy getting off the bus after school. But that couldn't be right, Tommy died before he went to school. Matt shook his head realizing that he was again confusing the boy, the new boy with Tommy. He had to stop that. But for a few minutes on the days he caught a glimpse of the boy, Matt had allowed himself to dream. That dream had gone too far, and now he was on the run. He had to stay out of sight, and what better place than in a cabin in the woods with a blind proprietor? Now he just had to send the police in another direction.

Matt found the tools he needed and loosened the screws on his license plates. He didn't take them completely off but left them loose enough he could easily switch them when he found the right replacements. With that done, he started the car and went in search of a busy parking lot and a few groceries.

****

Red heard the car come to life in the lot. Knowing it was Greg, he hoped the man was okay. Should he talk to him? Red knew what it was like to lose the love of his life, but not a kid. Would talking help? Or would the man resent him for prying? While Greg had only been there two days, Red enjoyed the company. He would wait and see if the man stuck around some. It was past time for supper, but the big lunch still sat heavy in his stomach. That, and he kept burping it up. The second time around was far less satisfying. "Two meals for the price of one," he said to the empty room, noting he was talking to himself a lot lately. Maybe Greg would want to take him fishing tomorrow, he wondered. That would be a great change in his solitary routine. This early in the season, he doubted there would be customers to sign in. That was at least a month away.

Chapter 32

The caravan left the Reed house like a small parade, minus the band, baton twirlers, and cheering audience. It created a stir in the small town. Seldom did government cars roll in and out of Middletown. Nothing gets news flowing like the mothers at an elementary school. By now everyone had heard of the attempted abduction and were keeping their children close by. Afterschool sports were no longer drop offs. Parents stayed and watched, eyeing anyone who looked the least bit unfamiliar. Trevor's friends and teachers had been questioned, asked if they had seen the man before. A few said maybe but couldn't be sure. Parents worried that their children were at risk too. Was it specifically Trevor Reed or would any child have done? The principal, school counselors, and the superintendent fielded many calls to help reassure the families that all were safe. At this point the rumors flying varied from a lone crazy man to an entire ring of pedophiles infiltrating their town. Children were inside long before the sunset with doors and windows locked, and double checked.

The Reeds looked out the tinted windows of the SUV and watched their small town go by. Steven cracking his knuckles, Jesse working on a nail, and Trevor kneeling, pressing his face against the darkened glass. He asked if he could roll the window down and wave, like the old guys in the Veteran's Day Parade. One look at his parents and the grim-faced agent in the front seat had him sitting down. When his mom whispered that he needed to buckle up he did so without comment. More confused than ever, Trevor turned on the iPad his dad offered and played a game.

The agent driving had confided in his partner that this was most likely a needless escort. The likelihood of the Reeds running into Matthew Stone was minimal. But he took his job seriously and would protect the boy and his family like he protected his own. Scanning his mirrors constantly, Agent Carl Morris increased his speed as they merged onto the highway. Taking Route 95 north, it was almost a straight shot to Lake Winnipesauke. The group would be in Wolfeboro in two and half hours, tops. They planned to drive straight through. His partner, Agent Maxine Black, almost ten years his junior and the first female partner he had, sat in the passenger seat reading the notes on the case. She was solid, didn't complain, and held her own in situations so far. Carl decided to sit back and take the cushy gig in stride.

The group travelled in relative silence. Jesse even allowed herself a cat nap. Steven was on his laptop discussing work matters with Jack. His heart was only half in it, his mind wandering like a ping pong ball in a tornado. Trevor bored of his game and watched the big trucks go by.

****

Karen found the small motel that Joe recommended. From the parking lot of the Motel 6, she could see a different hotel sitting atop a hill, overlooking a large green golf course. It also boasted an indoor water park. It was way out of her budget, so she trudged up to the office that held a blinking vacancy sign in a greasy window. Pulling the door open, she was greeted by a burst of coconut fragrance. Too much of the faux tropical scent, she wondered what it was trying to conceal. A pleasant young woman looked up from her dog-eared book with a couple embracing on the cover. When the girl looked up, Karen asked for a room.

"Staying long?" The clerk was friendly with a wide smile that reached her eyes. Karen smiled back.

"Not sure to be honest. Can I rent by the day?" Karen glanced at the chart with the rates. Forty-nine dollars a night, two hundred for the week. Complete with internet, free HBO, and list of local restaurants that delivered.

"Sure thing. If you wanted by the hour, I'd have to send you down the road." Delivered with a straight face and a wink, it caught Karen by surprise. The clerk was barely out of high school. The look of shock on Karen's face caused the girl to blush. "I, I didn't mean to offend you," she stammered.

"Oh, no. It's no problem. Funny actually, I just wasn't expecting it." Karen laughed to put the girl at ease. She signed her name and accepted the key, attached to a scarred plastic lobster. Faded letters on the crustacean said, "Lobstah."

"You recommend any place to eat? Not too expensive."

The girl drummed her chipped nails on the plexiglass that was covering placemats from a few local places. "This place has awesome sandwiches and the best pie ever!" She was pointing to the Rowley Diner.

"It's a fifteen-minute drive up Route One but totally worth it."

Hating to eat alone, she nodded, but took a stack of delivery menus as well. "Room 114?" The girl nodded. "Thank you. Enjoy your book." Karen went back to the lot to retrieve her bag. She hesitated before opening the door to her room but was relieved to see that it was clean and didn't reek of canned coconuts. Nothing fancy, like the officer promised. She could handle that. Karen sat on the bed and plugged in her laptop because it needed some juice. "Now what?" she said to the walls.

****

Matt pulled into the parking lot about forty-five minutes away in front of a Hannaford's and Target. He drove around checking the cars, looking for one similar to his. He found another Saturn, a few years newer, on the same green-grey spectrum, with Connecticut plates tucked between two large trucks. It was nearing dusk, and the car was close the back of the lot. Matt felt he could quickly switch plates, so he backed his car into a space a row away. Ducking down, he worked quickly. Soon the switch was made, and Matt jumped back into his car. He just broke another law. Sweat trickled down his neck and Matt was feeling sick again. Before he could change the tags back, he drove away. Hopefully this would give him the added layer of protection he needed. He headed toward the lake, surprised to be looking forward to chatting with Red again. Stopping briefly at a Rite Aid, he picked up the soda and snacks he craved. While there, he grabbed a bottle of Extra Strength Excedrin, thinking it might work for his headaches once his prescription ran out. Armed with new supplies, Matt headed back to the cabin. The sun had set leaving layers of pink and purple hanging just above the mountains in the distance. It was a beautiful sight. Maybe if the weather was nice tomorrow, he would try to go fishing. Red was sure to have a few supplies he could borrow. Pushing the theft of the license plates to the back of his mind, Matt allowed himself to enjoy the cool evening breeze through the open window.

Chapter 33

Joe didn't like letting Jesse and her family leave town, especially in the same direction they believed Matthew Stone went. Relinquishing control made him extremely uneasy. But at least he got his office back. Moving his things to their appropriate places helped lower his blood pressure a few points. Agent Buchanan had left his card, the names and numbers of the agents on the road trip, and instructions to call if anything new came up. Joe asked for the same in return and hoped the man would be forthcoming with information. At least Sarah was with them. She would let him know what was happening on that end. He was surprised to see that the day was nearly over. Tunnel vision for this case made him completely unaware of anything else that had happened that day. He went to check in with the other officers.

It had been a relatively calm shift. Just a few calls concerning the government caravan. Those inquiries were met a blank statement of, "Just some government folks passing through." Not everyone bought it, but surprisingly, there was no push back. Joe read over some reports from the day, a few traffic stops, a false alarm at the local pharmacy, and a deer found dead in the road. Every spring there were several deer strikes as new fawns tried to follow their mothers across roads. It saddened Joe to see new life end so tragically. All the reports looked to be in order and Joe signed off on them. As he was ready to leave for the day, he felt his phone vibrate in his pocket. He didn't recognize the number.

"Joe Marchand." He leaned on the edge of his desk.

"Officer Marchand? It's Karen Copeland. I hope it's okay that I am calling you. Your cell number was on the back of your card." Her voice was a mixture of hope and caution.

"Uh, sure, it's no problem. What can I do for you, ma'am?" Joe wondered what the reporter was looking for.

"First, please don't call me ma'am. It makes me feel like an old maid." She rushed on, "I was thinking maybe we could talk more about Matthew Stone. I was hoping to find out why he was after that little boy."

"I don't know what else I can tell you. I think you know almost as much as I do at this point."

"Where did the family go? They left today with escorts, my guess the FBI?"

This surprised him. "Where did you hear that?"

"The convenience store, the gas station, the girl checking me in at the hotel. It's all everyone is talking about. Small town, big mouths?" She sounded satisfied with herself.

Joe rolled his head from side to side, trying to release some of the tension that had built up during the past few days. "No comment?"

"I heard there was a good diner up the road."

He paused for a minute. He was hungry, she was cute and might have more to tell. Against his better judgement he found himself agreeing to meet for dinner. "I just need to shower and change. Meet you there in an hour?" Joe was smiling despite the niggling in the back of his mind that this might be a very bad idea indeed.

****

Karen couldn't believe that she actually just asked the cop out. She was barely paying attention to what he was saying. "Um, sounds good, thanks." A quick look in the mirror told her that she looked like hell. Rummaging through her bag she pulled out the least wrinkled pants and shirt, hung them on hangers and left them in the bathroom while she took a hot shower. Maybe the steam would pull out some of the worst creases.

****

Joe looked at his phone after she hung up and muttered out loud, "What the hell am I doing?"

"If you don't know we're all screwed, boss," Janette, the greeter, threw him a knowing glance. "Have a good night. You deserve some fun." Janette took the night shift and doubled as the dispatcher once the day shift went home. She was a widow, keeper of everybody's secrets, and mothered the whole crew. She even once tried to do the mother 'lick her finger clean the smudge off of his face thing' with him. Clear boundaries were set, and she was now limited to unsolicited advice, reminders of appointments, and delicious dinners packed and frozen once every two months. Living alone wore on her too, and once in a while she would go into a cooking frenzy. All the single officers, male and female, would get care packages. At Christmas time and Mother's Day, everyone remembered Janette. She would bring home some of the chocolates and flowers but leave the rest on her desk. With an open box of candy on her desk, she was guaranteed a few visitors throughout the evening. It was a win-win.

Joe smiled at her and mouthed 'thank you' as his phone began to vibrate again. "Joe Marchand."

"Marchand, it's Price. Did you get the info on the Dover tolls?"

"Um, no, nothing new since we saw his plate at the Hampton tolls. What's up?"

"Your guy, Paine? Saw the plate go through the tolls at four twenty the day before yesterday. Said he called you and left a message. I've been in meetings all day, so just got it now. That's the exact road the Reeds are on."

Joe pulled his phone away and looked at the screen. In the corner was an indicator that he had a message. He didn't know how he missed it. It must have been Paine. "No, didn't get it," he admitted. "Must have come in when I was with Buchanan. Stone's probably long gone. Our people would have passed through there at least an hour ago. Any word from them?"

"They report all clear." Avery sounded disconcerted. "We need to check the tolls farther up and notify the local and state police what we found."

"I can do that."

"No, it will be faster and hold more clout if it comes from me. No offense."

"None taken." Joe was seriously tired and mad at himself for missing the call. He wanted to talk to Sarah and was itching to get off the call with Avery. "Let me know if anything else comes up? I will call Paine and have him turn his eagle eye to the Rochester Toll Plaza."

"Sounds good. Keep in touch." Price signed off. Joe hit call back for Thomas Paine and was not surprised when the young officer picked up right away.

"Joe? Did you get my message?"

"Sorry, Paine, I did, but not until just now. Was crushed today. But great job. Did you by chance check the next toll?"

"I have been. One problem though, the right-hand toll camera is on the fritz. Nothing but grainy shadows. There was no sign of him in the other ones. It's EZ pass, and there's no indication Stone has one. Soon there will be no choice." Paine was referencing the changeover to all tolls being tracked through the EZ pass.

"Okay. Send that info to Detective Price. She will be talking to the New Hampshire police and updating the crew that went up. Good job, keep it up." Joe's head was spinning, and he was starving. The sandwich he bought for lunch lay half eaten in the conference room. Dinner at the diner was sounding even more appealing by the minute.

****

The whole family sat quietly during most of the ride. Just under two hours in, Trevor needed to go to the bathroom. Agent Morris looked at Steven through the rearview mirror. "Any way the little guy can wait?"

Steven looked at Trevor. Trevor replied, "I'll try," in a voice so small even the hardened agent cracked a smile.

"I'll look for a place to pull in. Have to alert the others though." He spoke into his headset to the car

197

behind. Two, two-man teams were a tad excessive, but they got paid either way. Plus, it doubled as a training measure for the newer pair. Agent Black looked for Sarah's number so she could let her know as well.

By the time the two SUVs and Sarah's Pilot pulled into the gas station/minimart, Trevor was all but literally 'holding it'. Then the two agents had to check the premises as discreetly as two men in suits could check out a place like that. The teenager behind the counter was on high alert. This didn't happen every day. He craned his neck to see who the VIPs in the other SUV were. The door opened and a man, woman, and child hopped out, looked around and were escorted inside. They went right to the back of the store. "Who the hell is that?" He wondered aloud while the man across the counter just shook his head.

"Maybe they are related to Romney, he running again?" The man was referring to the former Massachusetts governor who had run for president and was talking about running again. The kid behind the counter had no feelings for the guy either way but didn't approve of the constant presence of Secret Service when he did. Romney decides to get a pizza, and the whole town goes into a flurry. The customer tossed a ten-dollar bill on the counter for his roast beef sub, chips, and soda and walked out. The clerk called after him, softly, for his change but slid the dollar fifty into the front pocket of his jeans. The man in the suit standing near the bathroom door eyeballed him, and the teenager turned his back and pretended to organize the cigarettes.

The bathroom door opened, and the little boy and his dad walked out. "Wow, I was going to explode!" the child said.

Dad just ruffled his hair and said, "Glad you didn't. That would be gross."

"Can I have some candy?" The kid pointed to the rack that ran the length of one wall and was taller than him. At the far end, a woman who had come in with them was grabbing a Snickers bar. "She gets to."

She passed a guilty look to the dad and mouthed, "I'm sorry."

"No problem, just one. For each of us." The kid's dad smiled but looked exhausted. The boy selected mini M&Ms, the man placed a Kit Kat on the counter and, when another woman came out of the women's room, she added Skittles to the pile. "Agents?" the man asked the suits.

They shook their head. "We really should get back on the road." The shorter one nodded toward the parking lot. "We have a half hour more."

Chapter 34

Karen waited outside the shiny diner that looked straight out of the 1960s, an actual train car, transformed into a restaurant. Her father had always said that if you wanted a solid meal, to go to a diner. No fancy names, nothing pretentious, just good old-fashioned home cooking. She looked in her rearview mirror and checked her hair and make-up. She blushed. He was meeting her as a courtesy, nothing else. But damn, he was hot. The crunch of tires pulling off of the road alerted her to Joe's arrival. Just what she expected. He was wearing jeans and a button-down shirt. Cleaned up nice.

"Hi, found it all right?" Joe extended his hand and shook Karen's. Did he hold it for a moment longer than necessary? Don't be an ass. This is business, she reminded herself. She hoped her preppy chic ankle length pants with a loose top was appropriate for this date, meeting, whatever it was. He was saying something. "I'm sorry, I missed that."

"Oh, sorry, I just realized something. I don't know if anyone followed up on Stone's cell phone." He struck his forehead with his palm. "I have to call Agent Buchanan." Joe pulled out his phone and dialed. When the other man didn't answer he left a message. Hanging up, he held the door for Karen. They walked in and were greeted by an older woman sitting at a cash register.

"Sit anywhere you want. Good to see you, Sheriff." The old lady winked at Joe.

"Good to see you too, Dot." He led Karen to a corner booth and slid into the far seat so he could see the door and the entire diner. Old habits.

"Sheriff?" Karen asked as she sat down, setting her iPad on the seat next to her. Business could wait. The linoleum table had worn spots on each side. They bore witness to the years of friends sitting there, coffee cups in hand, elbows on the table, sharing stories, laughing. The seats had red duct tape to hide the wear and tear. Not a fancy place, but a welcoming one.

"Yeah, no matter how many times I tell her I'm not the sheriff, she insists on calling me that, even when I'm not in uniform. Been here for as long as I can remember. Her husband used to own the place, sold it to his brother just before he died. Dot stays on as a cashier and local gossip. Word will be out that 'The Sheriff' was wining and dining a beautiful young lady."

Karen blushed at the compliment and hid behind the menu which offered everything from omelets to prime rib. Daily specials were tucked into the sleeve, handwritten in shaky old school cursive. Dot no doubt. "What's good?"

"Everything. Best fries, awesome beef stew, sandwiches, everything. Can't go wrong. Well, maybe the liver and onions." Joe pointed to the daily special and wrinkled his nose.

A very cute nose. "I'll steer clear of the liver."

"You two all set to order?" Karen was startled by the waitress who appeared at her elbow. Thin, maybe forty, a smoker for sure, the voice had a gravelly edge to it. The smile was thin as she listened to their order. "Cheeseburger, medium rare, french fries, and Diet Coke, large."

Joe nodded, "I'll have an omelet, with mushrooms, cheese, and bacon. Wheat toast with butter, hash browns, and large milk." The waitress turned and returned to the kitchen where she belted out their order, verbatim.

"Good memory," Karen noted. "We'll actually get what we ordered?"

"Never fails. The owners don't allow them to write it down. The cooks have to remember it all too. No computers. Even the cash register is old fashioned. I couldn't do it." Karen was looking at the juke box attached to the wall of their booth. Joe tapped on the glass window. "Doesn't work, hasn't in like, forever."

"Why do they keep them?" She smiled as she read the names of the songs, "Billy Jean by Michael Jackson, Rumors by Earth Wind and Fire." There were several titles from Madonna and a few 'oldies' dating back to her grandfather's time.

"They don't like change I guess." Joe flipped the pages of the defunct juke and pointed to "Don't Stop Believing" by Journey. "My graduation song." He laughed, and he briefly remembered himself and Jesse holding hands as they walked into the field house as Pomp and Circumstance was butchered by the band. He shook his head to bring himself back to the present, sitting across the table from a very pretty woman. Joe focused on what she was saying.

"Our class was a wreck. There was a more than one threat to cancel graduation and just mail the diplomas.

Word got to the administration that several boys were going to streak across the stage as the class valedictorian gave her speech. In the end, the ceremony went fine, and we all just went to parties at our friends." Karen looked nostalgic as well.

The waitress returned with their drinks, napkins, and silverware. She plunked down ketchup and disappeared. "Just like a hummingbird," Joe commented with a smile.

They made small talk for a few minutes before Karen dared to approach the main topic. "So, what do you make of this whole thing? Do you really think he would hurt the little boy?"

"I have no idea. He's only gotten close to him once, that we know of. Hopefully Stone is found before we get proven wrong." Joe was folding his napkin in fours, unfolding it and folding it again.

"Is there anything you can tell me that you might have forgotten to say before?" She cocked her head.

"There really is nothing more, not that I could really share it with you if there were." Joe delivered the party line. Karen knew that historically, police and reporters butted heads. He probably didn't want to give the impression he would be forthcoming with private information.

"I know, but I am still hoping to do a story on him. I mean, it is a pretty wild story. First his wife, then his son. You can't help but feel something for him." Their meals arrived and were exactly as ordered. Karen was duly impressed. "Excuse me, could I have a side of mayo?"

The waitress was off and returned a second later with a small bowl of mayo. Karen took a hot French fry and dipped it in. She closed her eyes and almost groaned.

Joe gagged. "Don't knock it until you try it." She dipped another fry and passed it to him. He shook his head. "Chicken? It won't kill you."

"My arteries are hardening just watching you eat it." He took the fry and took a small bite. "Not bad, but I'll stick to ketchup." He grabbed the bottle and gave it a whack on the bottom. A huge blob landed on his hash browns. "Now this is gourmet." He stirred the mess and took an enormous bite.

"And cholesterol free?" She kidded him as she took a bite of her hamburger. The juice trickled down her fingers, and she unabashedly licked it off. "Back to the story, or what I hope will be a story."

"Karen…can I call you that?" She nodded with another mouthful of mayo covered fries. "I can't say anything that would put the boy and his family in danger."

"I wouldn't ask you to do that. I was looking for more information on Matt Stone. Stuff you might have that I can't get. Anything that happened down south, I think I have. It's just the stuff up here. Can you tell me anything?"

Joe thought for a moment. "Let me sleep on it." After a few bites he changed subjects. "So what's your story?"

"What do you mean?"

"You are from North Carolina and are a writer. What else?" Joe was steering the conversation away from the case. Was he playing by the books, or trying to get to know her better?

"Oh, not much. Lived there all my life, have a twin brother. Been working as a writer for the past few years." She left out the part where she was unceremoniously laid off. "Want that big story to get my name out there, stop writing fluff n' stuff." Karen was almost done with her burger, stopped and looked him in the eyes. "You know, so I can feel like I've done something important. You must feel like you do something good every day."

"Clever, the reporter, turning the conversation away from herself, onto the other person." Joe raised an eyebrow. "I like the job, usually pretty tame. It feels good to help people. And the lights and sirens are fun." He laughed.

"They must be, and they help you get to the front of the drive thru line at Honey Dew," she shot back playfully.

"Dunkin Donuts," he corrected her, "perks of the job. Ha, get it, coffee, perks?" Joe laughed again at his own joke. She used her fingers to give him the rim shot.

"You here all week?"

"Tip the waitresses." Joe leaned back. "You have heard my act before."

"Coffee? Dessert?" The waitress had reappeared and pointed at the pie case. "Got chocolate cream, banana cream, apple, blueberry, peach pie. Brownies, chocolate roll, turnovers, raspberry and apple and lemon squares." All said in one breath while looking bored.

"You have to try the chocolate cream." Joe didn't usually go for sweets, but this was an exception.

"You're the second person to tell me that."

"You guys splitting it?" The waitress inspected her nails.

They both immediately said, "No!" and raised two fingers. The waitress turned away, and an awkward silence was left.

"It's not that I don't like to share, but once you taste this pie, you will understand," Joe offered.

"Don't worry, I've never been known to leave much on a plate." Karen blushed again.

"You seem to have a good appetite." His turn, his cheeks flushed. "I mean, you look great, I mean, like you might be a workout freak. Not in a bad way, I mean…"

"Just eat the pie," the waitress said as she dropped the two plates on the table. She actually winked at Karen and was off again.

Karen looked at the pie, two inches of whipped cream topped with chocolate sprinkles sat on a thick layer of dark chocolate filling. She took the first bite and closed her eyes. "Omigod," she opened them, "that is amazing." Joe seemed to be watching for her reaction before he dug into his.

"Good huh?" He took a bite and smiled. "Worth every mile on the treadmill."

Treadmill? Karen wondered. Maybe she should try that one day. They ate in silence until the last flake of crust and final sprinkle were gone. Holding herself back from licking the plate, she leaned back into the cracked vinyl seat and patted her stomach. "That was the best pie I have ever had."

The waitress cleared their plates and asked if they wanted anything else. "No, thanks, I would literally explode," Karen said. "Just the check?"

The waitress walked to an old fashion cash register where she rung up their meal. As she breezed by the next time a small receipt fluttered to the table. Both Joe and Karen reached for it and when their hands met, they pulled back. With a nervous laugh she reached for her bag and pulled out her wallet. They each took out a twenty. "Before we go, do you have any suggestions for me in terms of the story? I have the background on him, you know, I know basically what the papers have already reported. But I really don't know what direction to go in given the new twist. Don't want to be one of 'those' reporters, flying after ambulances, dogging the court clerks."

"What if you sit on it for a day or so, until the Reeds get back and we know they are safe?" So, he wanted her to stick around, Karen thought and then she caught his slip. "Where did they go?" Karen asked casually memorizing the family name.

"Uh, family emergency," he spit out. Joe clenched his hands, he must have realized his slip. "So, you ever been to Massachusetts before?

"No, not much of a traveler, usually." Karen realized he was trying to change the subject. "This trip was very much an impulse decision. Needed to follow the story, you know." Steering the conversation back to where she wanted it to go, she added, "When do you expect the family to come back?"

Joe was beaten and she knew it. She was tenacious, hopefully he liked that. "No idea, really. But maybe things will be clearer concerning Stone by the time they get back. I would be patient if I was you."

"That sounds like the right thing to do," she said regretfully. Karen was trying to get away from tabloid reporting. And on another note, she was seriously thinking of pitching a tent in the parking lot of this diner. Save the drive, walk to breakfast, lunch, and dinner with naps in between.

They stood and walked to the lady sitting at the register by the door, another relic from when the place opened. "Enjoying your evening, Sheriff?" Dot said with a smile.

"Yes, ma'am. Very good. Like always." He took the change and placed it on the table for the tip.

They walked to their cars, and each stood there with a hand on their door handle. Karen cleared her throat. "Well, thank you. I was thinking I was going to be eating pizza in my hotel room."

"My pleasure. Why don't you check in at the station tomorrow? Maybe there will be news by then." Joe raised his eyebrows and smiled.

"That would be great. Thanks again." Karen hopped into her car with a grin that actually hurt her face. Was it the possible information or because the hot cop asked her to drop by? Pulling out of the lot she headed back to the hotel.

Joe was following at a distance. He had slipped up. But the whole town knew they left, so had he really? He needed to be more careful, but the reporter was easy to be around, and seriously cute. Once he saw her open the door to her room, he turned around and went home.

Chapter 35

It was getting late when the caravan arrived at the hospital. Hawkins was a low brick building, a few miles from the center of Wolfeboro. Steven had been there a few times growing up. Once getting stitches for a cut received when water skiing and another with a friend who broke his leg skiing. The SUVs pulled up front and the team in the second car went in first. Steven could see them talking to the receptionist, who was clearly frazzled by the men. In a few minutes a man in a suit approached the desk and checked their credentials. The small nervous party from Massachusetts could see him peering through the window at the car. "Um, my family has no idea what is going on with Trevor. I didn't tell them because I didn't want to worry them, especially now." Steven had leaned forward to speak quietly with the agents.

"You didn't tell them?" Maxine asked looking at her partner. "How do we explain our presence if they don't know?"

"I was hoping to just leave that out of it until we had to tell them," Steven admitted.

"Let me go talk to the administrator. Maybe we can be discreet." Carl got out and walked in, shaking his head.

Steven slid back with a mumbled apology. "I wasn't thinking I guess."

Jesse took his hand and rubbed his shoulder. There was nothing she could do to help him, his family, or Trevor. Just reminding Steven that she was by his side was the best she could do.

After a few minutes, Carl came back, opened the back door, and motioned Steven out. "Okay. The agents are doing a quick sweep of your father's floor. The receptionist and security have been given a head's up on our presence here. They wouldn't give me any info on your father, HIPAA, you know. I think it would be best if you and Mrs. Reed went in first. Your son can stay with Officer Dixon. I was told he knows her?"

"Yes, they've met. He seems to like her. Can I see my dad?" Carl nodded and led them to the main entrance. They called for Sarah to join them and explained that Trevor would stay with her for a while. She suggested getting something to eat at the cafeteria. Trevor slowly reached up for her hand and watched his parents enter the hospital flanked by the FBI guys.

"Come on, Champ, let's see what kind of treats they have." Sarah was starving herself, and really needed to use the bathroom. That would have to wait. She couldn't leave the boy unattended and felt awkward speaking up. She looked around and saw muted colors on the walls, shiny waxed floors, and a few staff walking with purpose in the halls. Following the arrows, they found the café, which had closed for the night fifteen minutes ago. Just around the corner they found two vending machines humming away. One offered waters and juice and the other sandwiches, fruit, hummus, cheese and crackers. Both Sarah and Trevor let out a disappointed sigh. "No candy, bummer."

"Why? All machines give out candy," Trevor replied as if by saying it candy would magically replace the healthy choices.

"A president's wife wants to get rid of obesity, people being overweight, in America," Sarah offered with little zeal.

"But I'm not o-beez." He lifted up his shirt to show her his flat belly. Sarah laughed.

"Well, these are the choices. You want anything?" Waving her hand like Vanna White.

"Um, raisins, my teacher says they are nature's candy." He pointed to the red box nestled between silver spirals behind the glass.

"Nature's candy it is then." She placed a few dollars in the machine and watched the boxes drop to the well. They took the snack and settled in a waiting room nearby. There the carpet and watercolors of local scenery did little to disguise the institutionalized setting. Sarah wondered how necessary this entourage was. What was the likelihood of Matthew Stone walking in here? Trevor was sticking the raisins on his teeth pretending to be a monster. She played along, happy not to be in the hospital room with a dying man. Hospitals gave her the creeps.

****

Matt pulled into the parking lot and stopped in front of his little cabin. After carrying in his bags, he went off to look for Red to see if he wanted to go fishing tomorrow. He was not surprised to see the older man coming into the office just as he opened the door. "That you, Greg?"

"Evening, Red. How was your day?" Matt was getting used to being called Greg.

"Not too bad. Sox lost. They need a new pitcher." Red propped his elbows on the counter and waited for Matt to get to whatever it was he came in for. Maybe he was moving on. Red liked the company. "How was your day?" Not one to pry, he waited out the silence.

Matt busied himself with some of the fliers for attractions around the lake. After a few minutes, he cleared his throat. "Um, I was thinking of going fishing tomorrow. Would you have any equipment I could rent?"

"Was thinkin' 'bout that myself. It should be a good morning for it."

Matt brightened. "You wanna come along?"

"You mind gettin' up early?" Red's face was bright with a smile.

"Usually up anyway. What time are you thinking?" Matt smiled.

"How 'bout six?"

"Sounds good. Where can we get bait?"

"There's a marina just up around the bend, we can stop in there and grab some. My boat's not fancy. Might take some convincing to start. Can't take it out without a driver, ya know."

"I'm pretty good with engines." Matt started for the door. "See you in the morning then?"

"Bright 'n early." Red was pleased to get to go fishing. He hadn't gone since last fall when one of his old friends stopped by. He paid a couple local boys to maintain the boat and run it every few weeks. They also saw to minor repairs around the property, including fixing the dock when the spring thaw took a few boards. The small cove off of the main drag into Alton Bay kept the rougher waves from boat traffic from damaging the dock, but the thaw would get almost everyone on the lake at one time or another.

He turned out the office light and returned to his quarters. There was a little pep in his step as he changed into pajamas and brushed his teeth. Just before he settled into bed, he kissed his fingertips and placed them on a picture of his wife. "Night, sweetheart." With a satisfied sigh, he rolled over and fell asleep.

Chapter 36

Steven walked down the hall to room 231. The room his father had been in for two days now, in a coma. He hadn't seen him in quite a while before this. They talked once every two weeks or so and got together for holidays and birthdays. The conversations were usually short, perfunctory. They exchanged pleasantries and went through the script. How's mom? Fine. How is Jesse, Trevor, work? Fine. New project, taking up a lot of time. You and mom done anything special? No, just the regular. Okay then. Talk to you soon. Bye. Dial tone. Not warm and fuzzy, but it worked for them. His mom would check in once in a while when there was something interesting to share. Usually, it was something crazy his sister was into, or the next accomplishment from his brother. Steven stopped before they reached the door and took a big breath. Jesse and the agents held back for a moment. When he was ready, he turned and went in.

What he saw almost took his feet from under him. His father, on the hospital bed with wires and tubes poking out of him. His mother and sister were stationed on either side of the bed. They both looked worn, drained. He didn't know Jane was already there and wondered if Tanner was too. His father looked grey, withered...empty. That was the only way he could think to describe him. A shell, chest moving up and down from the tube inserted in his throat. The monitors had been turned down, but kept a steady low beep, like the metronome on their old piano. He was speechless for a moment. Jesse spoke up.

"Jane, Lillian, how are you holding up?" She leaned down to peck her mother-in-law on the cheek. Jane stood and embraced her like a sister. They held for a moment then parted, and Jane went to her brother. Their eyes met, and instantly both teared up. Steven wrapped his arms around Jane and held her for a long time. Then moved for a big embrace with his mother. Pulling up a chair next to the bed, he gingerly took his father's hand. Steven's eyes moved over his dad's face, following tubes and wires to his chest and then to his father's large hand. Soft, weak, and pale. His dad had taught him how to shake another man's hand. Assertively, firm, confident, but not crushing. "Look him directly in the eye," he would say. "Let him know you are in charge." Holding this limp, cool hand now delivered a crushing blow. Steven had grown up regarding his father with a mix of respect, love, and fear. In many ways he wanted to be just like him. Strong, successful, dependable, for business matters. But he often wished there was a softer side, one that he could ask advice from, joke with, just sit in a comfortable silence. If he himself had been around for Trevor more, maybe this whole other mess could have been avoided. Staring at his hands covering his father's, Steven felt the enormity of it all. Matthew Stone, Trevor, his father, and now helping his mom. She would need him now too. Jesse's hand on his shoulder brought him out of his reverie.

"So, what are the doctors saying?" Jesse asked the difficult question.

Lillian pulled herself up straight and cleared her throat. "The doctor says he suffered severe damage to his heart that left his brain without oxygen for too long. They say he is..." Her voice trailed off. She was unable to say the words. Brain dead.

Jane took over. "The machines are keeping his body alive. The tests they have run so far have told the doctors that he will never be...him again."

Steven put his head in his hands. "Is Tanner here? Does he know?"

"On his way, should be here later tonight," Jane offered. "He knows pretty much everything, but we just haven't said the actual words."

"Lillian? Did you and Andrew ever talk end of life business? Does he have a living will? Do you know what he would want?" Jesse asked this quietly, knowing how difficult these questions were to hear. Steven looked to his mother, not wanting to put pressure on her, but they needed to know their father's wishes.

"We did discuss it after Henry died." She misted over again, thinking of her brother who passed away nine years ago. He had lung cancer. Never smoked a day in his life but worked with asbestos. He suffered for six years with debilitating pain, oxygen tanks, surgeries, and endless trips to the hospital. His wife wouldn't let go, and he basically shriveled before their eyes. "Neither of us wants to be kept alive by machines. We don't want it for us, or for you kids. It's no way to live." She pulled in a ragged breath. "It's so much easier to say that when you aren't staring at the love of your life, making that decision for them." The Reeds never spoke of emotions, and this declaration caught them all in the heart. A silence fell on the room.

A nurse knocked lightly on the door. "We need to get his stats and check on a few things. Why don't you all get some coffee? There's some in the family room just down the hall." Without seeming rude, she ushered them out. Jesse was familiar with the process, they would be changing IVs, checking his catheter, and probably drawing blood. Families often got upset when they saw their loved ones being handled, no matter how gentle you were. It was best to have them leave.

The agents were keeping a discreet distance as they filed down the hall. "Where's my grandson?" Lillian put on a brave face. Steven and Jesse exchanged an anxious look.

Chapter 37

After fretting and walking back and forth on the threadbare rug, Jim came to a decision. He would drive the car to the back of his property, behind the other abandoned trucks and cars that years ago Jim planned on rehabbing and selling for a nice profit. A few carefully placed branches and it would be nearly invisible to the casual eye. Taking advantage of the darkening skies, Jim grabbed the keys and set off to make his latest problem disappear. He nearly fell off of the top step when a state police car drove slowly by his place. The officer behind the wheel gave no indication of seeing him. Steeling himself with a deep breath, Jim walked to the car. The door opened without a sound, and he settled into the driver's seat. Could he be arrested for tampering with evidence? He carefully steered the car between a truck and some trees and threw a few branches on top, concealing the incriminating car. Standing back a few feet, he admired his work. At least in the dim light from the setting sun and the lone light in the front lot, the car all but invisible.

****

Steven looked at his sister and mother. After taking a deep breath he launched into an edited version of the situation. When he got to the part where Stone had actually grabbed Trevor, his mother paled even more.

Jesse went to her side and took an outstretched hand. Jane started to cry. "What the hell? Who is this guy? Where is Trevor now?" The questions came rapid fire. Jesse and Steven waited it out and then started to explain what they could.

"Trevor is with a police officer, here with us. We are being protected by agents," he nodded toward Carl and Maxine outside in the hall. They gave a small wave and looked uncomfortable. "They are going to stay with us while we are here, and other agents and police officers are looking for the guy as we speak."

Jesse took over. "They believe he left town once he knew we were on to him. Here comes Trevor now. Let's not discuss it in front of him?" She stood and caught her son as he jumped into her arms. "Hey there, howya doing?"

Trevor scrambled down as soon as he saw his grandmother and aunt. "Nono! Auntie!" The delight quickly changed when he saw the tears in their eyes. "Wumpy? Is Wumpy okay?" His brown eyes searched one adult then another. "Did he die?" Trevor's voice was trembling.

"No, nothing's changed, dear. Come here, give your grandmother a hug." Nono forced a smile and welcomed her grandson onto her lap. "You're growing like a weed. Look how big you've gotten!" She held his face between her hands and peppered him with kisses. It was a bittersweet moment as the family closed ranks and doted on the small child. Sarah quietly slid away from the group when her phone vibrated in her pocket.

As she was talking with Joe, the group in the family room got louder. Another man had come around the corner. The features were almost identical to Steven

Reed. "I think Steven's brother just showed up. I'll let you know what the family's plans are once I know." She hung up and returned to the doorway of the family room.

The family was embracing each other and then it was quiet. The sister said something, and all eyes turned toward the agents who tried unsuccessfully to blend into the hospital-green walls. Trevor called out, "Hi, Sarah!" She returned his wave and took the opportunity to insert herself into the family circle. She joined the group as they were sitting, pulling chairs from all corners of the small room. Sarah extended her hand and introduced herself to Steven's family. She leaned against the wall closest to Trevor and waited for someone to speak. The older brother spoke first.

"So, about Dad, any change?" Tanner leaned over and took Lillian's hand in his own. She shook her head and let out a weary breath.

Sarah understood that what wasn't being said actually spoke louder than the words that had been said. The family was not waiting on a miracle. Sarah wondered what they were planning. She glanced at the basket of treats, and her stomach growled. In the silent room, there was no hiding it. The elder Mrs. Reed was the first to laugh. "Oh, my, we must all be hungry. Can't remember the last time I ate. What about all of you?" A murmur passed through the room, and someone suggested they get a bite to eat from the café.

"It's closed," announced Trevor, "and the machines only have raisins." Sarah nodded.

"Do you want me to see if anyone delivers?" Sarah offered.

"Why don't we check in on Andrew, and then go back to the house. We can eat there." Jesse was waving them over, and Sarah broke from the group.

Tanner looked back at Sarah and whispered to his sister, "Who's the chick?"

Jane smacked him in the stomach. "Woman, you ass. And she's a cop." When Tanner's eyebrows lifted, she shushed him with, "Tell you later, it's a long story." The family disappeared around the corner unaware that Carl and Maxine preceded them to check out the room first.

When the family was ready to leave, Steven handed Jesse his phone and she found the number for Papa's Pizza Joint and ordered them all something to eat. It was pitch black by the time they arrived at the house on the lake, and the moon had slipped behind some clouds. Carl and Maxine held back to talk to the other team. Sarah went inside with the family, leaving her small duffle in the car. Until she was invited or told differently, she assumed she was spending the night in her backseat.

Carl and Maxine stayed outside and walked around the modest house. White with green shutters. A hand carved sign welcomed friends to the lake. Sliding glass doors led to a deck by the waterfront. For houses on the water, the doors facing water were considered the front doors and usually had a family plaque. Just as they expected, there was a hand carved sign painted with gold letters labeling the house as The Reeds' Retreat.

Carl walked down to the dock and let out a low whistle. Nice boat. One of those mahogany boats that reeked of old money. He walked the length of it and wanted to take it for a ride.

"Is your ego dreaming?" Maxine called from a rock near the point. "Look over here." She was pointing to a small, enclosed gazebo. It was situated on the point of the property sticking out into the bay a little. From there you could see the outline of a long, low island that jutted up at the end. She nodded toward it. "Looks kind of like an alligator."

"That's Rattlesnake Island. One of the largest in the lake. Supposedly snakes on the island sunned themselves on the top, hence the name."

"Rattlesnakes? Here?"

Carl laughed. "No, but Garter Snake Island sounds too wimpy, I guess." Then he resumed his role to protect and serve and turned to look at the house. "They should pull the blinds, be less visible." With the picture window illuminated by the lights inside, the family looked like they were on a movie screen. Clear, full color, and all the details from inside were on display. Like the door that was left open to the driveway, windows that had been opened to allow for fresh air. All mistakes from a security point.

"Yeah, we should tell Sarah to have them close them." Maxine started typing a text to the officer who stood off to the side, looking a bit uncomfortable. They could see Sarah receive the request, wander to the door, close and lock it. Then she pulled Steven aside and whispered into his ear. The man nodded and went to close the windows and blinds. As he closed the largest for the picture window, he signaled that he was coming out to join them. They nodded and waited.

Chapter 38

Joe came in from walking Mutt who was nuzzling his hand, looking for a treat. He shook out a few bones that promised fresh breath and healthy teeth. "Don't think they're working buddy, your breath smells like old man farts." Mutt gave him a disapproving look but disappeared behind his chair to devour the crunchy treat. Joe sat down to check in with the team. He texted Sarah, wondering why she hadn't called back. She called him back in a few minutes.

"Hey there, how's everything going?" Joe tried to sound casual, but the concern carried through the line.

"Sorry I didn't call you. The family is at the house right now, eating pizza. Met them all. Sister seems nice, mother is reserved, but very polite, and the brother is an interesting dude. Not sure what he knows of the situation. He keeps eyeing me."

"They haven't told the family yet?" Joe was amazed.

"I think they know the basics, but maybe not the brother. He came in later, and I'm not sure how much he's been told. Trev introduced me as his friend. Cute, huh?"

"Yeah, he's a great little guy. Any issues so far, in terms of Stone?"

S. Hilbre Thomson

"No, I got the update about the sighting at the next toll. He might have gone farther north. I would have. Why stop here? It's kinda close."

"Anyway, the family in for the night?"

"Seems that way."

"Keep your phone charged and let me know if anything comes up. Right away." Joe didn't like being so removed from the case.

"Will do. I will check in with you in the morning.".

Joe turned to his notebook, which was not revealing any new clues. He had a hard time concentrating. His mind kept wandering to Karen Copeland's soft accent and endearing smile. He reminded himself to be careful not to let it get in the way of him doing his job. But damn, she was cute. Even the manner in which she attacked the hamburger was cute. When she had a dab of ketchup on her cheek it was all he could do not to lean over and wipe it with his finger. He used the old trick of wiping his cheek with a napkin. Without even realizing it Karen took up her napkin and wiped her own face.

Joe shook his head. Why even bother? She didn't even live around here. Getting entangled with Karen could only lead to trouble, professionally and personally. Draining the last of his beer, Joe decided to go to bed. Mutt followed dutifully.

****

When Karen got back to her room, she called her brother and let him know where she was staying. He expressed his concern again for her being so far away from home and involved in a kidnapping story. Attempted kidnapping she corrected him. Didn't matter. When she reminded him that she was working with the

224

police and had spoken to the FBI, he was slightly impressed, but still worried. She felt like she was talking to her father, not her freewheeling twin brother. She was completely out of her comfort zone but kind of liked it. Plus, that policeman was not hard on the eyes. How she longed to be the whipped cream that stuck to his upper lip from that delicious pie. Flicked away by his tongue. What was that her brother was saying?

"Karen. Earth to Karen! I was asking what you were planning to do. How long do you think you will stay?" His voice had taken a slightly annoyed tinge.

"Sorry, something shiny." That was their code for situational ADHD. "I, um, will stick around and try to get more info from Joe."

"Joe? You mean the cop? So, now he is Joe. Two minutes ago, he was Officer Mayan, Mayner, whatever."

"Marchand. And yes, Joe. We had dinner tonight. Business, it was nice." Karen smiled in spite of herself.

"Nice. Like in nice ass, nice legs, nice kisser?" Her brother was the least tactful person she knew. And she loved it. When it wasn't directed at her.

"Don't be a jerk. We talked about the case. Some. But had some great pie."

"I'm sure it was great pie..." Her brother let the sentence hang.

"Yes, pie. You are a pig." Then she relented. Maybe two days in a car and then spending a good portion of this day alone left her craving conversation. "He does, you know, have a nice ass." She giggled.

"Oh, God, the giggle? Damn. I haven't heard your boy giggle in forever. What's he like?" Teddy could gossip like her high school girlfriends. He was the one she trusted with her secrets.

"Oh my God. He's gorgeous. Tall, fit, smart, and funny." Karen leaned back into the pillows and sighed.

"Damn, all your requirements. At least you know this guy doesn't have a record." He was referring to a guy she dated in college. Worked at the local bar, bouncing. Let her and her friends in even though they were underaged. After a few months he casually mentioned a meeting with his parole officer. Turns out he was caught stealing. How was he supposed to know there was a bag of pot in the trunk? Oops.

"Yeah, he seems nice. But really where can it go?" Karen tried to be logical. "He did say he would give me more information for the story as soon as he could."

"Could be putting you off."

"True, but I can be persuasive." Karen looked at the clock. Teddy needed to be up early. "Anyway, I'll check in tomorrow."

"Kare," he used his big brother voice, "please be careful."

"I will, promise. Love you."

"Love you too. Night."

She went through her beauty regime, which consisted of brushing her teeth and tying her hair into a high ponytail. Throwing on an old pair of sweatpants and a tee shirt, she was ready for bed. But sleep was slow in coming. Her mind alternated between the case and Joe. Joe and the case. Then just Joe. She could fall hard and fast for a guy like that. Closing her eyes, she hoped her dreams would give her insight.

Chapter 39

Steven's family had finished their late dinner and Jesse had taken Trevor to bed. His mom insisted that they sleep as a family in her room while she took one of the twin beds in the room with Jane. Tanner and Steven stayed up to talk. The brothers hadn't spoken in weeks. Not because of anything wrong, they were just both very busy. They had inherited their father's workaholic gene. Tanner headed up a financial group that represented many multi-million-dollar companies. Steven was swamped securing more clients and keeping the current ones satisfied. Both had families to take care of. Though truth be told, neither saw much of their wives or kids. Tanner was upset with Steven for not telling him about Trevor earlier.

"To be honest, Tan, this has all just happened in the last two days. Trevor had been telling us there was a 'Badman' for a while, but neither Jesse nor I really believed it. When I saw the footprints around our yard, I felt like a piece of shit. We assumed Trevor had just been looking for attention, and I felt guilty for not being around." Steven took a long swallow of beer. "What if this guy had actually taken him? Who knows what he would have done?" Steven slumped in a chair.

"Well, he didn't. Hasn't. But it seems as if the police feel there is a reasonable threat, or they wouldn't be going through all of this." Tanner waved his hand at the locked doors and drawn curtains. "Where do they think he is?"

"That's the kicker. Last time his car was seen it was going through the tolls on the way up here. I didn't think they would let us come."

"You mean he could be here? At the lake?" Tanner sat up and leaned closer to his brother. "Why are you here, Steven? That's a huge risk."

"What would you have done? With Dad and all. Could you have stayed away?" Steven was trying to convince himself that he had made the right choice. "Really, New Hampshire is a big state. Why would he come to a popular spot? There are so many other places to hide, the woods the mountains, or maybe he's going to Vermont?"

"Yeah, I know. You really were backed into a corner. Sucks, man." Tanner took a long swallow draining his beer. They batted around different scenarios in which Stone drove right to the border and tried to cross into Canada or veered off into upper state New York. Both seem much more likely than him holing up just a few hours from where the police were looking for him. "It doesn't look good for Dad, huh?" Tanner got up to get them another drink. The kitchen was dated. Their mother had fallen in love with the quaint appliances. The cast iron stove, large farmer's sink, and the teal blue refrigerator. It even had a bottle opener built into the door. Two bottle caps landed with a soft clink.

"When I asked Jesse her take on Dad, she was pretty straightforward. She doesn't think he has long, even with the ventilator. She says his kidneys are shutting down. Once that happens, the other organs fail, and he goes. She says he can't feel anything even though some folks believe that people in comas can sense those around him. Jesse thinks he's even beyond that." Steven took a sip from the new beer. "We have to let him go."

"I know, he would hate it if he knew we were all just standing around staring at him. He loathed the idea of people pitying him."

"You think Mom is ready? I mean as much as she can be?" What an impossible position to put her in. He was glad, at least, that his parents had discussed it. Now it was just a matter of making sure the rest of the family was ready.

"I don't know. How do you get ready for that?" After a minute he added, "Do you think she will stay here?" Tanner was pacing, downing the beer quickly. He set the drink on the mantel near a picture they had given their parents for an anniversary a few years ago. The whole family, at the lake. Everyone was on the dock. His parents front and center, Tanner and his family on the right, Steven and his on the left. Jane in the middle right in front. She sat cross legged, with Fiona, Tanner's youngest on her lap. Trevor and Andrew, Tanner's eldest, stood on either side looking up at their grandparents. Kendall, the middle child, stood near the center of the shot clutching her bear. The photographer was perched in the whaler twenty or thirty feet away in the lake, trying to get the perfect shot. She initially wanted them all looking right at the camera, but when she caught that moment, she stopped. Which was good because just seconds later the great Mount Washington boat cruised by. The boys jumped onto the antique Chris-Craft and ran to the bow where they jumped up and down trying to get the crew's attention. The captain rewarded them with a toot from the giant horn. Any picture taking was done for the day. Regardless of how many times it had come by each day, Andrew would stop and announce, "Here comes the Mount." At night Lillian would let them flick the lights and a search light from the helm of the big boat would flash across the camp.

Steven saw Tanner staring at the photo, which Jane had blown up and framed. Trevor and Drew were three or four. The white shirts offset their summer tans. Fiona, the little one, was laughing at something Jane had said. Everyone had an easy smile, and they looked like a Gap ad. Preppy, clean, tan, and happy. It was one of Steven's favorites too. He kept a copy in a frame on his desk at work. It was probably the last time the whole family had been here at the same time. Now they were here again. This would be the last time they would all be here again. Dad was just a few miles away, waiting for them to let go. Tomorrow would be a very long day.

"We should call it a day." Steven patted his brother on the back and left Tanner standing at the fireplace working on another beer. He slipped into bed, curling up to Trevor who held tightly to his blanket. Sleep evaded him, and he could hear the agents talking quietly in the yard. It made him feel both more secure and nervous at the same time. Once again, he was left feeling impotent, incapable of taking care of his own family. Memories of his dad filled his head. How many conversations were left unfinished, words left unsaid? Jesse was always trying to get him to include his parents more. Invite them over, call unexpectedly, just to say hi. He was going to do it. Later. And now it was too late. Just as he was giving into sleep, Trevor began tossing and turning. Steven reached over to rub his back and the boy sat up screaming. "Get away! I'm not Tommy! Leave me alone!" His eyes were wide open, and he was trying to run away. But Steven held onto him, and Jesse soothed him with calming words.

"Trevor, it's us. Mommy and Daddy. See?" She turned on the light. Trevor looked from one to the other blinking and shaking. "It's okay, honey. It's just a bad dream."

"No, it's not, Mommy, the bad man *is* trying to get me. That's why Sarah and the other guys are here." He held his blanket to his chest and cried. They all jumped when the door creaked open.

"It's just me, Nono." The woman was surprisingly fast getting to the room. She had on her bathrobe and slippers, and it was obvious that she hadn't been asleep either. Lillian sat on the end of the bed and rubbed her grandson's foot. "Can I get you anything, a nightlight? You know Daddy had one for years. We keep it in the bathroom, but I could bring it in here."

Trevor nodded, and she went to retrieve it. Steven and Jesse smoothed the covers and settled Trevor back into the bed. When Lillian returned, she had a faded light shaped like a baseball in her hands. "Why don't I plug it in right here? She bent down and found an outlet right by the bed. Then she leaned over, kissed her grandson, then Steven. By the time she closed the door on her way out, Trevor was asleep again. It took a long time for either parent to doze off.

****

Sarah, Max, and Carl took two-hour shifts, two people on, one asleep. They wandered the yard in pairs, listening to the night noises. This early in the season the lake was especially quiet. Here and there a lone owl called out to the night. A rustle in the leaves revealed a fox, just as curious of them as they were initially of him. Heart beats fluttered when these surprises came, but quickly settled again. On occasion a light would flicker on in the house, and they would see someone shuffle toward the bathroom through the curtains. Minutes later the house would go dark. Around three a.m. they were startled by cries coming from inside. Sarah and Carl were on, and they hustled to the side of the house. Through the walls they heard murmurs of Trevor's parents calming him down. "Nightmare?" Sarah suggested.

"Probably, let's check the doors just in case," Carl answered. A quick check assured them that the house was secure, and they went back to their pacing.

They spoke in hushed tones. "So, here's the cliché question... What made you want to become an agent?" Sarah asked the man several years her senior. She found him kind of stiff, but pleasant, nonetheless.

"The cliché answer? To protect and serve." He chuckled. "Truth of the matter is I went into criminal law in college. Loved the rules, regulations, and yes, the power. Went into the academy right after. Right out of there, I landed a job in LA. Scary stuff. Gangs and poverty superimposed on the rich and privileged. Turns out the haves are just as whacked as the have nots. Everybody out for themselves. The haves are just smarter about it. Money helps to hide evil. I moved over to major crimes, worked on a special task force that rounded up a drug ring. We took in everyone from the penthouses to the pavement. Suppliers to dealers to a group of private school kids deeply addicted. Must have impressed someone because I got the call from Quantico and haven't looked back." Carl was not known for sharing personal information. The lack of sleep must be getting to him. Quick to turn the attention away from himself he asked, "And you?"

"I don't know really. My older brothers are in the service. Broke my mom's heart to see them deploy. I am much younger and remember the way she spoke of them with a mixture of fear and pride. I wanted to have her be proud of me too. But I'm not much for traveling. Wanted to stay stateside. The academy seemed like a good compromise. After my bachelor's in psychology, I went right in. Love the job. And so far, it's been pretty tame, nothing compared to LA, I bet."

"I bet she still worries." They stopped and leaned against a large rock in the front yard. "Your mom, I mean."

"Yeah, now that my brothers are back, married with kids, she does worry about me. But I think it's more the fact that I'm not married and giving her more grandkids to fuss over." Sarah laughed, she never shared personal stuff either. Husband and kids would come when it was the right time.

"My mom worries too. Less now, but still wants the grandkids. My husband wants to adopt, teenagers. Says they have a harder time getting adopted." Carl looked pensive.

"Teenagers are hard, I'm sure. But he's right. Are you going to?" Sarah checked her watch.

"Think so, it's a matter of finding the right time." The older man was amazed at his confession. He did want kids. His watch beeped signaling the time to switch. It was Sarah's turn to rest. They went to wake up Max. Just as they reached the SUV something came crashing through the woods. Both officers pulled their guns as they reached for their flashlights.

Sarah flicked on her light as a figure leapt from the brush and pulled up short. The beam caught a pair of eyes staring at them. Her heart hammered against her rib cage. Carl stood down first when he saw steam rising from the animal's nose. The deer had no idea how close he had come to getting shot. Carl reached over and lowered Sarah's light. The animal darted back into the woods, making just as much noise as he had coming. They holstered their weapons and let out deep breaths.

"New Hampshire's version of excitement?" Sarah laughed in spite of her red face.

"If we're lucky." Carl knocked on the window of the car, waking Maxine. The women switched places, and Sarah drifted off. Her brothers were right, sleep when you can.

Chapter 40

Matt woke with a start. It was early, the sun wasn't up. For the first time in months, he had no dreams. He felt calm and was looking forward to fishing with Red but felt bad lying to the old man. Red was kind, relaxed and easy to be around. He reminded him of his own dad. Before things got hard. After he lost his job, Matt's dad drew into himself. Gone were the fishing trips, camping weekends. The focus switched to finding a job. His mom took on more shifts, and that left his dad feeling even more inadequate.

Matt swung his feet off of the bed and stretched, releasing the kinks. Spreading his arms out to his sides, he could almost touch the walls on either side of the small bungalow. Leaning forward, his back cracked, and he could touch the counter in the kitchen area. Matt had a fleeting thought that it was just slightly bigger than a prison cell. It came from nowhere and his mood crashed. What the hell was he going to do? He could turn himself in and explain the circumstances. Maybe the police would understand. "Just like they did back home," he said aloud remembering the interminable interrogations.

"Are you sure there was someone in the house?" The lights were bright, Matt sat facing two detectives who repeated the same questions over and over. All he

wanted was to be alone. He had shot his son. He wasn't allowed to see him after the EMTs took him away. They were working furiously on the little boy. Matt had tried to get into the ambulance, but the policemen grabbed him roughly and put him in the back of the squad car. He cried openly as the ambulance left, his cries louder than the screaming sirens. He continued after the sirens fell silent and the police car headed toward the station. It had been hours and Matt was trying to understand how the police could think he hurt his own little boy. Then they brought up Carol and the fire. "So, your wife died in a home invasion. But you got out?" The tone in the officer's voice struck Matt cold.

"You think I did this? That? I almost died too. And if it weren't for Tommy, I would have rather I did." Matt had worked hard to move on from the loss of his wife, his first love, and the brutality of her attack. The possibility of his involvement was quickly rejected due to the neighbors' accounts. Matt was a devoted husband and father, always loving, humble, and hard working. Matt raised his head and looked the detective squarely in the eyes. "I had nothing to do with that. See these scars?" He pointed to the jagged marks that ran down his left cheek. "That's nothing compared to the damage they did to me and Tommy, mentally. Every morning I wake up expecting to hear her voice. I roll over to see her side of the bed, empty. Tommy's first word was 'mommy.' " Matt sobbed into his hands. "He doesn't even remember her. It almost breaks me to have to try to explain where she is, in heaven. I love him, would do anything for him. Please, can I see him?" Matt pleaded with the men, who must have families of their own. Why wouldn't they let him go to Tommy?

The younger one cleared his throat. "Mr. Stone, you're so..." He paused. "Your son...died. The doctors were not able to do anything to help. There was too much damage." This was delivered with a touch of kindness which the other officer gave him a dirty look for.

Matt let his head hit the table. He cried for what felt like forever. The men waited him out. When Matt finally lifted his head again, his eyes were swollen, but empty. Matt spoke softly, "How did this happen? I want to die." Matt's lawyer convinced the authorities to let him go and see Tommy at the morgue. Stone did not speak another word for several days. He was held on suicide watch, while in lock up. When he was finally released, Matt had to be led by his friend John out of the station.

Matt never wanted to spend another day behind bars. Without Carol or Tommy, why was he even trying? He no longer felt like fishing with Red, and the all too familiar spots danced before his eyes. A migraine was coming on. He swallowed two more pills and lay back down on the bed. With any luck he could stave off the headache. Matt briefly imagined taking the whole bottle, to save everyone the hassle. Closing his eyes, he willed himself back to sleep.

Chapter 41

Joe woke to his phone buzzing. It was his alarm. Why was it going off so early? Then he remembered. Cheese, eggs, hash browns, pie. He needed to work off the sins of the previous night. Yup, the only sinning he was doing was eating fatty food. Lucky him. What he wouldn't give to have something worthy of a confession. He pulled on a pair of running shorts and a tee shirt. Mutt watched while Joe laced up his sneakers and pulled out his iPod. The dog scratched at the door. "You wanna come with?" The answer came in the form of a large yawn, three quick turns on his bed, and a large sigh as Mutt flopped down for his first morning nap. "Thought so." Joe let the door fall shut and he turned up his music. He found himself leaning toward country music lately with some classic rock sprinkled in. The songs had a good beat that upped his pace.

He ran around the small pond at the end of his street. Usually while he ran, he worked out any problems from the day before. Except today, his mind kept slipping back to Karen. She was sexy. Mostly because she didn't know she was. Talking to her was like talking to an old friend. They danced close to the line of flirting. He wanted to spend more time with her but knew it could pose a problem with the case. Hopefully the crew in New Hampshire would find Stone and they would get the answers they needed.

Things could go back to normal, stopping speeders, breaking up the occasional party, and catching young couples making out on dead end streets. But then, he realized, Karen would go home. He should check in with her, make sure she had a good night. That would be the polite thing to do.

As Joe ran, he went through his mental 'to do' list for the day. First, he had to check in with Sarah. Make sure everything went well last night. Then the office. Then Karen. He rounded the far edge of the pond and found himself face to face with Renee Poulee, the woman who almost hit Matthew Stone with her car. She was talking to him. Joe pulled his ear buds out. "Pardon? I missed what you said."

"Oh, I was asking if you found that man yet. I saw it on the news that he was still out there. Is he dangerous? Should I be worried? I mean, could he hurt me too?" She was waving a paint brush around. An easel stood off to the side. The woman appeared to be painting the sunrise over the pond. An apron splattered with color was loosely tied around her waist. Over that she wore an old jacket, spattered with paint too. She stood in front of him with her feet planted solidly in the path. The older lady wanted information and wasn't moving until she got it.

Joe was breathing hard. He wiped the sweat from his forehead and gave her the best answer he could at the time. "We don't believe he would cause you any harm. From what we have been able to piece together, he is a troubled man, who needs our help."

"But that little boy. I heard he was trying to kidnap him. Is he," she looked around and lowered her voice, "a pedophile?"

"No, we have no reason to think that."

"Then why would he want the child?" She was waving the brush back and forth. Joe stepped back to avoid the spray.

"Mrs. Poulee, I can't really get into the details of an ongoing investigation. But we are sure that he won't be coming back to hurt anyone. Thanks to you, we have a great description and picture for the public. If anyone sees him again, I am confident we will hear. That's a great picture. You're really good." Joe was getting quite adept at switching subjects.

"Well thank you. I am trying to get the same spot throughout the day. It's amazing what a change in lighting can do to a view. This will take on a whole new life once the sun is up, then again as it goes down. If I see an animal, I take a photograph and add it in later. One habitat, home to so many animals." She was staring out at the water. Just then a couple of geese landed halfway across the pond. As she reached for her camera, Joe said good-bye. She was caught in the moment, and he was long gone by the time she clicked the photo.

Joe turned up the music and his speed as he finished the loop. Six miles before breakfast. When he returned home, he went through a quick series of push-ups, pull-ups, and sit-ups. He cooled off sitting on his stoop drinking a protein shake. Mutt came up and sniffed the cup. Joe swore the dog gave him a condescending look and walked away in a huff. Leave it to the old dog to give him attitude. After a quick shower, Joe got into his uniform and headed to the station. It was seven on the dot. He could call Sarah.

"Good morning."

Trevor

"Good morning yourself. I bet you didn't spend the night in the backseat of your car."

"Oh, reliving your prom night?" Joe quipped.

"Yeah, yeah, funny. When I wasn't sleeping, I was busy squaring off with Bambi. Almost killed him. I would have received a summons for hunting out of season."

"Should I ask?" Joe laughed. "But I take that to mean it was a quiet night. The family awake yet?"

"They were up off and on all night. Steven and his sister are on the dock right now. Having coffee from the smell of it."

"Jealous?" Joe knew she needed her caffeine, or no one would be safe.

"Yes. Carl went to get us some breakfast. I told him to make mine extra, extra large."

"Oh, so it's Carl now, is it? Did he like the backseat too?" Joe teased her because that was what they did.

"Married," she answered back.

"Bummer for you. At least you will concentrate on the job." He added that because it was one of the reasons they decided they wouldn't work as a couple. They both lived and breathed work. No time for a relationship. He liked being in charge even if it meant having little time for anything else. At least that is what he tried to convince himself. Sarah had plans of her own. She was studying for the sergeants' exam. Because there was little room for advancement in this town, she had no problem with moving.

"Thanks, jerk. Anyhow. The family is going back to the hospital after breakfast. From what I understand, they are talking to the doctors today about the process

241

of taking him off of life support. Once that happens, he should pass quickly. They haven't discussed next step plans with us yet. Though they might have an idea. I just felt like an ass asking."

"Let Carl do that. He gets paid more and is ultimately in charge of the security detail. I need to check in with Buchanan and Price too. See if they found anything new overnight. How's Trevor holding up?"

"I haven't seen him this morning. Poor little guy had a nightmare in the middle of the night. Sounded terrified. He's got to be really confused with everything going on. I really don't think he knows just how sick his grandfather is either." Sarah seemed to be getting emotional. "He was so good all day yesterday. Beat me in a hundred games of Go Fish."

"Thanks, Sarah." Joe was quiet.

"For what?" She was confused.

"For watching over them. I can't be there, so I am glad you are." She heard the sincerity in his voice and opted not to give him a hard time.

"Don't worry, Joe, they'll be okay. The next few days will suck, but they will make it through. You just concentrate on finding Stone." She said good-bye for two reasons. She didn't like her friend and boss getting upset, and Carl's SUV was coming down the drive. She needed that coffee.

Chapter 42

"Steven, I don't know what I can do to help. Why is this man after Trevor?" Jane leaned back in the wooden chair and sipped her coffee. It was in a giant mug that read 'Do not approach until empty.'

"From what we can tell, Trevor looks like his son who died a few years ago. The guy shot him." Jane sat up straight. "Accidentally. There were robbers in his house, and his gun went off."

"Oh my God. How terrible." She sat back. After a few minutes she added, "But he really thinks Trevor is his kid?"

"Joe, Jesse's friend the cop, said that he is probably in the middle of a break down. Trying to change the past. Deal with his guilt. His wife died too. A home invasion, she was beaten to death. Just after the boy was born. I guess the whole family almost died."

"Jesus, it almost makes you want to feel bad for the guy."

"I do, on one level. On the other level I want to beat the hell out of him." Steven looked to his sister. Jane was not always the practical one, but she was really good at helping Steven work though his emotions. Growing up wasn't always easy. Their parents had such high expectations that they were often left feeling inadequate and angry. Somehow Jane found a way to ignore that and remain positive.

"To tell you the truth, I want to take a swing at him myself. Jesus, what a mess."

"You getting all religious on me?" Steven smiled. "God, Jesus, Hell. You been going to church?"

"Yeah, tried once, but lightning hit the building as I walked up. Took it as a sign that I wasn't welcome." Jane had gone through what her mother kindly put as her exploration years. She tried drugs, drinking, men, and women. There were times when Steven thought she was just trying to push her father's buttons. Once her folks stopped pushing her to become 'something special', she calmed down, found her niche, and was happy.

"Ha, yeah, don't think I would be welcome either." Their youth had been spent at private schools, forced to go to chapel every day, while the people around them were preaching one thing and living another. The school staff acted like a cast from a reality show. Tallies were informally kept as to who was sleeping with whom. Heck of a way to mold their minds into respectful, proper men and women. "How do you think Mom is holding up?"

"She didn't sleep a wink last night. We talked some, but then she got up to make tea. I heard Trev, he had a bad dream?"

"The Badman. That's what he calls Stone. He settled back down though. Mom was great." Steven looked out at the water. "Do you think we will do it today? You know, Dad?"

"Probably. We should, you know. Dad would hate this. But I don't know if I can be there when they do." Jane teared up. She turned so her brother wouldn't see.

Steven got up and put his arms around his sister. "I know. Me neither. But I think we should be, for Mom." They both turned when they heard Trevor burst through the door. "Dad, Auntie! Look!" He pointed to the pair of deer that had been grazing in the side yard. Until that moment. All Steven and his sister saw were the white tails bobbing away.

"Good morning to you!" Steven grabbed his son and held him high in the air. "I should give you a bath!" He held the boy over the edge of the dock. Trevor squealed in delight and fear.

"No, no! I don't have my bubble on!" He was in lessons at the local Y. His instructor was trying to get him to swim without it, but Trevor was still scared of going solo.

"I won't." Steven took him in a bear hug and inhaled Trevor's scent. His pajamas had dogs all over it and smelled slightly of sweat. The nightmare had worked him up. Underneath it was that sweet innocence of childhood. Johnson's baby shampoo, and sleep, if that had a scent. Steven held on as long as he could.

"Put me down!" He jumped into Jane's lap, spilling the last of her coffee. It landed on the dock and dripped through the wooden boards. She set her mug down and held her nephew. Over his head, she looked at her brother with eyes filled with fear and sorrow.

Jesse popped her head out the door and called them to breakfast. The three worked their way back to the house, holding Trevor by a hand and swinging him high. Sarah, Max, and Carl had caught the exchange.

"Damn. They seem like such a nice family," Maxine said as she polished off her bagel sandwich.

"They are. Any news on Stone?" Sarah turned to the two agents.

Carl spoke first. "I talked to Buchanan when I went for coffee. So far nothing new. No information either way from the toll cams. The New Hampshire authorities have his info, picture, license plate, and the car we believe he's in. Nothing so far. I just hope he stays away while we deal with this. Sarah, Buchanan wants you to talk to the family to find out their plans. Says you have more rapport than we do, so it might be better coming from you. We just need to be ready for what they need, services, et cetera."

"Jeez, Carl. Think that's above my pay grade," she said but smiled. This was an unusual situation. She did have more history with them, if only by a day but still wished Joe was here. He would have no problem with it. "After they eat, I will go in and ask to talk to Steven and Jesse." She finished her sandwich and downed the rest of her coffee.

"You gonna need seconds?" Maxine asked.

"And thirds, fourths maybe." Sarah laughed. Trying to work out the kinks in her back she leaned down to touch her toes. She pulled up quickly. "What's that?" Sarah was pointing to a cigarette butt on the ground, just under the car. She hadn't seen any of them smoke and it looked like the same brand they took from the Reeds' woods. Both agents knelt down to look at it.

"It's been here for a while, I think. Anyone know if it rained here in the past couple of days?" He took out a pen and pushed it back and forth. "Anyone in the family smoke?"

The women shook their heads. "Not that I've seen." Max walked around the car and looked for more.

"There's a couple more right here." She pointed to the edge of the driveway. "There's no way Stone was here last night. We would have seen him, especially if he was smoking." She pulled out a plastic bag and lifted the butt off of the ground with it. Carl handed her another bag and she dropped it in, picked up the others, and sealed the bag. "We should talk to the family, now."

Sarah went in and caught Steven's eye. She motioned him over. "Got a minute?"

He looked back where the family had stopped eating. "Uh, sure. Be right back," he called over his shoulder. Sarah saw Tanner get up too.

They met as a group by the SUV. "Anyone in the family smoke?" Carl asked the men directly.

They looked at each other. "No, not that I know of. Dad used to smoke but quit years ago. Why?"

Maxine held up the bag. "You sure? These were all over the driveway. Found them this morning."

Steven paled and went quiet. He recognized the butts too as his mind went back to the trail around his house. Matthew Stone smokes. Tanner answered for them. "Yeah, I mean no, no one smokes."

"I think we need to double check. Mind if we come in?" Carl asked not really expecting an answer because he was already walking toward the house. The rest trooped after him. Jesse, Jane, Lillian, and Trevor stopped eating again and stared.

Steven spoke first, "Um, they found some cigarette butts in the driveway. Mom, do you know if anyone was here and smoking?" Jesse knew what they were asking for and reached for Trevor's hand.

"Um, I can't think of anyone. Maybe it was the EMTs?" She was searching her memory.

"I highly doubt the EMTs would have stopped for a drag during their visit. Probably more concerned with Dad," Tanner offered.

Mrs. Reed sat quietly for a minute, searching her memory. "We've been the only ones here since the place opened. Oh, wait. The marina delivered the boat earlier this week. But they came by water. No need to be in the driveway." She went over to the calendar hanging on the refrigerator. Scanning back, she stopped on Monday. "The landscapers were here. They did a spring cleanup for us. Took a day and a half. Could it be them?"

"Very likely. Can I have their number? It's a quick check and will put us all at ease." Carl sounded less concerned. It was a probable explanation. How would Matthew Stone know they would be here anyway? The family didn't even know they were coming.

"I have their number right here." She reached into a drawer and pulled out an old-fashioned address book. Tucked in a sleeve was the card for the landscapers. 'Lakeside Landscapers, clearing the way to a perfect view.' Carl took the card and stepped outside. The rest seemed to hold their breath waiting for the agent to return. Within minutes he stepped back in.

"Spoke to the owner. He is checking with the crew that was here. Company policy is no smoking on the job. So, if it is one of his guys, someone is catching hell."

Trevor pointed at the tall man. "You said a bad word! A quarter for the swear jar." Laughter spread through the small group, and those with food left on their plates began picking at it. Carl walked over to Trevor and laid a quarter on the table.

"Sorry 'bout that. Forgot my manners."

"Nono says that manners make the man." He looked at his grandmother who just smiled.

"They do. I will try to be better." Carl actually blushed.

"Um, Mom, we have any more coffee?" Jane asked, missing the last dregs that had slipped through the cracks on the dock.

"We are all out. I wasn't expecting company. Usually just me and your father."

"Hang on," Carl offered and slipped out the door. When he returned, he was holding a Box of Joe from Dunkin Donuts.

"That's way better than a quarter!" Jane relieved him of the box and made herself a second cup. Within minutes, the box was drained, and polite chatter continued. Trevor was asking why Carl and Maxine didn't wear police uniforms, Sarah was asking Steven and Jesse what the plan for the day was as gently as she could.

"Um, not to be insensitive, but do you know your schedule for the day?" She felt pushy for asking, but they did need to know.

"We understand. This is complicated enough. From what I know, we will go to the hospital once everyone is ready. My mother plans on letting the doctors know that we are going to take him off of life support. I really don't know what to expect from there." Steven looked to Jesse.

"Usually when life support ceases, the patient drifts off peacefully. Once in a while the body does hang in there, almost out of habit. But within the hour, they pass." Jesse hoped she didn't sound too cold. She dealt with this situation at the nursing home often. She tried to be as clear as possible without being cruel. Most doctors let the nurses handle the families. It was the worst part of her job.

Sarah nodded. "I'm so sorry. This must be very hard for you." The couple nodded. "What do you think the plans will be after, after he passes?"

They exchanged a look then shrugged. "We haven't really gotten that far yet." Steven looked at the ground like he wished a giant hole would appear and he could crawl in and hide.

"No problem. But will you let us know as soon as you can?" Sarah left the couple feeling horribly. But she had a job to do too and wouldn't be doing it right if she didn't push.

Chapter 43

Matt woke again an hour later. He tentatively opened his eyes and was relieved to see no spots. The clock read 7:00 a.m. Red would be waiting for him no doubt. He quickly got dressed and went to the office/home of the one person he felt comfortable with at the moment. Not just because he was blind, but he was kind. Matt had a feeling Red knew there was more to his story but had the common decency not to pry. When his foot landed on the first step, the door swung open, and he was greeted with a big smile.

"Ready to go, lazy bones?" Red shuffled past Matt. "Bin up fer hours. Fish are gonna be gone if we don't get the lead out." Matt found himself trailing after the man. For an old blind guy, he certainly was spry. As they approached the dock, Red let Matt help him into the boat. "Gear's in the shed, if you don't mind gettin' it." Red hitched his head toward a small lean to. Matt opened it up and the musty smell hit him like a wave, bringing him back to the times he fished with his own dad. Matt smiled as he pulled out a tackle box and two rods. "Don't ferget the bucket!" Red called to him. Matt turned around to grab the bucket he did in fact forget.

"You said you have a special place to go?" Matt carefully set the gear down and got in front of the small outboard motor. The first tug caused the motor to sputter.

"Don't you worry. It'll start," Red chirped. "Just been a while." On the third tug it came around and roared to life. Matt untied the rope, and they were under way.

"Where to?"

"First we gotta get some bait. There's a small marina on the way. We can pull in there. Then off to the spot. I'm guessin' you don't have a fishin' license, so we have to be discreet. If we go north for maybe five to ten minutes, hugging the coastline, you'll see an inlet on your right. Looks like it's goin' nowhere but follow that. There's a narrow bit that marine patrol ignores most of the time. Long as we're quiet, we should be fine."

Matt forgot about the license and marine patrol. He tugged his baseball cap down tighter and scanned the lake for other boats as they pulled into the marina. It would be crazy if he got arrested for catching a bass. The two men puttered along in silence.

"When you see a giant rock on the right, start looking for a sign for the marina." Red broke the silence. When the rock appeared, Matt turned in. A sleepy boy around twelve years old trotted out to the dock. Red asked for some night crawlers, and they were back on their way in a flash. Matt loved the way the small boat skimmed the water, leaving a gentle wake. He looked at Red who was riding in the bow. His head was tilted up and found the sun that was still low in the sky. A smile crept across the man's face, and he looked at peace. As they passed other boaters, they each raised a hand in a silent greeting. The lake was very quiet, except for them and a few others out to catch a fish or just a moment's peace. Off to his left, Matt saw a loon pop up on the surface. It floated majestically for a minute and then dove under. He scanned back and forth, looking for it to resurface. Just when he was going to give up, the slender black head poked through the morning water and it sat, still as a statue. When was the last time he felt this calm? He couldn't remember.

"Beautiful, isn't it?" Red's voice surprised him, and he jerked the motor. "I can't see, but I do have a memory. The water, smooth as slate, clear. The trees, leaning toward the lake, like they are bowing to her beauty, unaware that their reflection on the surface tells a story of their own. Any loons out this morning?"

Matt was in awe. The weathered old man was a romantic. "Just one. Floating in the shade. Can barely see him."

"Preaching to the choir, Greg."

Red's use of his pseudonym shook him for a minute. He was doing so many things out of character that he felt like he was losing the last bits of his true self. Red grunted from the front. "Almost there, I think, you see a broken-down boat house?"

"Yeah, on the right?"

"Uh, huh. House burned down fifteen years ago, and the owners never rebuilt. Kids used to party on the dock. Once the boat house fell apart, it lost its appeal, I guess. Bet the dock looks like hell now too."

"Yup, sure does, falling into the lake." Matt slowed the boat more. "We there?"

"Yup, anywhere around here. We can drop anchor, or just float, up to you."

Matt pulled the small anchor off of the floor of the boat. The rope was old and grey, and he wasn't sure it would hold, but tossed it over anyway. Matt watched it fall and hit the muddy bottom, then turned to set up the rods.

"I kin' do it myself, thanks," Red said nicely.

"Sorry," Matt stammered.

"No problem, pass me those worms?"

They fished in a comfortable silence for several hours. Once in a while they got a tug, there was a little commotion, and then back to quiet. Both men seemed content to sit with their rods in the water. A turtle sunned itself on a long log jutting out of the lake.

Red broke the silence. "So, you findin' what you need here?"

Matt waited a moment, trying to sort through the question. Was he alluding to the boy? Had he heard something on the news to cause him concern? He decided on an ambiguous answer. "Yeah, this is just what I needed."

Red looked his way, and nodded, "Good 'nuff then."

Matt worried that he was suspicious. Did he need to pack it up and go? Matt felt the easiness of the morning ebb away. Tension creeped up his back and he no longer wanted to fish. He stared at Red. The old man sat, looking at the water. Seeing what? He seemed to be working on getting something out from between his teeth, making a whistling-sucking sound. As if Red sensed Matt staring, he turned to him. "So, whaddaya say we start wrappin' it up? I'm gittin' hungry." Maybe Matt needn't be worried. He grunted in assent and reeled in his line. They packed up in silence.

"You all set?" Matt asked when everything was tucked under the wooden seats.

"Yup. You pull anchor yet?"

"Nope, gonna do it now." Matt leaned over and grabbed the line. As he pulled the rope it caught on something. He tugged harder. Nothing. "Damn. Looks like it's stuck. Hang on." Matt stood and gripped the line with both hands. Just as he was about to pull, he saw a boy walk to the end of a dock a few camps down. Tommy? Matt was caught off balance, and the small iron anchor pierced through the water and flew over his head. The old rusty hook caught the older man squarely in the head. Matt gasped as Red pitched toward the water. He reached out and grabbed him right before he fell overboard.

Red was completely out. Setting the man on the floor of the boat, Matt leaned him up against the seat. There was a long gash with thick blood running from the temple to the jaw. "Red! Red! You okay?" Matt looked toward the shore for help. His companion lay still, moaning. "Someone. Help!" he yelled, looking for the boy who was no longer there. Shaking his head to clear it, he pulled off his tee shirt and tried to stop the bleeding. Once he had it wrapped around his head, Matt revved to motor and made his way out of the inlet scanning the camps.

He spotted someone on a different dock and sped up. Keeping an eye on Red, he pulled closer. "Hey there! I need help!" Matt's heart almost stopped. The little boy kneeling on the dock was playing with what looked like toy cars. His curly blond hair, the small frame, the way he moved. Tommy? Forgetting Red for a moment, he yelled, "Tommy!" The boy turned, startled at the intrusion. His face screwed up in confusion. Matt's heart sank. It wasn't Tommy, just another child. The boy was screaming and pointing to the boat. When Matt looked again at Red, the tee shirt had soaked through, blood was running down his friend's chest. "Please, get help."

There was no need to call for the parents, they were running from the house hearing the boy yell. They pulled up short when they saw the two men in the small boat. "Oh, my God! What happened?" The man was wading directly into the shallow water.

"Um, my friend, the anchor. It hit him in the head. He's unconscious." Matt cut the motor and allowed the man to pull him to shore where the boy was now crying, clinging to his mother.

"Shan, call 911," the boy's father called to his wife and then said to Matt, "Help me get him out of the boat. He needs to get to the hospital." Matt followed the man's orders while looking between Red and the young boy.

The boy's mother pulled out a cell phone and called. "They'll be here soon. Hospital is fifteen minutes from here." She ran into the house and came out with a first aid kit. Matt sat back and let them tend to Red. Between the accident and thinking he saw Tommy again, Matt found himself getting lightheaded and anxious. When he heard the sirens cutting through the woods, he was momentarily relieved. But when the patrol car pulled down their driveway and two officers jumped out, Matt felt the need to flee. Right behind them, an ambulance came to a screeching halt. Fortunately, their attention was on Red. He was asked questions. How old was the man? What was his name? What happened? Did he have any allergies?

Matt had few answers. They looked at him briefly. "Did you find him like this?"

"No, we were fishing together. I am staying at his place. His cabin, in Alton. I don't know him very well, he wanted to fish, so did I. I took him out, I mean to fish. He's blind, can't drive himself."

"He's blind? You could have led with that." The EMT leaning over Red gave him a look. Matt was flustered. After the attendants bundled the unconscious man up, they turned their attention to Matt. "That all his?" The dark-haired attendant was pointing at Matt's chest. He was covered with blood. He must have looked like hell.

"Yeah, I'm fine. Where are you taking him?" Matt took the towel offered from the woman and tried wiping off some of the blood.

"Hawkins. Can you get a ride there?" Red was taken care of with smooth efficiency, the EMTs taped the IV needle down and hung a bag of saline on the pole of the stretcher. Matt's tee shirt was tossed aside, and they loaded Red into the back of their ambulance.

Matt looked at the couple. "Would it be possible?"

The father nodded, "Just let me change."

The EMTs nodded. "Meet you there." The ambulance lumbered up the drive.

The police officers glanced at Matt. "We have a few questions, for our report." A heavyset officer pulled out a notepad to take notes. Matt's hat was in the boat and he wanted to get it, hide his face some. The younger partner looked from Matt to his partner to the boat. Then he wandered over to the boat to take a closer look. Matt had a hard time concentrating.

"Your name?" It was a simple question. But Matt felt panic rising in his throat.

"Greg, Greg Johns." He used Carol's maiden name. Sweat gathered on his brow.

Matt didn't hear the man at first. He was calling from the house. "Would you like some clothes?" he repeated.

Matt looked down at his blood-soaked clothes, he couldn't go anywhere like that. "I... I would really appreciate it." He dropped the end of the towel into the water to wash off the sticky blood, and to turn away from the officers. The young boy continued to stare at him.

"Mr. Johns. Do you have any ID? Where are you from?" The younger cop walked next to him.

"Why did you hurt him?" a small voice asked. Matt swung his head around to the child. He was standing a few feet away, asking an innocent question.

"What? I, I didn't hurt him, it was an accident." The words were familiar, he had said them before. Scenes flashed before his eyes. Carol, lying beaten, her eyes begging him for help. Tommy crumpled on the hallway floor, crying, asking that same question. Detectives, asking him the same questions, time and again. His head swam, he tried to sit down. But the ground met him before he could gain purchase on the nearby bench.

He heard one of the officers say, "I think we might need help. Call for another bus." Through the fog he heard the younger policeman calling for an ambulance. He tried to clear his head and sit up. "I'm fine. I just need a minute." Willing himself to full consciousness, Matt shook off the policeman's arm. "I can't stand the sight of blood. Guess it caught up to me."

"Um, hold on the bus. He might be okay," the lead policeman said to his partner. "You sure you're okay?" He was eyeing the blood, looking for wounds. What he did see were scars. Scars left over from the beating he took when Carol died. One below his ribs, right down to his belly button. His spleen had been removed due to internal damage. There was a long, jagged scar down his forearm, and a smattering of pale lines on his face. "What happened to you?"

Matt always tried to hide the scars. He took the towel, which Shannon had dipped in the lake again. As he washed off the blood, the scars came to life. "I was in a car accident. Got real banged up."

He was now sitting, and his color was returning. The man had returned with a pair of sweatpants and a new tee shirt. "They should fit. We look about the same size. Hey, I'm Eli by the way. This is Shannon and my son, Tyler."

Matt took the clothes. "Greg, nice to meet you. Sorry to just barge in." He was getting his bearings again. He tried to turn down the southern accent. "I had no idea where to go."

"Officers? Can I take him over to see his friend?" Eli asked as Shannon led Matt to the bathroom.

The police officers exchanged a look. The older one sighed and closed his notebook. "Yeah, we can follow up at the hospital. Thank you for your help." They gave one last look at the boat and then at Matt as he went into the house. Something was niggling at the back of the younger cop's mind. He and his partner got into their cruiser and backed out.

Once Matt could no longer hear the diesel engine, he breathed a sigh of relief. Dressed in a stranger's clothes, he wiped the last of the blood from his hand and went to find Eli. They were waiting outside. Matt looked at the family, mom, dad, son. It could have been his. It should have been his. He pushed back the sadness. "You sure you don't mind giving me a ride?"

"Of course not. We'll get you there and see what your friend needs." The men left in Eli's truck, Matt worrying about Red. The old man hadn't mentioned any other family, who should he call?

Chapter 44

Karen wanted to talk to Joe again. She needed more information on Matthew Stone, the Reeds, and what the FBI might have found out overnight. She popped open a Diet Coke and played Eenie, Meenie, Miney, Mo with the Pop Tarts and honeybun. Decisions, decisions. The honeybun won out. As she nibbled and sipped, she scrolled through her emails. Nothing. She googled Matthew Stone, nothing new. Then the Reeds. Still nothing. Then she had an idea. She typed in, 'attempted kidnapping, Middletown, MA.' The screen halted, then a few lines trickled down.

"Police searching for man in attempted kidnapping."

"Hit and Run, driver not at fault." In this short piece, there was a reference to the man who ran into a car and then fled, that might be connected to an attempted kidnapping at the local school. Karen stopped. The school. They might have some information. Information the police weren't giving her. She wrote down the school and the name of the principal, who was listed as a witness. Mrs. Shari Hemmingway. There were also pictures that looked like they came from cell phones. One was who she presumed was the principal talking to a policeman. Wait, that was Joe. He was there! Others were of parents walking away, holding their children tight. The last one was of a sign, bent and scratched. Ironically it said, 'Caution, Children Crossing'. Someone had set it on the sidewalk and, in the background, she saw the Reed family leaning against a police car. She decided that maybe she should go talk to someone at the school. With a sense of purpose, she finished her breakfast, took a shower, and got dressed. At least she had a plan.

As soon as Karen jumped into the shower, her phone began to buzz. She didn't hear it though and a message recorded.

"Hey, Karen, it's Wendy. Some guy called, a Buchanan, said he was from the FBI. The frigging FBI! He wanted to know what I know. I told him everything I told you. He kept asking if Stone was violent? Did I know anyone he would call if he were in trouble? Did he know anyone in New Hampshire, Vermont, or New York? I told him I don't know. How would I know?" a pause, "I don't think he believed me. I hope I didn't get you in trouble. Holy Christ! This is scary. Exciting, but scary. Okay, call me when you get this. I want to know if you're okay. If I don't hear from you soon, I'll call Teddy." This last part sounded a bit hopeful. The phone went silent as Karen stood underneath the hot spray.

****

At that precise moment, Joe was taking a call from Detective Price. Matt's license plate was spotted at a toll farther west, in Hookset earlier that morning. But it wasn't on the same car he had before. It was another Saturn, but a different model. The one they saw before was a LS, this one was an LW. And maybe a different color, grey or green at least from what they could tell. There was another small problem. There were two people in the car. Both appeared to be women. New Hampshire police were looking for the car now.

"So, he must have switched his tags. Damn. We need to find that car so we can see where it's been. What a major pain in the ass, but right now our only lead." Joe could hear Price tapping her pen. She was wired. Handling another case too. Homicide. Domestic. Avery was asking him if he had heard anything from the Reeds.

"Nothing much. Sarah checked in earlier. It sounds like the family is going to take him off of life support sometime today."

"Does she know anything else, service wise?" She was impatient. Too much to do. Wanted to get the pieces in place with this so she could get the family back in Massachusetts.

"No, she tried asking, but they didn't have answers."

"Tell her we need them. There's stuff to be set up. It takes time."

"I will ask her. She wants to be sensitive to the family's needs." Joe was trying to protect his officer and friend.

"Jesus, I must sound like an ass." The tapping stopped. Avery took a deep breath. "When I'm under pressure, I come off like a jerk." It was an apology.

"Hey, don't sweat it. This is new territory for all of us I assume. Crazy man after a kid, kid's grandfather dying in the same state we assume the suspect is in. It wasn't in my training either." Joe tried to sound easy going, but it was hard on him too. He wanted Jesse and her family back home. Not for the reason some might think. He owed the Martins, and taking care of Jesse and her family was the least he could do. "Well, keep me posted. I will let you know ASAP when plans are made."

"Thanks, Joe."

Joe sat at his desk trying to digest everything. They had to find Stone. The Reeds needed peace of mind. Karen was cute, sexy as hell. She kept sneaking into his head. While he really wanted to just daydream about the reporter, he pulled himself together and turned on his computer.

Chapter 45

The Reeds piled into cars, Jesse and her family with the agents of course. The rest of the family had resigned themselves to the presence of the FBI and basically acted like they were part of the group. Sarah followed in her vehicle and mused at the small caravan. Way to be discreet. Heads turned as they entered the small drive and pulled up to the visitor's entrance. The Reeds waited in the car as Carl and Sarah went in to check things out. The rest of the family waited uncomfortably outside the entrance. Obviously anxious to get inside, they kept checking watches and phones for the time. Just as Tanner was going to ask what the delay was, Sarah and Carl came out. They were given the nod, and Maxine let the Reeds out of the car. They were escorted into the hospital with questioning looks. Wolfeboro was an old-fashioned town. They had their excitement when Mitt Romney ran for office, but it had been quiet lately. Most didn't like it, and all had become quite adept to recognizing a federal agent. People whispered from across the room as they entered and waited for the elevator. The family felt the stares but were more concerned for Andrew and the decision they still needed to make.

After taking a deep breath, the group walked into the small room. Andrew lay there. The machines beeped and whispered as his chest slowly rose and fell.

Jesse looked down and the bag hanging by the bed was empty. No urinary output today. His skin was taking on a grey pallor and she knew, life support or not, he was not far from the end. Lillian went immediately to his side and grabbed a hand. Trevor tiptoed closer but stopped at the foot of the bed. Jesse searched the faces of the family and could see that the hope they secretly harbored overnight was gone. Their father was not really there. The man who lay there was a shell, like a mirage of his former self. Everyone jumped when the nurse passed through the door and said good morning.

"I'm so sorry. I didn't mean to startle you." She had a pleasant voice, with a hint of an accent. English? Irish? "He had a quiet night. No changes." The nurse moved around the room pushing a tissue box closer to Lillian, twisting a dial to soften the beeps. "Would you like the doctor to come in?" It was understood that the this would be the doctor's last visit. Lillian squeezed Andrew's hand, and a tear rolled down her cheek.

Jane inhaled deeply and her voice shook when she spoke. "Yes, I think that would be a good idea."

The nurse looked the group over. "Perhaps this little guy would like some juice?" She reached her hand out to him. Trevor pulled back.

"I will go with him, it's okay. Thanks." Jesse and Trevor left with the nurse.

"Mommy? Wumpy's not waking up is he?" Trevor's brown eyes looked at her earnestly. She shook her head. "So, he's gonna die, go to heaven?"

Trevor had been told there was a place called heaven, but he had never had to say good-bye to someone. He was quiet as they walked down to the family room. Sarah followed at a discreet distance and waited at the doorway. She listened as mother and son talked.

"Now he can know them, your mom and dad." A child's way of finding the good. One of Jesse's biggest regrets about her parents' deaths was that they never met Trevor. It was a heartache that never ceased. Did they really watch over her and her family like she wanted to believe? "Yes, it will be nice for them to get to know each other." Jesse looked up and saw Sarah standing there. "Come in, please."

Trevor gave her a small wave. "Wumpy is going to heaven."

Sarah was taken aback. "I'm so sorry, Trevor."

"He can meet my other grandma and grandpa now." He was wandering around the room aimlessly.

Sarah took the opportunity to chat with Jesse. "So, it will be today?"

"Yes, I believe." Jesse let her head fall into her hands. "This is so complicated! I can't concentrate on anything. I am worried about Steven, his family, and Trevor. How is he handling all of this? Most of all I am worried that Stone will come back and try to take him again! It's just unfair!" She looked up. "I am so sorry! You are here to help. And all I have done is complain." She wiped the tears from her eyes. "Do you have any news?"

"No, nothing new. Joe called this morning. He said it was a quiet night." The service questions could wait. She laid a hand on the other woman's shoulder. "Anything I can do for you? Hang out with Trevor? Maybe take him for a walk?"

"If you don't mind, I feel horrible not being in there." Jesse stood, kissed Trevor on the head, and said, "I will be back as soon as I can."

"Mom?" Trevor called after her.

Jesse turned back. "Please let me say goodbye to him before. Before, you know." Trevor's voice was small, and her heart broke.

"Of course. I will be back as soon as I can." She blew him a kiss.

"You want to take a walk? See if we can find any more raisin machines?" Sarah was hoping to keep the boy busy and his mind off of things.

"Okay." He took Sarah's hand as they began to walk away.

"Well first we need to let Carl and Maxine know where we are going. Then we can explore." They set off and met up with Maxine.

Sarah raised an eyebrow when she saw Carl on the phone. "Landscapers?" She remembered their discovery this morning.

"No, not yet," Maxine answered. "He was going to give them another hour and then call back. I have a feeling it's one of them. How on earth would Stone know where the family was?" All this was said in hushed tones to avoid oversharing with the young boy who was now tugging at Sarah's sleeve. A sleeve she had yet to change since yesterday. Gross. They headed off to explore the hospital. They were not to leave the building.

Chapter 46

Jesse slipped in just as the doctor was finishing up. "So, we will extubate him after you've all had some time with him. It should be quick, peaceful." Jesse sidled up to Steven and put her hand in his. He gave it a firm squeeze and didn't let go. When the doctor left, the air went still. The machines were no longer beeping, but the wheezing of the ventilator continued, like a slow march.

Tanner was the first to talk. "Remember that time Dad caught us trying to slip the bottle of rum into our bags when we went back to school?" He and Steven chuckled. "How were we supposed to know it was some sort of collector's item worth something like 500 bucks? Thought he was going to blow a gasket!"

Steven sighed. "Instead, he switched it with a cheap bottle. I couldn't believe it!"

"He did what?" Their mother turned with a look of surprise that made them all laugh.

"Yeah, we took it before he could change his mind." Tanner reminisced. "The next weekend, me, Steven, and a few friends ended up in the clinic with a nasty 'stomach flu'."

"I still can't stand the smell of it." They shared a laugh, then got quiet again.

"That time, I brought a boy home from college, Frederick. Dad gave him the third degree. Asked him about his plans for the future. Totally freaked him out. We got back to school, never saw the kid again."

"Frederick was a tool, Jane," Steven replied. "He flossed at the dinner table."

"In bed too," Jane giggled.

"TMI," Steven and Tanner said.

"He liked you, Jesse." Tanner looked at his sister-in-law. "You were grounded, and good for Steven."

"He did? Kept calling me Jessica. He couldn't believe anyone would name their child a nickname." Jesse rolled her eyes. "I always thought he wanted someone more sophisticated for his son."

The family told stories, laughed, and cried. When the stories tapered off, Jesse spoke up. "Um, I think Trevor would like to say goodbye. When do you think is a good time?"

Jane reached over and whispered to Tanner. "Will Tonya make it with the kids?" Tanner's wife was on her way from Florida. She had taken the kids for a vacation while Tanner went on a business trip.

Tanner shrugged his shoulders. "They missed their connection."

"Do you want to wait for them?" The nurse had stepped in quietly with the pastor. "This is a rare instant where you can choose."

Tanner just shook his head. "No, I think it would be better if we didn't prolong...this."

Steven looked at his brother. "We can, Tan, it's important for everyone to be okay with this." Jane reached for her brother's hand.

"No," he repeated. "I don't want to be the reason he suffers for a minute more." Tanner excused himself and Jane went after him.

The pastor reassured Lillian that it was all normal. For kids, young or old, to have a hard time dealing with their feelings at a time like this. She suggested that they go get a drink, or some fresh air and come back to say the last goodbyes. Funny how the advice from a perfect stranger is followed so easily. The family stepped out, except for Lillian. She wanted some time alone.

Jane found Tanner outside, standing mutely by a bench near the Emergency entrance. Sirens were getting closer, and they saw an ambulance go around the corner to the receiving bay. She sent a silent prayer to the person and their family. She found herself praying a lot lately. Tanner shook off her hand. "This sucks. Totally sucks. Why did the last time I spoke with Dad have to be an argument over where we would spend the Fourth?"

The Fourth of July was the start to the summer season. Families flocked to the lake to enjoy the fireworks and the parade. That was his father's favorite summer event. This year, Tonya wanted to visit her parents in Arizona. Tanner didn't care where they went, he would be working remotely anyway. That conversation took place a week ago.

"Tanner, we all fought with him. He could be difficult, we all know that." Jane was trying her best to relieve him of some of the guilt. She felt herself breaking down too.

"I'm sorry for being so selfish." Tanner grabbed his sister in a long hug. "He loved you. Kept a bunch of those art projects at the office, you know."

Jane looked up at him. "Really?"

"Really, even the sculpture that looks like a naked clown." A laugh escaped his lips. Jane kicked him lightly in the shin and they stood there sharing a combined laugh-cry.

Behind them, two men got out of a truck. "The emergency room is through here," the driver said. Jane raised her head and listened.

"Thank you for the ride," the other replied, "I should be okay from here. I sure do appreciate all of your help." Jane had a weakness for accents and looked up to see the man rushing in. No one showed up to the emergency room looking their best, but this guy looked ready to drop. His clothes didn't seem to fit right and the baseball cap on his head looked like it had blood on it. Tanner and Jane watched as other people filed into the hospital.

"You ready to go back?" Tanner was asking his sister when they both turned to a frantic knocking on the window. Trevor was standing on a low bench just inside. He was calling their names. The policewoman was behind him, ready to catch him if he fell.

Trevor's auntie and uncle joined them inside. "You guys okay?" Sarah asked, concern on her face.

"Just getting some air. Hey there, Bud." Tanner knelt down to talk to his nephew. "I think your mom and dad want to see you."

"Wumpy okay?"

"He's still here," Jane reassured. They each took a hand and led the boy back to the ICU.

Chapter 47

Matt went directly to the reception desk in the ER. "A man, he just arrived in an ambulance. He has a head wound?"

"Name?" The woman behind the desk barely looked up.

"Um, Red. He was just brought in. Can I see him?"

"Last name or first?" She snapped her gum as her hands hovered over the keyboard.

"I don't know his last name, or even what Red is short for."

She looked up, managing to look down her long nose at the same time. "You two close?" The sarcasm was dripping but he ignored it.

"Listen, I've only known him for a few days, staying in one of his cabins. He's old, blind, and as far as I know, he doesn't have any family. When he wakes up, he isn't going to know where he is or why." Matt pulled off his cap and ran his fingers through his hair. He felt a dry clump of blood and wondered how it got there.

"Mary, he's with us." The gruff voice of the older policeman came from around the corner. Matt quickly replaced the hat, pulling it low to cover his eyes. Side stepping the desk he followed the cop back through a maze of doors and curtains. From behind one of them he heard a woman describing the pain in her stomach like a "ten-inch knife coming right through her belly button." Next door a child was crying, and its mother tried to soothe it. In front of him was a curtain that was partially open. Red was there, a doctor, a nurse, and the EMTs were around him. They must have just transferred him to the bed because the bloody stretcher had been pushed into the hall. The officer spoke up. "This is his friend. The one with him when it happened." He pushed Matt closer, and the doctor turned to talk with him.

"Can you tell me what happened?" Red was groaning, the IV draining clear liquid into his thin arm. Matt hoped there were pain killers in there. His tee shirt wrap had been replaced with gauze and tape, but Red's face still had specks of dried blood on it. Someone had cleaned him up hastily.

"We were fishing. Red was ready to go back, so I pulled the anchor. It got caught on something, so I pulled harder. I don't know if the rope broke, or if it just pulled free. Somehow the anchor came flying through the air. Red couldn't see it of course, and it caught him square in the forehead."

"Was he conscious after, at all?" The doctor was taking notes on a clipboard.

"No, at least not when I was with him, maybe on the way here?" Matt looked to the EMTs. They shook their heads.

"Okay, so unconscious for at least half an hour to forty-five minutes, that fair to say?" Matt just nodded. "They tell me he is blind. We have no ID. You have no idea what his full name is?" Matt shook his head. "He tell you if he had any other problems, diabetes, heart?"

"No, I'm sorry. I just met him. Said something about cholesterol, maybe arthritis. I'm staying at one of his cabins. We were fishing. He asked me to take him." Matt rattled off the information and tried to step closer, but the policeman stopped him.

"We still need some information for our report," he said to Matt. Then he turned to the doctor. "Can I talk to him for a bit?" The man in the white coat just turned and ordered a few tests for Red. "Put him in as a John Doe for now." He glanced back at Matt with a curious look.

Matt allowed himself to be led into a small room with a door. There, the officer leaned against the wall. "You being straight with me? Just out fishing, barely know the guy. That's all there is to this?" Matt was familiar with the tone. They thought he had done something wrong.

"Look, I just came into town a couple of days ago." He decided to stick with the same story he told Red. "I needed to get a way. Divorced my wife, had to clear my head. Drove north to try to find some peace."

"Drove north from where?"

"South Carolina, Greenville. I was looking for a change of scenery." Matt brought his hands to his head to rub his temples. Partially to try to stave off the headache that was bearing down on him and partially to conceal his face from the nosy cop.

He was watching Matt closely. "So, Greg Johns, from South Carolina. You have any ID?"

"No, not here. It's back at the cabin. Didn't want it to get wet." He was starting to sweat again. The questions, the doubt, that hospital smell...it was all getting to him again. A migraine was fast approaching.

If he didn't get to his medicine soon, he could end up on a stretcher too.

"You okay? You're not going to pass out on me again?" Judgment was behind the fake concern.

"No, I don't think so. I get migraines. Horrible ones. My medicine is back at the cabin too. Listen, can I check on Red? I don't want him to wake up and be confused." The cop was conflicted. There was nothing to suggest that any foul play had occurred, but there was something about the guy. Had he been on time today he would have gotten the BOLO. But as usual, he coasted in just as his shift started and skipped the morning meeting.

"Let me check with the doctor and see how he is doing. You stay right here." Matt could hear the hushed conversation down the hall. But he couldn't make any of it out. Should he run? But where the hell would he go? That would make him look guilty of something. How would be get back to his car? He heard a voice cutting through the noises of the emergency room.

"Is that Red? Red? What the hell happened to you?" A woman in her fifties wearing scrubs walked down the hall, passing through Red's curtain.

"You know this guy?" the doctor asked.

"Sure, see him at the pavilion in Alton Bay for the summer concerts. He walks up there by himself and listens to the bands. Used to come with his wife, Celia. But she died sometime back. What happened?" Matt had peeked his head around the door and saw her fussing over the old man.

"Do you know his full name and perhaps any history?"

"Yeah, Red, short for Redman. His first name is Paul. He's been running a bunch of cabins down there for as long as I can remember. When Celia died, we all figured he would sell. Too much for him to keep up with when his sight started to go. But he stayed." She was lifting up a corner of his dressing. She let out a whistle. "By God, he must have twenty stitches. What happened?" She stepped away back into the hall and asked again.

"Fishing accident, got hit with the anchor. A friend got him to shore, and they called the ambulance from there. I am worried about infection. Any idea if he's allergic to antibiotics?" The woman shrugged her shoulders.

Another nurse had joined them. "He's starting to come around, doctor." They all disappeared behind the curtain. Matt stepped into the hall to try to hear some more. He couldn't make sense of the terms they were using but could hear Red asking where he was.

"Hate the smell of hospitals. Why am I here?" he demanded. "Where's Greg, what happened?" The doctors spoke to him again, but Matt couldn't make it out. "Ginny, that you?"

"Yes, Red, it's me. Missed me so much you had to come and visit?" Ginny must be the woman's name Matt figured. "How you feeling, old man?"

"Head hurts. What happened?" Red was insistent.

"Apparently you took an anchor to the head while you were fishing. You know they make small hooks for these lake fish." Ginny teased her friend but was using the conversation to gauge the level of his injuries. "You remember what day it is?"

"Of course, Thursday." The doctor and Ginny raised their eyebrows.

"What month?"

Red jumped. "Damn! Don't sneak up on an old blind guy like that! You'll give me a heart attack!" The young doctor mumbled an apology. "June twelfth, the day my Celia passed."

Ginny turned to the ER doctor. "I think he's going to be fine. Full of piss and vinegar, like usual."

"Well, that's not very technical, but it sounds promising. Now, Mr. Redman, I have some questions." Ginny promised to check back in on her friend and stepped behind the curtain with the crying child.

Matt closed his eyes and leaned against the wall. Thank God, Red was going to be okay. Now he just had to figure out his next step. Looking for the cop, he walked to the left then the right. He was nowhere to be found. So, he let himself into Red's room, curtained space, whatever it was and cleared his throat. The nurse looked up. The doctor was checking out the old man, peppering him with questions.

"Can I help you?" she inquired.

"I'm his friend. I was with him when it happened."

"Greg!" Red sat up, pushing the doctor's hand away. "You okay?" Red had no idea that it was him who sent the anchor flying.

"I'm fine. I'm just glad you are." Matt edged closer.

"Gonna have a hell of a scar though," Red said. "Don't know if I can handle seeing it in the mirror every day. Oh, silver lining! I can't see." He joked. "Celia probably would have found it manly." He looked toward the window as if to conjure up her image in his mind. He didn't speak for a few minutes.

"I heard you saying it was the anniversary of her death. I didn't know. I'm sorry." Matt sat down in a chair near the bed.

"Yeah, we used to go fishing each year together. Just once. Her and me that is. She never understood what the appeal was but went with me once each year. Now, I try to get someone to take me. Thank you."

Matt didn't feel he should be thanked for anything at that moment. He put the man in the hospital. "You're welcome, I guess. Sorry 'bout your head though."

"Hell, it was an accident. No worries. Hey, doc, can I get some pain killers?" Red turned to where the man was standing. "I'm not a wuss, but this is a demon." Pointing to the bandages, Red leaned back farther into the pillows. The doctor ordered medication for the pain and said he would need to stay for observation overnight. Red reluctantly agreed. "Hey, Greg, you watch over the place for me?"

Matt nodded. "Of course. I'll come back and check on you later."

He left the emergency room wondering just how he was going to get back to the cabin.

Chapter 48

Trevor, Jane, Tanner, and Sarah rode the elevator up to see Andrew. There was no conversation. Tanner and Jane didn't know what to say to their young nephew. A small part of Tanner was glad that he didn't need to juggle his own kids while trying to deal with his father's death. When the doors opened, Jesse and Steven were there to greet them.

"Carl wants to talk to you," Steven said to Sarah. "They went to get coffee."

She turned to go, stopped. "I can't leave Trevor though."

"He'll be with us, all of us. It will be okay for a few minutes." Jesse was eager to have her go so they could talk to Trevor privately. Once she was out of sight, she knelt down. "Hey, honey, we have to talk."

Trevor's lips trembled. His eyes filled quickly. "Wumpy's dead, isn't he?" His voice was rising. Steven sat down on the floor and took him into his arms.

"Hey, no. Not yet. But he will be. Soon." He pulled away so he could look him in the eye. "Do you think you want to say goodbye to him?" Trevor's reaction shocked them all.

"No! No! NO!" He jumped up, balled his fists, and continued to scream. "He can't die! It's not fair. It's the Badman's fault. Everything was good until he came!" Then he turned and bolted. Jesse and Steven scrambled to their feet but not before they saw the door to the elevator close.

"The stairs!" Jesse pointed to the door on the right. Steven fumbled with the knob and, when he finally pulled it open, slammed it against the wall. They took the stairs two at a time. Three flights tumbled by. Jesse felt a stab of pain when she slammed her hip into the railing. She ignored it and kept going. Trevor needed her. They burst through the door near the lobby. He was nowhere in sight. Steven called out to an attendant at the information desk. "You see a little boy come through here?"

He looked up. "Not that I saw. He lost?" As the man reached for the phone, Jesse saw him down the hall.

"There he is." They called his name, but he didn't stop. Trevor turned a corner and was out of sight again. They picked up their speed. People were staring.

A cleaning woman heard them yell and saw the boy. Putting it together quickly she dashed after him. "Hey there, sonny?" she called. When she caught up to him, she tapped him on the shoulder. The boy turned and looked up at her with the prettiest blue eyes she had ever seen. "I think your parents are looking for you." Jesse and Steven were just feet away.

A young couple just ahead had stopped as well, they were walking back to the cleaning lady and the boy, who was very confused. "Mom, Dad? This lady says you're looking for me."

Jesse and Steven pulled up short. It wasn't Trevor. Just another boy about his size, with blond hair. He wasn't even wearing the same clothes that Trevor had on. "It's not him." Jesse's hand flew to her mouth.

"Trevor!" She started to cry. "Where did he go? He must be so upset." A security guard caught up to them and began asking questions. Once it seemed they were not needed, Eli and Shannon took Tyler and went to find Greg. Shannon had followed them to the hospital to offer whatever support she could. With a tight grip on their little boy's hand, they made their way to the check in counter.

Chapter 49

Trevor ran. He saw the door to the elevator closing and he slipped in. If he wasn't there, his grandfather couldn't die. He just couldn't. So, he would run. Away from his parents. Away from the stupid hospital. Tears were running down his face and he wiped them as he ran. His breathing was ragged, and he was losing steam. He had no idea where he was. Trevor stopped to look for a hiding place. Making a slow turn, he saw a closet. He could hide there and then Wumpy couldn't die. Across the room a man stopped dead in his tracks. The baseball cap covered some of Matt's face and the beard was gone. The long wild hair had been cut and he looked like any other visitor.

****

Matt stopped in his tracks. Tommy? He clenched his fists to the point of almost making them bleed. He watched as Tommy rushed to a door and tried the handle. It would not turn so he stomped his little foot on the ground and looked around. Matt stepped behind a column. When he peered out again, his son was heading for the exit. Matt followed. Tommy was here. How? Why? He didn't care. In an instant he was thrown back into the past. He and Tommy out running errands. All sense of the here and now was gone.

The boy was looking up and down the drive, just as a delivery truck rolled to a stop. Fran's Flowers, Fresh,

Fancy, Fast. The flower-covered truck sat at an idle while the driver ran a bouquet inside. Without thinking, Matt ran out the door and scooped up the boy. "Tommy!" Matt hugged him so tight, no one could have heard the muffled cries. When the brown eyes looked up and saw Matt's face, it took a minute to register. Before the child could scream, Matt opened the driver's side door and plunked the child into the passenger seat. Then followed him into the vehicle, pushing the automatic lock, and putting the truck in gear. The truck peeled out of the entrance. Tommy was kneeling on the seat, banging on the windows. "Mommy! Daddy! Help!" On the main road, Matt turned left, trying to remember which way Eli had driven them. Tommy was crying in his seat. The look on his face was almost unbearable. Why was Tommy freaking out? Ignoring the cries and little fists beating at his arms, Matt drove on. He just kept saying, "It's okay, Daddy's here now." Anyone who had seen them might assume the driver had to take his unruly child along with him on the route. When Trevor tried to open the door that led to the back Matt scolded him, "Tommy! Sit down, put your buckle on. Right now." With fear in his eyes, Tommy slid down and slowly pulled the buckle across his lap. The tears kept coming, and Matt tried to figure out what was happening.

****

Sarah, Carl, and Maxine were running to the lobby where a crowd had gathered. In the middle, Steven was holding Jesse and was trying to explain to the security man that Trevor got upset and ran away from them because he didn't want his grandfather to die. A tall, thin man in a starched white shirt and blue polyester pants was trying to take charge. The radio on his shoulder was crackling away. Carl broke into the center and raised his voice and badge at the same time. "Excuse me! Excuse me! Quiet down." The man in the security uniform saw the shield and gladly yielded control.

"What's going on?" he demanded from Steven and Jesse.

"He ran from us. He got upset, scared. Jumped into an elevator, and just disappeared." Steven was trying to hold on but was losing his grip. "Where were you?" he yelled, accusing the agents and giving an especially scathing look at Sarah, who just minutes before he had told he could watch his own son. Sarah swallowed the retort at the tip of her tongue. She had broken protocol; it was her job to keep an eye on Trevor. She held her ground though inside she felt like crying.

Carl grabbed the security man who was slowly retreating to the outer edge of the group. "Issue a Code Adam or code pink, whatever you use here, no one in or out until we find the boy." He turned to Maxine and Sarah. "You two, outside, check the perimeter." They left at a run. Sarah left; Max went right. Sarah's badge was hanging by a lanyard around her neck. The bouncing annoyed her, so she pushed it aside. They were calling Trevor's name. A family was gathered peacefully underneath a tree visiting with a woman in a wheelchair. Startled they all looked up.

"You need help?" A tall red-headed man joined Sarah as she jogged, looking in the bushes. Before she could brush him off, he showed her his badge. "I'm on the job. What's up?"

"Missing boy, age six, blond hair, brown eyes. Blue shirt, jean shorts." Coming around the corner to another entrance her heart jumped. "There he is!" She pointed to a child just inside leaning against a window. She pulled at the door, but it wouldn't budge. The lock down. Damn, she banged on the glass panel nearest him. She could hear the announcement over the loudspeakers, "Code Adam. Code Adam. Six-year-old male, blond hair, brown eyes. Please report." The boy turned to her banging. Her heart sank again. "It's not him!" They continued their search, checking bushes, and in between cars. Sirens could be heard in the distance.

Inside, Tanner, Jane, and Lillian had joined the crowd. Andrew was forgotten at the moment, everyone was near panic. "Does he ever hide at home? When he's mad, or scared?" Carl was multitasking, alternately speaking to the family and hospital staff. "Every room, every exit. We will need the security tapes." The head of security, who had met them the day before, was now in front of the agent, asking how he could help. A sheepish assistant stood by, typing frantically at her tablet. Reports were coming in from different wings of the hospital. "NICU, clear. Telemetry, clear. Cafeteria, clear." With each announcement, Carl felt his blood pressure rise. He called Maxine. "Anything?" He sounded calm, but his heart was pounding.

"Negative. Nothing. He's not outside."

Damn, Carl thought, this better just be the kid hiding. What if Stone found him? But how? Scenarios ricocheted in his mind. He cleared them, and training took over. Focusing on the task at hand, he ordered the family to go in a small sitting area off to the right. He told one of the security men to stay with them. "Please, all of you stay there. The hospital is in lock down. The child can't get out." The words came with confidence he really didn't have. He was hoping the boy had gotten outside and was either wandering or hiding in a bush or something. They just needed to catch up with him.

Mr. Davidson took the tablet being held out to him by his assistant. The security tapes. The screen was split into four images. Each one was trained on an entrance. The ambulance bay, inpatient, outpatient, and a service entrance. His eyes flicked back and forth. Then it switched to four new images. This scrolled, showing the past ten minutes of activity at each door. A valet stepped forward, with a tall skinny acne faced teen.

"Excuse me, Mr. Davidson?" The man in the suit spun around.

"What?" Impatient and worried, he didn't need any interruptions.

"This man said his delivery truck is gone. He left it by the curb to bring in an..." Before she could finish, Carl cut in, "What door?"

"Inpatient. All patient deliveries have to come..." Again, he cut her off.

To the assistant he barked out, "Pull up that door, full screen." She took the tablet back and tapped the screen a couple of times. Carl looked at the tablet over her shoulder. When he tapped the forward button, the assistant handed the pad to him. The screen sped up. "There!" He pointed to the bottom of the screen. Trevor walked out of the automatic doors and stopped for a moment. The small child looked both ways, as if ready to cross the street. Without warning, he was picked up off of the ground and brought to the chest of his captor.

It was a man in grey sweatpants and a dark blue tee shirt. The baseball cap obscured a clear view of his face. They disappeared from the screen.

Carl played it back again. Although it didn't look like Stone, the mangy man who tried to grab Trevor at the school, it did look like the picture of the man before he shot his son. He took a screen shot of the frame and turned again to hospital staff. "Exterior cameras?"

The assistant timidly leaned in and tapped a few screens. Images of the driveways flickered on the tablet. "The quality isn't as good. We are waiting on upgrades." A look sent to the chief of staff seemed to allude to the fact that this was not a new subject. "Here's the view to the exit the boy took."

Fran's Fresh Flowers delivery van crossed the screen as it came to a stop. A few moments later a young man stepped out holding a giant bouquet. Carl could see Trevor's feet at the edge of the screen. The boy stepped forward until he was in full view. The anger and confusion were clear on his face. But soon it was replaced by fear as his head was tucked into the man's shoulder and he was taken to the idling vehicle. Even without a clear picture of the man's face, there was no question for Carl. It was Stone.

A cry from behind him startled the already edgy group. Jesse was being held back by her husband as they gaped at the picture, now frozen on the device. "Trevor!" She crumpled to the floor where her husband tried to console her while asking the officers what the hell they were doing standing around. Confusion broke out again as demands and accusations flew. A high-pitched whistle stopped them all.

It was the quiet assistant. In any other circumstance this might have been comical, but the look on her face was dead serious. "Look, here," she tapped a few commands onto the computer and new pictures appeared. She pointed to another view, from a camera at the corner of the building. "See? The truck turned left."

Carl sent her a grateful glance. The local police were arriving at that time. The chief of staff called off the Code Adam, leaving most to assume the child had been found. He asked for the family to again be escorted to a private room nearby. "I promise, I will be right in to update you. I need to coordinate with the locals to find him quickly." They left, Steven basically carrying Jesse at this point. He felt like hitting something, someone. Tanner, Jane, and Lillian stood by feeling useless. The reason they had come to the hospital lay forgotten three flights up.

As the agents talked to the local policemen, Sarah slipped away to make a phone call. She had to be the one to tell Joe first. How was she going to? It rang twice before he picked it up. "Did it happen?" Joe was referring to Andrew's passing. At this point that would have been news she would have been happy to share. She swallowed hard. "Joe, there's been a development." She leaned her head against the windowpane. He waited. "Um, Stone was here."

"What? How the hell?" He was stammering.

"He got him, Joe. Somehow, he found us and took Trevor." She was on the verge of tears herself. This was preventable. Her responsibility.

"How, Sarah? There are agents, and you are there to watch him. Never mind the whole damn family." She could hear him throw something and it land with a smash.

"Trevor got upset, managed to run off and slip into an elevator. The doors closed before anyone could get to him." Conveniently leaving out her role in it. Or more precisely, her lack of a role in it. "Stone was in the hospital. We had no idea he was here or how he found us. He just took him." She held her breath, waiting for more yelling or throwing of things.

A full minute went by, and she checked to see if he had hung up on her. "Sarah, what are they doing? Can I talk to Carl?"

She looked over at the FBI agent, who looked like he was gaining control. "He's crazy busy at the moment. I don't think he wants to hear anything from me."

"How's Jesse? Steven? They must be going nuts."

"She's upset, obviously, Steven is pissed. Yelled at me. Not that I didn't deserve it." Sarah banged her head against the window.

"Sarah, no time for blame, there needs to be a plan. Have Carl call me as soon as he can." Joe was making plans himself. As soon as they got off the phone, he was heading to New Hampshire.

"I'm so sorry, Joe," the apology fell on dead air. He had hung up. Pulling her shoulders up, she went to check on the family.

Chapter 50

Tommy had gone quiet. His legs were pulled up to his chest and silent tears rolled down his cheeks. Matt was talking to himself, trying to figure out what to do. "I need to find a place to get rid of this truck. Stands out too much." His mind battled back and forth. On one level he was aware that he was doing something horribly wrong. But on another, he had another chance with Tommy. Wouldn't that be the only reason they would meet again? If it wasn't meant to be, then he wouldn't have been in the hospital at the exact same time. His eyes darted from one side of the road to the other. There had to be a place he could pull off and not be seen. Thinking he would have luck again in a parking lot, he pulled into a lot of what looked like a mini mall made into a church. "Haven Saints United" a hand painted sign welcomed all for services on Sundays. Next door to that was a laundry mat. Matt watched while trying to comfort the boy. "It's okay, son, everything will be all right."

"I'm not your son." The words shot out of the little mouth like venom. "I am Trevor Andrew Reed. You are not my father!" Tiny fists hit at the big man. Tears and spittle splattered Matt's face as the boy lashed out. "I want to go home!"

Matt closed his eyes and saw Tommy, crying at a friend's birthday party. He was afraid of the clown that

was hired to entertain the children. He had cried out
those words, 'I want to go home,' repeatedly until Matt
apologized and left. Matt gently took the small hands
and held them between his. He patted the curly head
and shh-ed him like he had Tommy. The child
continued to cry and try to break away.

A woman drove up to the laundry mat and stepped
out of her car. Her head was bopping up and down to
music coming from her ear buds. Going around to the
back, she opened the trunk and unloaded her clothes.
When she entered the laundromat, the trunk was left
open. Without a second thought Matt dashed out of the
truck, Tommy in arms, and ran to the car. Looking into
the storefront, he could see the driver was busy loading
her clothes in a machine. He placed Tommy in the
trunk, promising he would be okay and that it wouldn't
be long. Shutting the lid, he walked around to the
driver's side door and drove away.

A moment later, the woman came out to find her
car missing. "What the hell?" she said to the empty lot.
She ran over to the flower truck to see if the driver had
seen anything, it was empty. She reached for her phone
to call the police only to remember it was sitting in her
purse on the floor of her car. "Dammit!" The woman
pulled out her earphones and kicked the side of the
truck. She ran back to the laundromat to make the call.
Of course, the pay phone on the wall was out of order.
The attendant was also missing. Did she take the car?
The lady was such a bitch. Always complaining that
customers overloaded her washers, causing them to
break down. So, the young woman ran next door and
tried the church next door. No one was there either. The
van didn't have anything in it but flowers. She sat on

the curb and cried hoping the delivery man would come back soon.

Matt drove as fast as he dared in the stolen car. While he wanted to get away, he needed to be inconspicuous as possible. He took the road that wound around the lake hoping it would bring him back to the cabin. He had no idea if the cops had figured out where he was staying. Hopefully Red was heavily medicated and unable to talk. He would have to be discreet and check out the place before going in. The windy road made the trip longer, but it was the only way he could get back. Matt looked in the mirror and saw the desperate man he had been a few days ago. Fleeing and in fear of going to jail. What the hell was going on? Was Tommy in the trunk? Why? Where was he going?

He put on the brakes, pulled off the road, and walked to the back of the car. When there were no cars in sight, he opened the trunk. There he saw a child, a shadow of his own son. Lying on a blue comforter and holding his head, which was now bleeding. When Matt stopped so quickly, the boy must have hit it on something. The little boy glared at Matt and cried harder. "You hurt me!" The words, so reminiscent of those uttered by Tommy just before he died, struck Matt in the heart. He saw his son, crumpled in a heap, blood seeping between his fingers. His head swam, the boy just stared at him. Panic closed in around him. Memories attacked, as vicious as the real thing. He could see Carol and the men beating her, the policemen questioning him over and over again after Carol, and then again after Tommy. But his son was right there with him now. None of it mattered if he could have his Tommy again.

Matt reached in and stroked Tommy's cheek. "We'll be home soon, buddy, real soon." But the boy was scared and pulled away. As Matt continued to talk to him, he squeezed back farther in the trunk, trying to get away. The sound of tires on the gravel behind him nearly gave Matt a heart attack. He turned to see another motorist coming to a stop. Where was he? Why was Tommy in a trunk? Like a slap in the face, he remembered the fire alarm at the school, running away. He needed to get rid of this guy and fast.

Matt casually closed the trunk and walked over to the man. "Hi there," his voice much calmer than he was.

"Car trouble?" The driver had rolled down his window, his own truck sputtering and coughing, threatening to die on the spot.

Matt looked back at the stolen car praying that Trevor would stay quiet. "No, just a jug of water rolling around. Driving me crazy. Needed to secure it. But thanks." Matt turned to walk away.

"Hey there." Matt turned back, heart in his throat. "Go slow, there are cops everywhere." With a friendly wave, the stranger pulled back onto the road and drove off. Matt waited until he heard the last of the wheezing vehicle and returned to his car. Matt leaned against the trunk. Cops, everywhere. They were looking for him and were probably close. He needed to get moving. He lifted the trunk lid again. "Just hang on. Be quiet, and everything will be okay.

Chapter 51

Joe was frantically making arrangements to cover his shifts and get on the road. Warren would come in for today and Daniels tomorrow. If he needed more time than that, he would figure it out later. He made a quick call to Price who agreed it couldn't hurt if he went up there and sent him back to his house to grab a bag. His phone rang and he answered, expecting Carl to be calling to explain what was going on. "Marchand." He was glad he had hands free, because he was driving fast and needed both hands on the wheel.

"Joe, I mean Sergeant Marchand? It's Karen, Karen Copeland." A silence hung for a moment. "Anything happening with the case?" She could feel that something was wrong even without him saying anything.

"Um, Karen. I can't talk right now." Joe didn't want to be rude, but he didn't want to tell her the details quite yet. Was that her driving on the other side of the road?

"Hey? Is that you?" Joe saw her car slow down as they approached each other. She held up a hand in a small wave. "Can you pull over?" Her head turned as he flew in the opposite direction.

"Uh, no. Got something I have to take care of." He shouldn't say anything to her but found himself spitting it out in a rush. "Karen, Stone has him. Took Trevor

295

right out of the hospital where he was visiting his grandfather. I'm going up there now."

Joe heard her gasp followed by the screech of tires turning at a high speed. He checked his rearview mirror, but she wasn't there. Yet. But she was peppering him with questions. "What? How? The family. They must be so scared. Is Trevor okay?"

"We don't know. Jesse must be going crazy. I can't believe this is happening. I have to be there." He was pulling into his driveway.

"I'll go with you," she was saying as he jogged into the house.

"No, that's not a good idea. I can call you with any details." Joe needed both hands now to get ready. "Hey I gotta go. I'll call you when I'm on the road." He didn't wait and hung up.

****

Karen looked at her phone. It was dead. Really? She had almost caught up with him and saw him turn off. When she saw his truck in a driveway, she pulled up to his mailbox and boldly got out. Dialing his number again, she waited until he picked up. "Why not? I wouldn't be in the way. Maybe I could help." She stood next to her car and waited.

He cleared his throat. "No, you can't. It wouldn't be right. Listen, I gotta go. I will call, I promise." She could hear the exhaustion in his voice and almost got back into her car.

"I've come this far," she spoke to the sky. Grabbing her bag from her car, she quickly walked over to his and let herself in. She was sitting in the passenger's seat when Joe came back out.

He rushed over and jumped in throwing his bag on top of her. Joe almost screamed when they came face to face. "What are you doing here?" He looked through his rear windshield and saw her car by the curb. The look on his face was thoroughly annoyed for the first few seconds. Then it slowly changed to slightly amused. "You can't come with me."

"Who said?" Karen sounded a lot more confident than she felt.

"Me, common sense, probably every rule in the book!" Joe hit the steering wheel. "Really, Karen, you can't come. You could get hurt. I will be distracted." He raised his eyebrows, pleading with her.

"I distract you?" Karen was pleased to at least distract him. She smiled. "Once we get there, you won't even know I am there. I'll just fade into the background."

"You could never fade. Trust me," he said with a flash of a smile. Then he looked at his watch. It had already been forty-five minutes since he talked to Sarah. Plus, another two or more hours up there. Against all of his better judgement he relented. "Okay. You can come. But there will be rules." He was already backing out. "First thing, we have no time to stop for your stuff and we are driving straight there."

She nodded her head. "Okay, that's not a problem," pointing to her bag near her feet.

He continued. "You will not talk to the family or any other officers. The FBI is there, and they will not be happy I brought you along. And most importantly, you will not print anything before we talk, and I okay it." The look he shot her gave her no other option than to agree. And since she didn't really have an outlet for her stories at the moment, she nodded.

"Girl Scout's honor," Karen held up three fingers and crossed her heart. Their conversation was cut short when his phone rang again.

"Marchand." He held the phone close, driving with one hand, so she couldn't hear anything. Still, she listened to his side of the conversation. "Yeah, I know." Silence. "What is happening now?" A pause. "How is the family?" Pause. "Can I talk to her? Or Steven?" A few minutes went by. He drove with an intensity that half scared, half thrilled her. Within minutes they were pulling onto Route 95. He sped up and went right to the fast lane. Cars on their right were just blurs of colors. A few motorists honked their horns and flashed their lights. Joe reached under his dash and pressed a switch. Cars in front of them pulled to the right. He must have dash lights. Karen reached up to make sure her seatbelt was tight.

"Steven? It's Joe." Silence. "I know. I am so sorry. They are doing everything they can." Karen could hear the man's voice coming through the phone. Joe held the device away from his ear, while the man ranted. She understood, anyone would be pissed. She glanced at the dashboard. They were going 90 miles per hour. Holy shit. Joe was trying to calm the father down. "I am on my way up. Will be there as soon as I can. You need to be calm, for Jesse, for Trevor." The father must be saying something, because Joe was quiet for a long time. There was a lot of umm hums, and I knows. He was using his calming policeman voice now. It seemed to be working. Then he asked to speak to Sarah. She came on, and his voice changed again. "Sarah, tell me what's going on. What do they have in place?" He listened intently, maneuvering the car deftly around a vehicle that managed to miss the flashing lights and ignore his horn. That driver received the same look Karen had been given about twenty minutes earlier. She almost felt sorry for the man. Joe was finishing with Sarah. "Okay, sounds like they are doing what they should. We are on our way."

Being in such closed quarters, she heard the voice on the other end go up. "We? Who is with you?" Karen waited to see what Joe would say. He gave no more information.

"ETA... 2:30ish. Call me if anything changes." He hung up and went back to his quiet place as they drove in silence. Karen was mentally composing a headline for the latest development. "Boy Taken by Bold Stalker." No. "Grieving Family Faced with Tragedy." No, the grandfather isn't dead, they aren't grieving yet. Jesus, that was cold. Karen gave herself a mental spanking. She had always promised that she wouldn't sensationalize to get printed. A well written story should sell itself without gimmicks. "Child Abducted from Hospital." Factual, but sounds like a baby napping. She shook her head; the title will come. She needed the story first.

"You okay?" She reached over to touch Joe's arm, but she held back and let it fall.

Joe looked at her. He was no longer mad, or at least didn't look it. He was worried. Frown lines appeared on his forehead and around his mouth. When he did speak it was soft. "Jesse and I basically grew up together. I became part of the family. Her folks took me in and basically kept me out of juvie." He anticipated the question she wanted to ask. "Yes, we dated. Through high school. I kind of thought we might get married, but she went away to college. We grew apart. She found Steven. That was okay. She was happy." He took a breath. "I stayed close to her family, helped out her parents as they got older, and sick. Losing the Martins was hard, it was like losing my own folks. I promised them that I would always look after Jesse. And I don't like breaking promises." His shoulders sank and his voice cracked. He looked away to hide what Karen believed were tears.

She gave him a minute. "This must be hard. But it's not your fault. No one could know Stone was there. It's too much to believe." This time she did put her hand on his elbow. He looked at it and then away.

"If I had been there this wouldn't have happened." He was angry, hurt, scared and on top of it felt guilty.

"Who knows? We aren't there and don't know how it all went down. I am sure there is a reasonable explanation for how he got so close."

"No, they were there to protect him. And they failed." Joe closed down again. The next hour passed in a near silence. Karen felt like an intruder of his private hell. She really wanted to slide closer and put her arm around his sagging shoulders. But it wasn't the time, and Joe's bag in the middle prohibited it. So, she concentrated on the scenery speeding by. Man, there were a lot of cows and wind turbines out there. And people said she grew up in the middle of nowhere.

Chapter 52

The APB went out for the flower delivery truck. No one had news of it, Stone, or the boy. Jesse was dry heaving in the women's room, Jane rubbing her back. Steven was being held back by Tanner. "You have to stay here. Jesse needs you."

Steven was straining against his brother's grip and mumbling that he would find Trevor and kill the son of a bitch who took him, when Agent Black walked up to him with a phone. "It's Officer Marchand. He wants to talk to you." She handed the frantic man the phone and stood back while he vented his anger. Black was glad it wasn't her on the other end. Steven was screaming into the phone and people were staring. His brother pulled him back into the little room they had been sequestered in. Before they shut the door, Max slipped in and listened. When Steven rose to give the phone to Sarah, she took it from him and left to find the cop. While not calm by any means, Steven was considerably less agitated after the conversation.

Carl was hailing her down and she raised a finger to tell him 'one minute.' Sarah happened to be walking toward her and she passed off the phone. She mouthed 'good luck' and went to see Carl. Carl's face was taking on a reddish hue. He hated not being in control, and this situation went from bad to crap in zero to sixty. Damage control was needed simultaneously with a manhunt for someone who could quickly become very dangerous. She was glad he was the senior agent on this one.

They stepped into the vestibule that Stone and the boy had left through. Carl looked at her and said, "This sucks."

"You're getting all technical on me again." Maxine tried to lessen the tension with humor. It was lost on him.

"We screwed up, both of us. We should have known the situation was too emotional for the family to be counted on. We let our guard down, and now the boy is in trouble."

"I know, but we can beat ourselves up or find him. What's going on as of right now?"

"Every officer in the county has his picture, the description of the van and the boy. Roadblocks are being set up on the major roads."

Maxine interrupted. "I think we would be better served to cover the side streets as well. Has an Amber Alert been sent out?"

"It's in the works. I can't imagine he will stay in the truck too long. It's too noticeable. But then he is either on foot, or he steals another car. All that's hard to do with a kid in tow. If he's trying to replace his son, I can't see him intentionally hurting Trevor. But he is desperate, and desperate people do stupid things." Carl pressed his fingers to his temples. "How are the parents doing?"

"Going crazy, pissed, they want to go look for him themselves. I can't say I blame them. You call Buchanan yet?"

Carl shook his head. "Was really hoping for a quick turnaround so we would not look like such assholes." He stretched his neck from one side to the other. Then walked away without another word. Maxine didn't have to imagine how he felt, her job was on the line as well. Hanging her head, she felt guilty of thinking of herself instead of finding the boy. How did Stone come to be at the hospital? It was entirely possible it was a coincidence that he was there not looking for Trevor, but it was more likely he had somehow found the family. Maybe this guy was smarter than they thought. She caught up with Carl. They decided to print out a stack of pictures and check with the staff. Maybe they had seen something and didn't even realize it.

Within fifteen minutes, pictures were circulating around the hospital. The usual shift change had been delayed due to the Code Adam. So, there were extra staff milling about, trying to understand what happened to the boy as well as pass off their patients to the incoming team. This added to the general mayhem. Meanwhile, Sarah was with the family, trying to calm them down. When Carl passed the doorway, she gave him a weak thumbs up. He would catch up with her later.

One of the security people was also tracking down where Stone had come from. He had to have gotten there somehow, so why would he need to steal the delivery truck? From what they could tell, he had come from the right, which was the Emergency Room. They were pulling those images now. A grainy video showed who they believe to be Matt coming in from the ER entrance alone. He then talks to the clerk and is led to

S. Hilbre Thomson

the bays inside. He must have been there for another patient. A few clicks more show him entering bay 4. Carl asked to speak to the patient but was being given the HIPAA run around.

"Look, I don't want to know why that guy is here. I don't care what's wrong with him. I just need to know what he knows in relation to my suspect." When the administrator shifted from foot to foot trying to decide, Carl merely added, "There's a little boy out there scared to death." He raised his bushy eyebrows and leaned closer. A tactic learned for intimidating witnesses. He found it, and guilt, worked in many situations.

"Okay, follow me. I need to talk to his doctor first." As he walked toward the ER, Carl was hot on his heels. The man looked uncomfortable but let him follow. Maxine watched him go. When she looked outside, she groaned. Channel 9 had just arrived. How the hell did they get here so quickly? She pulled her shoulders taut and went to greet the barbarians.

****

When they entered the little room, the old man was lightly snoring in his bed. A large white gauze wrap covered most of the side of his head. An IV was dripping into his right arm. "What happened to him?" the agent asked.

Red's doctor was with them. "Fishing accident. The anchor cut loose and hit his head. Seventeen stitches, he's here for antibiotics and observation."

"Why was this guy with him?" Carl pushed a photo of Matt in front of the lanky man.

"Um, he's a friend. Brought him in. He's the guy who took that kid?" The doctor squinted at the picture. "Looked different. Paler, and very concerned for Mr.

304

Redman here." This was said while the IV was checked.

"He medicated?" Carl was wondering why the man wasn't waking up. They weren't making any effort to be quiet, yet the man slept on.

Checking the chart, he nodded. "Yes, morphine, he might be groggy, but we can wake him." The doctor leaned down and lightly shook Mr. Redman's shoulder. "Mr. Redman? It's Dr. Orr. This man has some questions for you."

His eyes shot open but didn't seem to focus. Carl attributed it to the meds. "Who's that?" The man tried to push himself up higher on the bed but didn't make any progress.

"It's Dr. Orr, you're at the hospital. You hurt your head."

"I know that. Blind, not dumb," he was tugging at the IV line. "This hurts more than my damn head."

"I will have the nurse come and adjust it. Now this gentleman is from the FBI, and he has a few questions about your friend. The one that came in with you."

"Greg? Why? He didn't mean to. It was an accident." Red was searching for the other man. Needed him to speak to track him.

"Mr. Redman," Carl spoke up.

"Call me Red."

"Okay, Red. This man you call Greg. How do you know him? He a friend of yours?" Carl had pulled out a chair and sat next to the bed.

"Greg? He's staying at my place. Been there a few days. Nice guy. Whaddya want with him?" Red appeared sharp as a tack now. A hint of concern. "Who are you anyway?"

"Oh, I am sorry. I am Special Agent Carl Morris with the FBI. We have been looking for a man named Matthew Stone in conjunction with an ongoing case in Massachusetts."

"What'd he do?" Red's eyes were slits, looking toward Carl with suspicion. "How does he know Greg?"

"We aren't sure. How did Greg pay for his room? He give you a credit card? Did you check ID?" Carl said, catching his mistake as soon as he said it.

"Yeah, I looked at it real close." Red grimaced and smacked his lips. "He paid cash. Kin I get a little somethin' to drink? My mouth feels like lint."

Dr. Orr reached for a small pitcher of water and plastic cup. He went to bring it to Red's lips, and the old man pushed his hands away and took the cup from him. "Not a baby, thank you." There was an edge to the voice. He downed the water and felt for the tray that had been pushed up against the bed. Once the cup was safely on the table he turned back to the agent. He was trying to piece together why they believed Greg knew this Stone guy. "He was just passing through. From down south somewhere. South Carolina."

That made sense to Carl, he would probably have an accent and switching states was easy enough. Especially where this guy wasn't able to check ID and he paid in cash. "Do you have any idea what he was driving?"

Red shook his head. "A smaller car, not too noisy."

"And he was traveling alone? You're sure?" Carl was putting the details together to form an explanation. The most likely one being that Greg and Matt are one and the same. It was becoming evident that Red was not going to be able to give them too much more. They needed to go to the cabin and see if there was anything that would help. "Red, we need to see Greg's car and belongings. We believe that he is connected to the man we are looking for."

"You're gonna go anyway. So, you really don't need my permission." His wry smile let them know he didn't like the situation but couldn't fight it.

He gave them the address. Carl thanked the injured man and was on the phone before he left the room.

As Dr. Orr was leaving, Red called to him. "Hey, why are they looking for this guy?"

"A little boy was kidnapped. Taken right from the hospital. He was here with his family and an FBI escort. Must be some sort of VIP."

"We'll they're barking up the wrong tree. Greg, he was really nice." Red kept the cries he heard coming from Greg's cabin last night to himself.

"Hope so, Mr. Redman. You need anything else?"

"Wouldn't mind something to eat, if that's okay."

"I'll send a nurse in. She will take care of you. We will have a room for you soon.

Red was left wondering if Greg was in trouble or was he actually the trouble? Must have something to do with the nightmares that kept his guest awake at night.

Chapter 53

Matt pulled up to the parking lot of the Lazy Man's Inn. It was quiet. His head was pounding. The medicine was right inside. Banging came from the trunk. Matt turned the car around to back up to his cabin. He called through the trunk lid, "Tommy, I'll be right back. Be quiet and I will get you right out."

"I'm not Tommy!" the muffled voice returned, and the kicking from the inside the trunk continued. Matt looked around. No one was there. He darted into the cabin and pulled his duffle out from behind the bed. Then he glanced around quickly and grabbed his coat and car keys. Stopping at the counter, he took the bag of snacks and a couple bottles of water. He popped two pills for his head and drank half of the first bottle to wash them down. Then he twisted off the top of the other water, broke open a capsule, and emptied it into the bottle. Putting the top back on, he returned to the car shaking the bottle. Tossing the items into the back seat of his car, he approached the trunk of the car he had just stole. He knocked on the lid.

"Hey, there, little guy. Shhh," he waited a second. When it was quiet, he said, "I will let you out, but you have to promise not to scream. I have food and something to drink. We will talk and figure this out." Another moment of silence. He cautiously lifted the lid. The face looking back at him was red with fear and drying blood. Matt reached in and pulled him out. Just the weight of him in his arms brought more memories flooding back. With one smooth movement, he had Tommy settled into the front seat and slid in next to him. He locked all of the doors and kept one hand on boy's leg. "You're okay. I've missed you. But we need to go now, somewhere else. You remember how Daddy told you we could go on an adventure? We're going on one now. You want something to eat? Drink?" He spoke quickly and offered the crumb cakes and water. Tommy's hand snaked out and grabbed the cake. Plastic rustled as it was opened. Tommy took a few small bites before pointing at the water.

Matt took the cap off and handed it over. He hoped the boy would drink enough of it to get the medicine in him. The pills would make him sleepy and then Matt could figure things out. He watched as Tommy took a few big gulps and went back to the cake. Within minutes the crumb cake and half of the water were gone. Matt had left the cabins and was heading north. He needed to get away and out of sight. His eyes flicked back and forth, checking his mirrors and jumping at any oncoming traffic.

If his memory was right, the road went around the lake winding by numerous houses and cabins that were more likely than not empty this early on. Need be, he could pull into one of them, hide the car, and hole up for a while. Tommy sat quietly in the passenger seat, stealing looks at him. After twenty minutes, a little voice startled him, "Who are you?" Then the figure slumped to the side and the boy was asleep. With his head tilted that way, Matt could only see the profile of his long-lost son. A smile crept over his face, and he turned his attention to finding a way out of this.

They drove on, keeping to the speed limit. Matt reached back and put a new baseball cap on his head. That was the best he could do for a disguise at the moment. Matt kept stealing glances at the little boy sleeping next to him. He and Tommy were together again. Everything was going to be okay. With each passing moment Matt was slipping farther into his delusion that he had his son back.

****

Carl and Maxine led the group quietly onto Red's property. There were six cabins, sorely in need of repair, a nasty pool, and a small dock next to a shed. The only sign that anyone was or had been there recently, was a car in front of one of the cabins. The place was shut up tight. Maxine reached over and touched the hood of the car. It was very warm. A thumbs up to Carl meant it had been driven recently. He signaled the assembled group to surround the cabin closest to the vehicle. He had given everyone the strict orders that there would be no shooting because of the child. But they were armed nonetheless, this was a dangerous situation. The boy's safety was number one priority.

The officers crept closer, moving silently like ghosts. To the pair of squirrels that were chattering in a nearby tree there was nothing amiss, but to the officers on the property these were high stakes. Soon there was a person on either side of each window and the door of the small cabin. Their elbows were practically touching, and tensions were high. Not everyone had the full history, and speculation was almost worse than the truth. But the unknown is what kept them on their toes. They peeked through the windows; the curtains were drawn but thin as tissue paper. When Carl and Maxine went through the door, it was easy to see that the place was empty. With a stand down order, the officers leaned on the fences or rocks while the FBI agents checked it out. They were left to wonder where the man had gone. Within minutes, Maxine stepped outside leaving Carl to do a more thorough search and walked to the car. She looked inside, finding nothing. Then she lifted the lid to the trunk. When it sprang open, she saw an indentation on some bedding. It was about the size of a child if he was all curled up. Her stomach seized when she saw a stain the size of an orange, a red smear staring out at her. "Carl!" Her voice brought everyone on the property to attention. All conversation ceased. Carl's footsteps thundered across the small lot. As he approached his partner, he could see the change in her stance. He steeled himself for the worst news.

He wasn't sure this was any better than his worst fear. They spoke in low tones. "There isn't that much blood. Could he have cut himself?" Maxine pulled out her flashlight and waved it around the interior of the trunk. Seven inches above the stain was where the hinge would hang when the lid was down. She took a gloved finger and ran it over the edge of the metal piece. It came back a dark red, blood just starting to dry. "I think he must have hit it here. And then maybe rubbed his head to try to clear the blood?" She looked around. Spotting the chief, she called him over. "We need this whole thing dusted for prints and then a blood sample. And we need it yesterday."

Maxine stepped away to update Sarah back at the hospital. She made it very clear that the Reeds were not to know about the bloodstain. She could tell them that they found where Stone had been staying and were on his trail. It was the truth; they just had no idea where the trail was leading them and if it would bring them back a healthy little boy. They also needed to call Buchanan, now. It was not a call she was looking forward to.

She didn't need to worry any longer, for Carl was holding the phone away from his ear. Max could hear her boss' voice from where she was standing. "Why didn't you call me?"

Carl was holding the phone about a foot from his ear as their boss hollered at him. "A. Giant. Flowered. Truck." Carl saw her and motioned her over. When the conversation got quieter, he switched it to speaker so she could hear everything.

After the verbal spanking, Buchanan was all business. Lucky for them, everything he was telling them to do, they had done. "Okay, so the net had been cast, far and wide. What you need to do is think about all of those empty houses. It is a perfect place for someone to hole up." After a moment, he asked, "How's the family?"

"How you would expect them to be," Maxine offered.

"Okay. Do whatever you can to keep them calm. Tell them we are doing everything to get the boy back."

"Will do, sir." Maxine and Carl hung up and looked at each other, then the people who were obviously listening. Carl cleared his throat. "Okay, so we just got our asses chewed up and spit out. Now let's pick up the pieces and get back to work."

Maxine spoke to Carl off to the side, "Jesus. This is so screwed up. We still employed?" Max raised an eyebrow. Carl shrugged his shoulders.

Chapter 54

Steven and Jesse sat in numbed silence. Their family tried to offer words of hope, but they fell on deaf ears. Each parent was caught in a hopeless loop of questions. Why hadn't they believed their son from the beginning? Why weren't they home more often? What would this man do to their little boy? The need to do something gnawed at them until it physically hurt.

****

In the midst of all of this was Andrew. Lying upstairs, in a room alone, seemingly forgotten. The machines continued to whir and beep in a sad, slow melody. His nurse had come and gone a few times. "It's okay, Andrew. You do what you need to do." She was aware of the drama unfolding downstairs and believed that somewhere deep down, the old man felt their pain and fear. His family was caught in a nightmare far worse than this. She told the other nurses on the floor that Andrew would wait until his family was ready.

****

Lillian fussed around the small waiting room they had been shooed into. Straightening the magazine stacks, she noted they were over a year old. She paced but sensed it was making the kids nervous, so she perched on the edge of a seat. "Why are these seats so uncomfortable when everyone knows whoever is sitting there is likely to be sitting for a long time?" She mused out loud and looked over to her son and daughter-in-law. They were clinging to each other like if they let go, one or both would be sucked out into space. That touch kept them grounded, and it was vital as air. She longed for Andrew to be there, helping her get through this ordeal.

Tanner and Jane had been speaking to Sarah. The young lady looked as torn up as the rest of them. They were nodding and glancing at the parents on the couch. Sarah broke off to take a call, and Tanner excused himself to use the restroom. Jane came and sat near her mother and whispered, "Nothing new."

An elderly woman pushing a cart full of magazines rattled by the door. "You folks need any reading material?" Sarah appeared at her side, pulling the phone away from her ear, she asked the woman to move along.

When the woman and her cart were out of view and earshot, Jane spoke up. "Sarah said that there was nothing new to report. They have an Amber Alert issued statewide." It was meant to make them feel better, but it left the room flat. "I, uh, am going to the bathroom.

On the way there she saw Sarah talking animatedly into her phone. Wanting to catch some of it, she wandered over to the welcome stand. There was hot coffee, crackers, and small water bottles. Jane fussed over the coffee, pouring in the creamer and sugar packets deliberately. She could hear nothing but Sarah's sign off. "Of course, not a word to the family." When the officer turned around and saw Jane's startled expression, both women knew they were caught. However, Sarah was saved by her phone ringing again and stepped a few more feet down the hall before she answered. Jane was left to wonder what was not to be spoken of, and her imagination was more than helpful in filling in the blanks.

With nothing left to stall her, Jane returned to the little room empty handed, the decoy coffee left to cool on the table. All eyes met her when she walked in, and she tried to smile encouragingly. Failing, she sat heavily next to her mother, who held out a hand that Jane graciously took.

****

The Amber Alert had posted about fifteen minutes before. There had been a small rush at the gas station and Pearson had been running about. Some guy was trying to pass off an altered scratch ticket, saying he won fifty bucks. After some back and forth and a threat to call the police, the man left angry. Then the toilet overflowed. His least favorite part of the job. He opted to tape an out of order sign on the door and returned to his post behind the counter. Once the place cleared out, he wiped off the counters and sat back on his stool. His phone was buzzing beneath the counter. Even though it was against policy, he checked it. The picture of the little boy who had been in the store the day before with the special escort was next to a picture of an older guy with ragged features. Pearson's jaw dropped, and he read the scant details.

Missing six-year-old boy. Blond hair, brown eyes. Wearing a blue shirt and jean shorts. Believed to be with Matthew Stone. Aged 37, brown hair, grey eyes. Possibly driving a grey/green four door. If seen, contact New Hampshire State Police right away. "Holy shit!" the teen said out loud to the nearly empty store. There was a TV in the corner near two small tables where customers who needed a break could eat and rest. He reached for the remote and turned the channel to local news, Channel 9. Then he turned up the volume. There was nothing at that moment except for the running announcement on the bottom of the screen.

Feeling connected to the story, he shared the Amber Alert to everyone in his contacts, with the tag line, "They were in the store yesterday!" It started its journey zig zagging across the state. He was on his phone non-stop, tending to customers as they came in. Pieces of his conversations were overheard by the customers and word was spreading quickly. Everyone who left the store picked up their phones to look for more information and talked about the breaking news. Heads were turning as cars passed each other. The public was doing their part.

Chapter 55

Matt knew he needed to get out of sight. He desperately wanted to turn on his phone and see what was on the news but wasn't willing to take that risk. There was no way to know if they had this number and could track it. Just how crazy was this thing getting? Watching Tommy sleep next to him brought back a flood of memories. His first words, first steps, favorite book, and the blue blanket he carried with him everywhere. Matt's most cherished memories were when they snuggled at bedtime, Tommy asking him a million questions. The stalling tactic worked, Matt often fell asleep, clinging to the side of the twin bed. He could tell from the questions that Tommy asked that he was going to be a scientist, a teacher, or maybe a zookeeper. He would be something cool, helping people or animals. A kind, sweet soul. Flashes of the funeral snuck up, and Matt pushed the memory away. Placing a gentle hand on the boy's foot he whispered, "You're safe now. I promise. No one will ever hurt you again." The boy stirred but didn't wake. Matt's mind was cloudy, probably a mixture of the medicine and the last threads of reality trying to hang on. He turned his attention to the houses and cabins along the windy road. There were so many, but he knew he needed to get farther away to be safe. The car continued down the winding road, not nearly as far from the authorities as he thought.

****

Almost three hours had passed since the little boy was swept away by Matthew Stone. It was agreed that returning to the family home might offer the group a modicum of comfort. That was suggested by the hospital chief, reminding the FBI agents that personnel were on edge, as well as patients and their families. After a very brief visit up to Andrew's room, they moved in a tight formation. The security tapes were copied, and the entourage left. Special Agents No Longer Wanting To Be In Charge, Max and Carl, had the foresight to have someone pull their SUV down to a loading dock. The family went out that way, to avoid the news crew that had shown up from WMUR as well as a few stringers for local papers. There was even one from a Boston newspaper. The agents were tight lipped on the drive back to the house. Sarah left in her personal car, and Lillian's Cadillac remained at the hospital.

Jesse and Steven sat clinging to each other and to hope. Their imaginations took them to places no one should go. Their only saving hope was that Stone believed their son to be his own. Would he harm his own son? Assuming the shooting was in fact an accident like they said, there was no reason to believe he would hurt Trevor. But the man was not acting reasonably, so who's to say what he might do?

Lillian fussed in the small kitchen trying to put together some sandwiches for a meal no one really wanted. It gave her something to do. Tanner was on the phone outside with his wife. Jane was working alongside her mother in an uneasy silence. Fear and hope were a relentless cycle that made Lillian dizzy. She hadn't slept in a few days, and she leaned against the counter.

"Mom? You all right?" Jane placed her hands under her mother's arms and guided her to a chair at the table.

"Yes, yes, I'm fine. Just a having a moment." Lillian fanned her face with a napkin.

Steven was by their side. "Mom? What's wrong?"

"Just got woozy for a moment. I'm okay." She tried to stand but Steven held her there.

"I'll finish up. You sit and rest." Jane and Steven finished up the sandwiches and set the platter on the table.

Jane called Tanner in and invited Sarah to join them. "It's not your fault you know," she whispered to the young officer.

"Thank you, but it is." Sarah closed her eyes for a moment, then added, "We will get him back." She took the proffered lunch but opted to eat it outside where she could keep an eye on things and take any calls without fear of them hearing. That call came just after she filled her mouth with the first bite. She struggled to chew and swallow before the call went to voicemail. "Joe? You almost here?"

"Yeah, service is crappy, so I'll be quick. We're maybe twenty minutes out, if the navigation is correct. I am planning on coming to the house and checking in on Jesse and Steven, then joining the manhunt."

"Sounds good. Have you spoken to Carl or Maxine? And who is with you?

"Um, Karen Copeland. I'll explain that later. Feds are chasing down a few leads. They found where he stashed the flower truck. Stole some girl's car while she was in the laundromat. They have a crew there, but I told them not to bother, not that they'll listen to me. He's long gone, either heading for the border or hiding out in one of the houses around the lake." He sounded like he was going to say more but the line cut in and out.

"Joe? Joe?" Sarah tried to tell him they would talk when he got there, but the line was dead. Why the hell was the reporter with him? She set the phone down and finished her sandwich wondering how the dynamic would change once Joe arrived.

Sarah stood on the dock for a while looking out at the calm lake. So smooth it reflected the sky in perfect symmetry. The occasional fish surfaced to catch a bug and then disappeared. Like Stone. Surfaced for a second, took what he wanted and poof, gone. Across the water were a few islands. Off to the left was an island with a single house on it. Not for her. She liked her alone time, but that would drive her batty. A lone boat puttered across the lake, trailing a fishing line. Soon, in the middle of summer there would be tons of boats zipping back and forth. She shook her head in disbelief of how totally screwed up this had all gotten. Feeling restless, she called Maxine for an update. "Anything?"

"No. Not really. But what I can tell you is where Stone isn't. They are doing a slow and steady search of the houses along the lake. At the same time, blocking off the roads leading around and away from the lake. That is a nearly impossible task, because there are literally hundreds of roads, many that lead nowhere. I think he's sticking to the side roads and looking for a place to hide with the boy."

"Me too. Is there anything I can do from here? I feel useless."

"Heard your guy, Marchand, is almost here. Catch him up to date. Check back in with us. If there is any news, I'll call you." Maxine signed off quickly, leaving Sarah to wait for Joe. She decided to go back inside where the five faces turned as one.

"Anything?" Jesse asked.

"No, not yet. They really are throwing a net around this place, the lake I mean. Roads are being blocked, houses checked, and the Amber Alert is out. We'll find him." Again, Sarah felt the words coming out were hollow, with no substance behind them. Her job was to serve and protect. The best thing she could do for the Reeds at the moment was to protect them from the truth. They were no closer to finding Stone and Trevor than they had been an hour ago.

Chapter 56

"So, when we get there, I will need a few minutes to talk to the Reeds and Sarah. I need to do that alone." Joe looked over at Karen.

Karen nodded. Though it would be great writing to capture the raw emotions of the family and people involved, however, to get Joe to trust her and keep her in the loop, she needed to play by his rules. During the ride he had given her a little background on Trevor's family. Without asking, she had gotten some great color for her story. The all-American dream, two hard working people meeting, falling in love, getting married, having a kid. Right on track, until the train was derailed by Stone. Now, his story was tragic, no way around that but now the victim had turned into the criminal. Just how far had he gone, or would he go? She shook that idea from her head and asked if Joe had ever been involved in a kidnapping before.

"No. Nothing like this happens in a small town like ours. We've had a few custodial issues, but no one has ever actually taken a child before." Joe's jaw tensed. Karen guessed he was thinking that this wouldn't have happened had he gone with the family.

When he hit the steering wheel with a fist, Karen jumped. "Are you okay?"

Running his hands through his hair, he blew out a long breath. "Just pissed. I should have been watching them."

"Sounds kinda creepy, Joe," Karen replied with a smile meant to break the tension.

Joe laughed in spite of himself. "Yeah, I'm a creeper." He rolled his head back and forth. Karen resisted the urge to lean over and rub his neck. He caught her looking and she blushed.

Changing topics, she asked him if he had ever been to the lake before. "When I was younger, once a summer, my friends and I would drive up here with a cooler of beer and rent a boat for the day. All day long we would beat the hell out of each other on the water skis or tube. Can't believe we actually made it home alive." He chuckled at the memory. "Who in their right mind would rent a boat to a group of teenagers carrying a full cooler?"

"That was long before driving and drinking was enforced, huh."

"Way before. It was like no one thought it mattered because it was a boat." Joe slowed down as they traveled through a rotary. Even with the flashing lights, it looked like he was going to have to wait to merge. He flipped the siren, and cars pulled aside as they sailed straight through. A few minutes later they arrived at the base of the lake. Keeping the lake on their left, they followed the road. Not surprisingly, they were slowed at a roadblock where Joe stopped to talk to one of the locals. The officer repeated much of what Sarah had told him and pointed the way to the Reeds' house. "Careful when it comes to the bend. Keep left but slow down. It's not a paved road and the winter left it a mess." Joe thanked her and moved on.

When they did turn off, Karen spilled her Diet Coke down the front of her shirt. "Damn!" The soda splashed on her chest, and it trickled between her breasts. The stain was spreading, and Karen blushed again.

"Lucky soda," Joe mumbled loud enough for her to hear. It made her laugh but was horrified of the brown spot. She stuffed some napkins inside her shirt and dabbed at the blot. It dried it up some but left the ugly mark. Ugh, she would have to change. Distracted by the spill, she didn't notice that they were turning into the driveway. When the car came to a stop, she looked up to see a young woman half jogging to the car. Then she remembered it was the officer Joe's department sent. Sarah, he had said. Joe let himself out and Karen busied herself with pulling a new shirt over the old one and twisting out of the old one. It was the trick she learned at Girl Scout camp. "Ta dah!" she announced to the empty car. Karen wished she had lowered the window before Joe got out. It would have been a whole lot easier to accidentally hear what was being said. Every so often the pair turned to look at her sitting in the car. She felt like a child waiting outside of the principal's office. Sarah didn't look pleased, and Joe was shaking his head. When the front door opened and another woman jogged out, Karen was shocked to see her embrace Joe. Must be Jesse Reed she deduced. Damn, she's pretty. Joe mentioned a history. What did it mean? Tired of sitting in the car, the reporter opened the door and got out. All eyes turned to her, and she felt out of place. She was going to have to get thicker skin to be an investigative reporter.

Joe spoke first, "Um, Karen, you remember Officer Dixon?" She nodded and extended her hand. "And this is Jesse Reed, Trevor's mom." Karen looked her directly in the eye and immediately felt her pain.

"Nice to meet you. But I am very sorry for the circumstances," she offered. Jesse nodded and remained quiet.

"Karen is along because she gave us some information about Matthew Stone. She was researching him for a story back in North Carolina," Joe explained.

Karen felt it warranted more explanation. "I was doing a human-interest piece on him, Stone. To see how he was coping after losing his family like he did. I had no idea it was going to turn to this."

"No one could." Jesse's voice was soft and dripping with pain.

Chapter 57

Matt was getting tired and hungry. He also needed to go to the bathroom. Stopping wasn't smart, but mother nature was calling, no screaming, at him to stop. He spotted a rundown cabin down by the water with a large shed off to the side. It looked like no one had been there for years, so he parked behind the shed to take a leak. Matt turned the car onto the bumpy narrow drive. The jolt made Tommy start to wake up. Matt put a hand on his leg and tried to soothe him back to sleep.

"It's okay, kiddo, I am just stopping for a minute. We'll be on our way again soon." Tommy mumbled something incoherent and curled up again. Matt brought the car to a stop in back of the shed, that looked close to falling down. The place was a mess but that reassured Matt that no one had been there for a very long time. After waiting a minute to be sure Tommy was back asleep, he quietly opened the door and stepped out. Not wanting to take his eyes off of him, Matt stepped to the front of the car and relieved himself. Feeling much better, he stretched his legs and back. Being with his Tommy again, he felt calmer but had a sense of urgency to stay out of sight that he couldn't completely understand. Matt's mind flitted between reality and his twisted imagination. When he looked at the boy sleeping in the car, he saw him as he did that last night.

The blue shirt became Tommy's blanket, and Matt was next to him reading a story.

A loud noise from a few houses over made Matt jump. He ducked behind the car and saw a van door open and several boys tumble out. They hopped and jumped and shouted, running around the property and down to the dock. That was enough to bring Matt back to survival mode and get back into the car. When he turned the key, it made that loud metallic grind that told Matt it was already running. He looked to the neighbors, but they didn't seem to hear the noise at all. Matt turned the car around and edged up the drive. From out of nowhere, a chocolate lab dashed in front of the car. Right behind him was a boy around ten years old, calling the dog, "Buster, come."

Matt was going slowly so he easily rolled to a stop, but the boy stared right at him. The dog was on Matt's side of the car now, nosing the window. It stood on its hind legs and lapped at Matt's arm. He tried to shoo the mutt away.

"Buster, stop." The boy caught up to his dog and pulled at the collar. "Sorry, mister." He eyed Tommy, who was stirring again. "You guys live here?"

Matt cleared his throat. "No, just visiting some friends, took a wrong turn." Tommy was rubbing his eyes and was almost awake. Matt patted the dog on the head and gently lifted the paws to get him out of the window. "Gotta get going though, hang on to your dog." He pushed the window button and the glass slid up.

"Okay, sorry about Buster." The boy pulled the dog down and backed away from the car as it rolled up the driveway. Matt was sweating and wanted to punch the gas to get the hell out of there but had to stay in control. Tommy had woken up and turned to look at him, his eyes widening in fear.

"Let me go!" He was trying undo his seatbelt, but his hands weren't working well. His small body twisted easily beneath the strap, and he wiggled to his knees. "Let me out! You're not my dad!"

"Tommy, sit," Matt said calmly, but with force. Why was Tommy acting this way?

Matt tried to force Tommy to sit as he peered over the seat out the back window. When he saw the kid and the dog he started screaming, "Help me!" Then he scrambled for the door handle. Matt saw him and hit the automatic lock on his door and held his finger on the button. He glanced in the rearview mirror and saw the boy let go of the dog and run back to his house. It was then Matt put all of his weight on the gas pedal, heading the car up the little incline and onto the poorly paved road. Tommy was thrown to the floor as the wheels touched the asphalt. His head banged off of the dash and he was crying again. Matt's eyes darted back and forth from the boy to the road to the rearview. So far no one was coming, and the road was empty other than him. Damn, he would need to get out of sight now. Tommy continued to cry in the well of the front seat. Matt's eye caught a birthmark on the boy's back. When did that get there?

He kept his eyes peeled for a good place to stash the car and hide. Now that he had Tommy back, there was no way he would give him up again. The back roads were too windy, hard to navigate. Maybe he should switch to a main road. Matt took a right thinking it would bring him to a main road, but it seemed to only get narrower. The road wound around and around and now Matt could see water on both sides of the road. Where in the hell was he?

Chapter 58

The Badman had him. He needed to get away. Trevor was trying to calm himself down. His teachers said something about deep breaths. It was hard, all scrunched down on the floor. He wanted to climb back into the seat but didn't want to be any closer to the man. When he reached up the man said, "No, son, stay down. It will be safer." The man's voice was like his dad when he had run into the street one day and almost got hit by a truck. Trevor remembered that his dad yelled at him then held him tightly and almost cried. Maybe this guy wouldn't hurt him, he hoped. Trevor kept his head down and tried to be brave. That's what Mommy and Daddy would want him to do, right? If he hadn't run away from his grandfather's room at the hospital, this wouldn't have happened. It was all his fault, and his parents would be very mad at him. Trevor bit his cheek to keep himself from crying more and tried to think of what he should do.

He swayed back and forth as the man drove the car on the bumpy roads. His head felt weird, and his stomach hurt. The strange man's big hand reached down and touched his shoulder. When he tensed up, the man took it away. Trevor didn't want to look or talk to him, but he had to go to the bathroom. Only little kids wet their pants. He wasn't a little kid. Trevor summoned up his courage and turned to talk. "I have to go to the bathroom."

The man looked down at him. "You have to wait."

"But it's really bad. Please? I don't want to pee my pants." The Badman looked angry, which Trevor didn't like. "Do you have a cup?" The man looked at him weirdly. "Sometimes Mommy and Daddy have me pee into an old coffee cup, so we don't have to stop on long rides." With the words Mommy and Daddy, the man glared at him. "Please?" The Badman turned around and looked in the back seat. The blaring of a horn made the guy jerk the wheel. Branches from an old pine tree scraped the passenger side as the car jerked to the right and the man jerked it back to the left. A Jeep narrowly missed them, passing them with the naughty finger held up.

"You should get into the seat and put your seatbelt on." The man was sweating and breathing hard.

Trevor climbed the rest of the way up in the seat and tugged on the seatbelt. The angry man reached over and placed the belt into the clip. Trevor sat as far away as he could get, his back pushing against the door. He was scared, and he still needed to pee. Something told him that asking the man to stop and let him go to the bathroom didn't sound smart. Trevor looked around trying to see if he could figure out where they were. All of the houses looked the same, and when he could see the lake, none of the islands looked familiar. He didn't know most of their names, just the one called Rattlesnake. And the one near it called Sleepers, where Daddy's friends lived. "Mister? Where are we going?"

When Trevor spoke, it seemed to startle the guy. The man smiled. "We're gonna find a place to stay, for a while. Then we'll get cleaned up, get something to eat, and take a rest." Trevor just looked at him. "Remember? I used to tell you how I wanted to bring you to New Hampshire and take you fishing?" He reached over and squeezed his knee. "Here, have some more water. We will get something to eat soon."

Trevor tried to keep himself from flinching from the man's touch. The Badman had never said anything about fishing. They had never talked before. But at least his voice was softer now, not as mean. Trevor took the water, even though he had still had to pee. Maybe the guy was just confused. "Mister, why did you take me?"

The dark flash came back to the man's eyes. Then it disappeared. "Tommy, stop fooling around. You know we were going to take this trip. If you don't want to fish, we can hike, or swim, or swing in the hammock." The man was looking at him, but not focusing on him. "Just have to find the right place."

"I'm not Tommy." Trevor whispered to the window.

"It won't be much longer. I'll know it when I see it." The Badman wasn't talking to him, Trevor realized. He took advantage of the man tuning out to look around the car more. He could see the man's phone, sitting between them on the little shelf. Could he get it and call 911 like his mom and dad taught him? As they drove, the guy actually started humming a song. Trevor didn't recognize it, but he was getting sleepy again. The rocking of the car on the uneven road and the last of the medicine in the water lulled Trevor back to sleep.

Chapter 59

Matt looked over at Tommy and felt a rush of emotion. They were together again. It had been so long. He would never let his son go again. His thin grasp on reality was slipping more and more as the miles rolled on. He had no idea how long he had been driving when a parking lot appeared at the bottom of a small hill. A sign for Ash Cove Marina pointed down a winding road on his left. There were only a few cars there, and two small garages. Matt drove slowly around the lot and stopped on the far side of one of the buildings. He quietly slipped out of the car and peeked at the docks. There were a couple of twenty-foot bowriders and one small dinghy with an outboard motor. He hoped it was one with a pull start. He checked on Tommy, who was still asleep. Grabbing his duffle, he jogged down the dock and jumped into the small boat. It took a couple of tugs, but the motor finally caught and roared to life. Leaving it to idle, he tossed the duffle in and went to get Tommy. After placing the boy safely in the bottom of the boat, Matt untied and steered away from the dock. With one last look around to make sure no one saw him, he headed down the small inlet that led to the lake. Once he was on the main lake, he kept his eyes peeled. He still needed a place to go. Slowing down, he took a moment to look around, and he spotted a group of islands up ahead. With a turn of the throttle, the little boat surged ahead. Matt guessed it would take around five or ten minutes to get there. Then it was only the matter of finding a house they could get into. The sun was high in the sky and the day was clear. Only a few boats were on the water, which could be good or bad. Hopefully they wouldn't find his car any time soon and assume he was still trying to drive away. Tommy moaned from the floor of the boat, so Matt leaned down and rubbed his back while steering toward the islands.

A blue flashing light caught Matt's eye off in the distance. He forgot about Marine Patrol. Dammit! He needed to get onto an island and out of sight quickly. Revving the engine, he decided to go to the far side of the bigger island and pull in somewhere to hide until dark. Maneuvering to the side farthest away from where the Marine Patrol boat was coming from, he could see that the trees created a shadow that would hide him even more. Going closer to shore, Matt looked at each camp he passed to see if there was anyone around. As he turned the point, there was another little inlet that looked promising. But it could also box him in if Marine Patrol came this way. The boat puttered along, until it started to spit and sputter. Matt toed the gas tank sitting next to the motor. Crap, he was running out of gas.

About a hundred yards up, he saw a rundown boat house and steered the boat toward that. So far, he had seen no one, nor any other boats nearby. When the motor finally quit, they were only fifty feet from the dock, so he picked up the oar and paddled. Beyond the broken-down boathouse was an A-frame camp. The windows were boarded up, so no one was home. He looked to the houses on either side and felt comfortable that there was no one there as well. The door to the boat house was really just a flap made out of an old tarp, so Matt pushed it aside and floated in. Once the boat was tied off, Matt looked around the small structure. There were a couple of gas cans up against the far wall, and a few orange life preservers hanging from the rafters. Climbing out of the boat proved trickier than he planned on. The old boat house had an even older dock. He tested each board before putting his full weight on it and made his way around to the back where the two gas cans sat. The first one was empty, but the second was heavier, maybe it was half full. He used that to switch out the tank on the boat and decided to check out the rest of the property.

Matt didn't want to risk Tommy waking up while he was gone so he gently lifted the boy up to his shoulder. Holding his son again was not something Matt ever imagined he would be able to do. It took a moment for the wave of emotion to pass. The sound of a motor in the distance reminded him that he needed to move. Relieved to see that it was not Marine Patrol, he walked up the small hill to the main house. The door and windows in the front of the house were boarded up with thick plywood. He tugged on the edges to find that they would be tough to remove without tools. Walking around the side, he was surprised to that the back door was not boarded over. Maybe it wasn't exposed to as much weather? Either way, it was good news for him. Surprisingly, it wasn't even locked, or maybe it had been at one time, but had broken some time ago based on the rusted edges.

When he walked into the small house it was obvious that no one had been there for a very long time.

The only light came from the window at the peak, but it was enough to see the layers of dust and cobwebs. It was not a huge stretch to think that the place housed many mice and possibly more creatures. Tommy was mumbling and squirming around in his arms, so Matt laid him down on the couch near the wood stove. He needed to see what was in the cabin, and if they might be able to stay for a while. The kitchen was no more than a few steps away, so he checked the cabinets to see if by chance there was any food. There was none, but there was a flashlight, a few candles, and one of those long lighters. They would be able to light the candles come nighttime.

"Mommy? Daddy?" The voice came from behind him, and Matt turned to see his little boy sitting up. Rubbing the sleep from his eyes, Tommy looked around him with wonder, and then fear. When he saw Matt, he burst out crying. "I want my mommy!" He stood up but was wobbly on his feet. As Matt rushed to his side, the boy shrank away from him.

"Tommy, you're okay." Kneeling in front of the couch, Matt tried to take the child into his arms.

"No, I am not Tommy! You are the Badman! I want my daddy!" When he tried to run, Matt grabbed him around the waist and held tight.

"It's okay…you're okay. I won't hurt you."

"You are the Badman. You are hurting me!"

The screams were getting louder, and Matt was concerned that someone might hear them. He put his large hand over the boy's mouth and said forcefully, "Don't scream. You have to be quiet." What was wrong with Tommy, Matt wondered.

The tone of his voice and the pressure on the boy's mouth, brought the screaming and struggling to a halt. Matt held tight a few moments longer. "You promise not to yell?"

A tiny nod was the answer, so Matt cautiously removed his hand. "Tommy, it's me. Daddy. Everything will be okay."

Tommy shook his head and tried to say, "I'm not Tomm—"

"NO! You are Tommy. My boy." Matt gripped the boy's shoulders harder. "You will be safe with me. I will keep you safe. No one else."

When Trevor shook his head the grip got tighter, so he stopped. A few moments later he said, "I still have to pee."

Matt looked around and saw a door. "That might be the bathroom. Let's see." They walked across the floor, and he could see another small room off in the back. A bedroom? The door was ajar, and the edge of a mattress came into view. The bathroom was simple, as expected, but the bowl was empty. "There's no water. Just go, I'll will figure it out later."

Chapter 60

As Trevor relieved himself, he saw a small window over the sink. It was really small, but so was he. He snuck a look at the Badman who looked different now. No messy hair, but the eyes still looked crazy, sometimes. When he turned to leave the bathroom, Trevor caught a glimpse of himself in the mirror. He gasped and leaned closer to see that there was blood all over the side of his face and ear. "I'm bleeding!"

Matt turned to see Tommy crying and trying to rub off the dried blood. There was a towel hanging off of a peg, so he turned on the faucet, only to remember that the water wasn't on. There was an entire lake outside, but he couldn't risk being seen, so he spit on the towel and wiped the blood off. "The cut's not bad, heads just bleed a lot." After most of the blood was gone, Matt used his fingers to try to comb out some of the blood in the hair. "See, just like new."

Trevor was caught off guard by the kind voice and the hug the man gave him. His eyes weren't scary now. Trevor was starting to see when he let the man call him Tommy, he was much nicer. He could play that game. For a while. Until his mommy and daddy came to get him. "I'm hungry."

"I know. I haven't figured that out yet. We just need to wait a little bit then we can go outside and get some water at least." Matt continued to look through the cabin and found a Rubbermaid container in the closet that had a few bottles of water, a box of rice, two cans of soup, and a can of tuna. Whoever lived here in the summer had either forgotten the box was there, or left it there just in case they ran out. Before he went looking for the food, he had jammed a chair under the doorknob and told Tommy to stay on the couch. He came back to his son yanking on the chair. "Tommy! What are you doing?"

"I want to go home. Please, mister. Just let me go."

Matt was instantly brought back to the county fair the year Tommy died. He wanted to go on The Flying Bobsleds ride but was just an inch too short and was begging the man to let him on.

"Please, Mister? Just let me go." Tommy turned and looked up at Matt, his big eyes pleading with the man.

"Can't let you go. It's not safe. I'll lose my job." The teenager turned to the people behind them in line. "Next!"

"It's okay, Tommy." Matt said walking toward the cotton candy. "We'll go next year."

"Next year, son. You'll be all set." Matt said this aloud.

"Next year!" Tommy screamed and began running around the cabin, banging on the walls, climbing on the furniture, trying to get away. Confused for a moment, Matt couldn't figure out the reason for the tantrum. It didn't take long for him to catch Tommy who reached back and threw his small fist at Matt's chest. "I." Punch. "Am." Punch. "Not." Punch. "Your son!" A

340

kick to the shin was not hard, but a surprise. When Matt looked down, Tommy jumped down and ran into the bedroom. The door slammed shut, but Matt knew the windows were boarded over, so he set himself in front of the door. He could wait it out.

What had set Tommy off? Matt wondered. He had these fits once in a while and often they were because Matt himself was acting off, missing Carol. When he tried to play back the afternoon in his mind, nothing made sense. He was at home with Tommy. He was fishing, then in the hospital. Home with Tommy, then back in a boat, with Tommy. Wait, why was he at the hospital? Matt's head hurt. He kept hearing Tommy cry, "Why did you hurt me?" Matt got up and walked around the cabin, trying to sort things out in his head. In his mind he kept seeing Tommy in his pjs, looking up at him. Blood spreading across his chest. His head was pounding. Throbbing. He could hear and feel every heartbeat. Where was his medicine? Where was his bag? A wave of dizziness overcame him, and he stumbled. His foot caught on the corner of the chair that was blocking the door, and he tumbled to the floor. Matt hit his head on the fireplace hearth on the way down. When he reached up and touched his head, it came away bloody. As the blood dripped down his face, flashes of Carol's beating and death overcame him. Watching as the men raped and beat her one last time as he sat helpless, bound, tied to a chair. Watching the life drain out of her eyes, he yelled, "Carol!" He heard Tommy crying in the bassinet, then came the smell of gasoline, and the heat of fire. In the cabin, Matt had curled up into a ball on floor and started keening. Softly at first, then louder.

****

Trevor had stopped yelling; his throat was starting to hurt. He had already pulled the curtains aside and seen that the windows had boards on them. Nono and Wumpy did that too. The Badman was talking in the other room, but Trevor couldn't figure out what he was saying. The door had one of those old keyholes like at his house. He crept over and peered through it. The man was walking back and forth. Then he was crying. When he yelled something, Trevor fell backward onto the bed. The guy sounded crazy. As he lay there, he saw a shelf high on the wall.

Actually, it looked like the ledge at the beginning of the crawl space in his attic at home. The one at home led to where his parents put the Christmas decorations. On the other end of the space at home there was a trap door that opened up into the garage. Trevor remembered his mother telling him how she and her friends used to play spy games and use the trap doors to sneak around on Uncle. Maybe this house was the same. There was a dresser next to the door, so he opened the bottom two drawers to make some steps to climb on. Once he was there, he was able to jump up and see that there was a space. The man in the other room was crying now. Trevor thought about getting down to see what was going on but wanted to see where this space went. Trevor gripped the edge and tried to pull himself up. He was too short. On the other side of the bed there were a couple of books. He got back down and tossed the books on top of the dresser. Then he climbed back up and tried again. That did it. He was able to grip the ledge and pull himself up.

Once he was up, he stopped because he couldn't hear the Badman anymore. Trevor held his breath, the man was crying softly now but he couldn't hear him moving anymore. Crawling on all fours, he made his way over to where a few cracks of light were coming in. As his eyes adjusted to the darkness, he could see that the people who owned the cabin put things up here too. The problem was there didn't seem to be another trap door. He felt around and caught his finger on something sharp. There was the corner of a metal frame wedged into the floor. It was a screen of some sort and when Trevor looked through it, he saw that it led to the bathroom. The bathroom had a window! He could get out and run for help. He tried pulling at the edges, but they were screwed down too tightly. There was thin screening over the slats, so he pushed his fingers through that and was able to grab the frame better. It started to pull up but was making a lot of noise. He stopped, held his breath again, and listened for the man.

Trevor could hear the man calling for Tommy. He wasn't Tommy, so he didn't have to answer. He sat completely still and listened as hard as he could. He heard footsteps and what sounded like a vitamin bottle being shaken. Then the door to the bedroom opened. Trevor stifled a gasp and shrank away from the light the ceiling fan was letting in. "Tommy? Where are you?" The voice was so close and so loud, he was sure the Badman could see him. Trevor could hear him rushing around and a small thud. "You under the bed?" Trevor was no dummy—monsters lived under beds, he'd never hide there. The man got up and rushed out of the room. He heard the bathroom door open with bang and then close again. "Tommy." Trevor waited until he heard the door to the outside open. Once he heard the leaves crunching in the yard, he allowed himself to breathe. What should he do now? One last tug on the ceiling fan let him know it wasn't coming out. He decided to try going down and getting out the same door the man had gone out of. Backing to the ledge, he slowly lowered himself down onto the dresser, then jumped down to the floor. Peeking around the cabin door he could see the ground outside. Just as he reached the door frame, he heard the man coming back. He had a split second to make up his mind. Should he hide in the house, or make a run for it? That split second was too long. Matt saw him standing in the doorway and ordered him back in the house. Any courage Trevor had fled when he saw the look in the man's eyes. The Badman was back.

****

"Tommy? Where are you?" Matt woke up on the floor with a dreaded sense of déjà vu. He saw the blood on his hands and shirt and looked for his son. The shooting replayed in his mind taking his breath away. Once his vision cleared, he saw that he was in a cabin. Snippets from the day came back to him. Tommy was mad and was in the bedroom. Standing took some effort and his head spun. The headache was there and worse than ever. "Tommy, are you okay?" There was a chair on the floor by the door, and his duffle on the kitchen counter. He needed his medicine.

Matt's heart thundered in his head, almost blinding him. He needed to lie down, but he had to find Tommy first. Why was he being so naughty? A quick search of the cabin revealed that Tommy was no longer there. He must have run outside. Matt moved the chair on the floor and stepped outside. The dry leaves crunched underfoot, making it harder to hear where Tommy might be going. Darkness came quickly in the mountains, and he was losing his footing in the dusky light. He needed that flashlight back at the cabin. Just as he turned the corner, he caught sight of Tommy's face peering out of the door. "Tommy! Get back in the house! Now!"

Maybe he was just playing hide and go seek. Tommy loved to play that. Matt kept his eye on his son as he made his way back to the cabin. Why did his head hurt so much? That medicine needed to start working soon, or his head would explode. Out of breath and trying to slow down his heart rate, Matt climbed the two stairs into the cabin. Tommy was standing in the middle of the room, with his eyes darting side to side. "We can play hide and seek later," Matt mumbled as he lurched to the couch after closing and blocking the door with a heavy chest. "Daddy has a bad headache. I just need to rest for a few minutes."

****

Trevor stood in the middle of the room staring at the man who was holding his head and rocking back and forth on the couch. His mean voice was gone. He seemed to be able to switch it off and on. When he was angry, his eyes got all black and his forehead got red. When he wasn't, he had a smile, and nicer eyes. Trevor just couldn't figure out how to keep the Badman from getting mad. Well, he did know, he had to let him call him Tommy and act like he wasn't afraid. He didn't want the man to call him Tommy, but it might make him less scary until Daddy and Mommy and Joe could find them. "Okay. But I'm kinda hungry. Can I have something to eat?"

Trevor watched as the man went to the box he had found and pulled out a can of soup. It was the red soup. Yuck, and he was going to say something but caught himself, remembering not to make the man mad. There was an opener screwed to a beam by the refrigerator and once the can was open, the soup was poured into two mugs. It was cold. Double yuck. Trevor sipped the soup and tried not to make a face. The man sat at the table and kept looking over at him. Trevor stole glances as well. There were a bunch of scars all over his face. That must have hurt. The guy didn't say much. But when he looked at Trevor, he smiled and sometimes his eyes got wet. When the soup was all gone, they sat in silence for a long time. The cabin was getting dark, so the man lit a candle and set it on the table. Trevor tried to think of ways to get out. If the Badman went to sleep, he could sneak out. No, the door was blocked. Maybe he could get that window in the bathroom open. Trevor looked around from where he was sitting for anything that could help him.

****

Matt watched Tommy who was being very quiet now. Should they spend the night there or try to get farther away? He couldn't look out the windows and didn't want to go outside again until it was totally dark. He had Tommy back, but he couldn't understand why people were chasing him. That had happened before, when Tommy was little, and the reporters wanted to get a story on Carol's murder. Once they found out where Matt and Tommy were staying after the fire, reporters were outside for weeks, until the man hunt for the intruders died down. Then they were back again, after the shooting.

The shooting. Tommy. Matt's head whipped up and he stared hard at the little boy across the table.

"What are you looking at?" The little voice was loud in the silent cabin.

"Huh?" Matt shook his head, trying to make sense of the ideas swirling through his mind. Carol dying, Tommy dying. Tommy sitting there, right in front of him. How could that be?

"Why do you keep looking at me like that?" The boy shifted in his seat and leaned forward toward the candlelight.

The blond curls, the brown eyes, the freckles. Where are the freckles? Tommy had freckles on both cheeks and his nose. The same as Carol. They would count them sometimes. Matt leaned in to get a better look. "Tommy?" Standing up he got within inches of the boy's face. Then he pulled the candle over. "Where are your freckles?" Matt used his hands to turn the boy's head back and forth, closer to the light. His head was throbbing again.

"I'm not Tommy," the boy said quietly. "I'm Trevor. Trevor Andrew Reed." Matt pulled back sharply and sucked in a breath. It was like he was punched in the stomach.

"But you are. You have to be. I've been looking for you." Matt reached behind him and pulled out his wallet. Tucked away behind his license was an old photo of him and Tommy on his first day of preschool. There he was...his boy. Blond curls, brown eyes, and a spray of freckles across the bridge of his nose and cheeks. Looking back and forth between the picture of the boy and the child in front of him, the fog began to clear. His Tommy was gone. Carol was gone. He had

S. Hilbre Thomson

not been able to keep them safe. It was all his fault. "Oh my God. What have I done?" He stood so fast, his chair fell over causing Tommy, no the boy, to jump. The sudden movement made him dizzy. Matt reached down to the table to stop the room from spinning.

"Mister, what's wrong?" The little boy, the one without freckles, stood up too and backed away from the table. They stood like that for several minutes. Matt's chest felt like it was going to cave in. The police were after him. He had kidnapped this little boy, someone else's son. He knew the loss of a son was unbearable, and he couldn't put another family through that.

The sound of motors could be heard on the lake. "We have to go."

"Where?"

"I don't know. The cops are looking for me. We have to go." Matt was grabbing the duffle and the flashlight.

"But we can just tell them that I am okay." Tommy, no his name is Trevor, was not moving.

"We have to go. Promise, I will let you go once we get to the mainland. I can't leave you here on the island."

"We're on an island?"

Matt had forgotten that he was sleeping the whole time they were in the boat. "Uh, yeah. C'mon." Moving the heavy chest out of the way, he opened the door. The little boy didn't move. "Look, I'm sorry. I am messed up, got confused. You look like my little boy. I'll take you back to your parents."

Trevor didn't know what to do. Should he go with him, or run? The man held his hand out, the mean eyes were gone. The promise of seeing his parents was too much. Trevor let himself be led out of the cabin and down to the lake.

Chapter 61

The Reed family was on edge. Any pretense of small talk, eating or even drinking was abandoned. The locals offered to call a doctor to get Jesse some tranquilizers, but she refused. While the state and local police widened their net looking for Trevor and Matthew Stone, each report brought a deeper sense of dread. A second shift was brought in to retrace previous routes, in case Stone doubled back or got lost. Joe and Karen stayed outside sitting side by side on the picnic table. Joe understood that he needed to let the locals do their job. Or more importantly, he was told to stand down and stay with the family. His boss wasn't too happy that he brought the reporter along. Sarah hung back too but was walking around the yard. Karen had the common sense to be still and quiet, which was unlike her. They checked their phones often, hoping for news. There was none.

****

Buchanan and Price, who had driven up on the news of the kidnapping, joined Maxine and Carl licking their wounds and tried to help the locals. Buchanan was conferring with the New Hampshire Feds that had been brought in and Price was talking to the State Police and Marine Patrol. Even though the TV shows make it seem like police forces and the feds don't like to work together, it was 'all hands on deck situation.' There was a heightened sense of urgency because a child was involved.

Egos were put aside, and all ideas were listened to. There had been no sightings on land, so they had added the lake and islands to the search. Marine Patrol brought in all personnel, but so far, no boats were reported stolen. Everyone agreed that this early in the season most people are home during the week and wouldn't notice a missing boat until Friday or Saturday. Most boats weren't even put in the water until July Fourth so empty slips were not uncommon. The authorities were flying blind, and it was getting dark. Marine Patrol Captain, Lane Porter stood in front of the tired group of men and women that had assembled near the Moultonborough barracks just a half hour away from the Reeds. "I know this is discouraging, but no one knows this lake like you. We have a little boy and his family depending on us to get him home safely. Air support will be around for another hour, but beyond that we are on our own. We know he was on Elkins Road four hours ago. No one has spotted Stone on land, so it's likely he took a boat and either crossed the lake or is hiding on one of the islands. My bet is he's hiding. It's hard to travel with a scared kid. So, what makes sense is to check out the nearest islands first. We are going to split into teams and check all docks for boats that look out of place. Check all boat houses, and overhanging trees that could hide a boat, or a kid. We don't know what we are dealing with." Nods all around as assignments were handed out.

Buchanan stepped away from the group to update his boss and to call Marchand. He wanted the family kept in the loop. Boats were starting up, lights flashing, and the mood was somber. Everyone was wary, once the sun completely set, they would be flying blind.

****

Joe took the news to the family who weren't sure how to take it. Anything short of bringing Trevor home was not good enough, a failure. He left the family huddled and crying.

Chapter 62

Matt stood in the shadow of a giant pine tree and surveyed the lake. He had no idea where he was but was able to use the setting sun to figure out that he was facing west. He remembered that Red's cabin was in the southern tip of the lake, so he didn't want to go back that way. That meant he should head toward the west and hope he could get to the mainland without getting caught. Then he would leave Tommy, no Trevor, at a store or something and then disappear. He couldn't face another round with the police and media. There were boat sounds from what he thought was behind him, on the other side of the island, but he couldn't be sure. Holding tight to the boy's hand, they darted into the boathouse. Once there, Matt turned on the flashlight so they could see to get in and untie. Just as he was stepping into the boat, he saw one of those molding, orange lifejackets hanging from a nail on the rafters. "Put this on," he said flicking it over the post into the boy's lap.

"Okay." Trevor tried to put it on. He fiddled with it for a minute until Matt leaned over to help him. They were ready and the boat spit and complained the first few tries, but then kicked to life. Backing up wasn't smooth, but soon they were on their way. The air was cool and there was just enough light that Matt could see clearly for 200 yards or so ahead of him, but beyond that, not much. It was more likely that the water was deeper, and he could avoid hitting rocks if he left the edge of the island. But that put him in plain sight. He also didn't know how long the gas would last. They cleared the edge of the island, and Matt could see a fleet of Marine Patrol boats fanning out nearly a mile back. Swallowing the panic, Matt tried to continue calmly. He squinted because he saw some lightning bugs up ahead, but soon found it was just the lights on boats. He was supposed to have a light on. Which would draw more attention? A light or no light?

He would have to just go without. He hadn't seen any on the small boat anyway. He steered toward the distant shore and kept scanning for boats, and rocks. The boy, Trevor, was sitting in the bow on the small seat. Matt's emotions threatened to take over again, as he flashed back to times with his dad, and the plans he had for him and Tommy. The sun was going, and it was getting trickier to see what was ahead. "Can you hold this, keep it pointed in front?" Matt stretched his arm up with the flashlight and the boy took it. With a click, they had a bobbing beacon shedding a weak beam across the top of the water. Suddenly the boy gasped and sat up straight. His eyes were trained on something behind Matt off to his left. Looking over his shoulder, there were the telltale blue lights of a patrol boat. Then two, then three. Instinctively, he gunned the motor, causing the boat to lurch. The flashlight fell overboard, and Matt looked back at Trevor. "Hold tight."

****

Harold Caldwell was a twenty-year veteran of the New Hampshire Marine Patrol. Over his tenure he had been a part of many search and rescue operations.

Usually, they were looking for someone who wanted to be found. But once in a while some yahoo took to the islands hoping to evade capture. There was only one that got away, the rest were found inside of a day. This time he was pissed. He had his whole team out here in the dark searching for a deranged kidnapper. There was no telling of his mental or physical status. He had a young boy with him. That could slow him down, but it could also make him more desperate, more dangerous. The department was waiting for infrared cameras to be able to check the cabins faster. Stopping at each one, looking for an entry point, and keeping track of it all took time. At this point they had to share the machines with other search and rescue teams. The ones they wanted to use were still an hour out.

Both Ragged and Sandy Islands had been checked and cleared. Now they were moving onto Welch and Round. If only it wasn't dark. His men were familiar with the lake, but this area was strewn with rocks and shallow waters. Access was tougher, and he wanted to call it for the night. But knowing the child was out there kept him going.

"Lieutenant? I have a small craft between Welch and Fish. No running lights, going really slow. We're gonna check it out." It was Fitch, a second-year patrolman. Good man, still somewhat green. His partner, Turner had a few years on him, but the common sense of a trout.

"Fitch? Hang on. I'm on your six, want to go with you." Caldwell swung the boat to his right and sped toward the patrol skiff. Could this be the guy? They approached the boat slowly. Turner pulled out the spotlight and lit up the small boat. The man on board raised his hand to cover his eyes.

"Marine Patrol, coming portside," Caldwell instructed, meaning the driver needed to stop and let them come to his left. The guy on the boat nodded but kept his hand over his face. The Lieutenant didn't like that and instructed the man to lower his hands.

"Can't see a damn thing," the man on the boat yelled. Turner lowered the light slightly, keeping it steady on the man's hands and torso. "What seems to be the problem, officers?" He was slurring.

As they tethered their boats together, it was clear this was not their man. But it was even more clear the guy should not be on the water. "I don't need this crap," Caldwell mumbled to himself. "Fitch, hand this over to the next boat. I'm heading toward Welch. Catch up as soon as you can." Assured the situation was under control, the Lieutenant was back on the hunt for Matthew Stone.

Chapter 63

Matt's heart hammered in his throat as he saw flashing lights behind him. Panicked, he debated going back to the island and hiding there. But he could move much faster on the water. As he increased his speed the police boat peeled off to his right. Matt let out a huge sigh and continued on his way. The moon shone brightly on the lake as they skimmed the surface of the water. Under any other circumstances, he would have enjoyed the view. The mountains were rolling black shadows miles away, giving him some guidance. Gunning the engine, Matt picked up speed and turned to the left to keep going the way he thought he should be going. The buzz from the motor tickled his ears as the boat bumped its way across the lake.

****

Caldwell had one of his feelings. Those instincts he had learned to follow, because more times than not, they led to something good. He sent a message over the radio for all patrols to kill their engines so he could listen. Sound carried over the water. After the motors wound down, they sat in the boats waiting. With a keen ear tuned to the night sounds, he heard the tell-tale whine of a small outboard. It took a moment, but he homed in on it. Ahead and to his right. "I hear something, one o'clock. Gonna check it out." It meant swinging around the point of the island and turning a little to his right, but he could just make out the ripples in the water from a boat up ahead. He picked up his speed, lights flashing.

****

Matt had been looking behind him every minute or so, to make sure no one was chasing him. When he checked this time, he saw the lights flashing over the water. It took him a moment to figure out if they were coming toward him or away from him. When he realized they were coming his way, he panicked. Twisting the throttle to its highest point, the boat took off. Matt was basically steering blind, for the clouds had shifted, covering the moon again. The boy's head bobbed up and down. In the distance, he saw a glow on the horizon. Mainland was that way. Every time he looked over his shoulder, his boat steered to his right without his knowing it. Matt watched as more boats pulled up behind him. Their engines were much larger and there was little hope to outrun them. But he would try.

****

Caldwell grabbed his radio. "In pursuit, I believe it's our suspect. No running lights and he's not stopping for our blues. All units, he is heading northwest. Looks like he's heading between Timber and Governor's." Four or five boats flew toward the chase. He signed off with a warning. "Remember where you are, keep your eyes peeled." They were entering a tricky part of the lake, and darkness only made it more dangerous.

****

When Matt looked behind him again, the lights multiplied. The wind was now whipping at his face, bugs pinging off of his cheeks and forehead. His motor roared as he pushed it to the limits. He wondered again how much gas was in the tank. Couldn't worry about that now. The boat skimmed across the surface and Matt felt as if he was flying. He wished Tommy was sitting next to him and not in the bow. No, it wasn't Tommy, he reminded himself and yelled to be heard above the noise, "Sit down, in the bottom of the boat." Adrenaline coursed through his veins and before long, there were at least three boats on his tail, two, three hundred yards behind him. Land seemed too far away, and Matt briefly considered just giving up, killing the motor and letting them get him. The next time he looked backward he saw two boats veer off to the right and one to the left. Matt didn't have time to wonder why. The clouds shifted once again.

He turned back around and saw what looked like the silhouettes of a bunch of birds sitting on the water. Why weren't they moving? That's when he saw they weren't birds, but a bunch of pointy rocks sticking straight out of the water right there in the middle of the lake. Before he could react, there was a gut-wrenching sound of metal on stone. He felt and heard the impact as the boat scraped the top of one of those jagged rocks. His boat jumped into the air launching the boy overboard and himself onto the floor. It crashed down bow first into another set of pointy rocks. Matt was thrown again, this time out of the boat and into the pitch-black water.

Matt felt himself flying over the bow of the boat. He reached out for anything he could grab, but he only got air. The dark water and blinding lights made it impossible for him to see where he was landing. Not that he had a choice. He somersaulted once, his foot clipping something hard, and then he landed, headfirst onto one of the rocks. There was an instant of pain, and then nothing. He slid silently into the dark water.

****

"All units, pull out! He's heading right into the Witches!" The Lieutenant called everyone off. He pulled the wheel to the right while yanking his throttle back. His boat lurched to a stop. The others did the same. One of the other officers trained the spotlight on Stone's boat. The tiny boat hurtled toward the most dangerous spot on the lake. In the bow of the boat there was an orange blob, the boy? Caldwell turned up his speaker and yelled, "Stop!"

Marine Patrol watched in horror, there was nothing they could do to stop what was happening. None of the men were optimistic enough to believe that the man would be able to stop. Hurried prayers were sent from those who believed and a few that didn't. A small figure in with an orange life jacket was hurled overboard and within an instant the closest patrol boat was approaching the scene cautiously. The thunderous crash echoed off of the mountains followed by the whining of a propeller in air.

Fitch had just pulled up and played the spotlight over the surface of the water. Several black tips protruded from the water, an unexpected shallow area in the otherwise deep section of the huge lake. Dubbed The Witches, because the rocks resemble their pointy hats, the outcropping had been responsible for many accidents and several deaths over the years. The search light stopped on the boat, half in, half out of the water. The motor was whirring away, uselessly spinning in the air. After a minute it stopped altogether. Caldwell pulled out his own light and moved his boat as close to the wreck as he dared. Even a seasoned boater like him knew not to venture into that wicked maze. His light searched in a grid like formation. The oar, a life jacket, and the gas tank were floating near the boat. Stone was nowhere to be seen. Caldwell brought the light back to a spot of orange. It was the boy! Before he could react, Fitch was in the water swimming toward the little boy. The Lieutenant ordered the other boats to look for Stone while he maneuvered his boat to the left, ready to take the boy on board. Green was radioing for more help as his partner reached the boy and flipped him over. He swam, towing the boy, over to Caldwell's boat as quickly as he safely could. The limp body was gently lifted onto the floor of the patrol boat. CPR was started right away. Soon the rescue boat could be seen coming from the Gilford base. Once they reached the wreck, the paramedics took over and were off toward Wolfeboro and the nearest hospital. Focus returned to finding Stone and taking him in, if he was still alive.

It only took a few minutes of searching for the officers to spot Matt. He was floating on his back, most of his face smashed and bloody. He wasn't moving, eyes open, but not seeing. They swam over to the wreck and confirmed he was dead. Lieutenant Caldwell used a long pole to help retrieve the body. Once it was on the boat, he swept the water once more. He gathered up some of the debris and then saw a square of fabric caught on one of the rocks. Curious, he pulled it in as well. It was a six-by-six square of blue fleece. He tossed it next to the man. Then he attended to the details of trying to contain the site. One dead, and one in serious condition. Sometimes he hated this job.

Chapter 64

Joe's phone buzzed and he looked down to the display. He jerked his head toward Sarah and the pair stepped away from the group that had gathered outside to get some air, they said, but all eyes were on the lake.

Sarah tried to listen but couldn't really hear much. But she could tell from the tone that something was up. Joe was moving farther away from the family and listening intently. The only thing she could hear was a few 'You sures,' one 'Oh my God,' and one 'how bad.' Joe was agitated, shaking his head, nearly snapping the cell phone in half. She turned to see that the family was watching them carefully. She held up a hand, hoping to hold them off until she could talk to Joe. No luck. They rushed over, Jesse in the lead.

"Joe," she grabbed his arm. "What is it?" Tears were streaming down her face and Steven stood rock still next to her.

Joe took a deep breath and faced the group. "They found him. Trevor."

Jesse looked him in the eye. "Oh, thank God." Joe was silent, he looked to Steven, then Sarah.

"What aren't you telling us?" Steven was in Joe's face. "What aren't you telling us?" Sarah stepped closer ready to intervene if needed.

Joe took Jesse's hands in his. "He's alive." Then looking up at Steven and the rest of the family. "There was an accident on the water. Stone was trying to get away and his boat hit some rocks. Stone didn't make it, but Trevor is on the way to the hospital."

Jesse collapsed to the ground and Steven collected her in his arms. "How bad?" Jesse croaked out between sobs. "Joe, don't lie to me. Tell me."

"I don't know. They didn't have a lot of details. He's unconscious. We should get to the hospital."

Behind them on the lake, the rescue boat flew by. Everyone stopped in their tracks. The sirens echoing across the otherwise still lake. An anguished sob escaped Jesse's mouth while Joe led her and Steven to his truck. All the others piled into Jane's Tahoe. Joe looked at Sarah. "Can you stay here, with her?" He nodded toward Karen, who was standing awkwardly in the middle of the yard.

"Yeah, sure." Sarah patted his shoulder. "Let me know what you find out." She went over and explained the plan to Karen.

****

Karen was in no position to complain. Was she right to come? Stone was dead. The boy was hurt. This family was suffering. Then the reporter in her kicked in. There is still a story to be told here. She just needed to figure out the best way to write it, without being an asshole. Which would make the better story? Family reunited, or the aftermath of a madman? Could she combine the tragic lives of the Stone family, the impact of human suffering, and the Reed family drama into a meaningful piece?

Sarah's question surprised her. "You hungry?" The look on Karen's face made the officer laugh. "Stress eater." She pointed at the plate of sandwiches that had gone untouched on the picnic table.

"Yeah, actually I am." The women sat down across from each other and picked at the plate. After a while, Karen tried to break the silence. "So, how long have you been a police officer?"

Sarah looked at her. "Five years. How long have you been a reporter?"

"The same." They fell quiet again.

After they ate, they moved to the dock.

"So, have you worked with Joe all that time?" Karen tried to sound causal.

The other woman just shook her head and smiled. "That took longer than I expected." Sarah's comment made it clear that Karen wasn't fooling her, so she shrugged her shoulders. "Yeah, he's a great guy. Good cop, good friend." Sarah was distracted by something on the lake. There were a few boats buzzing by, including the Lake Tow and a few more Marine Patrol boats heading over to where she assumed the boat crash was. "God, I hope Trevor is okay. He's a great little kid." Sarah tried to hide the tears forming at the corners of her eyes.

****

Jesse's heart was in her throat the entire ride to the hospital. She was hoping they were telling her the truth. That he was okay. That was what mattered. But what had he gone through? What did that man do to him? Oh, God. She hoped he didn't molest him. There wasn't enough time, she told herself. He was on the run. How would Trevor get past that? "He's okay, he's okay. Calm down." Those were Steven's words; he was talking to her. She turned to see his eyes filled with tears of relief, but with fear behind it. Was he thinking the same things? Before the car came to a complete stop, they were opening the doors.

"He's okay, Jesse, he's okay," Steven repeated the words like a mantra until they heard the sirens in the distance. Jesse gripped his arm like a vise, but he hardly felt it. Joe held them back from running to meet the ambulance as it turned into the emergency bay.

Joe led them inside and spoke quickly to the doctors. "These are the Reeds, Trevor's parents."

The doors opened and the EMTs rushed in. As the gurney turned into a curtained slot, they caught sight of Trevor. He had tubes in his arm and an oxygen mask on, but his eyes were open.

"Mommy! Daddy!" The little voice was muffled and weak, but it was the best sound they had ever heard.

They tried to rush to their son's side, but the doctors waved them off. One doctor looked at Trevor and then his parents. "Just give us a few minutes with him, to make sure he's okay. We will go as fast as we can."

"Trevor, we're right here!" Steven called out. Jesse stood silently praying to God, her parents, anyone and anything that might help. Nurses and doctors were busy checking him over, taking some x-rays, drawing blood. Joe stood back and talked to the EMTs, Max and Carl who had shown up shortly after the ambulance did. The crash site was being cleaned up, evidence collected, and Stone was on his way to the morgue downstairs. Joe held off calling Sarah until he had more information on Trevor.

****

Even in the dark, Sarah could see Karen's mind whirling and needed to drop the woman in Joe's lap ASAP, either literally or figuratively. She didn't want to babysit any longer. She wanted to know how Trevor was. Not wanting to bother Joe, she decided to turn the tables and ask the reporter a bunch of questions. "So, how did you get involved in all of this? I know you are a reporter and all, but you are a long way from home."

Karen did her best to explain how she had locked onto Stone. She openly admitted she had no idea it was going to turn into this. Sarah had to respect the hustle, the leap of faith it took to drive almost a thousand miles to get the story. But she needed to protect Trevor, the Reeds, and her friend. "So, what are you going to do now? Stone's dead. Is there still a story?" Sarah was trying to do two things, pass the time, and get an idea if this woman was one of the good reporters.

"It's tricky. Both sides need to be told. The Reeds are suffering right now, Trevor has been hurt, physically and likely emotionally. Stone? There's layers and layers of shit there. Mostly beyond his control. Losing his wife, watching her raped and killed? Then almost dying himself from the beating and fire? Who can survive that without serious baggage? Then to accidentally kill his own child? That would drive anyone over the edge. Not to point fingers, but where was the support for him? Once I start feeling bad for him, I get reminded of the crap he pulled here. Could that have been avoided?"

Sarah could see some of the logic. She felt responsible for the death of the fireman. However, the department had hooked her up with a psychiatrist. She talked to Joe and her family, and it still haunted her.

But to take a kid? "Let me call Joe. He can tell us how Trevor is." She was going to walk away, but Karen would find a way to listen anyway. Joe didn't answer but sent a 'Can I call you later?' reply. "No answer." She felt helpless and needed to do something. "I'm going to clean this up." Picking up the tray of sandwiches, she walked into the house.

Chapter 65

After what seemed like an eternity, the people around Trevor's bed slowed down and the mood relaxed. A doctor signaled for them to come in. Jesse and Steven rushed to Trevor's side. "He's medicated, so he will be in and out." Trevor moaned softly. "He's sustained quite a few injuries from what we can tell. Obviously, there's concern that he has a concussion. We will send him up to CT soon. The x-rays show a couple of broken ribs and a fractured ulna." The doctor pointed to his own arm. "We will have ortho look at it again in the morning. His lungs look clear, I don't think he was in the water long enough to cause any damage there. One laceration on his skull was closed with a couple of stitches. Bloodwork's not back yet. We will keep him overnight for observation and see where we go from there when we get all of the test results." The doctor looked from parent to parent and then back at his patient. "Overall, he was really lucky. Most people don't survive a crash like that."

Another doctor stepped forward. "Do you have any questions?" He motioned for a nurse to bring in two chairs.

Steven cleared his throat and looked the doctor in the eye. "He will be okay though, right?"

"He should be." A different nurse walked over with an iPad and held it out to the second doctor. He checked it over. "The first round of blood work looks good. We will try to rush the CT, but meantime, have a seat, hold his hand. Give him a hug." With that, the nurses and doctors stepped out of the room to give them some time. Jesse and Steven finally allowed themselves to breathe. Joe had overheard the update and walked down the hall to call Sarah back.

****

"How is he?" Sarah blurted out. Once she had the update, she gave Karen the thumbs up sign. Karen's smile was genuine. Stepping outside, she closed the door behind her, hoping the reporter would take the hint. "I can totally see why you let her come. The reporter. Cute, funny, and smart. But be careful, Joe. She's also very hungry."

"Huh?"

"For the story. Remember why she is here in the first place?" Karen was looking at family photos on the mantel. "Make sure you are thinking with the right head!" She said goodbye and hung up.

****

The rest of the family had gone in to see Trevor, then went up to see Andrew. Steven's phone was vibrating in his pocket. Seven missed calls. Five from Jack and two from a client. He really should call Jack and let him know Trevor is okay. But he just didn't feel like talking. A quick text it would be. *Good news. Trevor is okay. Banged up a bit and scared but safe with us. Will call later with details.* "I should go see my dad," he whispered. Jesse nodded, so he went.

It was time for Steven to tell his dad what he never had. Leaning his head on the railing, he started. "Dad, I should have said this a long time ago. But thank you.

Thank you for giving me, Tanner, and Jane everything we needed growing up. Thank you for pushing me even when it pissed me off. I wouldn't have made it without your help." He wiped a tear. "Or pressure, however you want to put it. I wish I had understood it more. Maybe then I wouldn't have been such a jerk." Then he thought of Jesse's parents. "I am so thankful that you had the chance to know Jesse and Trevor. You and Mom are his only grandparents. And he is lucky. I think you were lucky too. Trevor has taught me a lot. I think he taught you too, like how to be silly, how to laugh more. It was great to see you with him. He made you laugh. You have a great laugh, you know. I wish we laughed like that." Steven choked back some more tears.

"You did." Steven jumped. Lillian was there. She had walked up behind him and hugged him. "When you guys were little, he would come home early from work and take you outside. He rolled around in the yard and you three would tackle him." Steven's face betrayed his surprise.

"I don't remember that. He was always at work."

"When you kids were very young there was a huge crash in the market. We almost lost everything. Your dad lost his job, and we almost lost the house."

"You never told us. Why?"

"Your father was a proud man. He believed it was his job to keep you guys safe." Lillian pulled up another chair. Holding one of Steven's hands and Andrew's other one, they formed a tight circle around the bed. "He never wanted us to worry. He would leave each morning and look for a job. Not come back until dinner time. Some days he felt broken, but he never gave up.

Finally, things turned around. When they did, he worked even harder, afraid to have it happen again. He worked to provide for the family and so we would always have a nest egg. Just in case."

Steven looked at his father again. How did he not know all of that? It had always been taken for granted that his dad would be there for them. Now, would he ever know that Steven appreciated all that he did? The tears fell freely as they sat together. He stayed for a while and then went back down to his wife and son.

****

The next morning, all the tests had come back, and Trevor was going to be all right. The bones would heal, and while there was a trace of a sedative in his blood, the doctors assured them there would be no lasting effects. They were strongly urged to find someone to help them process and heal emotionally. "From what I understand, the guy who did this, he needed some help dealing with his tragedies." The social worker who worked with the hospital had told them this, handing over a list of referrals in the Boston area. "I understand there is also the issue of his grandfather. Do you want me to talk to him about that?"

Jesse and Steven agreed that it might be good for a professional to check in on Trevor. In that conversation, Trevor revealed that he really wanted to see his grandfather before he passed, so they made the arrangements. Later that day, with Trevor in a wheelchair, Jesse and Steven went to see Andrew. The small boy asked to be wheeled right up to the bedside. His arm was fully encased in a cast, and his ribs were very sore, so it took a lot of effort for him to wiggle out of the chair and lean over to kiss his grandfather. The rest of the family was gathered around the bed. "I'm sorry, Wumpy. I messed everything up by running away." He gulped back his emotion. "Thank you for waiting for me. I love you." Tears rolled down every cheek in the room. Lillian put her arms around Trevor and kissed the top of his head. "He loves you too. And you're right. He is ready." With that, Jesse passed him off to Joe who had not left the hospital. He agreed to wait with him while Andrew was taken off of life support.

****

Joe watched a movie with Trevor back in his hospital room. But he wasn't really watching it. He was recalling the conversation he had with Karen a little earlier that day.

"Hey there. Crazy day huh?" He tried to sound casual.

"Oh, no. Just another day in the office. This kind of stuff happens all of the time," Karen laughed uneasily.

"Um, this is really wrapping up here. Trevor is safe and sound and Stone won't be bothering them again." Joe coughed and said what he had to be said. "I can arrange for a ride back to your car so you can get going."

"No thank you," Karen replied. Going no further.

"No thank you?" Joe half laughed, half grunted. "What's that mean?"

"I want to stay. Follow through. I came for a story. I think there is something worth telling here. This guy kidnapped a kid, led police on a multi-state manhunt, and died in a horrible accident. There is something people can learn from this mess." Joe could hear the conviction in her voice. There was compassion underneath it. He liked her, and wouldn't mind her hanging around, but his first allegiance was to the Reeds. "Listen, we will deal with that later." Trevor had fallen asleep, so Joe took a moment to rest himself.

****

The family took turns giving their final kisses and stood silently around Andrew as the nurse turned off the machines and the doctor removed the tube. With a last breath, he passed. Quietly, painlessly, and quickly with his family around him, surrounded by love. It was the best they could hope for in that circumstance. When the family was ready, the group went up to Trevor's room feeling lighter for the first time in days. The boy would be released the next morning. It was decided to have a small private ceremony for Andrew right there at the lake house. Jack, Jen, and Tanner's family finally made it, and even Joe was invited. Karen waited back at the hotel room she had rented. It was the right thing to do plus she had scored an interview with Red, the guy who Stone rented a room from.

When everything was said and done at the house by the lake, Joe and Karen said their good-byes to the Reeds who stayed on for some needed relaxation. On the way back to Massachusetts Joe looked over at Karen. "What are you looking at?" she asked.

"You. You're kinda cute, ya know." He smiled.

"You too, but don't let it go to your head." She took his hand and they drove across the border, her outlining the story she was going to write.

****

Matthew Stone's body was returned to North Carolina, where he was laid to rest next to his wife and child. Just before the lid of the coffin was sealed, his friend John begged the mortician for a small favor. After a great deal of arguing with the New Hampshire police, he had been given the one thing that still mattered. He lifted up the lid and placed a small blue piece of fabric on his friend's chest. "Rest in peace, my friend."

A word about the author...

S. Hilbre Thomson grew up in Massachusetts with three older sisters and a younger brother. While she has had a career in education as an elementary school teacher her entire adult life, she has always dreamed of writing suspense novels. *Trevor* is her first published novel. Her love of writing comes directly from her love of reading which she enjoys almost as much as spending time with her husband, three daughters, and their dog, Tucker. Summer vacations allow her to spend time with extended family at Lake Winnipesaukee in New Hampshire where she loves to read on the dock and look forward to a great thunder and lightning storm. Thomson is an exceptional baker (but not a good cook). Whenever she asks what she can bring to a party, the answer is always chocolate chip cookies. She enjoys making other people laugh with her sarcastic sense of humor. Her favorite authors include John Grisham, James Patterson, Patricia Cornwell, and Jennifer Nielsen.